Anthologies

EDGE OF DARKNESS
(with Maggie Shayne and Lori Herter)

DARKEST AT DAWN
(includes DARK HUNGER and DARK SECRET)

SEA STORM
(includes MAGIC IN THE WIND and OCEANS OF FIRE)

FEVER
(includes THE AWAKENING and WILD RAIN)

FANTASY
(with Emma Holly, Sabrina Jeffries, and Elda Minger)

LOVER BEWARE
(with Fiona Brand, Katherine Sutcliffe, and Eileen Wilks)

HOT BLOODED
(with Maggie Shayne, Emma Holly, and Angela Knight)

Specials

DARK CRIME
DARK HUNGER
MAGIC IN THE WIND
THE AWAKENING

DARK PROMISES

A CARPATHIAN NOVEL

CHRISTINE FEEHAN

JOVE
New York

A JOVE BOOK
Published by Berkley
An imprint of Penguin Random House LLC
375 Hudson Street, New York, New York 10014

Copyright © 2016 by Christine Feehan
Excerpt from *Power Game* copyright © 2017 by Christine Feehan

ISBN: 9780515155594

Berkley hardcover edition / March 2016
Jove mass-market edition / February 2017

Printed in the United States of America
1   3   5   7   9   10   8   6   4   2

Cover art by Larry Rostant / Bernstein and Andriuilli
Cover design by George Long
Cover handlettering by Ron Zinn

For Joan Colbert

FOR MY READERS

Be sure to go to christinefeehan.com/members to sign up for my PRIVATE book announcement list and download the FREE ebook of *Dark Desserts*. Join my community and get firsthand news, enter the book discussions, ask your questions and chat with me. Please feel free to email me at Christine@christinefeehan.com. I would love to hear from you. Each year, the last weekend of February, I would love for you to join me at my annual FAN event, an exclusive weekend with an intimate number of readers for lots of fun, fabulous gifts and a wonderful time. Look for more information at fanconvention.net.

ACKNOWLEDGMENTS

With any book there are many people to thank. In this case, the usual suspects: Domini, for her research and help; my power hours group, who always make certain I'm up at the crack of dawn working; and of course, Brian Feehan, who I can call anytime and brainstorm with so I don't lose a single hour. Thank you to Chris Tong for his help with the language when I can't remember what I'm doing! This time I want to thank my community members, who have such passionate and fun discussions on the Carpathian walls—in particular those who always answer the newcomers when I'm not around and who keep the discussions going on the discussion walls and at FAN.

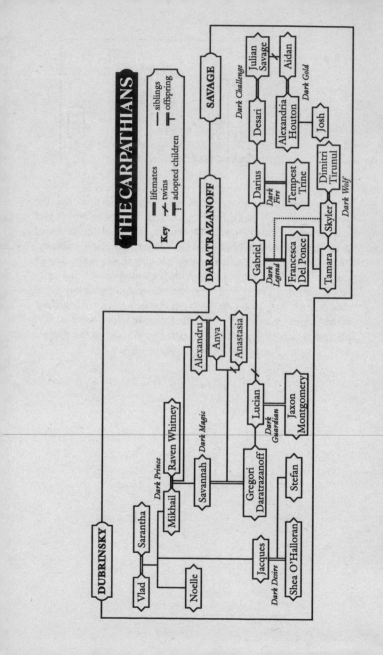

THE CARPATHIANS

Key
— lifemates
⋏ siblings
⊥ offspring
⊤ adopted children

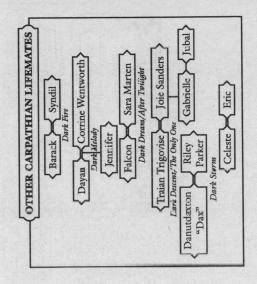

OTHER CARPATHIAN LIFEMATES

Barack — Syndil
Dark Fire

Dayan — Corinne Wentworth
Dark Melody

Jennifer

Falcon — Sara Marten
Dark Dream/After Twilight

Traian Trigovise — Joie Sanders
Lair Descent; The Only One

Danutdaxton "Dax" — Riley Parker
Dark Storm

Gabrielle — Jubal

Celeste — Eric

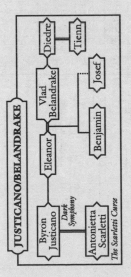

JUSTICANO/BELANDRAKE

Byron Justicano — Eleanor — Vlad Belandrake — Diedre
Dark Symphony

Antonietta Scarletti
The Scarletti Curse

Tienn

Josef

Benjamin

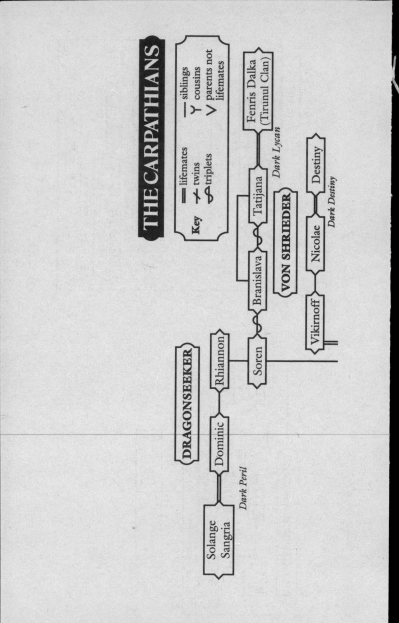

THE CARPATHIANS

Key
= lifemates
= twins
= triplets
— siblings
Y cousins
V parents not lifemates

Fenris Dalka
(Tirunul Clan)
Dark Lycan

Tatijana

Branislava

VON SHRIEDER

Destiny

Nicolae
Dark Destiny

Vikirnoff

Soren

Rhiannon

DRAGONSEEKER

Dominic
Dark Peril

Solange
Sangria

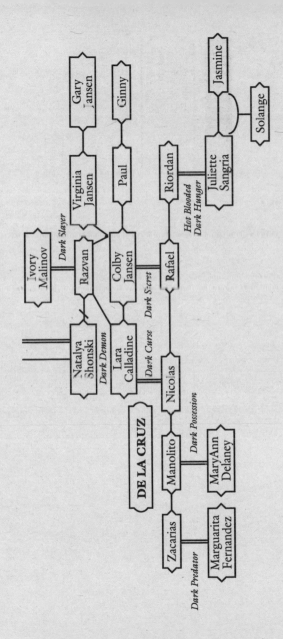

DARK
PROMISES

I

Joie, can you believe this night?" Gabrielle Sanders stared out the window at the stars scattered across the sky. The night was almost a navy blue, with so many stars overhead it would be impossible to count them. The moon was rising, a beautiful half crescent of shining light. "It's perfection. Everything I dreamed of."

Her wedding night. She'd dreamed of it for so long. At last, this was the evening she'd waited for, and the weather was cooperating, just as if it knew she was marrying the man of her dreams.

"We've got to get you ready, Gabby," Joie answered. "Come back here. I need to make certain you have everything you need and give you the 'talk.'"

Gabrielle turned back with a short laugh. "I'm marrying Gary, Joie, the love of my life. I certainly don't need the 'talk.' I love Gary Jansen with every breath in my body," she whispered, as her sister smoothed a hand down the filmy ivory and lace gown and stepped back to survey her handiwork.

"Daratrazanoff," Joie corrected, a hint of worry in her voice. "You still persist in acting as if you're human, Gabrielle. You aren't. Neither is Gary. Both of you are fully Carpathian. When Gary rose Carpathian, he rose as a true Daratrazanoff. He's from one of the most powerful lineages the Carpathian people have. You can't pretend he isn't."

"He's still Gary," Gabrielle protested gently. She took both of her sister's hands in hers. "Be happy for me. Truly, I've never been happier than this night. We waited so long to be together."

"I am happy for you," Joie said immediately, smiling at her sister. "You look so beautiful. Like a princess."

Gabrielle looked at herself in the mirror. Her dress was exactly right. The perfect fit, a lovely fall to her ankles, swirling around her so that she appeared to be ethereal. She loved the square lace neckline and the fitted bodice showing off her small waist. She was tall enough to pull off elegant, and the gown did just that.

Joie didn't understand. None of them did. Only Gary. He knew. He saw inside of her. Way down deep where no one else had ever looked.

"Joie, I'm not like you or Jubal," she admitted, referring to her brother. "I'm not a woman who craves adventure. I'm not a warrior who wants to go fight the injustices of the world. I'm just Gabrielle, no one special, and I like my life simple. Peaceful. I like to sing when I wake up and hum all day long. I like picnics. Horses. Galloping across the fields and jumping over tree trunks and streams. I love sitting on a porch swing and talking quietly with someone I love. That someone is Gary."

"Oh, Gabby." Joie put her arms around Gabrielle. "I didn't realize you've been so unhappy. You have, haven't you?"

Gabrielle hugged Joie back, feeling lucky to have a sister and brother who loved her so much. She felt their love at all times. Their support. More than anything, she wanted Joie's support now in the biggest moment of her life.

"I don't fit in this world, Joie," she said gently, trying to find a way to carefully explain. Joie pulled back and looked at her with liquid eyes. Gabrielle's heart beat louder. She didn't want to hurt her sister, but she wanted to be honest. "I like to observe people from a distance, not be in the middle of some kind of crazy battle between vampires and shifters. I didn't even know there were such things as shifters or vampires in the world. Carpathians. Lycans. Mages. Jaguars. It's all crazy, like a mad nightmare, Joie. Violence and war aren't big on my agenda. In fact, the entire Carpathian way of life is totally foreign to my nature."

She had, thankfully, never heard of Carpathians when she was growing up. And she'd always thought vampires were a myth. She wished she still thought that. Carpathians never killed for blood, but they slept in the rejuvenating ground, couldn't be in the sunlight, and existed on blood. They hunted the vampires who lived to kill their victims.

Gabrielle gave a little shiver. She'd had enough of battles. Of wars. Of seeing someone she loved—such as Gary— nearly lose his life when it wasn't even his fight. She had nearly lost him. Gregori had converted him, bringing him fully into the Carpathian world—as if they hadn't already brought him there.

Gary had somehow become an integral part of Carpathian life, so essential to them that even the prince sought his opinion on matters Carpathian. Gregori, second to the prince, was always with Gary now. It wasn't as if Gary was born a Dara-trazanoff. He was born Gary Jansen, a genius, off-the-charts intelligent, a tall, thin reed of a man with glasses and a thirst for knowledge. A geek. Like her.

Now he was a tall, completely filled out, walking warrior. He went into battles without flinching. Even before Gregori had converted him he had. She'd watched him slowly change from her nerdy geek to a completely different man as the Carpathians put more and more demands on him.

Joie moved to a chair, as if Gabrielle were delivering a terrible blow, and she probably was. She hadn't told anyone but Gary her true feelings. Her beloved Gary. He was quiet and solid. He could always, *always*, be counted on. Everyone counted on him, but especially Gabrielle.

She kept trying to make her sister understand. "Joie, you and Jubal belong in the Carpathian world. I don't. I don't even want to be here. Not anymore."

Joie inhaled sharply. "Gabby . . ."

Gabrielle shook her head. This had to be said. She wanted Joie to understand just what Gary meant to her. What he'd been for her in the past and what he would be in her future. "I hope, after tonight, after I marry Gary, we'll go away together and live in a beautiful little house. Nothing big. Nothing fancy. Just small and snug and filled with love. That's it. That's my dream. Gary and my little house tucked away someplace where there are no such things as vampires, and women carry their children to full term and give birth to healthy, happy babies. No wars. Just peace and happiness."

There, she'd said it. That was the strict truth, and Joie needed to know how she truly felt.

Joie's eyebrows came together as she frowned. "You mean you want to move away from here? Where your laboratory is set up? You love working here. You want to move away from the Carpathian Mountains? From the prince? From Gregori?"

Gabrielle straightened her shoulders and lifted her chin. "*Especially* away from the prince and Gregori."

Joie shook her head, looking shocked.

"I don't belong in the Carpathian world, I just don't. Only Gary seems to understand that about me. He doesn't mind that I'm not a fierce warrior woman. The thing is, Joie, I don't *want* to be different. I'm a book person. I like to live quietly."

"Gabrielle, you are so far off track about yourself and Gary. Where is this coming from? You love adventures. You've gone ice climbing with Jubal and me a million times. You've gone caving. Hiking in remote, third world countries."

Gabrielle nodded. "I went caving because you and Jubal did, and I enjoy spending time with you, but I don't live for adventures the way you do. I'm really a homebody."

"Are you crazy, Gabby? You're a genius who thrives on studying hot viruses. News flash, sister. Playing with that kind of virus without a way to fight it can get you killed. If you didn't like adventure you would never, under any circumstances, study them."

"You fight the world's injustices your way, and I fight them mine. Viruses make sense to me. I can solve the puzzle and try to help with things like finding a way to stop the Ebola virus from being let loose on the world. Vampires make no sense. None." She gave a little shudder. Joie would never understand that she escaped into a lab, that once she focused on whatever she was studying, everything around her disappeared and she didn't have to think about anything else at all.

"You have crazy, mad skills in a lab, Gabby," Joie said. "You're a genius. It isn't just Gary. He isn't smarter than you."

"Actually he is. Most men bore me silly after two minutes alone in their company. I can talk to Gary for hours. What's more, I can just listen to him when he talks to others. He's brilliant. He's also the kindest, sweetest man I know."

Joie shook her head. "He's a Daratrazanoff. Every bit of power, of knowledge, their blood, their ancestors, all of it was given to him in the cave of warriors. You know that. You were there. He was powerful before, Gabby. He's even more so now."

Gary always had the back of the hunters and he'd never let any of them down during a battle, not once. Gabrielle knew it because when he'd nearly died, their best hunters came in to give blood and to pay their respects. She knew it because Gregori Daratrazanoff had made him his brother, his own flesh and blood. The power of the Daratrazanoff family ran in his veins. Was in his heart and soul. Was there, in his mind.

Okay, she had to admit to herself she shied a little away from the sheer power there at times, but still, he was always her Gary. Gentle and kind with her. Seeing her when others couldn't—or wouldn't. She'd tried to tell Joie and Jubal that she was different, not at all wild or willful, but they laughed and said she didn't know herself very well.

Maybe she didn't. But she knew what she wanted—what she'd always wanted—and that was Gary. "I don't care what his last name is, or whose blood runs in his veins, he's *mine*," she declared firmly. "He's always been mine, and I want him back. His life shouldn't be fighting vampires. He's such a genius and I miss him in the laboratory. I want him back there. Once we're married and we find a home, we can set up a lab and he can research for solutions to all the Carpathians' problems *away* from the Carpathian Mountains and vampires and anything else that is monstrous."

Joie cleared her throat, and Gabrielle's gaze jumped to her younger sister.

"Just tell me, Joie," she said. "We've always talked straight with each other."

"You can't change him, Gabby. Gary is a man who will put himself in harm's way over and over if it comes to his sense of right or wrong. He has a clear sense of honor, of duty, and that's why Gregori accepted him from the start—from the very beginning when he first met Gary. Gregori didn't associate with humans, but Gary already had the same values. He was willing to put himself on the line. Like Gregori, he's a man of action, and he's decisive about it."

Gabrielle shook her head. "They've forced him to become like them. He belongs in a laboratory. He loves research and he's got the mind for it, Joie. You know he does, but more and more they're pulling him off that work to go hunt the vampires with them. He's with the prince and Gregori all the time."

"Because they value his advice, Gabby," Joie said gently. "You should be proud of him."

"I am, superproud," Gabrielle assured her sister, and she *was* proud of Gary. "He's a brain. *Gregori* changed him."

Joie bit down on her lip, her eyes shadowed. "He didn't, Gabby. Gregori wouldn't have changed him—he couldn't. Fundamentally, Gary is the same man he always was. Gregori looked into his mind and he saw a brother—a man who thinks as he thinks. Gregori accepted Gary because Gary is exactly like he is. Of course Gary didn't have the skills or knowledge to fight the undead, but he does now. He is Carpathian through and through. You have to be very sure you know him and you accept who he is, not just a small part of him."

"They almost got him killed. In a way they *did* get him killed." She ducked her head and twisted her fingers together. "I was there when he was dying. I was *right* there. Do you know what he said when Gregori told him he was going to convert him? Gregori explained that Gary was *dying*. We all knew."

She pressed a trembling hand to her mouth as the

memories flooded in, the ones she tried so hard to keep at bay. She actually felt sick to her stomach. Her lungs refused air and her heart accelerated to the point where she was afraid she might have a heart attack. She would never forget the sight of Gary, torn and bloody in so many places. He'd saved the life of Zev Hunter, lifemate to Branislava of the Dragonseekers. Zev was *Hän ku pesäk kaikak*—guardian of all and a very needed member of their people. But in saving Zev's life, Gary nearly died. So close. It had been a terrible few hours. The worst. She never wanted to go through that again.

She wasn't a healer like some of the women. That wasn't her gift. She didn't even know what her gift was, other than a party trick or two. So she could look at a map and locate things. What good was that? Her family—and the Carpathians—said she was psychic, but she wasn't. Not like Joie, not like Jubal. She was just plain Gabrielle. No one special. But Gary was a gift, and he saw her that way as well. She'd nearly lost him to the madness of Carpathian life.

"He said he could better serve the people as human," she whispered, her fingers covering her mouth as if she couldn't say the words aloud. "He was ready to die for them. He didn't make the decision to become Carpathian. Gregori made it for him."

There was hurt in her voice. She knew Joie heard it. The Carpathian people had been put above her. Everything in her life had changed when she'd been nearly killed. A member of a human society of vampire killers had stabbed her repeatedly, a vicious, brutal attack. She still had nightmares, although she didn't share that with anyone, not even Gary. She had been brought into the Carpathian world in order to save her life.

Had it not been for Gary, she would have wished they hadn't saved her. She didn't belong. It was that simple. Mikhail, the prince of the Carpathian people, had given her the choice. Live or die. Of course, it had been her own decision to be converted, but Gary was a huge part of that. She'd never had regrets because of him. At the time, terrified and in pain, she had been happy for the chance. Mostly because she knew *this* day would come. Her day. The day she married Gary.

"Gabby," Joie said. Her tone said it all. Compassionate. Sympathetic.

Gabrielle blinked back tears. "I know he has a sense of duty. I know that. I love that about him. When we're bound together as lifemates, my soul to his, that sense of absolute duty and honor and love will be for me. I'll be first. Traian puts you first. Even Gregori puts Savannah first. Lifemates are always first."

"You're absolutely certain that Gary is the one for you, Gabrielle?" Joie asked.

Gabrielle had always chosen to think before she spoke, especially to her sister and brother. She loved them both fiercely. She turned what Joie said over and over in her mind. Was she fooling herself? Was her love for Gary real? Did she see him the way he saw her? Because she knew, without a doubt, Gary saw her. Inside of her. He knew her better than anyone else had ever known her.

She moistened her lips. She had never really used her abilities as a Carpathian to look into Gary's mind. That was true. She could. He would have allowed it, but she wanted that human aspect of finding out slowly about her partner. She even needed it. She was lost in the mountains, amid the wars going on, wars she didn't understand and wanted nothing to do with.

"I love Gary, Joie. I always have. His mind is so incredible. He starts working on something and it's breathtaking to watch him. He gets a scent and he's like a bloodhound. It's such a beautiful and mind-blowing thing to see. He's always going in the right direction. I love that about him. I love that I don't have to talk down to him. Or dumb it down. When I talk, he listens to me, and he believes I'm intelligent. Together we can accomplish so much."

"You already have," Joie said gently. "Give yourself credit. You and Shea were right there with Gary trying to find solutions and coming up with all sorts of things."

"But it was really Gary who pointed us in the right directions. It could have taken years or longer to figure things out," Gabrielle said. "I love his mind. I love how it works. I love how gentle he is and how kind. I love how sweet he is."

"What about his sense of duty?" Joie said. "That's a *huge* part of him. His sense of honor. His integrity. Those things make up his character. He'll put others before his own life. He'll put himself in a dangerous situation in order to protect others. He, like Gregori, is a shield."

Gabrielle felt her stomach settle. Her heart slowed to normal. The breath moved in and out of her body naturally. "Once we're lifemates, that shield is mine, Joie." She knew that was the absolute truth. She'd known it practically since the moment she'd laid eyes on him. He was hers. After tonight, she would be forever grateful she was Carpathian. Tonight was her night. The wait was finally over.

Joie smiled at her. "I can see you're absolutely certain. I can tell Dad and Mom I had the 'talk' with you and you passed with flying colors."

"I'm so in love with him I can barely breathe sometimes when he's around," Gabrielle admitted.

"You really are breathtaking," Joie reiterated. "I've always thought you were beautiful, but the way you look tonight, Gabrielle . . . Gary is a lucky man."

Gabrielle smiled. Her heart leapt. *She* was the lucky one. She and Gary would exchange their vows and go away, far from the mountains where every single night Gary was asked by the prince or Gregori or someone to perform some monumental task that no one else could possibly do but him. Some terrible thing that put his life in jeopardy. She couldn't bear that, not ever again. Being proud of your partner was just fine until they died in your arms, then pride wasn't all that great anymore.

Gabrielle smoothed her hands down the line of her filmy gown and took a deep breath, pushing her fears away. Nothing was going to mar this special night. Nothing at all. Tonight was hers. Once more she glanced out the window up at the night sky where the stars glittered like a ceiling of diamonds. The rest of the tension coiled in her stomach slid away.

There wasn't a single cloud. Not one. Just a beautiful blanket of stars, and she knew why. Gary. That was the reason. Carpathians created storms easily. They could also bring beautiful, perfect weather when they needed it. Gary had brought her this night. She didn't feel the subtle pull of power, but she knew it was there.

"He's waiting for me."

"He can wait. You need something borrowed," Joie said. She pulled a necklace from around her neck. A small pendant hung from a thin chain. "I keep this with me most of the time." Her fingers wrapped around the pendant. "Well, *all* of the time. I found Traian in that cave and when we were escaping, I found this embedded in the ice. I think it belonged to one of the mages. Maybe even Dad. I've never showed it to him because I love it and feel very drawn to it and I really don't want to lose it. It feels as if it should be mine."

Gabrielle understood that her sister was giving her something that was important to her. She took the pendant and chain on her open palm, studying it from every angle. It was made of rock. It looked like quartz to her, but it was shaped into four circular corners with lines in the middle of each circle. It was highly polished, but still appeared crude. Gabrielle closed her fingers around it and felt warmth instantly. More, she felt her sister's presence—as if she held a small bit of her in her hand.

"I can't take this," she whispered, her heart fluttering as love for her sister overwhelmed her. "This is meant for you. I feel you in it." She could feel the way Joie loved her. Fiercely. Protectively. Unconditionally. She had that. Tears filled her eyes. Joie gave her that.

Joie reached out and gently put her hand over Gabrielle's. "Just for this night. For *your* night. I want to be there with you in some way. I can't go to the field of fertility with you, but I can give you something that matters to me so I can travel with you and know how happy you are. And you deserve to be happy, Gabby."

"Thank you, Joie, I'll wear it, then." Gabrielle carefully slipped the chain over her intricate hairdo and let the pendant rest between her breasts.

"Something blue," Joie said, and grinning, fashioned a lacy garter to slip under the wedding gown and onto Gabrielle's thigh. "Gary will be happy to discover that."

Gabrielle blushed. "Lovely. He will."

"Something old," Joie said, sobering a little. "Jubal gave me this for you. He said it was Dad's, an ancient bracelet from an ancestor we've never heard of."

"Dad gave this to Jubal? It's for a woman," Gabrielle said, her eyes on the delicate links, all fashioned by a brilliant ancient jeweler. The bracelet was made from a material she was unsure of, but the links were locked together and couldn't come apart. She couldn't see the clasp.

She wanted it instantly. It was beautiful. Primal. It held power. She felt it in the delicate links. "Why would Dad give this to Jubal?"

"He said Jubal would know who it belonged to and when to give it to her. Jubal says it belongs to you and now is the time," Joie said.

Gabrielle bit her lip and took the links from Joie's palm. Instantly the bracelet felt alive. Warm, like Joie's pendant, but there was a surge of power, almost like an electrical current. The links moved, snakelike in her palm. She should have been afraid, but she wasn't. Her heart beat faster, but only in anticipation.

This was hers. Just as the pendant was Joie's and her brother had a bracelet that was really a weapon, this delicate piece from ancient times was meant to be part of her.

She closed her fingers around it, accepting it. Accepting that it held power and would somehow become a part of her. She felt the ancient links move again, slipping out the side of her fist to curl around her wrist. For one moment the links blazed hot, changing color from that strange metallic to a glowing red. Her wrist felt hot, but not burning, just the sensation of heat—a *lot* of it. Then the bracelet was there. Closed. No clasp. No way to take it off. It was as if the links surrounding her wrist were a part of her.

Joie caught her hand. "It's beautiful, but, Gabby, it's some kind of weapon like Jubal's is. I think my pendant is for protection, but I think this is a weapon."

"I don't know what this is or who it was made for," Gabrielle said softly, stroking the links with the pads of her fingers. "But I know it belongs to me. It's *supposed* to be mine. I love this, Joie. It feels right on my wrist, almost as if it's part of my skin." She lifted the bracelet to admire it in the moonlight.

As soon as the beams of light hit it, the bracelet lit up, moving of its own accord, a glittering warmth that surrounded her wrist, snug, but not at all tight. She loved it. More, she loved the fact that it had belonged to an ancestor before her and that Jubal had been the one to pass it on to her.

"You have something old. Something borrowed and something blue. You still need something new. You said you wanted to blend traditional with human, so we need to cover all four bases," Joie said.

"Everything is perfect, Joie. I couldn't ask for anything more."

"Shea, Savannah and Raven had something made for you. Something brand-new. Byron made it. Do you remember him at all? He lives in Italy with his lifemate, but he's a gem caller, and they asked him to make you something special for your wedding."

Tears clogged Gabrielle's throat. She knew she'd become bitter toward the Carpathians ever since Gary had nearly died—ever since Gregori had brought him fully into their world. She felt like she'd lost him twice. First in death, and then to the prince and his second-in-command. Gary was fully a Daratrazanoff, and with that name came the power and responsibilities given—and those were huge. Still, she'd pushed aside the friendships she'd forged with some of the women, and that had been wrong. Very wrong.

"I don't deserve anything from them, Joie," she admitted in a low voice. "I've been standoffish."

More than that, she'd been restless and irritable, as if something deep inside her called to her. Wanted. No, even needed and recognized that time was growing short. She'd pushed for the marriage because she knew if she didn't do this now, something terrible was going to happen.

She pressed both hands to her churning stomach. She'd woken up from her sleep—the terrible paralysis of the Carpathian people—deep beneath the earth. She could hear her heart thudding dangerously loud. She felt the echo of the nightmare, the vicious stabbing as the knife blade penetrated her body, slicing deep over and over. She relived it, but the moment she woke, there was an echo of something else. Something she couldn't quite catch. So elusive, but so important. The feeling of dread built in her until every rising she wanted to run away and hide.

She still couldn't tell Joie, as much as she wanted to. She could only tell Gary. He didn't look at her as if she wasn't quite up to the standards of the Sanders family. Joie and Jubal could kick serious butt. Gabrielle had stood over Gary's broken, wounded body and cried her eyes out. She had nightmares when other Carpathians said they didn't dream—as in ever. She was growing afraid as each rising passed. She had to be somewhere, and the need in her was so strong, she feared she would take off on her own soon. She didn't make sense. The Carpathian way of life was definitely not good for her and she had to find a balance before she went crazy. Gary was her balance.

"Shea, Raven and Savannah love you, Gabrielle. All of us noticed you've been withdrawn, but it's entirely permissible and even understandable, after what happened to Gary. Everyone knows you love him. How could that not affect you? Of course you've been moody and withdrawn."

"Don't make excuses for me," Gabrielle said. "They're my friends, you're my sister, and I shut all of you out."

Joie hugged her tight. "I'm the queen of shutting people out, Gabby. You're a Sanders. When we have problems, we tend to keep them to ourselves until we figure out a solution. It isn't possible with your lifemate. I'm warning you right now. He'll know when you're upset and he won't mind in the least getting into your head and reading what the problem is. Males want to fix everything."

Gabrielle smiled. She couldn't help it. It was the truth. The good thing was, Gary knew her. He knew how to fix her. He didn't have to invade her personal space, and she liked it like that. Although, since he'd risen as a Daratrazanoff, she'd noticed he was far quieter—and he'd always been quiet. Much more serious, and he'd always been serious. He had the same look that Gregori sometimes got, or Darius, Gregori's younger brother— one bordering on command, as if everyone had better do as he said when he said it. Still, he never looked at *her* that way.

Joie showed her the ring. It was beautiful. Elegant. Breathtaking even. It was to be worn on her right hand, the ring finger, and the moment Joie slipped it on, Gabrielle knew there was more to the ring than platinum and gemstones. She loved it just like she loved the bracelet, the pendant, and her blue garter. Perfection for her wedding. She knew that each of the gems set in her ring were power gems and each would have a purpose. She'd learn about them later. For now, she could enjoy the fact that her sister and her three best friends were sharing this monumental event with her.

She stood there for a moment, feeling radiant and lucky. She actually felt beautiful, like a princess about to meet her prince. She'd never been happier than that moment, knowing he was waiting right outside for her. She felt him. She always knew when he was close to her.

"He's here," she said softly to Joie. "He's waiting for me."

Joie hugged her again and kissed her cheek. "You've never been more beautiful than you are at this moment, Gabrielle. I hope you always stay this happy."

"I'll be with Gary. How can I not be happy?" Gabrielle asked, and hugged Joie back.

She turned toward the door, a lump in her throat. She wanted to see his face when she stepped through. That would tell her everything. She would know if he felt the same way. Joie, staying to one side of the door, pulled it open for her, and Gabrielle picked up the sides of her dress and stepped outside. Her crystal shoes and ivory gown were all lace and crystals so that the moment the beams of light from the moon hit her, she sparkled like the stars overhead.

Gary turned toward her, and she drew in her breath. He was gorgeous. Every time she looked at him, she felt as if she were seeing him for the first time. He looked older than when she'd first met him, but it suited him. He had a few scars, but they suited him as well. His hair was long and thick, growing like the Carpathians' hair seemed to do. That gave him a more primitive, ancient look, but she found she liked it. He had a few streaks of gray spun into his dark hair.

Gary was a few inches shorter than Gregori, but no less commanding. She'd never seen that in him before. He'd always been a man to slip into the shadows and let others take the spotlight. She couldn't imagine him in the shadows now. His eyes were glued to her. He no longer wore his glasses. In any case, because he was so often in battle, defending the children against vampire puppets, he'd long since settled for the contacts Gregori manufactured for him. Now he was fully Carpathian and didn't need glasses or contacts, and she could see the amazing green of his eyes.

She loved the expression on his face. She couldn't have asked for a better manifestation of his love. His entire face lit up. His mouth went soft. His face went warm, and his eyes went hot. *Really* hot. A million butterflies took wing in her stomach. Her lungs felt a little as if they couldn't quite get enough air. She moistened her lips with the tip of her tongue. He was so beautiful to her. Inside and out. Everything about him. Especially his mind. She loved his mind, although, right at that moment, when he was looking so handsome in a dark suit, so appropriate for a wedding, she thought maybe she could love his body even more. Well. Equally.

He held out his hand to her. "You look beautiful, princess."

He always called her princess when they were alone. Never in front of others. He made her feel like a princess in a fairy tale. Always. No other person in the world was so gentle with her in the way that he was. When violence swirled around them, Gary was always her rock.

"Thank you. I think you're quite handsome tonight as well," she said, a little shyly. She felt shy with him. She didn't know why. Gary knew her better than anyone else did, but still, it was their wedding, and after tonight, they would be bound together in the Carpathian way. Not just in their hearts, but in their very souls. She secretly loved that idea. Being his other half. She *loved* it, knowing it was better than any fairy tale.

Gary drew her to him, his eyes still drifting over her face. Over her body. Slowly. Taking her in. Appreciating the time she'd spent getting ready. Human time. Not Carpathian. She had carefully put on every article of clothing manually. Taking her time, making it right. Wanting this night to be a mixture of both cultures, human and Carpathian.

Her hand was trembling, and he knew it. He immediately enveloped her hand in both of his.

"You're safe with me, Gabrielle. Always."

She knew that. She had always known it. She loved the timbre of his voice. So gentle, like a caress. He was such a good man. As much as Gregori intimidated her and she didn't want Gary to be *anything* like him, she couldn't help but admire the flashes of Daratrazanoff in Gary. The confidence. The ability to keep her safe.

Maybe it wasn't so bad that he was a Daratrazanoff, especially if they could move away from the prince. Always Mikhail Dubrinsky and his family would draw vampires and now, rogue Lycans. To eliminate the prince was to eliminate the Carpathian people. Mikhail now had a daughter and a son. Both were threats to the vampires and rogues.

The attacks would never stop, and Daratrazanoffs

protected the prince. If they remained, no matter that she was his lifemate, even putting her first, Gary's life would always be in danger, and she didn't want that. She couldn't have that. And that made her *so* not a Carpathian. It was ingrained in every man, woman and child to protect the prince and his heirs. Even she felt it. Gary, as a human, had always taken on the protection of all the Carpathians, from unborn children to the prince himself. Now, as a member of one of the most powerful families of Carpathians, he would be twice as in demand.

"Gabrielle?" Gary prompted softly. He didn't tug on her hand or try to hurry her in the least. He never did. He was never impatient with her. She knew he was capable of impatience because she'd seen him giving orders to some of the other males, and he did it in a voice that meant business—and they obeyed him.

"I'm ready." She lifted her chin, pushing aside the weird urge to run that kept getting in the way of her happiness. Run where? To what? Everything she wanted or needed was standing right in front of her. She just had the vague, persistent feeling of dread, as if something terrible was going to happen any minute. The feeling was growing stronger every day. Another war? Another moment when Gary would save a life at the expense of his own? In saving Zev Hunter, Gary had been eviscerated by the rogue Lycans. He waded in where no other human—well, except her brother—would dare to go.

"Are you ready, Gary?" she asked, needing his reassurance. Needing to know he wanted her with the same urgency that she wanted him. She'd waited so long. Everything Carpathian had gotten between them. They had never had a moment to themselves. It was as if fate had conspired against them.

"More than ready, princess. This is our night. Our time. I want to give you everything you ever wanted." Gary snapped his fingers, and a horse emerged from the trees.

Gabrielle caught her breath. The horse was a good seventeen hands. Pure white. Tail and mane flowed like so much silk with every move the graceful animal made. He came to them, prancing as he did so, his eyes on Gary.

Gary put his hands around her waist and lifted her onto the horse's back, sidesaddle, her dress flowing around her much like the horse's mane. The ivory lace settled in a beautiful drape. Her breath settled in her lungs as Gary took the reins and began to lead the horse through the trees toward the mountain where the fertility flowers grew in abundance—another thing Gary had contributed to their people. He had planted and cultivated the flowers until an entire field grew once more wild up the mountain.

White petals drifted around them and settled on the trail so that there was a carpet of white for the horse to carry her over. Overhead, the leaves rustled as they went under the canopy of trees. She glanced up and swore some of the branches bowed toward them as they passed, setting the leaves swaying so that they appeared a beautiful silver in the moonlight.

Wolves began a serenade, and she knew they sang to them. She loved that. She loved that nature surrounded them and seemed to bless their joining. The horse's gait was so smooth she didn't even have to hold on, but could balance without effort. She felt as if she were floating through the air toward their ultimate destination.

The hoofs made a light sound on the rock as they started up the mountain, adding to the beauty of the moment. She couldn't have asked for a more perfect way to make the ascent. Her man—no, lifemate—leading her to an incredible field of flowers on the back of a white stallion. Who had a man like that? Only Gabrielle Sanders, soon to be Daratrazanoff. Only she did.

2

The scent of the Night Star flowers permeated the air. Gabrielle found the perfume potent, almost an aphrodisiac. As Gary lifted her from the back of the horse and set her on the ground, the feeling of his strong hands at her waist sent a thrill through her, even as a strange tingle of fear crept down her spine.

She looked around at the field of white. Above them was a ceiling of sparkling stars and surrounding them were the beautiful flowers that had been thought to be extinct. Gary had discovered them in South America with her brother, Jubal, and brought them back to help with the fertility problems the Carpathian women were experiencing. It had been Gary who had discovered the existence of the flower in centuries past and realized it was a vital part of the Carpathian courtship.

The blossom was large, shaped like a star, but the petals and texture were much like that of a lily. The inside filaments were striped and the ovary was ruby red. Joie had told her the blossom took on the scent of the Carpathian male and female, adding to the need for consummating the lifemate bond. Gabrielle had waited so long for Gary she didn't need a flower to make her any more ready for him, but she couldn't find one fault with the setting.

In the center of the field of flowers was a four-poster bed, draped in white. Petals from the Night Star flower were strewn over the white satin sheets. Her breath caught in her throat. She lifted one hand to Gary's chest. Her fairy tale. The outdoor bed in a field of fragrant flowers with the stars shining

down on them. He had remembered the one time she told him
of her dream wedding night.

The moonlight hit the bracelet on her wrist and it seemed
to come alive, going warm, looking like a ring of fire, the links
glowing red and gold. It looked beautiful on her wrist, so delicate, and yet she knew the bracelet was far more than that.

Unexpectedly, Gary's hand came up under hers to pull it
away so he could inspect it. "There's power in this. Where
did you get it?"

Her stomach somersaulted. He sounded . . . dangerous.
Not at all like her Gary. Gabrielle pressed her lips together.
Gary sounded fully Carpathian, a male hunter refusing to be
denied an answer. When she glanced up to look into his eyes,
they were glittering down at her. Her heart jerked.

"You're scaring me, Gary," she said. He really was, but
she didn't know why. And she didn't know why the bracelet
felt as if it was a threat to him, but it, too, had gone from
beautiful to deadly, just as Gary had.

Gary didn't touch the bracelet and his gaze didn't leave
her face. "It's a weapon, Gabrielle. Where did you get this?"

"My brother. For the something old. You know," she persisted. "Something old. Something new. Something borrowed
and something blue. This is something old. My father gave it
to Jubal to give to me when the time was right. Jubal told Joie
the time was right."

"On our wedding night?"

"I don't understand what's wrong." She didn't, and yet she
did. Her bracelet had begun to hum. It was low, but it was
there. She heard it. Gary heard it. She pulled her hand out of
his and put her arm behind her back to quiet the bracelet. She
didn't know how to take it off or she would have. She didn't
want her beautiful bracelet to ruin this night for her.

"What is wrong is that that bracelet is looking to slice me
to pieces. Take it off."

She bit her lip hard. "I can't, Gary. I don't know how."

He drew in his breath, his eyes going electric green. He
looked more of a predator than she'd seen in a wolf. She drew

in her breath and willed the bracelet to behave and stop humming.

"You put an object of power on without having any idea how to remove it or how to make it work or stop working?"

That was a blow. A huge blow. She could hear the sarcasm in his voice. He looked down at her as if she wasn't quite bright, when, in fact, she was brilliant. Okay. Maybe he had a point, it wasn't the smartest move, but it was her wedding night and a gift from her brother. And father. It was hers. It felt right on her wrist, and she knew it was hers. Just as the pendant was Joie's and Jubal had his weapon from the mages.

"I shouldn't have," she conceded. "But it was a gift from Jubal, and I was caught up in the wedding traditions. When Joie gave it to me, I thought it was a bracelet, a piece of jewelry, not a weapon."

She didn't want to take the bracelet off. She kept willing it to connect with her as Jubal's weapon connected with him. She knew Jubal could control his weapon with his mind.

Gary studied Gabrielle's face. She was beautiful. She had always been beautiful, but since being converted to a Carpathian, she was even more so. It was difficult to resist the look on her face. Her eyes, a true dove gray, stayed on his, held captive there. He wanted her with every breath in his body. He had since the moment he'd laid eyes on her. The Carpathian people had been facing extinction and he had worked day and night to help ease those problems, hoping to buy them enough time to actually find ways to solve them permanently.

Without children no species could continue, not even one with the longevity the Carpathians had. He had put aside his own emotions, wants and maybe even needs in order to help them. Then the prince had sent him on countless errands and given him so many tasks, both dangerous and not. When he wasn't learning to fight the enemy, protecting children during the day or researching, Mikhail and Gregori asked him to join their strategy meetings.

There had been no time for himself or Gabrielle. He had thought this day would never come. His beautiful bride. She was smart and funny and so beautiful it hurt to look at her. He reached for her hand again. Both of them. In the Carpathian culture, the male was imprinted with the ritual binding words before birth. In essence, Gary had been reborn as a Daratrazanoff, a full Carpathian, and the words were there, along with the power and knowledge of his ancestors.

Saying the ritual words to Gabrielle would bind his lifemate to him for all eternity. His soul to her soul. Simply put, he loved her with every cell in his body. He loved her mind and the compassion and empathy in her. He loved the way her mind worked, focusing completely on a problem and working it out piece by piece. He could talk to her and she understood what he said. She caught on quickly when he was trying to explain a resolution and why he was certain his solution would work. When they worked side by side, the research went so much faster because they made a good partnership. He didn't have to direct her. Her mind followed the same path his did.

It was impossible not to love Gabrielle. She lit up a room with her laughter. With her sunshine. With the possibilities of her brilliant mind. If they disagreed over a problem, she always had a sound argument and reasons why she thought they should choose a different way.

He knew she had struggled with the Carpathian way of life ever since he was nearly killed. She'd grown quiet and moody and he could see the worry in her eyes. She had begun to pull away from her relationship with Shea, her best friend. Shea was lifemate to Jacques, the prince's brother. He knew that was on him. He didn't like it, and he was determined to rectify it.

Gabrielle wanted a wedding. She wanted their relationship finalized. He hadn't lost his emotions or his ability to see in color as the Carpathians did over time, so there had never been that exact confirmation that she was his lifemate, but he knew he loved Gabrielle Sanders. He would defend her with his last breath and he would do anything to make her happy.

He was certain once they were lifemates, their souls bound together, she would relax a little and realize it wouldn't be so easy to kill him. He had lived through countless battles as a human. He could live through many more as a Carpathian male. She would see that once she shared his mind.

"Say it," she whispered. "Right now, Gary, with the moon shining down on us, in this perfect field of beautiful flowers. Bind us together for eternity."

He smiled down at her. "I was just thinking what a lucky man I am to have found you, Gabrielle. To have you right here in front of me. To know you before either of us was converted. I know a few of the Carpathian males have known their life-mates from childhood, but it is rare. We have a past that binds us even closer."

She smiled up at him, her smile reaching her eyes, taking his breath. This was finally their time. He tightened his fingers around hers, ignoring the still glowing bracelet. At least it had stopped the warning hum.

"You are my lifemate. I claim you as my lifemate." He said the ritual words decisively. He had wanted to say them before he was even Carpathian. She was everything he'd ever wanted in a woman. "I belong to you. I offer my life for you." He did belong to her. He loved her with all his heart. He would lay down his life for her in a heartbeat. "I give you my protection. I give you my allegiance. I give you my heart. I give you my soul."

The moment he uttered the words, something shifted inside of him. Fingers of dread crept down his spine. His gut knotted. Tight. Tension slid in. The bracelet burst into flames, the red dancing through the gold ominously, leaping around her wrist and humming a warning.

Gabrielle bit her lip, pushing at the bracelet with her hand, trying to get it off. It wouldn't budge, clinging as if a part of her body. She did her best to ignore it, feeling desperate, her stomach somersaulting while everything in her screamed she might lose the most important person in her world. "What's wrong? Why did you stop?"

He had been reborn Carpathian. Fully Carpathian. He was no longer human. He loved Gabrielle Sanders with all of his heart. She loved him in the same way. With her heart. All of it. But this vow was to bring two halves of the same soul back together. She had to hold the light to his darkness. Gabrielle was definitely of the light. He could see it shining in her eyes. He could almost see her soul in those beautiful eyes. But not now. Not at this moment—he saw reluctance. He saw the same dread in her that was there inside of him.

"No, Gary," Gabrielle said. "Finish it. Say it in the ancient language, maybe the ritual needs to be recited in the ancient language. They aren't going to take you away from me. Not that. You're all I have left. I can't make it without you. Say the words to tie us together."

She knew. On some level she knew. The knowledge was strong in him even when he wanted to deny it. Her soul would not bind itself to his.

"Gabrielle . . ."

"Don't." Tears swam in her eyes. "For me. If you love me, do this. I need you, Gary. I love you. Please, finish it. Say it in the ancient language."

Gary took a deep breath. His world was crumbling around him. He couldn't imagine Gabrielle with another man. He wasn't even certain he would remain sane if he ever saw such a thing. He'd lose his mind and try to kill her lifemate. She belonged to him. He belonged to her. She looked . . . devastated, just as he was devastated.

"Please, baby, please, for me, try again," Gabrielle pleaded.

"Te avio päläfertiilam. Éntölam kuulua, avio päläferti-ilam." The moment he uttered the binding words in the ancient language, the dread increased tenfold. His stomach lurched. The knots tightened. He drew in his breath, shaking his head.

She shook her head again and tried frantically to tear the bracelet from her wrist. Her nails dug into her skin, leaving bloody tracks.

"I won't let them do this to us. They've taken everything from both of us. Over and over, bled us dry. They can't have you. It isn't working because we were both human. Their rules don't apply to us. We helped them, Gary. If it wasn't for you, and also for me, their children would still be dying. I know Lara helped, but it was you who pointed everyone in the right direction. You were the one who saved their children. We deserve to be happy."

He drew her into his arms, fitting her body into his. He held her tightly. "Honey, it isn't them. There is no *them* versus *us*. They want us happy." He stood in the middle of the field, blinking as he looked around him, noting uneasily that the white petals of the flowers were no longer so white. The green of the leaves on the flowers had faded as well. He took a breath. Closed his eyes. Opened them, his heart bleeding for both of them. "This isn't their fault."

"How did this happen? I don't understand how this could happen," Gabrielle cried against his shirt.

He understood. He had been reborn. His soul was no longer the soul of a human, but that of a Carpathian male. Gabrielle had always belonged to another man. Another Carpathian. She was the keeper of that man's soul. Whether he was alive or already gone, whether he would actually find her, was a moot point. Her soul still reached for his—her true lifemate's.

"I don't care," Gabrielle said, pulling back to look up at his face. "What are the chances of either of us finding our lifemates? Seriously, Gary, calculate the odds. We can live as humans. We can go far away from here, build a life together, have our children and accomplish all the things we talked about doing for the world."

There it was. She would go away with him. His heart stuttered in his chest. It wasn't the right thing to do, not for either of them, but, God, he wanted her. She was there, under his skin, in his heart, his everything. But she wasn't his lifemate—and he wasn't hers.

"Don't," she whispered. "I see it on your face. Don't do this, Gary. We belong together. In the human world we'd get married and have children and live out our lives together. We'd be happy. You know we would."

Her fingers curled into the lapels of his jacket. His suit jacket. His wedding suit. Gary closed his eyes again, the need for her so strong in him, it shook him. She was giving herself to him. No man, not even a Carpathian male, could be offered the love of his life and turn it down. No one.

He opened his eyes slowly, his gaze hooded. Sensual. Needing her. Wanting her. Loving her with every breath he took. He just had to take her hand and lead her to the bed and she would be his. She would go away with him, and he knew without a shadow of a doubt that he'd be happy with her. She was everything.

Still, the night was dimmer. The color in the world around him had faded significantly. He tried not to be alarmed, but the white flowers were now dull. Her hair wasn't a rich black but a softer gray. Her lips, always so red, had faded in color as well. All around him, he could see that he was losing his ability to see in color. The vibrant shades weren't fading over time, like they did with most Carpathians; they were being wrenched from him all in one night. His brain processed the information even as he rejected the idea of it.

He hadn't considered what rebirth meant. What the pouring of wealth into his mind from all the ancients in the Daratrazanoff lineage would actually mean. He received all the power. All the skills and knowledge acquired in centuries of battles, of living, were in his head. All of it. But with that came the darkness. Overwhelming. Terrible. Descending on him as if he'd lived those centuries, but again, overnight. Robbing him of his humanity. Taking this woman from him. His one love.

His hand tightened convulsively around Gabrielle. He stepped closer, needing to feel her body against his. Needing to hold her. He put his arms around her and held her tight. One hand cupped the back of her head, pressing her face against him. He ignored the rising hum of the bracelet.

"Honey, you are just as Carpathian as I am." The words, as true as they were, tasted bitter in his mouth. It was too late for them. She didn't understand what was happening to him. He was hurting her. He knew he was, and that just added to the sorrow in him. She had chosen to live because she thought they would be together. Now she had to feel as if he was deserting her.

"Don't, Gary. Please. *Please*, don't let them take you away from me." Gabrielle wept uncontrollably, her arms around him. Clinging. Pressing herself even closer.

If there was a hell, this was it. Gary dropped his head down to rub his face in her soft hair. Breathing her in. Breathing in her sweetness. Trying to make a memory that couldn't be ripped from him in just a few moments.

"I can make you happy," she whispered softly. "I can, Gary. I know it. We can leave here, go far away and marry. Have a family. We can live a human lifetime together. After that, after we're supposed to be dead and gone, maybe then we'll have had enough of each other, but I can't imagine my life without you. I can't."

"I know, Gabrielle. I feel the same." He heard the regret in his voice. She heard it, too, because she stiffened.

Gabrielle pulled back, putting space between them, her hands curling into two tight fists. Her face tipped up toward his and he could see the anger and hurt there. He could feel it vibrating in the air between them.

"You're refusing me. Rejecting me. On. My. Wedding. Night."

"It's a matter of honor, honey. You know it's the right thing to do."

"For *them*. It's always about them. I can't believe you're willing to sacrifice us. Sacrifice me. For *them*."

Tears ran down her face unchecked, breaking his heart further. More color bled away. Gary reached for her. She stepped back, shaking her head.

"I have to tell you what's happening, Gabrielle, so that you'll understand." If his ability to see in color was fading so fast, it stood to reason he would lose his emotions just as abruptly. He couldn't risk her.

"I *know* what's happening, Gary. This is our wedding night. You made promises to me, and now you're walking away. Rejecting me. Jilting me."

She sounded close to hysterical and she jammed a fist in her mouth, stepping back even farther from him. His gut tied into hard, bitter knots. Gary murmured her name and stepped toward her. Gabrielle threw her hand between them, palm out.

"Don't. Not unless you're going to leave with me. Go away from here and live out our lifetime as humans while we can. We can have that. At least that, Gary."

He wanted to give that to her. He wanted to give that to himself. She was right there, standing in front of him, everything he'd ever dreamed about. He loved her with every beat of his heart. Every breath he took.

"Honey, just for a moment, listen to me. I'm already losing my ability to see in color. It's happening fast. Everything's fading to gray. When the ancients in the Daratrazanoff lineage accepted me as theirs, they poured their knowledge into me. They gave me tremendous gifts, their power, their skills, even their abilities to fight vampires. All of it, just as if I was born with those abilities and power."

She bit her lip, her gray eyes swimming with tears. He could see the teardrops sparkling on the ends of absurdly long lashes. At that moment, with the flowers surrounding her and the night sky above her, she was more beautiful than ever. "How can that be?" she whispered.

His heart turned over at the concern in her voice. "I don't know how it's done exactly, I only know they have a collective conscious. Mikhail has access to them there in the cave of warriors. When they come together like they do, all the warriors, past and present, they are very powerful. That power runs through Mikhail. I felt it. He's some sort of conductor, or rather, a receptacle for that combined power."

Gabrielle stepped into him again, her arms circling his waist, her head on his chest. "What have they done to you?"

"I love you, Gabrielle," he admitted. The words felt wrenched from him, leaving him naked and exposed. He couldn't have her. He would have to allow another man to have her, and that would kill him. The warrior in him protested.

"I know you do," she whispered. "I love you, too. There

has to be a way. If you feel love for me, you can still feel emotion, even if you're losing your ability to see in color. We could still go away and live together. Have that life. Most humans get forty, fifty years together. We can take that time for ourselves, couldn't we? What would be so wrong about that?"

He held her close, feeling his body heat surrounding her. Inhaling her scent. The temptation of keeping her—having her for himself—was alarming in its strength.

"We can't make a decision like that without really thinking it through, Gabrielle. We would have to leave. Live far from here, far from other Carpathians. If your lifemate came along, or mine . . ."

"I once asked Mikhail what would happen if a Carpathian male found his lifemate and she was human, married with a family and happy. He said a man of honor would either meet the dawn or wait it out, hoping her spouse died before she did. He would never come between them. A lifemate makes his other half happy."

"Exactly, Gabrielle. You're not thinking how *you* would feel. If your lifemate happened to find you, you would be compelled to make him happy." He kept his voice gentle as he explained a reality he was certain she hadn't considered.

"I wouldn't know because I'd be happy with you and he wouldn't reveal himself," she pointed out.

He'd always known she had a stubborn streak. That was part of what made her so good in a laboratory. She fought so fiercely for them. She would make a fantastic mother, one who would fight for her children with a ferocity that he would admire always. She took care of those she loved.

"No, he wouldn't, Gabrielle, but he would suffer. He might even take his own life because we were giving ourselves a few years together selfishly."

She lifted her head and stared into his eyes. "You're a genius, Gary. What are the odds of both of us finding our lifemates?"

He knew so many of the ancients were still out there, looking, hoping. Hanging on by a thread. She had been in the

Carpathian Mountains and met many of them. None had claimed her. The odds were far less for him. She saw the answer in his eyes.

"*Exactly,*" she said. "Gary, we have a right to be happy. Both of us. We've helped the Carpathians. You know we have. This is our time."

His hands came up to frame her face. "And if I lose my emotions? My ability to feel love for you, what then, Gabrielle? What happens to you? To our children?"

"I don't know. No future is ever certain, Gary."

He took a breath and then he kissed her. Hard. Hot. Hungry. She tasted incredible. She kissed him back, opening her mouth to his, taking him just as hungrily, just as in need. Just as filled with despair. They clung to each other in silence until he lifted his head.

"Gary, I honestly don't know if I can make it without you," she whispered against his throat. "I don't know how to live without you in my life."

He understood because he felt the same way. He tightened his arms around her, pressing her body tightly to his. Even though he feared he might be in danger of crushing her, she didn't protest. She held him just as tightly.

"Please come away with me," she whispered. "I'm afraid without you. You steady me. You make me feel as if I have an anchor in a world I don't understand. If you leave me alone, I'll just dry up and blow away."

He closed his eyes, his heart weeping. "Give me time to figure out whether we'll have the time to raise a family and be together before I lose my ability to feel. I won't put you through that, Gabrielle. I need to talk to Mikhail and Gregori . . ."

"No," she said sharply, her hands going to the lapels of his jacket. "You know they'll tell you to let me go. You know they will. This is between the two of us. Our decision, not theirs."

"Honey, you persist in thinking they're the enemy."

"In a way, they are, Gary. They're my enemy. They've taken you from me. You were always mine, the only person I've ever really had."

"Gabrielle." He caught her chin and tilted her face up toward his, compelling her to look into his eyes. "You come from a loving family. You adore your sister and brother. You love your parents."

"Very much," she admitted. "But I don't fit anywhere. Not with them. They don't know me. They don't understand me. They never have, as much as they'd like to. These people"—she swept her hand around the field to indicate the Carpathians—"they don't even try to get to know me. I do research and I keep to myself. I don't mean anything at all to them. But you . . . you see me. I matter. I exist." She shook her head, tears swimming in her eyes again. "You can't take that away from me, Gary. What will I have left?"

He took a breath. "All right, honey. I want you to take some time and think about this realistically. If in a week you still feel like we can make a go of it, we'll revisit the issue, but you need to really think about what could happen if I lose my emotions so abruptly and have all the past history of hundreds of years of loneliness poured into me all at once. That could be dangerous to us."

"You're a man of honor, Gary. You would tell me what was happening and we'd face it together. You know that's what you'd do." She was absolutely certain.

He crushed her to him again, knowing he would have to give her up, that she wasn't his. She believed that much in him. He was the one who didn't have a family anymore. He'd given up being in the human world in order to try to help Gregori. He admired him. At first he'd been intrigued by the Carpathians, but then it became a compulsion, a need to aid them. The species was in danger of extinction in spite of their longevity. With no women and their inability to conceive or carry children, something had to be done, and Gary had been determined to do it. He'd led the research projects, with Gabrielle and Shea, a doctor, to aid him. In a short time, they'd come a long way.

He was in the middle of working on how to permanently remove all the mage-mutated microbes spreading throughout the soil. Xavier, a mage the Carpathian people had believed was their friend, had plotted to bring the entire species down and had nearly done so.

Carpathians were diligent about cleaning the soil where they slept, and about removing any of the microbes they found in their bodies that would kill the unborn children or the babies in their first year. Gary was certain, if Xavier could mutate the microbes to do his bidding, they could reverse the process. He was close, too. He felt it. He always felt something before a major breakthrough.

Gary had never once regretted his decision to help the Carpathian people. Never. He was fully committed to them. Until now. This moment. Giving up Gabrielle was nearly impossible. He took a deep breath and brushed his mouth over the top of her head, savoring the feeling of her in his arms. He wanted to commit this moment to memory. The scent of the flowers. The night sky. The way she looked in her gown. Her hair done so intricately, flowers woven through the silken strands. Even the bracelet, burning red-gold flames captured in the links, circling her delicate wrist.

"I know what you're doing," Gabrielle whispered. "I'm doing the same thing. I won't change my mind, Gary. I choose you. Every time, I choose you. It will always be you."

He didn't answer. He was a Daratrazanoff, and he felt the heavy responsibility of his bloodline. He had a duty to the prince, to his people. He was a shield now. A protector of his people. He had all the power and skills, but he also had the brain he'd been born with. He knew he was a huge resource to the Carpathians, and Mikhail and Gregori recognized him as such.

Gabrielle was correct when she said the prince and Gregori would discourage any romance between them. Still, he also knew, when he dropped from vivid, real emotion to absolutely nothing at all, they would try to cushion that fall. It would be brutal. He was intelligent enough to know why the Carpathians' emotions faded over time and why, when they were restored and their lifemate was taken from them, that abrupt nothingness sent them into a dangerous killing frenzy known as the thrall.

He wouldn't endanger Gabrielle. He had to find out when it would happen. How much time he had. If he had fifty years, he would take those years and give them to her. If he didn't have at least that many, he would have to give her up. She wouldn't forgive him. That would be the price he would have to pay to keep her safe. She would always feel as if he abandoned her. Rejected her.

"Think about it, Gabrielle. I'll do some research and see what we're looking at. We'll talk in a few days."

She shook her head, clinging to him. "If I let you go now, I'll lose you. Make love to me. Give me that."

Sheer torture. He felt as if his heart was being ripped out of his body. "Honey, if I touch you, I will never have the strength to walk away. I think you know that. We have to know what we're getting into before we make a decision."

She tore herself out of his arms. "You've already made up your mind. God. I hate them. I hate what I am. I hate that I have to live my life according to their rules. That some man I don't know or love can dictate to me what I can or can't have. I don't know if he even exists and he's ruling my life."

She turned and ran away from him, charging through the field of Night Star flowers. The stalks bent toward her, as if bowing as she passed, and then sprang back up. Gary watched her flee, hearing her weep as she raced down the mountain, her gown flowing behind her. He wept with her, his tears bloodred, dropping on the petals of the flowers surrounding him. Even as he looked at the droplets, the red faded to a dull gray.

Gary blinked rapidly to clear his vision. With Gabrielle's departure, all color was gone from his life. She'd taken it with her. He stood there a long time. Minutes. Hours. He didn't know. Staying still. Knowing if he moved, he might shatter. She took her bright light and left him in darkness.

"Gary."

He closed his eyes. The voice held too much compassion. Mikhail Dubrinsky, prince of the Carpathian people, stood to one side of him. Gregori was on the other. Guarding. Watching over him. To protect the others, or defend him? He didn't know, but Gabrielle must have returned while he stood alone and they had come to him.

"You knew." It was an accusation.

"I suspected," Mikhail corrected. "I hoped, for your sake. I feel the love you have for her. It is very strong. I wanted it to work out, but the chances were . . ."

"Zero," Gary said, tasting bitterness. "She couldn't have held the other half of my soul, nor could I hold hers. I had hoped she wasn't another man's lifemate. That she was psychic but that she wasn't a lifemate. Not all psychic women are. When she was converted, I held on to that. I didn't make a move, waiting for another to claim her. They didn't. She was mine. She belonged to me."

"Gary," Gregori said, his voice gentle. "I'm sorry."

"I gutted her. She's so hurt."

"She'll come to terms with it," Mikhail said.

For the first time Gary looked at the prince, met his eyes. He knew there was fury in his gaze, but Mikhail didn't flinch. "She was *gutted*. I did that to her. You both knew I would lose my ability to see in color immediately. You should have warned me."

He was looking directly at Mikhail so he saw the shock on the prince's face. Mikhail looked to Gregori. Gary followed his gaze. Gregori looked just as shocked.

"You've lost color?" Gregori asked.

Gary nodded. The sense of betrayal faded with the shock on their faces. "Yes. Tonight. Nearly all at once. When she left, she took the last of the color with her."

"That isn't good," Gregori said. "If it happened to you, it will happen to the others as well. Not Zev. He has his lifemate. But Luiz. And he's a De La Cruz. That's going to be brutal."

"How long before I lose my emotions?" Gary asked.

Gregori's gaze sharpened. "Do not even think about living with Gabrielle, Gary. Do you have any idea how dangerous that would be?"

"'That's for us to decide. I want to know how long I've got."

"Gary," Mikhail said, turning Gary's attention back to him. "We had no idea you would lose your ability to see in color, at least not for a couple of hundred years. We should have known better. You have the blood, the memories and experience of the ancients. Of course you would also have the loss of emotion and color as so many of them had no lifemate—and neither do you."

Gregori swore in the ancient language. "Gary. When you lose emotion too fast, it is dangerous. Horrendous. You cannot be with Gabrielle when that happens. You will need help through those first dark months."

Gary cursed his own intellect. He had known. He didn't want to know, but he had. He had lost Gabrielle. "I can't face her. If I see her cry one more time, or if she pleads with me, I won't be able to resist the love I have for her."

Mikhail let out his breath slowly. "Andre has found his lifemate. She believes she has the ability to extend the ancients' time before they become so dangerous they cannot hunt the undead or feed from innocents. Gregori was going to go to the monastery up in the mountains to talk to Fane, who seems to run the place. We were hoping that if Andre's lifemate could really do such a thing, the other healers could be taught as well. Perhaps you should go in Gregori's place."

Gregori stirred as if to protest, but Mikhail's gaze lifted to his just once, and Gregori subsided.

It is possible she can aid him as well.

Gregori took a deep breath, glided a step closer to Gary as if he would shield him from what was coming in the future.

Gary glanced at Gregori, held his eyes for a long moment and then nodded. It would give him time and distance, something he needed to separate himself from Gabrielle. He would either find a solution in that time, or he would learn to accept that he had lost her forever.

3

Gabrielle streaked through the dark sky. She was going to be too late. She felt it. That terrible buildup of tension. Of dread. It was there, a tremendous pressure in her chest. Her belly was in knots. Her heart hurt. An actual pain. No one would tell her where Mikhail had sent Gary, but he'd definitely been sent away. He was gone the following rising when she went looking for him. She'd done what she'd never attempted to do before. She'd used her deep connection with him to call to him—and then she had tried shapeshifting on her own. Flying on her own.

The echo of his answer was faint—very faint. She knew he was a very long distance away from her, but it didn't matter, she could follow his psychic trail. She'd had time to really think about what her life would be like without him, and she knew she didn't want to live in the Carpathian Mountains. She would go away, far from everything and everyone she knew. Disassociate. That was what she did. She lost herself in her research so she didn't have to face life. A lonely life. Gary was the only one who "saw" her. She needed him to be real. To exist.

She didn't even care if she was chasing after him, needy as hell. Psycho ex-girlfriend. Because she knew without a shadow of a doubt that he loved her. He would walk through fire for her. If she didn't get him away from the prince and Gregori, she would lose him forever, and she would lose herself.

Below her the mountains streaked by. She caught glimpses of the dense forest and craggy mountaintops. Ahead were the mists surrounding the monastery where the ancients went when they wouldn't walk into the sun but could no longer be trusted around humans or Carpathians. When they could no longer safely hunt the undead. They were dangerous men.

Gabrielle didn't want to go anywhere near the monastery. She didn't want anything at all to do with them, but if that was Gary's destination, then she was going to be there first. She knew, from sliding into her sister's mind, that he had gone to see Andre and his new lifemate, Teagan. Together, the three would approach those in the monastery to see if they would be willing to have Teagan try to help them. Gabrielle intended to catch them outside the gates. She had followed Gary's psychic trail and found her way.

The air had gone cold, unnaturally so. She could feel the safeguards woven into the mists broadcasting a warning that got under her skin even when she knew why and how it was there. Inside the mist things moved. Shapes. Voices whispered warnings. The mist swirled, dense and heavy, so that even in the form she'd taken, she was saturated, the water penetrating her feathers, a nearly impossible feat.

She could easily see how the ancients had stayed undiscovered for so many years. Their warning system was brilliant and cleverly in play all year round as well as both day and night. The actual location of the monastery appeared to change as well. She'd catch a glimpse of it, the mist would close over it and when the veil parted again over what she could swear was the exact same spot, the buildings were gone.

She was fully Carpathian with all the powers. She had never really utilized her gifts before. No one had really talked to her about what she could and couldn't do, and she hadn't asked. She should have asked. She knew most humans were converted by a lifemate and their lifemate taught them everything they needed to know. She'd been converted, and although grateful to be alive, she had disappeared into her work so she wouldn't have to face a life that was very alien to her.

Perhaps if someone had worked with her, she wouldn't

have felt so cut off, but no one thought to do so, and she couldn't ask. Not the prince. Certainly not Gregori. She had counted on Gary. She had always counted on Gary. He would teach her what she needed to know.

Now she used her mind to keep herself in the air. She knew everything started in one's mind. Her feathers might be soaked, but she could shift in the air if she had to. Whatever the ancients tried, she would not be afraid. She would not back down. Gary belonged with her. No one was going to take him away from her. She'd seen in his eyes that he was close to capitulating.

The owl began to falter in the center of the mist and she forced a shift, one she'd never attempted before, but she was very familiar with molecules and the molecular structure of the human body, so she wasn't as afraid of becoming molecules as she had been when she'd first learned how to shift into the form of an animal or bird.

The veil of mist parted again, and way down the mountain she caught a glimpse of four men and a woman hiking the mountain trail above the human village. They looked tiny, like ants. She was grateful they couldn't possibly see her in the thick, swirling clouds of living fog miles and miles above them.

Without warning a wrenching sickness took her over, so that even in her present state, without a body, she felt as if she might tumble from the sky and be sick over and over. Fear seized her. She couldn't tell why. It was unreasonable. She knew that, but it didn't help to lessen the effect on her. Fortunately, the veil parted again, and this time, she actually saw the gates of the monastery. More. She saw Gary. He was with Andre. She recognized the Carpathian others referred to as "the Ghost." With him was a woman. She was shorter than Gabrielle and had beautiful, mocha skin. Her hair was a deep ebony, and even braided it was very thick and hung to her waist.

Relief flooded through her and she dropped down fast, afraid if she didn't get through the small hole in the mist, she would lose the location again. She saw Gary turn his head toward her as she came out of the mist to shift only feet from him. Andre stepped in front of his lifemate.

"Gabrielle." Gary breathed her name.

The unguarded look on his face was everything she could ask for right before a mask dropped down.

"Gary. I've had enough time to think about everything, and I'm willing to take the chance. We have too much for me to be afraid of reaching for what I want," Gabrielle said hastily, moving right into him.

She ignored Andre and his lifemate, Teagan. She ignored the fact that she was nearly pressed against the huge, thick gates of the monastery. She knew better than to touch them, but she stayed firmly inserted between Gary and the gates. She knew she only had a few minutes before everything was lost. She knew because she felt the two Carpathians trailing after her. If they arrived before she managed to convince Gary they deserved their time together, she would lose everything.

"Gabrielle." Gary said her name softly. Just that—her name.

She closed her eyes at the love in his voice. So real. So raw. So honest. How could anyone ask them to give up each other? As humans they would have married, had children and lived a happily-ever-after life. She knew that with every breath she took. She could hear the same knowledge in the sound of Gary's voice. In her name.

She held out her hand. "Come away with me. Right now. Andre can do the prince's bidding. We can take fifty years. Fifty. That's all we're asking for ourselves. We have an endless amount of time ahead of us." She couldn't think about that long eternity of loneliness stretching in front of her—not without Gary. "Fifty years isn't too much to ask, Gary."

She held her breath. Looked into his eyes. Let him see how much he meant to her. How much she loved him. They deserved to be together. They belonged. She felt it in her heart. No, in her very soul, the soul she supposedly shared with another man.

"Gabrielle." The melting sensation in his heart told Gary he was so far gone in this woman he was going to lose the battle. He didn't want to ever hurt her. Not again. The look on her face before she ran down the mountain, the rejection and pain so plain in her eyes, had gutted him right along with her.

"We've given to them. We both have." She stepped closer.

Her scent was elusive, mesmerizing, beautiful and delicate like she was, wrapping him up and surrounding him with *her*. Gary always got lost in her when she was so close. He couldn't help it, he had to touch her. All that soft skin. It felt as soft as it looked. He framed her face with both hands, ignoring Andre, who had stepped close, his lifemate, Teagan, who had tears in her eyes, one step behind her man.

Gary stared into Gabrielle's dove-gray eyes and fell hard. He always did. She was right. They both had given much to the Carpathian people. Both had suffered. Nearly died. "Fifty years," he whispered.

Her eyes searched his, hope creeping into her expression. "We'll come back after and give the rest of our lives to them. If we find lifemates at that time, fine; if we don't, we had our time."

"Honey," he said, still trying to do the right thing. "I could lose my emotions. Any time. Any day. What then?"

"You'll know before it happens. They fade away. Over time. We have time. That's one thing we do have."

"My ability to see in color left when you did on our wedding night." He would always remember the sight of her running from him, taking the vivid colors with her, leaving his world gray. "My emotions could go the same way."

"I get that you're saying there's a risk. I know you would never hurt me, Gary. I *know* it. If you lose your emotions, we'll deal with that. But it should be *my* risk. *My* choice. I should have that right. I work with hot viruses; do you think I wouldn't risk everything for you? I'm fighting for us, Gary. I need to know I'm just as important to you as you are to me. I need you to fight for me."

She laid it all out. Courageous. Right in front of Andre and Teagan. She bared her soul, leaving herself exposed and vulnerable to him. There was no resisting that. He felt the smile start somewhere deep inside of him. She was right. She was *so* right. Fifty years in a Carpathian's life was nothing. For them, it would be everything they wanted.

"I love you, Gabrielle," he stated. "I love you with every breath in my body. And honey, never, for one moment, think you aren't worth fighting for. I'd die for you. You aren't second to anyone. You're my number-one priority."

Her face lit up. Like sunshine. Like the stars over his head. Lighting his world. He might not be able to see in color, but he could see the light shining like a beacon—for him. His heart jerked in his chest.

"I think Andre and Teagan can handle this assignment without me. I was here to observe, if the ancients even wanted to try Teagan's experiment. We can leave now. Go to the States, live out our time there."

Gabrielle flung herself at him with a glad cry, her mouth turned up to his. He caught her in midair, wrapping his arms around her at the same time she wrapped her legs around him. His mouth found hers, tasting her. Tasting the wild in her. The wild she never let anyone see, but he always knew it was there, under the surface. His. She'd been his from the moment he'd laid eyes on her.

He kissed her. Hard. Wet. A kiss that promised there was a lot more to come. Her mouth was a kind of paradise, her taste addicting. Sweet. Pure honey. Her body jerked hard, nearly pulling her from his arms. He lifted his head. Saw her eyes wide with shock and fear.

"Gary," she whispered. Scared. Terrified.

Her body jerked again. Hard. Hard enough to tear her from his arms. She screamed as she flew backward, slamming into the thick wooden gates of the monastery. Vines, like snakes, circled her wrists and drew her hands above her head. More vines wrapped around her waist, pinning her to the massive wall, holding her there, a prisoner.

She screamed again, her eyes on him. "Help! What's happening? What's wrong? Help me!"

A voice woke him. A soft musical murmur. Sound. Melodic. The notes pushed through the darkness of his mind. Silvery notes that left a small trail in their wake. He could almost see them, tiny, narrow streams of liquid silver penetrating the dense sheet of unrelenting darkness. The streaks left trails through his mind, much like a comet. The light spread. Sank deep.

Aleksei waved his hand to remove the soil surrounding him. The musical notes went from silver to gold. *Gold.* Not gray. Not a dull, dingy white. *Gold.* Silver and gold. He could see the notes dancing through the sheet of darkness, bursting like stars, ripping the sheet to shreds. Each note tore more of the dark from his mind, letting in the light until the backs of his eyes burned.

He blinked rapidly and looked around slowly, his eyes hooded, lashes fanning down to protect his vision. The carefully cultivated plants were in bloom and he could see the riot of colors. So bright. So vibrant. His eyes burned and the intensity of the colors caused a lurch in his belly. Disorienting. Still. *Colors.*

He took a deep breath and drew in the air she breathed. His lifemate. She was close. Right outside the gates. He heard her, that soft murmur. Plea. She was arguing with someone. He drew her into his lungs. Deep. Deeper. Holding her right there with the miracle of silver and gold notes burning through his shredded soul. Cauterizing. Attempting to repair the damage done by centuries of killing. Of being alone, hoping and then losing hope. The darkness didn't win and yet it had—until now.

He forced his eyes to shutter, to reduce the vivid colors enough that he could rise without the lurching, disorienting feeling that was so disturbing. Her voice rose outside the gates, carried to him on the wind. Soft. Pleading. Tears in her voice. A man's murmur followed. Rage hit him. Deadly. Dangerous.

Help! What's happening? What's wrong? Help me!

Emotion was something he didn't even remember, and the intensity was overwhelming. He could barely contain elation at finding his lifemate and fury that another man hurt her enough to make her cry. The storm inside him was violent, relentless and demanding. He did his best to tamp it down. He had to be in control. He was far too dangerous not to be.

Aleksei took to the sky, something he hadn't done in a very long while, whirling like the mist, carried on the sudden forceful wind. His lifemate's screams tore at him, sent streaks of pure rage rushing through his bloodstream. He had never heard the fear and anguish in anyone's voice as he did in hers, and it ripped him apart, ripped away the last veneer of civilization, leaving him solely what he'd always been—a predator at the very top of the food chain. There would be no escaping him. Not for her. Not for the man who caused her tears.

From the air he saw the woman he knew belonged to him and the man she faced with tears running down her face. She was beautiful. Absolutely beautiful. Her back was against the gate, both arms stretched above her head, wrists bound by the guardians. Another binding circled her slim waist. She wore a man's garb, something he didn't care for at all, especially when another man was looking at her as if she was his entire world. It was too form-fitting, revealing her luscious curves. The plants Fane used as safeguards to protect those in the monastery had done their job, recognizing that this woman belonged and holding her. Should any approach her, the vines would protect her.

He immediately noted Andre was there with his lifemate—a woman he recognized from a few days earlier when she had tried to heal Andre after he'd battled a master vampire. Fane, keeper of the monastery, had given them aid, but Aleksei and two others had stayed close to protect them.

The stranger stepped toward Aleksei's lifemate and

something animalistic in him roared a protest. He dropped from the sky to insert his body solidly between the stranger and his lifemate.

"You dare to touch my woman? My lifemate? You dare such a thing?" He switched to English, realizing they had been using that language. "I am Aleksei, and the woman is *mine*."

Aleksei was utterly confident in his skills but he was surprised and a little taken aback to recognize that the man—his enemy—was a Daratrazanoff. There was no mistaking one from that lineage or the power emanating from one of them. He had never known a Daratrazanoff to be a man without honor, but to try to take another man's lifemate was a crime punishable by death—even for those second-in-command to the prince.

He exploded into action, and he was fast. These last years in the monastery could never take away the speed and experience of his centuries of battle. To keep fit and in practice, each evening the ancients gathered to fight, using weapons and hand-to-hand combat. They stayed sharp that way, and it helped to occupy their minds.

He knew he was risking his honor to go into battle; that risk was the very reason he had entered the monastery in the first place. He was far too powerful. Had lived too long. He would be a vampire few could kill. This was his lifemate, and he would defend her with his last breath even if he risked the ultimate dishonor.

Gabrielle screamed and fought the vines holding her in place. Andre barked a command to Teagan and she disappeared, obeying him instantly. Gary was only barely aware of those things. His attention was centered on the raging beast claiming Gabrielle. The man was tall and strong—abnormally so, even for a Carpathian. His shoulders were broad, his chest heavily muscled. His eyes glowed red, vicious, predatory. He hit like a jackhammer, slamming his fist straight at Gary's heart, his white teeth exposed. His teeth showed his state of mind, and it wasn't good.

Gary dissolved fast before the fist could penetrate his chest. He came up behind the Carpathian, reaching to circle his neck with his arm, to lock around him in an effort to break his neck. Thick black hair spilled down the intruder's back, and the hair went wild, became alive, slashing ropes of razors that cut flesh when touched.

Around him, Gary could feel the frenzied energy spilling out in every direction. Gabrielle, nearly hysterical, desperate to be free, terrified for him. Terrified of the predatory creature that had attacked him. He could feel the energy pouring off the stranger, so broken, so far gone, the darkness in him absolutely crushing. Surprisingly, Gary's own emotions were much easier to control in the face of the threat.

He had no idea who Aleksei was, but so far, Andre hadn't made a move toward them, which he would have had the crazy ancient been a vampire. Still, Gary wasn't about to allow anyone to hurt Gabrielle, and this man had to be responsible for the vines holding her prisoner. She'd been jerked backward a good fifteen feet and slammed hard against the monastery gates.

With Aleksei's razor-blade hair, Gary had no choice but to release him and jump back. He needed to keep his distance and use modern weapons. This was an ancient Carpathian, possibly a vampire, and no matter how much power and knowledge Gary possessed, he didn't have this hunter's experience. He needed to use intellect to defeat him, not brawn. He was outmatched and he knew it, and that meant he had to press and press until he was completely played out. The one thing he couldn't allow his opponent was time.

He leapt back and pulled his weapon. He'd been developing ways to fight vampires since he'd first become Gregori's friend. He'd perfected several. He flew back, his body now protecting Gabrielle, as he drew and fired his weapon. Aleksei simultaneously whirled and came at him, his features sheer stone, eyes blazing with fury.

The small gun was lightweight and fit in the palm of Gary's hand. To kill a vampire wasn't all that easy. One had to extract the heart and incinerate it. The gun rapid-fired several lethal circular bullets—claws of steel. The discs, high velocity, were sharp enough to penetrate through flesh and bone and designed to burrow deep.

Once fired, the disc locked on to a target—the withered low-level beat of the undead's heart—surrounded the organ and clamped down. As soon as the claw had the heart in its grip it emitted a high-pitched screech that signaled, even during a loud battle, the heart was ready for extraction. The second trigger on the gun activated the extraction. The entire process took the same amount of time it took to fire a bullet.

The disc hit true. Aleksei stumbled back under the impact, his hands going to his chest. Gary fired a second disc as Aleksei reached into his own chest to pull the claw from inside his body. The ancient didn't make a single sound. Not one. He didn't even blink. If he felt pain, he didn't show it, but he did dodge the second disc with blurring speed, coming at Gary so fast there was no time to move, no time to think of anything but survival. All the while Aleksei rushed, his hand continued to remove the claw from his chest.

Aleksei had no time to puzzle out the reason his lifemate continued to cry out for his opponent's safety. He couldn't take the chance that Gabrielle would be hurt in the battle, and a Daratrazanoff was between them. Close to her. Far too close to her. He felt Andre moving in his mind, telling him to stop, but that didn't make sense either. Andre knew that a lifemate was never to be touched by another man. Never. To break that sacred rule was punishable by death, no matter the lineage of the offender.

As he whirled toward Gary, using both speed and movement to prevent the crazed Carpathian from using his weapon, Aleksei sent the wind rushing around them, driving the man away from Gabrielle with a series of fireballs aimed at him, raining out of the night sky. The two combatants came together in a fury of blazing fire. The flames came out of the wind, firebombs dropping to surround them, to hold the two in the center, moving them back away from Aleksei's lifemate. He was careful that the fireballs were well away from her, but the flames prevented Gary from getting near her.

"Stop them, Andre," Gabrielle shouted, terrified for Gary. She struggled against the vines, and the more she struggled, the harder the tough wood bit into her skin, until blood began to trickle down her arms. "He's going to kill Gary."

She could see nothing now but the wall of flames. Strangely the fire wasn't in the least bit hot to her skin. Still, not seeing what was happening between the two men was far worse than witnessing it.

"I cannot," Andre said quietly, and indicated something to her left and then to her right.

Gabrielle turned her head, and her breath left her body in a rush. For a moment she went still, her heart pounding so hard it nearly came out of her chest. There were others. Others like the one called Aleksei who had claimed she belonged to him. She felt their darkness. It was oppressing. Frightening. Sad. So sad that even in the midst of her fear for Gary, she felt the weight of their sorrow pressing down on her.

She could see they were watching the combatants intently, and they also were very aware of the blood trickling down her wrists. They could smell it. Sometimes eyes would move over her and then become riveted on her wrists. Terror mounted. If Gary didn't save her, these horrible ancient Carpathians were going to feast on her. Devour her. Drink her blood until there was nothing left of her.

"*Gary.*" She whispered his name. Her only salvation. Her love. Her fear. "Please, God, help him."

She didn't care if every one of these horrible ancients ripped her to pieces. If Andre wouldn't help Gary, then she would. She turned her head and stared at the bracelet on her wrist. She'd seen her brother Jubal's bracelet become a weapon. He did it by tuning himself to the metal. It worked only for him.

Gabrielle closed her eyes and tried to block out what was happening around her. She concentrated on the delicate links of metal surrounding her wrist. At once she heard the low hum that she'd noticed before. Instantly she locked on to that and sent her own command. She needed the vines gone. Right. This. Moment.

Gary Daratrazanoff hit Aleksei with the force of a freight train, driving him back toward the wall of flames. Aleksei dissolved and came up behind Gary, re-forming, catching at his head and wrenching with enormous strength to break the neck. Gary shifted out from under him, becoming a huge, powerful python, coiling around him fast, the head eye to eye, the constriction deadly.

Aleksei didn't fight it; instead, he shifted his body to that of a python as well, a feat many Carpathians weren't able to do. Few could shift when they were being held captive in any form. The two snakes coiled and thrashed, upright, standing on their tails, facing each other with big, angry, curved teeth. Once those teeth sank in, it would be difficult to extract them, even in his present form.

The head of the python came close and, without warning, small, wiggling snakes erupted from its mouth, leaping to fill Aleksei's. Aleksei allowed the rain of fire to stop in order to combat the multitude of snakes leaping at him, trying to get inside his body. He turned his snake's head to buy a couple of seconds, all the while following the beat of the heart inside the snake. There was always a heart, no matter how one tried to protect it. No matter how withered and black it had become.

He concentrated on the sound until he pinpointed it perfectly and then he shifted, one hand shooting out from his python's body to slam into Gary's python, his fist penetrating deep.

Gabrielle screamed, the sound piercing the night. A wail of utter despair and terror. Her terrified screams filled his mind. Filled his heart and soul. Still, to fight a Daratrazanoff with the kind of power and skills they had, he would have to shut her terror out. He couldn't feel anything at all. Nothing. Only the power running through his body. The confidence born of centuries of battles. He knew fighting and killing this man was dangerous to him as well. One more kill, even with his lifemate to anchor him, could send him over the edge into madness. He was in the monastery to prevent having to hunt and destroy lives—even the undead.

Once he penetrated the chest cavity, he shifted, and to his shock, Gary shifted as well, something extremely difficult under the circumstances, but it didn't matter. Aleksei had him now. He knew it. And then Gary's eyes held triumph, and Aleksei knew he was fighting something altogether different from the vampires he had fought over the centuries.

Gary's fist smashed through his chest toward his heart, coming from an altogether different direction, and the form in front of him simply disintegrated. Gary had deliberately misled him with the python, with the heartbeat. A genius in battle. Now it really was life or death, and Aleksei had no intention of dying now that he had found his lifemate.

Genius didn't mean experience in battle. Aleksei slammed his head into Gary's forehead, shifting just enough to put a sledgehammer there. Gary fell back and down, and Aleksei went down to one knee, his fist going in for the kill. Something hit him from behind and he caught the attacker with one arm behind his back, circling the small waist and nearly hurtling the featherlight body toward the gate of the monastery. At the last moment he realized his attacker was his own lifemate. Simultaneously he heard the low protest of his brethren and Andre's sharp command to stop.

He set Gabrielle down gently and rose slowly, shocked at her behavior. He could see that his brothers were stunned as well—all but Andre, who appeared to stare at her with compassion. Her wrists were bloody and he could smell her, the faint, almost elusive feminine scent that called to every cell in his body.

She had *betrayed* him. With another man. The man she was trying to protect. The man that wasn't him. No Carpathian woman would do such a thing. She stood there, staring at him with huge, frightened eyes. He knew why. Everyone knew why. There was absolute silence. Even the wind held its breath while he decided whether to kill her, or keep her. She didn't deserve to live, and neither did Gary Daratrazanoff. He had been betrayed by his own kind. By a family he knew and respected.

He let his breath out slowly, his eyes on her. She was beautiful even in her fear. Her entire body trembled. She lifted a small, delicate hand to her mouth and he could see that it shook. She was tall, with a lot of curves, but she seemed fragile to him.

He heard the murmur of his brethren and turned his head to see Mikhail Dubrinsky, the reigning prince of the Carpathian people, and Gregori Daratrazanoff, his second-in-command, materializing close to him. Close enough for them to be a threat to him. He felt that threat emanating from Gregori, and his brethren did as well. They moved closer, ringing the newcomers, forcing Andre into the middle. Andre was a wild card, but the others would stand with him. None of the ancients residing within the monastery had sworn allegiance to the prince. Not him. Not the others.

Mikhail stepped closer but Gregori and Andre closed ranks instantly, preventing him from moving toward Aleksei. Mikhail held up his hand as Aleksei remained over Gary, holding the man down with his mind, his fist ready to remove the heart. He heard his lifemate make a single sound. Low. One of terror.

"They deserve death." Aleksei made it a statement, but he knew he didn't want to kill her. He wanted to keep her. He wanted the prince to perform a miracle for him. He had thought Gabrielle was his miracle, but he was wrong and the bitterness in his mouth, in his mind, had turned an ugly, dark flavor.

He planned every move in his mind. The speed he would need to kill Gary and then Gabrielle. His brethren would end him when he went into the thrall and he would still have his honor. Still. He waited. For a miracle.

"I know what this appears to be," Mikhail said. His voice was soft. Low. The sound alone carried power. Not the challenging power of a male hunter, but a magnetic, compelling sound that got into one's mind and took away anger. Rage. The driving need to kill. "I assure you, my word as the prince of our people, this is not what it looks like."

"She is mine."

"I am aware of that," Mikhail said, in that same calming tone. "She does not understand, and the fault does not lie with her, or with Gary, but with us." He indicated Gregori. "We are solely responsible for this mess."

Gabrielle cried out. Low. Afraid. Mikhail half turned so he could try to reassure her without putting himself at risk. She looked terrified. "Don't," she whispered. "Mikhail, don't."

"You are his true lifemate, Gabrielle. He won't harm you. He will cherish you and protect you."

Gabrielle shook her head, tears running down her face. "No. I won't accept him. I can't. You can't ask me to do that."

She really was frightened, and it was clear to Aleksei there was something he didn't understand about the situation. She was breaking his heart standing there, one pleading hand out toward Mikhail, the blood streaking her soft wrist. Imploring him.

Aleksei sought to reassure her. He spoke in the ancient language. Clearly she didn't understand, continuing to stare at him with frightened eyes. How that could be, he didn't know, but he switched to English and translated for her. "There is no reason to fear now. I am here, your true lifemate. This man will not touch you again."

She shook her head, tears spilling down her face. "No, you don't understand. I refuse. I refuse to be your lifemate. I *love* him. I'm *his*."

Fury filled him. He'd spent centuries looking for his woman. Centuries of bleak loneliness. Hope faded, and all he had left was his honor. She would not take that from him because she was afraid. Carpathian women knew their duty. They understood what could happen when a lifemate was stripped of his other half.

She dared to love another man? Choose another man? She was *his*. His reward. His anchor. His only hope. She had no right to refuse him. He felt the bloodlust rising in him, felt his teeth lengthen. He didn't hesitate, not when a Daratrazanoff was trying to take his woman. Not when she was too frightened to do right by him. Not when dishonor was a breath away.

"Te avio päläfertiilam. Éntölam kuulua, avio päläfertiilam. Ted kuuluak, kacad, kojed. Élidamet andam. Pesämet andam. Uskolfertiilamet andam."

"Stop! Stop it!" Gabrielle screamed the words. Frantic. "Mikhail, please. Stop him. You have to make him stop."

He heard the tears in her voice and that tore at him, but he couldn't stop. There was no way to stop. Not even to comfort her. Not even to reassure her that she would be safe with him. Rage was still there. The bloodlust hadn't subsided.

"Sívamet andam. Sielamet andam. Ainamet andam. Sívamet kuuluak kaik että a ted. Ainaak olenszal sívambin. Te élidet ainaak pide minan. Te avio päläfertiilam. Ainaak sívamet jutta oleny. Ainaak terád vigyázak."

He spoke firmly, in a deep, commanding timbre. He used his ancient language and felt every word ripped from his soul. Even as he uttered the binding words imprinted on him before he was born, he felt the ties binding them together. His soul to hers.

She cried out with each completed vow. As if he'd struck her. As if, somehow, he'd ripped out her heart and soul. Before he could step close to her to soothe her, he heard the warning growl from the Daratrazanoff on the ground. And it was a growl.

"Gabrielle." The single name was spoken softly. The raw love was so strong it hurt to hear it. The sound made the man exposed, vulnerable, and showed his loss. His despair. The knowledge that she was lost to him for all time.

Aleksei jumped back as Gary Daratrazanoff leapt from the ground. He was even more shocked when he looked at the man's face. He'd witnessed the killing thrall of a Carpathian male who had lost his lifemate on more than one occasion. Each time, he'd been the one to deliver the mercy killing to prevent him from dishonor.

"Gary!"

His woman—Gabrielle—cried out, more frightened than ever. She couldn't fail to recognize the way the man shut down completely. It was a terrifying thing to see darkness claim a good man. Aleksei moved his body squarely between Gary and his lifemate. The man was in a killing rage. The thrall was impossible to stop, but it was only brought on when a lifemate died. What was going on? Surely his woman couldn't have been Gary's lifemate as well.

He'd had enough. He'd taken all he was going to take from any of them. He whirled, snatched up his woman, tossed her over his shoulder and was inside the gate before anyone could stop him. Behind him, his brethren joined him, sealing the safeguards against all outsiders.

He cared little what the prince, Gregori and Andre would have to do to the Daratrazanoff who had tried to take his lifemate from him. Lock him down, send him to the earth to heal or simply kill him. None of that mattered now. Only his lifemate. The woman who had betrayed him with another man.

He set her down, and she flung herself back toward the gate. He caught her in an iron grip around her waist and walked her backward. Her back hit the wall of their gathering building. Instantly he caged her there, using his large frame to hold her in place. He put one hand on her belly and the other beside her head. She looked up at him with tears swimming in her eyes and a look of utter terror on her face.

His eyes blazed down at her. He refused to be swayed by her fear. "Now you will explain your unseemly conduct, and know this, woman—you will suffer punishment should you not obey me."

4

abrielle glared defiantly up into Aleksei's face. She *hated* him with every cell in her body. She detested the fact that his face was purely masculine and she noticed. She hated that she felt the heat of his body, or saw that his eyes were a clear, startling green. He wasn't handsome in the accepted sense of the word; he was far too dangerous and rough-looking for that. He didn't try to hide the fact that he was a predator from anyone, least of all her. And she didn't care. Not one little bit.

"*Obey* you? That's what you expect? That's *never* going to happen." She spat the words at him, hoping to goad him into killing her. "You took everything from me. I will never do anything you say."

His breath hissed out and his eyes went flat and cold. Hard. Terrifying. His hand wrapped around her throat, and for one moment she thought he'd actually break her neck. Or strangle her. Her pulse beat into the palm of his hand. She held his stare, but it was difficult. Very, very difficult. The gaping wound in his chest was already closed, his shirt clean of all blood. How he'd managed that she didn't know, but it made her all the more angry at him.

"Do not ever say I did not give you a chance to explain."

She stuck her chin in the air. "I don't owe you an explanation. I have nothing at all to say to you. Nothing." She nearly spat the last word at him.

Her heart nearly stopped beating when he transferred his hold from her throat to her hair. He bunched the long strands in his fist, and there was nothing gentle about the way he twisted his hand so that his grip was anchored close to her scalp. He turned and walked rapidly in the opposite direction, forcing her, by her hair, to go with him.

She bit back a scream of pain and beat at his hand and arm. When that didn't slow him down—in fact he didn't even appear to notice—she tried to concentrate on activating the bracelet. Even that let her down. She fought, but the hold on her hair was relentless and every movement she made, from attempting to kick him to hitting him as hard as possible, only increased the agony in her scalp.

Aleksei thrust his lifemate inside the walls of his home. Each of the ancients had their own personal space, and this was his. The bare bones of a house. Nothing on the walls. No furniture. What was the need? The ground was the floor. The soil his bed. He waved his hand and instantly there was a soft carpet covering the dirt. That was all she was going to get.

He would have killed her outside. *Before.* Before he'd uttered the ritual binding words and bound her soul to his. He should have. Another mistake on his part. A big one. Now he couldn't kill her. It was impossible to kill one's lifemate after the ritual words bound them together. He either had to keep her or meet the dawn, something that was so against his nature that he had come here to this monastery, where others like him viewed it as a cowardly act.

He'd lived a life of honor to be brought to this, so close to his downfall he could feel it. The darkness spreading like a virus through him. A breath away. Waiting to take him. He had lived too many centuries and had skills not many had. He would make a terrifying vampire, one that would kill hundreds if not thousands before he was brought down. He knew that. He knew it with every fiber of his being.

He shoved the woman away from him, down to her knees. *She* had brought him to this. She was Carpathian and she knew the consequences of her actions to her lifemate should she betray him. Even her tear-streaked face couldn't stop the rush of fury at her. Not only would she bring him down, but she would be indirectly responsible for the innocents he would kill should he turn. And he would turn if he didn't finish this and make this treacherous wench fully his.

He tried to shut down his emotions so her tears wouldn't get to him, wouldn't soften him, but his fury was too great, the darkness taking hold of him so firmly he feared if they didn't complete the bonding he would lose it and kill her and as many others as possible. Should the ancients have to destroy him, they would turn as well. Because of her. This harlot. She put them all in danger.

"Take off your clothes."

Every vestige of color drained from her face, leaving her skin pale and her eyes enormous. She shook her head, wrapped her arms around her body and bit hard at her lip.

He wasn't about to repeat himself. He stepped close to her, caught her hair in his fist and dragged her to her feet. It took a moment with her struggling to get her feet under her. He didn't help her. The moment she was up, he leaned in and sank his teeth into her neck, right over that tempting, pounding pulse.

She cried out, but he let go of her hair and jerked her tight against him. Her blood spilled into his mouth. Saturated his cells. Ruby red. The finest he'd ever tasted. *Ever.* In all the centuries of living, of surviving, of taking blood to sustain him, there had been no other blood that tasted so amazing. Nothing had prepared him for the taste of her. She burst on his tongue like fine bubbles, teasing and eluding his ability to name the mixture of tastes.

He knew he was instantly addicted. He would crave her for eternity. And that was just fine with him. She was his, and she'd earned her place as his slave. No more. No lifemate status for such a treacherous woman. He would feed on her. Enjoy every drop he took from her.

As he fed, he stripped the clothes from her body with his mind, taking great care not to enter her mind. He didn't dare. He didn't want to see her treachery, what she'd done with this other man. That would send him crashing over the edge. He knew it, those images, her feelings for another man. Her *betrayal*.

Deliberately he remained fully clothed, so that she was completely naked and helpless in his arms. He wanted her to know that there was nothing she could do. Nothing. He controlled her. He would have control of her life for eternity. She didn't deserve kindness or love. She deserved humiliation and to serve his every need. Her blood was exquisite. He hoped the rest of her was as well.

He didn't try to soothe her as he aroused her body. He wanted her to know he could bend her will to his. He was an ancient. She was very young for a Carpathian lifemate, but that was no excuse for her adulterous behavior. His hand went to her breast, to her nipple. Even as he rolled and tugged hard, he sent the impression of his tongue lapping over her breast, drawing her into his mouth and suckling.

She cried out. Squirmed. He smelled her heat and still he took her blood. Let himself indulge in his needs. Needs that were sharp and terrible, clawing at him now. His body was hard. A steel spike between his legs, growing into a monster of need. For her. For this woman who had betrayed him.

He closed the wound on her neck, but didn't take away the evidence of his ownership. His gaze dropped to the circle of lacerations on her wrists and, in spite of himself, he raised first one hand and then the other to heal them with his tongue. The fact that he had to do that—that he couldn't stand her hurt—made him even angrier. He opened his shirt with a flick of his wrist. "Feed." He uttered the command coldly.

She swallowed hard and shook her head, blinking up at him. Her tears continued to flow. He bent his head and deliberately licked up the trail of tears, drawing the flavor into his mouth. Just like her blood, the taste was exquisite. He caught the back of her head with his palm, opened his chest with a single fingernail and pressed her head ruthlessly to him. Again, he gave her no choice, and he knew, once the taste of him was in her mouth, on her lips, she would be just as addicted to his taste as he was to hers.

Her mouth moved against him and the spike between his legs grew even more monstrous. Thick. Greedy. So hungry for her he felt the darkness sliding closer. He had to get her body aroused, in a state of frenzy. His hands roamed over her, not gently, but demanding a response. He felt every swift intake of breath when he found an erogenous zone and he capitalized on it. Still, this was never going to be about her. This would always be about him, and he wanted her to know that from the start.

She could withhold her love and loyalty from him, but he would always have access to her blood and her body. He found both extremely pleasurable. Her body was all soft curves. Her breasts were extremely sensitive. He liked her nipples and knew he would spend hours playing with her body. No. *His* body. She belonged to him—all of her—and no other man would ever touch her again. He knew he could tie her to him through sex. He knew he could make her want him with every breath in her body. Not love, but sheer hunger. Maybe in a few hundred years he'd get past her betrayal. But for now . . .

His fingers slid down her belly. He loved the feel of her skin and wanted more against him. He got rid of his clothes with a single thought and allowed his hands to take in more of her. Heat emanated from the junction of her legs. Her body moved restlessly against his. Still, he wanted her more aroused. He wanted her to *need* to obey his every command in spite of the fact that she claimed she detested him.

He swiped his finger along her damp entrance, and her entire body shivered. He smiled above her head. She was definitely sensitive, and he was going to enjoy himself. He kept her feeding, knowing his blood would be an aphrodisiac to her. He slid one finger inside her slowly, feeling her slick heat, the grasp of her delicate muscles, surprised at how tight she was. Her protest was another moan, and the sound vibrated straight through his cock.

She protested, but in spite of her detesting him, her body wanted his. He had made certain of that. He controlled her senses. He wanted her to know he could do that. That he would become her world. The only things she would want were his blood and his body. He would be the only man she craved. She would do anything to have him by the time he finished with her. And he would never finish with her. This was a sentence for eternity—for both of them.

He took his time, circling her sensitive bud, watching her body shiver in reaction. Watching her face go soft and sensual. Her eyes fought him, but her body responded to the heat and hunger he created.

"Enough," he murmured. He wouldn't put it past her to try to drain him dry. He kept a hold on her senses, still refusing to enter her mind in the way of lifemates. He didn't want to see that man there—not ever. Daratrazanoff. Just the thought of him had him snarling. Growling. A nearly animal response. He was long ago gone from civilization. He was from ancient times and knew nothing of modern women. But she would learn her place.

Gabrielle licked at the small wound on his chest and just that lapping of her tongue sent heat curling through his cock. He wanted more. He pushed her off of him. Away from him. Arrogantly, he walked away from her, to the center of the thick carpet he'd installed.

"Get down on your knees."

Her eyes blazed defiantly. He smiled. Slow. Mean. Wanting her to defy him. Wanting her to hate this, because that would make her surrender all the more sweet. She couldn't talk. He'd given her the chance to talk and she hadn't taken it, so there was nothing more to say. Her eyes remained on his, and the defiance turned to despair when she could do nothing else but go to her knees and crawl toward him.

Aleksei watched her body move. She was truly beautiful. Had he seen her somewhere, he would have noticed her immediately. Picked her right out of a crowd. He would have known she was his even before he heard her voice. What he would never have guessed was that she could be so beautiful on the outside and so rotten on the inside.

She was at his feet, moving up his legs, her hands sliding

up his thighs. He caught her wrists and held her still, an ugliness rippling through his stomach. Churning. He didn't want to see her like this. He was angry, and he was unfamiliar with such an emotion. He was close to turning, and he had no idea what to do with the dark whispers and need for violence welling up in him. But he couldn't see her like this. He couldn't do this.

It didn't matter that she was rotten inside. That she had betrayed him. She was still his lifemate and doing this—taking her will, forcing her to complete the binding by sharing her body with his when she clearly didn't want to—was every bit as dishonorable as becoming the undead.

He closed his eyes and drew her to her feet, his hands gentle. He had to let her go, and there was only one way to do so. One. He wasn't going without memorizing every inch of her. Without holding her body against his. He deserved at least that much. He didn't want to see her eyes. He didn't want to know she hated him with every breath she took. Or that she wanted another man.

He was going to do what every ancient in the monastery had refused to do because they felt it was wrong. It was cowardly. Somehow, some way, they had to be strong enough to overcome that terrible darkness shredding their souls. He had vowed to live until they figured out how. He didn't have that choice now. He would meet the dawn and free his lifemate to find her way in the world. Perhaps the ritual binding words hadn't worked on her as they were supposed to. In any case, he wasn't going to look into her eyes again.

He took his time, savoring the feel of her very feminine body. Her skin was softer than anything he'd ever touched. His hands were big. Calloused. Rough. She felt wonderful beneath his exploring palm and fingertips. He committed her to memory, and he did it slowly. From her face to her toes. Front and back. She had lush curves and he spent time shaping and committing them to his memory. He would know her blind.

He didn't release her from his control while he explored

her body because he didn't want her hatred and venom to take this one moment from him. He would walk into the sun with her scent surrounding him. With the feel of her soft skin on his hands and her body imprinted on his mind. He could do that.

Because she couldn't control her body's reactions to his exploration, he learned every sensitive point of her. Sometimes her hips bucked against him. Sometimes her breath caught in her throat and a small moan escaped. That was all her. Not him. He didn't feed her body's reaction to him. He didn't try to make this about sex or about her. It was his goodbye. His reward.

He was as gentle as possible, knowing she detested his touch. He didn't want her to feel worse than she already did. It wasn't as if she was trying to seduce him and every other man around them. She had told him straight out she was in love with Daratrazanoff. Had he not been so far gone, he would have let her go, at least he'd like to think he would have. His emotions were too new, too overwhelming, and the darkness had pressed so deeply into him that there was little goodness left.

Aleksei knew he had misread the signs outside the gate. He'd been in the monastery for well over a hundred years. He had heard her cry out and thought she was being attacked. Everything in him had him flying to her rescue. It had never occurred to him that a Carpathian woman would turn against her lifemate, but it had been Daratrazanoff she'd worried about, had even tried to fight for.

He was sickened by her actions. By Daratrazanoff's actions. But mostly, he was sickened by his own. Never in centuries of living had he stooped so low. No one deserved what he had done to her, least of all his lifemate. His despicable actions only served to show him how far gone he truly was. She might deserve the justice of his people, certainly what she'd done was punishable by death, but not this.

He inhaled her scent, her amazing fragrance, and then he dropped his hands and stepped back, clothing her and releasing her at the same time. She sank to the ground, wrapping her arms around herself, her hair in disarray, her beautiful gray eyes swimming with tears, but still glaring defiantly.

"Do your worst," she hissed.

He bowed to her, a low courtly bow. "I apologize for my behavior."

"I could put a stake through your heart and not even think twice," she spat. "You *controlled* me. Forced me."

He nodded, taking another step back. She wasn't safe. He wasn't safe. No one was. "I have not felt any emotion in over a thousand years. Longer. Much longer. It is no excuse, but being so close to the undead, walking that edge and then finding you, the woman I . . ." He broke off. Shook his head. "I fear I could not see anything beyond your treachery. On the next rising, I give you my word, you will walk out of here a free woman. I will leave you now and no one will harm you. Seek the ground in one of the unoccupied buildings. Do not take a chance on open ground."

Gabrielle studied his face. He sounded like he meant what he said, and hope blossomed. She licked her lips, trying to stop the strange reluctance blooming along with the hope she felt. "If you mean what you say, why not allow me to leave now? The others are still close by. I would be escorted to safety."

He sent her a quelling look. One of disgust. Almost a sneer. Gabrielle didn't want to feel it, but she did. That look hurt. The look made her feel guilty when she had nothing to feel guilty over. He was still holding her prisoner. Gary and the others were still outside the gates. He just had to open them and she would be free.

"I have lived my life in honor. I will not allow one such as you, so deceitful, a selfish Carpathian woman who is willing to force her lifemate to choose between dishonor and death, to have her way. You know what that bond is, and still you broke it. I am far too close to darkness to watch you go to him. You can wait one rising. I will walk into the sun, and you can go to ground satisfied that I will no longer keep you and your lover apart."

Gabrielle stared up into his face. She could see the sorrow in him. She *felt* it, a great weight pressing down on her. She felt the centuries there, centuries of darkness. Of loneliness. Of a barren, cold world without color, emotions, family or caring. He had endured all of that. At the end there was . . . nothing. Nothing but Gabrielle. Nothing but a woman who didn't want him.

She saw that there in his eyes. In the lines carved in his face. That knowledge shamed her, even as she sought to excuse herself. She wasn't Carpathian. She was in love with another man, and she had been for a long time. She didn't know the first thing about lifemates, only what she'd observed. When she was working in the laboratory, they talked work. Since she'd been converted, no one had given her any advice. She felt human, not Carpathian.

She knew the rudiments. She could shift, which she rarely did. But she couldn't feed. Someone always provided for her. She slept above ground and someone always opened it after she fell asleep and before she awakened. She wasn't really Carpathian. Still, all that aside, she felt a deep sorrow in him and she had a terrible inkling of what could happen if she left. She didn't know what exactly, but there was something about the set of his shoulders. The mask on his face.

He turned away from her. For some insane reason she didn't understand, she couldn't let him just walk away.

"He isn't my lover. He's never been my lover. I don't have lovers." She blurted the truth out in a low voice. So low it was a mere thread of sound.

He turned back to her slowly. His eyes found hers. Searching. She knew he didn't believe her. His face could have been carved from stone, but his eyes were alive with contempt. That shamed her more.

"Do not speak. It is best that no more lies come from your mouth. I am uncertain how strong I am. You . . ." He trailed off and shook his head, turning away from her a second time.

She tightened her arms around her middle, terrified her churning stomach would let loose and she'd be sick everywhere right in front of him. She had no idea why it was important to her he knew she wasn't lying to him.

"I'm not lying. I've worked in a laboratory and I get caught up in my research. I've never had time for relationships. Or the inclination. I've never had a lover."

Gabrielle bit down on her lower lip. She bit down so hard she actually drew blood, all the while fighting the desire to run from him—or from herself. Suddenly she was terrified. Terrified of herself. Of what was inside of her. What Gary kept at bay. It was right there in her stomach, rising up, reaching out, threatening to consume her. She gasped, and he turned again, his frown deep as his burning gaze took her in.

Aleksei noted the drop of blood on her lip. He wanted to lick it off. Kiss her better. He couldn't help but see the way her arms held her midsection tight. He felt the need to go to her and hold her gently. She appeared the epitome of a woman in distress. What's more, her voice rang with truth.

She also appeared lost, and in spite of himself, in spite of the danger, he couldn't help the sudden surge of emotion for her. His lifemate. He had vowed to put her happiness before his own. She had betrayed him, but he had retaliated in a way that was far, far beneath him.

"I believe you." Clearly it was important to her to give her that. Still, it changed nothing. She wanted another man. She'd refused him. She'd made it clear she despised him. The choices were still the same, and she wasn't in a frame of mind to share her body with him. Without completing their binding, he wouldn't make it through the rising. "Thank you for that." He turned away again. Each time was much more difficult, but he knew it was the right thing to do.

"Please. Just wait. You can't do what you're thinking of doing." Her voice shook.

Aleksei closed his eyes. He had to get away from her. From her scent. From the intimate knowledge he had of her body. He had time to think. To process. A lifemate was about caring. About having a home. A family. Someone to love you as you loved her. To take you as you were. Accept you. This woman wanted no part of that. She kept reaching out to him, but there was nothing there for him. He couldn't look at her again. She was asking too much of him.

"It is too dangerous for me to stay and talk." And truthfully, there was no reason. There was nothing else to say. "I will get Fane to come to you. He will watch over you until the others go to ground." His voice was gruff. He could hear the growl coming close to the surface and he swallowed it down. He was close. Too close. "It is best you go to ground immediately to be safe. Next rising, walk out of here. Fane will open the gates for you."

He heard movement and then she was right there, stepping in front of him, blocking his way. He kept walking and she was forced to step back, her hands out, coming into contact with his chest.

"Stop. You have to give me a minute. You're not letting me even think," Gabrielle said. "You can't just tell me calmly you're going to commit suicide and then walk away. That's not right."

"What is not right is my lifemate choosing another man over me," he said quietly. "This is dangerous to both of us. I refuse to lose my honor. Without you, I cannot live. You know that. Your duty was to me. You refused. You chose another."

"Stop saying that. Stop thinking that." Gabrielle caught his shirt desperately. "You aren't listening."

"You are not saying anything."

"Because you won't give me time to think."

He caught her chin, forcing her head up so he could look into her eyes. "Are you willing to share your life with me? Your body with mine? To give yourself to me? In order for us to be lifemates, these are the things that have to be."

She licked her lips, smearing that small bead of ruby red. Her lashes fluttered and then dropped down to veil her expression.

"That is what I thought." He gently removed her fists from his shirt and stepped around her.

Gabrielle watched him stride away and nearly collapsed

on the ground, but that wouldn't do any good. This couldn't be happening. She couldn't be responsible for this man's death. She'd wanted him dead just minutes earlier, but the reality of his *being* dead was something else altogether.

She stood undecided, watching him as he waved his hand toward the door. Instantly it obeyed him, flying open. Outside she could see the night. Feel the breeze. The cool air. The mist enclosed the monastery in a gray veil. She sucked in her breath and went after him. There was no real thought in her mind, just that she *had* to stop him.

She couldn't think about Gary right now or what was happening to him. She'd already lost him. She lost him the moment she'd agreed to become Carpathian. Aleksei was right in believing she had known about lifemates and that she could be one to someone, but he was wrong in thinking she had betrayed him. Or was he?

"Stop. Aleksei. Stop." She couldn't prevent the tremble in her voice, but there was also pleading. "Just give me another minute of your time."

He didn't turn around this time. He kept walking. Desperation set in. She ran after him. "I'm not Carpathian. I'm human. I knew Gary before I was converted. When I was converted, I thought . . ." She was almost up to him and she was still talking to his back. He needed the truth, so she had to face it. Deep down inside her, where no one looked, not even her, she had to face the truth to save this man's life. "I thought they would teach me what I was supposed to know. I thought someone would help me. Instruct me, but they didn't."

She halted. Put a hand to her mouth, found her fingers were trembling and bit down on them in an attempt to still them. To stop talking. He didn't want to hear her. He didn't want to see her. Whatever transgression she'd made, and she could admit in his eyes she'd made a huge one, he didn't want to hear what she had to say.

She *hated* being Carpathian. She couldn't just take off, because she didn't know even the basics of caring for herself.

Her sister was gone all the time so there was no asking her. And then that stupid, stupid war with the faction of Lycans that wanted to destroy Lycans and Carpathians both. She hated feeling incompetent. She had stayed longer and longer in the laboratory, and she knew she had clung to being human more and more as time passed. How could she not? No one took the slightest interest in her or treated her as if she was worth anything—other than Gary.

"Aleksei." She whispered his name. She had too many sins on her soul already and she didn't know if she deserved them or not.

She knew Gary was in trouble. She couldn't save him. She was responsible, and she couldn't save him. Now this man, innocent in the entire horrible mess, was going to die as well. Because of her. Because of her inability to adapt.

She sank to her knees. *"Don't do this."* She whispered that as well.

How had she messed up her life to this point? She wept inside for Gary. Sorrow pressed in so deep she could barely see with the tears in her eyes. She could barely breathe with tears clogging her throat. But still. There was Aleksei. There had to be a way to save him. She didn't want to think too hard on what that way would be.

Are you willing to share your life with me? Your body with mine? To give yourself to me? In order for us to be lifemates, these are the things that have to be.

She licked at the small laceration in her lip. *These are the things that have to be.* Was she such a coward she couldn't give him those things to save his life? Would it be impossible? She closed her eyes, feeling the caress of his hands on her skin. Her body reacted, coming alive, just as it had done earlier. As if it had a life and will of its own. To share her body with Aleksei would be such a betrayal of Gary.

She closed her eyes. She had blamed everyone for this mess, but she'd chosen to be Carpathian. She bit her lip again, shaking her head. Her sister, Joie, hadn't been Carpathian and she'd still been a lifemate to Traian. She'd been human. Gabrielle squeezed her eyes closed tighter, not wanting to face the reality of what was happening to her.

She didn't understand the lifemate bond. She only knew it was intense. Very intense. Very sexual. Very everything. Lifemates were always together. And the men were very domineering. The women didn't seem to mind, in fact they usually just rolled their eyes and did what they wanted, but the male Carpathians scared her.

Gabrielle took a breath. The life frightened her. The violence. The blood. The intensity of their lives. She was *such* a coward. She had seen vampires up close. Her entire body shuddered. They weren't the only enemy. She touched her back, down low, where her kidneys had taken the knife slicing through them. The pain had been excruciating. And then the Lycans had come. She wanted her safe world back. The cocoon of her laboratory where she could hide away. Gary would have given that to her.

She covered her face with her hands as realization dawned. She loved Gary with all of her heart because he would have given her exactly what she wanted. Not what she needed. What she wanted. She wanted to hide away. Be safe. Be happy. No bumps. No scares. Just a sweet, easy journey through life.

Joie and Jubal could easily handle their mother's intense meltdowns. Her father just shook his head and grinned. When she was young, Gabrielle would hide under the bed, her fist jammed in her mouth, her heart beating hard. When she was a teenager, she had learned not to say a word. She would disappear in her mind. As an adult she hid herself in work. She hid. Period. From everything and everyone. Including herself.

Hiding had led her to this moment. To the possible deaths of two good men. She was a researcher, and yet she hadn't asked any questions about life as a Carpathian. She hadn't lifted a finger to acquire knowledge when knowledge was her world. Why? That alone should have raised a red flag for her.

Gabrielle wrapped her arms around herself and began to

rock back and forth, trying to soothe herself. Trying to think what to do. She was intelligent. Highly intelligent. She couldn't save Gary, and that tore at her. Ate her up. Left her grief-stricken with that terrible weight of guilt pressing squarely down on her. But what about Aleksei?

Truthfully, he terrified her. He was violent. Dangerous. Definitely domineering. He would expect her obedience. Her loyalty. Her participation in blood exchanging. In—well—*everything*. Her body did another shiver, almost in anticipation. Her mouth craved his taste. Her body craved his touch. What did that make her when she loved Gary? How could she want another man when her heart belonged to someone else?

Nothing made sense to her anymore. She'd never talked to her mother about anything that was important to her. There was *always* drama with her mother. She knew her mother loved her children—loved them so much she wanted to run their lives. She had no problem with tantrums in public, and that had always humiliated Gabrielle. Like their father, Joie and Jubal had found their mother amusing.

She had shut down as a child. Refused to live life. Afraid. She was still metaphorically under that bed, shaking, her fist jammed in her mouth to keep from making a sound. Holding herself still. She'd locked herself in a laboratory because she would rather face a hot virus than live her life. Gary was safe. He saw how fragile she was. How afraid of life she was. She wanted a controlled environment, and he was willing to give that to her. She loved him for that. She loved him because he was a kind, gentle, *protective* man. But she couldn't have him. She couldn't save Aleksei if she clung to her safe world. If she clung to loving Gary.

She took another deep breath. "I'm sorry, Gary," she whispered. She had to let him go if she was going to save Aleksei and herself. She didn't mind dying, but she couldn't live with Aleksei's death on her conscience. She couldn't. That meant she had to let Gary go to his own fate, and she had to try to figure out her own.

Gabrielle stood up slowly and followed Aleksei out into the center of the monastery grounds. She didn't hurry. There was no point. She knew he would be waiting out there for the sun, and it would be a long wait. The sun wouldn't rise for several hours.

She felt the other ancients watching. She couldn't see them, but she knew they were there. Her stomach clenched. Knots formed. Terror kept her from breathing, but she forced her body forward. She knew the ancients had surrounded Aleksei—from a distance—but they were there to destroy him if the dawn didn't. He had been telling her the strict truth.

She walked straight to him and sank onto the ground beside him. Close. Her thigh touching his. Just that small brush of her leg against his sent a shiver of awareness through her. She saw his body jerk and knew he was just as aware of her.

"What are you doing?" he demanded. "Get back inside and put yourself in the ground."

His voice was scary. The look on his face was even scarier. She shook her head and stayed.

"I will not allow this, Gabrielle. I am capable of forcing your obedience, as you well know."

She lifted her chin and looked at him, really allowing herself to see him for the first time. Up close, he was all male. All hard edges. In a way, a very scary way, he was striking. She couldn't imagine anyone fighting this man and coming out on top. He appeared extremely lethal, and she was very certain he was every bit as deadly as he appeared. Still, she looked him straight in the eye.

"I'm your lifemate, Aleksei, whether or not you or I like it. That means you don't get to sit here and wait for the sun without me. Whatever happens to you, happens to me. I'm willing to do this if it's what you want to do. With the mistakes I've made, I think you deserve to make that call—but know, whatever you decide, it's for both of us, not just for you. As your lifemate, it's my right to make the decision to follow you, wherever you lead."

She made the statement quietly. Firmly. In a low tone, so that he had to listen to hear her speak. She meant what she said and she knew he could hear it in her voice. It was the first time in her life, outside the laboratory, that she had ever been confrontational, scared out of her mind, but determined.

5

H ave you got him?" Andre asked. "We cannot lose him. What happened? How could this happen? She was not his lifemate. This is not supposed to happen."

"Gary lost everything all at once, just as if he had lost his true lifemate," Mikhail explained. "Colors and emotions are gone. All. At. Once."

"Do you have him?" Andre asked again.

Gregori jerked his head. "Not without Mikhail. He's strong. I did not expect this."

"We did not factor in the possibility that a human's love can be as strong as that of a lifemate. We do not see it that often," Mikhail said. "But this loss is from the ancients, not from the loss of a lifemate. It happened far too quickly. We were saved such an event because we lost emotions and color over a long period of time, so we barely realized they were fading over those two hundred years. To have everything wiped away in a moment would send a man insane."

Gregori shook his head. "That is not going to happen. We have to get him out of here. We are vulnerable here."

"I felt them, too," Mikhail said grimly. "Human hunters. The society is on this mountain, trailing after someone. Still, they are miles away."

"I can stay behind and hunt them," Andre offered. "You take Gary home and put him in the ground. Try to heal him, Gregori. We cannot lose him."

"There is greatness in him," Mikhail said softly. "He is destined to do great things for our people. I should have sat

Gabrielle down after I converted her and explained her duties as a Carpathian woman. I did not. I thought her sister would. I thought others would aid her in learning, but ultimately it was my responsibility and my failure."

"None of us could have foreseen this," Gregori said, reaching down to pull Gary to his feet. Gary's eyes burned with dark fury. He could hold his brother in check with Mikhail's help because they shared the same bloodline.

"No, but we could have helped Gabrielle adjust to our way of life so she would not have felt so dependent on Gary. We practically threw them together. From the beginning, I was uneasy over their relationship, but still, I did not interfere," Mikhail admitted. "I thought, once Gary became fully Carpathian, they would understand they were not destined for each other. I did not factor in human love, which is very real."

"Mikhail," Gregori warned. "We have to leave now."

"They are a distance away." Mikhail glanced toward the gates of the monastery, a frown on his face. "I do not like leaving her to her lifemate. Aleksei did not understand what was happening, and he is very close to turning."

"None of those inhabiting the monastery have sworn allegiance to you," Gregori said. "You cannot risk going in there. Gabrielle has a lifemate, and how they choose to fix this mess is on them, not you. We have to leave. Right. Now."

A stirring in Gregori's mind startled both of them. The thrall was there, a killing frenzy brought on by the sudden loss of all emotion and the pouring in of centuries of too many battles, too many deaths, far too fast for one mind to cope with.

I feel them. Down below us. Eager to kill. Leave me behind and I will keep them from the prince. Gary used the more common telepathic path of all Carpathians, so that not only could both Mikhail and Gregori hear him, but so could any other Carpathians in the area, including the ancients.

Gregori heard his brother quite distinctly. He was still there. Different. But his mind was there. Gary's intelligent mind was quick and fearless.

It is too dangerous for you, right now, Gregori responded. *Andre can take care of this threat. You come with me back to our home to guard Mikhail.*

They have new weapons. Weapons Andre has not yet seen. I have been researching the society and found some of their schematics. They could kill him or those inside the monastery.

They knew Gary spoke of Gabrielle. Already, his memories would be fading fast. She would be the last for him. The memory of love that most Carpathians tried to hold on to. Love of family. Of siblings and friends. He would lose even that, and if it was anywhere as fast as the loss of color and emotion, his memories of those emotions could go at any time. He would be left with only his honor to sustain him. And he would hold the darkness of all the ancients that had gone before him.

They will not kill me, Andre assured. *Nor will they kill the ancients.*

"We need to get word to the De La Cruz brothers. They need to watch over Luiz. The same thing will happen to him," Mikhail said.

"I'll call them on my cell." Andre flashed a faint smirk. "Imagine Zacarias with a cell phone. His brothers call him just to make him crazy. And Josef texts him. How do I know this? Zacarias had a few words to say about it to me the last time I saw him."

The idea of anyone calling Zacarias De La Cruz on a cell phone gave even Gregori pause.

We need to get the prince out of here. Gary was clearly pulling it back, taking control back.

Gregori was a little shocked that he was already strong enough to do that. He exchanged a long look with Mikhail. He had taken hold of his brother with the prince's help, keeping him from moving, preventing him from killing anyone. It had taken both of them, and both together were exceedingly strong. Still, it was a struggle. Now Gary was exhibiting signs of that strength by thinking clearly when his brain shouldn't be able to process anything but killing.

"Gary's right, Mikhail," he agreed. "We need to get you out of here. Andre, no trace of us left behind."

Mikhail sighed. "You will never change, Gregori."

"Not when it comes to your safety."

"And Gary is going to be just as bad."

Release me.

Not with a threat so close to the prince. Not with Gabrielle trapped in the monastery, Mikhail answered Gary, sparing Gregori.

I can do nothing to help Gabrielle. I can help to guard our prince.

Mikhail raised an eyebrow at Gregori and shook his head slightly. It was there, that clarity, but Gary was also an extremely intelligent individual. He worked out many of their battle strategies. He could so easily, even in his present state, lull them all into a false sense of security. He was thinking and that was a good sign, but they were too near Gabrielle, and if those starting up the mountain truly were members of the society hunting them, Gary could easily be tipped over the edge into permanent darkness should he kill, even to save the prince.

"We are leaving." Gregori jerked his chin toward Mikhail, and the prince shook his head, a small smile softening his hard features.

"Andre. Good to see you. I hope to meet your lifemate soon. Raven was very pleased when word came down that you had found Teagan. She is very fond of you."

"Mikhail." Gregori growled his name, patience gone. "Your enemies are everywhere. We have no idea how close any of those in the monastery are. And we need to get Gary into the ground." He played his trump card, knowing Mikhail was fond of Gary. Fortunately, Gary understood what he was doing and remained silent.

Mikhail shifted immediately and took to the sky. Gregori waited for Gary's body to shift, staying in his mind, just as Mikhail was. Gary did so with such speed and precision, Gregori found himself wondering just how much of the information the ancients in the Daratrazanoff line had given him the man had already processed. He was "getting it" at an alarming rate of speed.

Mikhail is correct, Gary, Gregori said. *You will do great things for our people, more than you've already done. Hold to your honor, brother. Hold to it, and when there is nothing else for you, you will have that.*

I will.

Two words, but Gregori felt the truth of them. The sincerity. He'd always known. From the moment he'd met Gary, when they had walked down the street together in New Orleans, he had known then that this man was connected to him. He shifted and took to the sky, the two Daratrazanoffs doing what they always did, positioning themselves on either side of their prince for the long flight home. They were many, many miles from Romania, where they all resided, and it would take a good part of the night to return.

Far off, they heard the sound of a rifle. They were too high, in the mist, and the shooter was closer to the lower part of the mountain, but still, all of them knew that was no hunter, but one of the society members eager to make a kill.

How would they know we are not anything but what we appear? Mikhail asked Andre through their common telepathic path, suddenly worried about the ancients in the monastery.

Teagan can tune herself to vampires and follow that path straight to their lair, Andre admitted, if a little reluctantly. *I believe that is her grandmother with those men and she has the same talent.*

Andre. Teagan breathed his name. Filled it with anguish. A sense that he had betrayed her. *You do not know that.*

Teagan, our first duty, always, is to the prince. Without him, our people are lost. His son is still too young to assume the mantle. He is too small to be a vessel for our people. The prince must stay alive or all of us will die and our species will be extinct. Andre did his best to explain to his lifemate.

Teagan was young. She had been human and he had very recently converted her. She had come to the Carpathian

Mountains in search of a particular stone that would help her to "cure" her grandmother's growing insanity. Her grandmother believed in vampires and had gone so far as to order a vampire-hunting kit off the Internet. Her family had tried to convince her to stop talking about them and then sent her to professionals. In the end, Teagan, afraid for her grandmother's sanity, took matters into her own hands and made the trip to the Carpathian Mountains, only to find that her grandmother was right and everyone else was wrong.

The problem was, her grandmother didn't discriminate between a vampire and a Carpathian. She had no idea the dangerous, ruthless people she traveled with.

Teagan came out of the mist, walking toward him, taking his breath away like she always did when he laid eyes on her. She was beautiful, no doubt about that, but more, she was alive as in *alive*. She lived life large. Right now, she was very unhappy with him, and there was no misreading that look on her face. With Teagan, what you saw was what you got. She adored her grandmother. Family was all-important to her.

The danger, Andre decided, of bringing humans into their world was that it would take a long time for them to realize the importance of protecting the prince and his children. They couldn't understand that one man held the entire future of their species, which made him vulnerable to outside attacks.

Her grandmother was being used as a pawn, or she was just plain fanatical. If it was the latter, Andre knew he would have to kill her. If he killed her, Teagan would have a difficult time forgiving him. Still, it would have to be done, and lifemates didn't lie to each other.

"She isn't vicious," Teagan greeted. "She's misled."

"Regardless, she's with four men, Teagan. Four men who have come here determined to kill us. You. Me. The men in the monastery. She's leading them right to them. We are going to have to stop them."

"I didn't know you were different when I met you, Andre, and she won't, either. We can casually meet them on the trail and say we've been camping for our honeymoon. Because we've just gotten married, it will seem natural for us to want to be alone, even in the daylight hours." Teagan stepped close, putting her hand on his chest and looking up at him.

His heart did a slow somersault when he looked down into her eyes. He would give her the world if he could. He wanted to give her this. They'd be walking right into the enemy's camp. He had no doubt that he would have done that on his own, but to bring Teagan along was sheer madness.

"It is dangerous, *sívamet*. These people have killed many of us. They find our sleeping places and murder us when we have no way to fight them. They kill the innocent. I doubt they've ever killed a real vampire in their lives. Your grandmother is the one leading them to us, abusing a special gift."

"But she doesn't know that's what she's doing," Teagan insisted. "She's funny and smart and loves to be snarky, but she wouldn't kill an innocent person. She just doesn't know."

"Teagan." He said her name gently. Lovingly.

She shook her head. "Don't. She's my grandmother, Andre."

She blinked up at him with her dark, chocolate eyes and those luscious eyelashes that never failed to catch his notice. She was pulling out all the stops, and because she was the world to him, he knew he was susceptible. Still. It was dangerous.

"Even if you were to convince her, Teagan—and I am not saying I will allow you to take that risk—her friends will not care one way or the other. I have seen their kind many times. They will not tolerate different. I am different. You are different. The ancients up in the monastery are different. And they will not come at us at night. They know better. They will strike during the day, when we are vulnerable."

Andre knew he wasn't convincing her. She loved her grandma Trixie and she wasn't going to back down over the issue. He took her hand and brought the tips of her fingers to the warmth of his mouth.

"*Csitri.*" Again he used his voice on her. Soft. Mesmerizing. Loving. Pure silk and velvet with the rasp that always shook her. She wasn't immune to his voice.

"She's my grandmother. She raised me. Imagine how you would feel, Andre, if you had to even think about killing someone you loved."

He closed his eyes briefly. He had destroyed several people he cared for. Friends he'd grown up with. Friends who had lost the fight against the darkness in them—darkness Teagan had saved him from.

"You cannot ever be blinded by love, Teagan. By anything. We will be in danger every moment we are in the company of humans. Unless you can feel the threat—such as we do now, because they are in that mode—you could be right next to a member of the society and not know it."

"She isn't evil."

"I did not, at any time, say your grandmother was evil, Teagan." He framed her face with both hands, tipping her head up so she was forced to meet his eyes. "You love her. You want her safe. I will move heaven and earth to accomplish that for you. But, *csitri*, you have to get what I am saying to you or I cannot have you anywhere near those people. They are dangerous. They would kill you without even thinking twice about it. I have to know you are with me. Me. Your lifemate. Not your grandmother."

"Can't I be with both of you?" she asked in a small voice.

He ran his finger down her soft mocha skin. Beautiful skin. His beautiful empath. "No, *sívamet*. Not this time. This time we have to go into this situation with the knowledge that things could go wrong. If that happens, I have to know I can trust you to have my back—that no matter how difficult, you can accept my decisions."

Her eyes searched his. He liked that about Teagan. She thought things out for herself. She liked to chatter when she was nervous, something he found he liked far too much, but she was always serious when it was called for. She knew what he meant. She knew her grandmother could be facing a death sentence and he wouldn't hesitate if she stayed with the members of the fanatical society. Still . . . She bit her lip. It was her grandmother. The woman who had raised her.

Trixie had had a difficult life. She had her only child at fifteen. A child raising a child. She loved her daughter with all her heart and poured every waking minute into seeing to her care and education. She wanted her daughter to have everything that she didn't have. She'd named her daughter Sherise and loved her more than anything else. When Sherise fell in love in high school and repeated Trixie's downfall, getting pregnant at sixteen, Trixie loved her through it. Fortunately, Sherise's man loved Sherise and stuck by her, marrying her. They moved in with Trixie.

Teagan bit her lip nervously. Her grandmother was an extraordinary woman, quite brilliant, and had she had the chance for a good education, in a different place, Teagan knew she would have excelled. As it was, she excelled at making a family. She worked hard until she had enough money to move Sherise, her husband, Terence, the baby and herself into another, much better part of the city. She worked so they could continue their educations.

Sherise had three daughters eighteen months apart. Terence got his education and a good job as an accountant, and they happily raised their girls until he grew fatigued and sick. He died of cancer when he was barely twenty-four years of age. Sherise and her three daughters moved right back in with Trixie, and she never once protested having to help her daughter raise more babies.

"Teagan."

Teagan closed her eyes. She could barely resist Andre's voice. Not when he said her name like that. A silk and velvet rasp she felt caressing her skin. She leaned into him and pressed her lips to his flat belly, right over his belly button. She loved him. Pure and simple, she loved him.

"I showed you what my grandmother did for her family in my memories. My mother didn't go near other men for years. And then she met Charles at a place where she worked. He was Caucasian, but it didn't matter to her. She thought they fell in love. She got pregnant with me. After so many years of not being with a man, she finally chose one, and he left her the moment he found out."

She stared at Andre's hard chest. She didn't want to look into his eyes. She knew, when it came to matters of safety, he was implacable. Still, it was her grandmother, and she had to try to make him understand. "She died in my grandmother's arms, Andre. Giving birth to me. She died. My grandmother's only child."

She traced circles on his chest. "She took us all in. My sisters and me. I was a newborn baby. My father was Caucasian." She finally lifted her eyes to him. "She loved me, Andre, in spite of the fact that her only daughter, her only child, died giving birth to me. I took away her beloved daughter, but she loved me anyway. She's all about family. She loved my sisters. And once again, she worked her butt off so we could have educations. She wanted us to have choices she never had. She gave that to us."

She was desperate for him to understand. "If you have to do it, you could separate her from them. Take her somewhere safe, like our cave, to give me a chance to explain the difference. She couldn't possibly hurt me with you close by."

She felt Andre take a deep breath and she knew she had convinced him. He nodded his head. "But, seriously, Teagan. You know me. If I tell you to do something, you do it with no questions."

That was a total warning and she knew he meant it. She nodded her head, because if she didn't, he wouldn't drop it. She knew him now, inside and out, and there were certain things he didn't give an inch on. In his mind he was making a great concession even taking her along, so she had to give him something back.

"You will have to trust me that I will look out for you and your grandmother."

She nodded her head again. She did trust him. There was no doubt in her mind if he gave his word, he would do exactly what he promised. She went up on her toes, her arms going around his neck to bring his head down to hers so she could brush her lips over his. He slanted his mouth over hers and took control of the kiss, sending her stomach plummeting into a roller-coaster dive.

She *loved* his kisses. Seriously loved them. His kisses should have been an inspiration for all mankind. They were electric, shooting little charges of white lightning through her veins straight to her sex so all she could think about while she was kissing him was ripping off his clothes. Quite frankly, that part of being Carpathian, the ease of getting in and out of clothes—and stylish boots—was one of the best things ever. That and not having to pay for the clothes and boots. How cool was that?

"Teagan."

There it was. Her name. That voice. Curling her toes. She loved that. She just plain loved Andre.

"Um . . ." She lifted her eyes to his face.

"*Sívamet.* When I am kissing you, you might consider forgetting about clothes and boots for a moment. I would prefer your mind was on me."

She laughed softly. "Andre, a little FYI. My mind is *always* on you. Let's go before I forget everything but you and leave my grandmother too long hiking on this mountain. I mean, really, what in the world is she doing thinking about hiking and camping in the wild at her age?"

Andre took Teagan's hand and they walked together away from the gates of the monastery. They were up in the mists and he had no fear of being seen, but already, his warning system was going off. He reached out, this time to one of the ancients inside the monastery, an ancient who had given him blood. It had established a more private telepathic communication between them.

Fane.

There was a small silence. Andre wasn't certain whether or not the ancient would answer. All of them within those walls were far too close to turning. He had almost entered that monastery himself. Fane was the acknowledged gatekeeper and that said a lot for his ability to stay in control. He wasn't as far gone as the others.

I am here.

Andre flinched a little at the tone. Fane didn't want to communicate with him. None of them did. They needed the distance between others, and now with a woman inside the safety of their gates, they all had to be on edge.

Two things, and then we will leave this place. A warning to all of you. There is a group of travelers led by a woman— a woman related to my lifemate. She can tune in to us. Lead others straight to us. A gift. Teagan has used hers to find the resting place of vampires. Her grandmother has fallen in with the society members. They have new weapons. Ones that even the playing field when they attack us. They also, with this woman, have the ability to find this place.

Kill her.

I hope to avoid that, but if I have no other recourse, then I will.

Thank you for the warning.

Andre knew if he didn't kill Teagan's grandmother and she made the mistake of leading the others to the monastery, the ancients would kill her. Sadly, for any of them, engaging in a battle where they were forced to take more lives could send them over the edge.

One more thing. My woman—and you have met her so you know she is genuine—believes she has found a way to bring all of you a little relief and buy you more time. I found her when I gave up. I believe there are human women with psychic abilities who hold the other half of each of your souls.

Fane was silent again for what seemed a long time. *Each of us has searched the world over, down through the centuries, and have not found the woman who would save us. Even as we speak, we are all aware of the rejection by Aleksei's woman. If there is no hope for him, a man of such honor, there is none for the rest of us.*

There is always hope, Fane. I learned that lesson. Teagan taught me that. We have access now to a database of psychic

*women. We intend to find them before society members do.
They were the ones who put together the database.*

*I have been away from the outside world for a very long
time, old friend. I do not understand what you mean.*

*We have learned that human women with psychic abilities
can be lifemates to our males. We believe that Vlad sent those
of us out whom he knew to have these women as lifemates in
other times so they would not be killed in the wars. He had
precog. We all know that. If he knew each of us had a lifemate
and we just had to endure until the right time, you know he
would have sent us out.*

He felt Fane suddenly come alert. Sending them out to
endure until the time their lifemates were born would be something Vlad would do. He had asked for volunteers when he
sent the hunters out into other worlds, but he was very specific
about others, Andre being one of them. Each of the ancients
inside the monastery, he had asked for personally.

That is so. There was speculation in Fane's voice. *And your
woman can help us to hold out a little longer?*

*We believe so. She has not had the opportunity to try, but
she is willing if one of you would allow her.*

Teagan tightened her fingers around Andre's. Fane had
also given her blood. He had said they had a strange connection he couldn't explain, but maybe this was it. Maybe she
was the one to give him hope as well as bring it to the other
ancients. Andre hoped so. The three ancients closest to him—
triplets whose family had taken him in when he lost his own—
were far too close to the edge. They had gone to the United
States and he intended to follow. He hoped Teagan could ease
them as well.

Explain this database. What is it?

*The society compiled names of women with psychic abili-
ties and kept it all in one place. We managed to take it away
from them. In the process we discovered that vampires had
infiltrated the society . . .*

*Vampires would never associate with humans and not
destroy them. They do not have that much discipline.*

Fane. They do have it now. Master vampires have been collecting followers—lesser vampires. They use them as pawns. The master vampires formed an alliance in South America and planned to assassinate Mikhail Dubrinsky. They practiced their plan first on the De La Cruz brothers. They are a very big threat to our people now.

There was another long silence as Fane tried to process how the world had moved on while he and his brethren had kept themselves locked away in the monastery. *This cannot be. Vampires are vain and would never be able to resist killing one another.*

Andre didn't argue. He didn't ever argue. He'd told Fane the truth. Some of the master vampires had grown crafty, and they sought power. Having lesser vampires surrounding them fed their egos and allowed them more power.

This is not good, Andre. We had no idea.

Warn the others. I will do my best to eliminate the threat to you, but should any get past me, understand what you could be dealing with. The society members also use drugs— drugs that can paralyze us.

Fane remained a presence in his mind. And then Andre felt him reaching for Teagan. Instantly he was there, a shield, preventing Fane from doing more than a cursory examination. He allowed his ancient friend to see her resolve, but refused to let him into her mind any further. Fane seemed to respect the boundaries because he didn't push.

When you have rid us of this threat, bring your lifemate back. I will allow her to try her healing skills on me. If she succeeds, no doubt a few of the others will allow her to try it on them as well.

Andre couldn't ask for anything more than that. He knew that living in complete darkness, one century after another flowing into one another until there was no difference and no way to mark time, took its toll. When you added hunting and killing old friends and even family, the toll got worse until it was one's very soul that paid the ultimate price. When one could no longer even hear the whisper of temptation, it was time to go. One more battle. One more kill. That could easily be the one pushing an ancient over the edge. After living a life of honor, that would be the worst possible fate.

Arwa-arvo olen isäntä, ekäm—honor keep you, my brother, Andre whispered telepathically in the language of his people. Meaning it. Asking Fane to hold out just a little longer.

Sívad olen wäkeva, hän ku piwtä—may your heart stay strong, hunter, Fane replied back.

Andre took Teagan's hand. "Remember what I've told you. They shot at the owls flying. We cannot take any chances. We will hike down as humans. I will set up a camp off the path, down in the rocks where you climbed the boulder. We will meet them accidentally. We are spending our time alone up here after our marriage."

"They can check anything with the Internet, Andre," she cautioned. "We haven't gotten married."

He gave her a look. One that said she was married. She was bound to him in the way of his people. The vows had been said. They were married. More than married. It was impossible to separate them. One could not survive very well without the other.

"Josef filed our papers, Teagan. We are officially married. I once told you I never used surnames that meant anything to me. Not until I met you. You have my name." He looked down at her, his gaze moving over her face. "It matters."

He watched her eyes go soft. Melt into dark chocolate. Her lashes fluttered, and he wanted to kiss her upturned mouth, so he did. She was irresistible. Her mouth was a haven wiping out his past, a dark lonely period that had gone on century after century, just as Fane and the other ancients suffered.

She slipped her arms around his waist, pressing her front to his, her breasts tight against him. She was much shorter and he always found that when her soft breasts brushed against his groin, his cock leapt to life, looking for a warm place to rest.

"It matters," she murmured against his mouth. "Nice to

know to the outside world we're married, but my grandmother is *not* going to be happy. I'm certain she's come here to prevent me from making a mistake. She thinks you're involved with a human trafficking ring or some sheik who will put me in his harem in the desert."

He ran his hand over the back of her head. Teagan always braided her hair when they were outdoors. Rows and rows of cornrows that were tight over her head and drawn back in a thick ponytail that fell to her waist. He objected on principle. He loved her hair and preferred it down. She complied when they were alone inside the cave where they had a resting place, and he was content with that—for the moment.

"We'd better keep going down the mountain, *sívamet*. We need to know what we are dealing with, and they are a good distance away. I want to travel as humans, just in case. If they can shoot at owls, suspecting them to be more than the natural wildlife in the area, they have someone other than your grandmother assisting them." His voice was grimmer than he wanted it to be.

She gave a delicate shudder, holding his gaze. "Do you think there's a vampire traveling with them?"

"I think it is unusual for them to spot three owls winging out of a mist that is as thick and filled with safeguards as the one surrounding the monastery. Your grandmother can hear musical notes, and maybe detect the monastery, but when we take the form of an owl, we *are* that creature. The notes would be in perfect harmony. She was not the one pointing out Mikhail, Gregori and Gary as they flew away."

Teagan turned and began moving down the mountain fast. "Is Grandma Trixie in danger, Andre?"

She already knew the answer or she wouldn't have been practically running. He reached out and caught her arm.

"Slow down. We are on our honeymoon and we have to play that part. Your grandmother knows you like to hike and climb. She will think that is what you are doing and she will convince anyone else with her who might be suspicious."

"How much danger?" she demanded.

"She is traveling with at least four members of a society that kills indiscriminately. They are fanatical, and that means there is no reasoning with them. Most likely there is something else at play here. A vampire. A vampire's puppet. Maybe both. If there is a vampire, by now your grandmother will know she's in trouble. In order to stay alive, she will have to be very, very careful."

"She's highly intelligent, Andre. Grandma Trixie didn't have a formal education but she's brilliant. If there's something not right, she will know immediately."

"Then she is in more trouble than ever." He wasn't going to lie. He couldn't lie to her, not even to remove the anxiety from her mind. "But, *csitri*, we will make certain she is safe."

6

Gabrielle held her breath. She'd never seen a man quite as scary as Aleksei, and she'd been around Carpathians, even ancients, for a long while now. The very air vibrated with his darkness. With his fury. He was definitely at the very edge of his control, and that alone nearly had her running from him. His eyes blazed fire. As in flames. She could see them.

She breathed out, emptying her lungs, pretending she was doing meditative breathing, sitting tailor fashion as if he weren't scaring the total crap out of her. She wished she was like her brother and sister and could find amusement in any situation as they did, but her heart pounded and her mouth went dry. Still. She held herself firm. She wouldn't flee. She would follow him wherever he led. She owed that to him, and she was determined to see this through.

"Put yourself in the ground, woman." Aleksei bit out each word, his green eyes glittering and his mouth set with absolute menace.

She lifted her chin. "I will follow wherever you go. It is my right as your lifemate whether you reject me or not."

He growled. Not low, but a rumbling, scary, mean, threatening growl. Like a tiger might do right before he pounced on you and tore you to shreds. She blinked and dug her fingers into her thighs. His gaze dropped to her hands. Inspected her white knuckles.

"*O jelä peje terád, emni.*" He said the words low this time, in his own language, and for some reason, that was worse than the growl.

She lifted her chin, trying hard to keep from trembling. "I don't know what that means. I don't know the Carpathian language."

Something moved in his eyes. Something different. Not gentle. Not softening, but still, she had gotten that much through to him. She *didn't* know the language. A few words maybe, but those words hadn't sounded very nice.

"It means, 'sun scorch you, woman.'"

No. Definitely not nice. She flinched. "I suppose that's what we're doing here, isn't it? Sitting out in the open, waiting for the sun to come up?" She tried a faint smile. "At least you know I'll obey that order."

"What is wrong with you? Are you a lunatic? Insane?"

She moistened her lips, and that small action had his gaze dropping to her mouth. She saw his body jerk as if she'd punched him. She probably was a lunatic. Otherwise, what would she be doing in the middle of the monastery yard, surrounded by ancients who were there to ensure Aleksei did in fact kill himself? They believed she had betrayed one of them and deserved death. She felt the weight of their eyes, although she couldn't see them.

Her fingers twisted tightly in the fabric of her soft vintage jeans. "I don't think I am. But I'm so confused I could be."

"Put. Yourself. In. The. Ground."

Her heart nearly stopped beating. She'd really, really made him angry. He was terrifyingly angry. She'd seen him like that already and she didn't want to go there again. Her fists tightened around the material of her jeans.

"Not unless you do as well. I told you. Your decision is my decision."

He glared at her. The air thickened. Vibrated with his anger. He was from a different time, she reminded herself. Women didn't talk back to men in his time. They *obeyed*.

Suddenly he was on his feet. He reached down and caught her arm, yanking her up, yanking her into him. His body was hard. She couldn't find a soft place on him. He was enormously strong and his fingers shackled her just as well as any chain would have.

"If I really had a choice, I would throw you down and bury my cock in your body. I would taste you, eat you up, drink your blood. Claim every inch of you for my own. I would not let you rest until the sun began to climb and then I would put you in the ground with me and hold you while we slept. When we awakened, I would start all over again."

He was deliberately scaring her. She didn't doubt that he meant every word. Every single word. She could barely breathe. Barely draw in a breath. She caught her lower lip between her teeth, trying to assess her own reaction. Her brain screamed at her to run, but her body melted at his words. Really melted. She actually went damp and her breasts ached.

She didn't understand how it could happen when she knew she really loved another man, but strangely, she was *physically* attracted to Aleksei. The chemistry was off the charts, even when he was holding her captive like he was. She wasn't wild. There wasn't anything the least bit wild about her; normally she would have run for her life, but she couldn't. Not if she was going to save Aleksei, and he deserved to be saved.

"Is that your decision, then?" She couldn't look up at him. She just couldn't. Not with her heart pounding and her body reacting and her mind screaming at her.

Her question was met with silence. She stared down at the ground, terrified to look at him. Terrified of his answer. They would either return to that horrible carpet on the ground and he would take her body, or they would sit together and burn in the sun.

"Look at me."

She swallowed hard, studiously staring at the ground. "Aleksei. This is your decision. I told you I would do whatever you wished and I will, but I'm really scared. If I look at you, you're going to see that and it might influence you one way or the other."

"When I tell you something, Gabrielle, you are to do it."

His tone was gentle for the first time. His voice soft. Compelling. But there was no give there. No concession. He meant it. She closed her eyes briefly, summoning the courage she would need. In truth, she had caused this innocent man harm. She'd nearly pushed him over the edge right into the darkness. She knew that. She was responsible. She felt the darkness rising and she should have been able to pull herself together to calm him instead of inciting him further.

She'd been too upset at losing Gary to think straight. She'd been clinging to a way out. There was no way. Not even with Gary.

Aleksei's fist bunched in her hair in a clear warning. Gabrielle swallowed the terrible burning lump in her throat and lifted her gaze to his. The moment her eyes met his, her heart thudded wildly. She felt the darkness in him, and that was bad enough, but she could see it, too. The demons driving him. His implacable strength. This was a man the complete opposite of the one she'd fallen in love with. He was hard and scary and would demand things of her she wasn't certain she was capable of giving. Still. Without her, he wouldn't survive.

"You would tie your life to mine for all eternity." There was sarcasm in his voice, and she winced as if he'd struck her. "You would give your body into my keeping."

She couldn't look away. His eyes were such a piercing green, and they seemed to look right through her. She nodded.

"That is not good enough, Gabrielle. Say it."

She swallowed hard, afraid she might get sick, but not because her body didn't want his. In fact, she was growing warm. Too warm. Her breasts ached and she was damper than ever between her legs. But quite frankly, her terror was escalating with every word he said.

"Yes."

Impatience crossed his face. His fingers tightened, pulled her a breath closer. Her hands landed on his chest and she gasped at the heat pouring off him.

"Yes, what?"

She stared up into that pure green. No gold flecks. No hazel. All burning green. She took a deep breath and threw herself straight into the wolf's jaws. "I give my body into your keeping."

Her declaration was met with silence. He stared down into her eyes for what seemed forever. She was terrified he would take her up on her offer. She was just as equally terrified that he wouldn't.

His fingers went to her chin. "I am very close to the darkness. Too close. I know nothing of modern women. I will expect complete loyalty from you. Complete honesty. And obedience."

She forced her gaze to remain steady on his. She would not lie to him. "I will give my complete loyalty to you. I will give you complete honesty. I cannot promise obedience."

Something moved in his eyes. Something hot and wild. Something that sent heat curling in the pit of her stomach.

"You are afraid of me."

"Yes."

"Of giving your body to me. I will not take a woman who does not want me. To do that would be pushing myself completely into darkness. I cannot make it through another rising without completing our binding. It is best you put yourself in the ground now and stop tempting me."

She took another breath. "I do want you. That doesn't mean I'm not afraid. I am. I've never had sex. I don't know the first thing about pleasing you or what I'm supposed to do. That doesn't mean I don't want you. It means I'm embarrassed and inexperienced."

She clenched her teeth. She couldn't do this. She couldn't stand there and convince this man to take her body without love. Without care. She started to turn away from him, but his hands prevented her from moving.

"Look at me."

She knew better than to disobey him right then. His tone was back to an almost snarl. Her gaze jumped to his, and her breath caught in her throat. She couldn't read his expression, but her heart stuttered as his thumb slid very gently over her cheek. His touch was at complete odds with his tone.

He was beautiful in an entirely masculine, *savage* way. She found herself trembling. His touch, as light as it was, as sweet as it was, felt like a brand against her skin. There was a part of her that screamed that she was betraying Gary. The man she loved. The man she had planned to spend her life with. The other half of her screamed that she had betrayed this man. She'd left him to complete darkness. To dishonor.

"I cannot merge my mind with yours," he said, and this time his voice was as gentle as his touch. "I cannot risk seeing him there."

"I know."

"That means you have to talk to me."

"I know." Her voice was a thread of sound. "I'm so scared, Aleksei." Her gaze clung to his. She knew she was willing him to keep her safe.

He suddenly leaned down and wrapped his arms around her back and thighs, lifting her easily into his arms, cradling her against his chest.

"There will be no going back from this. Once I make you fully mine, there will be no room for anyone else."

"I know," she said again. She couldn't find air to breathe. Those two words were all that would escape through her pounding heart and burning lungs. She circled his neck with her arms, not knowing what else to do. "I'm really, really afraid," she admitted.

"He will not be with us," he continued, his green gaze blazing down into her eyes. "Not in your head. Do you understand me? When I am inside you, there are only the two of us there. Not him. You think of me. You say my name when you give me your surrender."

That was a decree. More, an ultimatum. She recognized it for what it was. She bit at her lower lip nervously. She didn't think any other man would dare to enter her mind when she was with Aleksei.

"Gabrielle." He growled her name in warning.

"No one else." She whispered her agreement.

It was just sex. Hopefully really, really good sex. She was saving him from the darkness. He needed her. He needed her to save him. She'd worked in a laboratory since her eighteenth birthday. She'd been in college at twelve. Then her masters. Her doctorate. She'd never had the chance to be with boys. To date. To experiment. To think she was in love. To know.

He turned and strode across the yard to the building they'd left earlier. His home. A shell of a building. No house. No white picket fence. No neighbors who would drop by for coffee and chat. Just four walls, a roof and a dirt floor.

His resting place was the death of her dream. Her only dream, since she'd been a child and her mother had been throwing things in the kitchen and she'd been under the bed, building a fairy tale to keep from hearing the shrill voice, her father's soft murmur and then softer laughter. She didn't understand their crazy relationship, but it was theirs, not hers.

Gabrielle buried her face between his neck and shoulder. At once she could hear the steady, rhythmic beating of his pulse. There was something solid about that beat, something rock steady, as if nothing would ever elevate it. Shock it. Stop it. That pulse would be steady through everything and it could be counted on.

Aleksei set her on her feet in the middle of the room. He framed her face with both hands, forcing her to look up at him. "You have to be certain, Gabrielle. Very certain. I will not be able to stop once I have started. I am too close to the darkness. With what has happened this rising, I am at risk, and now so are you. There will be no going back."

She swallowed hard. She could see the darkness in him. See it stamped on his granite features, the ruthless set of his mouth, but mostly, it was there in his eyes.

"I don't know what I'm doing, but I want to make it good for you. You'll have to help me." She knew they had chemistry, which convinced her they were in fact lifemates, but she didn't love him. She didn't expect that she would enjoy their joining, but she was determined that he would.

He stared down at her for what seemed an eternity. He took a breath. She did, too. Her heart was beating so hard she was afraid she might have a heart attack, but she would save this man. She could see him struggling. She could see he was afraid for her. She knew, without looking into his mind, that he was a good man. She'd brought him to this, and if it was the last thing she ever did, she would fix it.

Something flickered in the depths of his eyes. Something very frightening. She knew that was the moment he made up his mind. "I know you do not know me, Gabrielle, but you will be safe in my care. I will make this good for you. I am more animal than man right now. There is no light in me, but I will do right by you."

She knew that was a warning, she just didn't quite understand what it meant. Still, because he was the scariest man she'd ever met—and many of the Carpathian males were very scary—she nodded her head.

He stepped back from her and at once she felt the loss. He had been her anchor. Her protector, as strange as that sounded. Now she felt alone and more frightened than ever. His masculine features were hard, his eyes so green they actually appeared to be green fire.

"Remove your clothes for me."

She looked around the room. The stark, cold room, devoid of all furniture. Devoid of all signs of life or love. No warm fire. No field of flowers. No white horse . . .

A long, slow growl rumbled through the room. He was on her in seconds, his fist bunching her hair, dragging her head back. "What did I say to you? That man will not be in this room with us."

"He isn't. I wasn't thinking of *him*," she denied, tears gathering because her scalp *really* hurt. There was darkness in him. Set deep. She could see it. She could see he was battling it. "Just leftover childish dreams. Please, don't hurt me."

Instantly he loosened his hold on her hair. To her shock,

his fingers massaged her scalp, easing the ache. He leaned forward and shocked her further by brushing a kiss over first one eye and then the other. His mouth followed the trail of her tears, sipping at them, removing them with his tongue. It was . . . intimate. So intimate, the brush of his tongue and lips sent another wave of curling heat to her stomach.

"I am sorry, *o jelä sielamak*, it is difficult to control intense emotions after so long without them. You have said you will not tell me an untruth and I choose to believe you. I will have more care with you." His gaze dropped to her eyes. "I have need of you. Right. Now."

He said the last two words against her mouth and then he was kissing her. Not just kissing her. *Kissing* her. She hadn't known a kiss could be like that. Demanding. Rough. Nearly savage it was so rough. She thought she wanted gentle. She *needed* gentle. Maybe her mind did, but her body responded to the hunger in his mouth, the harsh, near violent way he devoured her. Flames danced through her body. There was no slow smoldering; his kisses took her straight to the fire.

Her body moved against his restlessly because there was no controlling her response to him. Her clothes hurt her skin. She needed to feel his skin, and she did, slipping her hands under his shirt to slide up his broad back. She could feel every muscle, and that heat—that incredible heat pouring off of him. All the while he kissed her. Claimed her. Put his brand on her. With just his mouth.

He kissed her like a starving man. He kissed her like he owned her. His mouth was hot and demanding. He tasted like paradise. And her body . . . Her body forgot who was in charge. Her brain just shut down. Short-circuited. She kissed him back. Really kissed him. Not just let him sweep her along, but she kissed him, her hands taking in as much of his smooth, hot skin as they could. She couldn't stop herself. She had no idea what she was doing, but somehow, following his lead, she learned fast.

She could tell he liked her kisses because when their tongues tangled, his arms tightened until she was afraid she'd be crushed under his enormous strength, but she didn't want him to stop. Her body had come alive with just his mouth on hers. *Alive.* Singing. Screaming for more. Every single cell was aware of him. An electrical current seemed to have taken up residence in her bloodstream. She'd never felt anything like it in her life. She hadn't known a woman *could* feel like that. He moved and she tightened her arms, whimpering a little, trying to keep him there.

He smoothed his hand down her hair as he lifted his head, removing the intricate braid so that her dark hair fell in clouds around her face and down her back. His green eyes were darker. Filled with hunger. Her heart thudded. Her sex spasmed.

"I like your hair down. Wear it down for me."

His mouth was back on hers before she could protest. Not that she was going to protest. She couldn't think past the need to kiss him again. His kisses burned even hotter. His hand went to her throat, tipping back her head, while his other arm became an iron bar at her back, pulling her tightly into him.

He lifted his head again. Just inches. Green eyes blazing down into hers. She went up on her toes, trying to follow his mouth.

Aleksei brushed her mouth with his but held back. "Are you going to give me that, Gabrielle? When it is just the two of us, will you give that to me? Your hair down where I can feel it on my body? Against my skin?"

God. God. He robbed her of breath.

"My woman does not say no to me. Not ever. She trusts me to do right by her. Are you going to give me what I want?"

Mesmerized, hypnotized by his dark sensuality, without taking her gaze from his, she nodded.

"And you will not say no to me."

Could she give him that? She didn't know if she was strong enough to make herself into what he wanted or needed. She was so afraid of him. Trusting him was going to be very difficult.

"Gabrielle." His tone told her he was losing patience.

She swallowed her fear and shook her head. "I'll try, Aleksei," she promised.

Instantly he rewarded her, his mouth at hers, breathing fire down her throat so that the flames reached her breasts. So sensitive. So aching. So needy. Just with his mouth on hers.

He tugged at her tee and it disappeared right off her body. Her bra was next. Both of his hands went to her breasts, cupping the soft weight in his palms. A small cry escaped. His touch was rough, not gentle. She didn't expect gentle from him—his kisses were far from that. But she hadn't expected that rough would only make her hotter. Her legs threatened to give out as his mouth traveled over her chin and down her throat.

"I don't think I can stand up," she whispered truthfully.

He took them to the floor, stripping them both as they went down, cushioning her fall, but just barely, his mouth already on her breast. His hand was at her other breast, his fingers rolling and tugging while his mouth suckled strongly. Her hips bucked, the heat building in intensity, forks of lightning streaking from her breasts straight to her sex.

Deep inside the tension began to coil tighter and tighter. Her breath came in gasps. His mouth went to her other breast and his finger was at her nipple. She arched her back, giving him more, needing more, her arms wrapping around his head to cradle him there. The feel of his hair, all that black, salt-and-pepper silk, drove her wild. The sight of him feasting on her was erotic. The strength in his arms and the heat of his mouth fed the fire burning so deep inside.

His mouth left her breasts and began to travel down her body. He kissed under both breasts, her ribs and down to her belly button. His tongue tasted every inch of her as he made his way down her body. His hands were everywhere, his palms sliding over her skin possessively.

Her body was restless. It was too much, yet not enough. Without thinking, she dug her heels into the carpet and tried to slide away. She didn't know where she was going or what she was going to do, only that if she kept feeling this way, her entire body was going to come apart.

Aleksei growled deep in his throat and his hands went from gliding to gripping. Hard. Her heart jumped at the sudden aggression. She thought he'd been aggressive, but obviously she'd made a mistake and triggered the very dangerous side of him. His head came up and his green eyes glittered at her.

The look on his face frightened her as nothing else could have. She didn't dare move. His features were hard, aroused. His gaze dropped from her face to completely and utterly focus on the junction between her legs. Just the way he looked at her, all that darkness. Stark. Raw. Erotic. *Hungry.* She couldn't quite get air through her lungs and past her throat.

He was naked. Muscles everywhere. His body hard and hot. His erection was long and thick, throbbing against his stomach. One hand circled the width of it, just for a moment, and she couldn't take her eyes from the sight of that steel spike wrapped by his fist. She didn't see how it could possibly fit inside her. Fear mounted but at the same time she wanted him even more. The hunger and burning need inside of her kept building. Higher. Hotter. Delicious. Terrifying.

"Be still," he growled.

His voice was raspy. Harsh. Still, there was a silky quality to it that was mesmerizing—that stroked over her like a caress. She wanted to obey him. She had promised herself she would give herself to him, any way he wanted, but the sensations were too much. Mind-destroying.

He lowered his head again, and her breath was trapped in her throat as his large hands went to her inner thighs to spread her legs open for him. Wide. So wide. So exposed. So vulnerable. She cried out, trying not to writhe against the carpet. Trying to do what he wanted, but just lying there so exposed to his fierce, lust-filled, *hot* gaze nearly destroyed her.

His hands felt rough and hard against her soft inner thighs and she heard a soft moan escape, the only evidence that she could still breathe. She couldn't take her eyes from him, from the harsh lust etched there in his face, so sensual, so raw and beautiful. His fingers moved close to her center and she gasped. Whimpered. Struggled to stay still when she needed him inside of her, putting out the terrible fire that he'd built. That was still building.

Then his mouth was on her. Right there. His tongue stabbed deep, then circled her hard, tight little bud in torturous circles. Then he lapped at her, lapped at the cream spilling from her body. There was no way to stay still. Her hips bucked, jerked. She arched her back, pressed tighter against his mouth. She desperately needed to hold on to something to keep from screaming and flying apart, so her hands settled in his hair, fists bunching that thick silk tightly.

Aleksei didn't protest or snarl at her movements this time. He gripped her thighs in his strong hands, an unbreakable grip holding her open to him as he devoured her. Gabrielle was afraid her heart would burst it was pounding so hard. The pleasure was so intense, it skirted the edges of pain. His mouth was relentless, taking what he wanted, driving her ruthlessly up until she was shaking with need. Pleading. Begging him. Terrified she was going to lose her mind.

His breathing was harsh, ragged, his face a mask of pure sensuality. His mouth suckled, his tongue flickering over her clit, and the fire rushed over her. Before it consumed her, he pulled his mouth away, his eyes piercing hers. Dark. Glittering. Filled with lust. With hunger.

"Who is with you, Gabrielle? Who is giving this much pleasure to you?"

Pleasure? She wasn't certain that *pleasure* was the word she would use. The sensation was too intense, skating too close to pain. Still, she didn't want him to stop.

His fingers plunged into her aching, melting flesh. Her head tossed back and forth. *"Aleksei."* She managed to gasp out his name, only it came out like a plea. "You have to stop. Stop."

"O köd belső." He spat the curse out in his ancient language, fury burning in his eyes, heightening the lust there.

His mouth was on her immediately, his tongue flickering and laving, his mouth relentless, sending her crashing over the edge. She bucked, her low cries filling the room. He didn't stop. Didn't give her time to recover. His tongue drew the honey from her body, drew her clit into his mouth and attacked the raging nerve endings even harder. Even rougher. More insistently.

She bucked her body, trying to move his head. He was building the fire inside of her, too hot. Too fast. Pushing her too high. When his hands held her hips still, she tried pulling his head away from her by using his hair. He snarled at her. Like an animal. A wild, feral creature. His mouth never stopped feasting on her. *Ravenous*. Devouring her. Sending more sensations crashing through her.

She cried out, needing more. Feeling desperate. She tugged at his hair. "Please. Aleksei. I need you. Right now." Because she was unraveling. Coming apart. Feeling empty. She needed more.

His tongue stabbed deep and her sheath convulsed. The shock waves spread out from her core throughout her body. Up to her heaving breasts. Down to her jumping thighs. She opened her mouth to scream but another wave hit her, this one stronger than the last, and she couldn't catch her breath. Couldn't think. She just fragmented, and still, it wasn't enough.

Aleksei rose above her, holding her thighs apart, his face a harsh mask as he lodged the broad crown of his heavy cock in her entrance. She tried to push down, tried to impale herself on him.

"Are you going to tell me to stop now?" he demanded. His voice and hands were rough. He bit the words out on a snarl, his teeth white and bared. He appeared untamed, dominant, totally savage. The devil himself. And she couldn't resist him.

She bit her lip, her gaze clinging to his. She shook her head, and he pushed deeper. It burned. It stung. She gasped as he slowly invaded her body, stretching her impossibly. She mewed softly, insanely, and turned her head away from him. He stopped advancing. She could feel him *inside* her, pushing against the tight muscles, forcing her body to accommodate his. It was sexy. Sensual. Erotic. And it definitely was somewhere between pain and pleasure. She couldn't decide which, but she didn't want him to stop.

"Look at me," he commanded harshly. "Keep your eyes on me."

She didn't know if he wanted to see her eyes to see what she was feeling because he wasn't in her mind, or because he wanted her to see him and not another man when he took her. Maybe both. Either way, he wasn't going to move until she did as he demanded. She brought her gaze back to his face. She would have sworn, at the moment, he looked like sin incarnate. The lines in his face were cut deep. His green eyes were filled with lust and a ruthless intent. He looked every inch the predator.

"Do you feel me inside you? The way I feel you wrapped around me. So tight. So scorching hot. Your body is mine, *kessa ku toro*. Now look at me and ask me for what you need. Say my name."

She had no idea what *kessa ku toro* meant, but she didn't think it was a curse word. Not like the one he'd spat out earlier.

"I didn't mean . . ." She trailed off, watching his gaze drop to where his body met hers. He looked so huge, intimidating. Still, it was sexy. Seeing him stretching her like that, his finger moving over her lips where they wrapped around him so tightly.

"You said it." He was implacable, his voice going from harsh to guttural.

She knew he was at the edge of his control. She knew when he took her he would be just as savage, just as rough as when he kissed her. His fingers slipped through the slick heat at her entrance, the slick liquid fire that coated his cock, her thighs, and gleamed on his jaw. His other hand went to her left breast, gripping her nipple and tugging roughly. Fire shot straight to her sex. Blood rushed hotly through her veins. Her sheath spasmed around him, sent more liquid bathing the thick, broad head buried in her.

His eyes were hooded, heavy-lidded, his teeth bared as he waited for her to obey him. It cost him, that wait, and she knew one word would shred the last of his control. Not movement. Her surrender. That's what he wanted from her. Total surrender.

She had nothing left. Nowhere else to go. No one else to turn to. There was only this man, the ancient she'd wronged. An ancient who was more feral than tame. An ancient who was not in the least civilized. There was only Aleksei and the things he was doing to her body.

"Don't stop, Aleksei," she whispered, because she needed him desperately.

His eyes changed. Dark. Dangerous. Breathtaking. Staring into her eyes, he took her, slamming his cock home, tearing past her thin shield to bury himself to the very hilt. He seemed to lodge in her womb. His heavy sac pressed tight against her buttocks. Pain warred with pleasure as her body struggled to accommodate his size, her tight muscles stretched beyond belief. It was too much. The pleasure rushed over her, catching her by surprise until she didn't know what was pain and what was paradise.

She lifted her hands to push him away, her body flinching from his, but he caught both wrists in his viselike grip and slammed them to the carpet on either side of her head, his eyes glittering in warning.

"Do not take back your word," he hissed. "Fighting me now is far too dangerous."

She didn't have time to tell him that wasn't her intention. She just needed a little breathing room. A little time for her body to assimilate the streaks of lightning, the fire gathering like a terrible storm. The pressure building too fast. Too hot. His mouth came down on hers, a wild, savage kiss that took what was left of her sanity. Then he was plunging deep, setting a harsh, ferocious pace that jolted her body with every stroke, sending streaks of fire straight to her core.

She gasped and caught at him for an anchor, the pleasure so intense she feared she might actually pass out. She couldn't breathe. She couldn't find a release. He just never stopped, pushing her higher and higher until she was certain she couldn't take it. She was being pulled somewhere else. It was terrible. It was beautiful. It was terrifying.

"Stop fighting me," he hissed, going to his knees. "*Kessake*, you like this. You want it. I can feel your need, your hunger. Your fighting only makes me lose all control. Relax for me." He growled the words, but she could tell he was trying to settle her. There was an underlying plea in his command. "Let me help you."

She hadn't realized her body was thrashing under his or that her fingernails were digging into his skin. She could see the scored rake marks on his chest and knew they had to be on his back as well. She was just as out of control as her own body.

"O jelä peje terád, emni." He bit the curse out between his teeth. "Sun scorch you, woman, stop fighting me." He swore again savagely, in English this time, his hold transferring to her inner thighs.

He held her thighs with a bruising grip, his cock relentless, never stopping, slamming deep and hard with every stroke, burying himself over and over, his face a mask of pure lust, robbing her of all breath. She felt him everywhere. Surrounding her. Taking her over. His body a piston, a jackhammer, driving deep, sending the fire, the flames, through her entire body.

Her tight sheath pulsed and spasmed. Her inner muscles gripped his thick spike viciously, clamping down like a vise, holding him, increasing the friction as he drove into her. Then it was there, exploding through her, tearing through her body, roaring with a life of its own.

She chanted his name. Giving him that. He'd given her the stars. She tried to take him with her, but his green eyes were trained on her face and he plunged into her again and again, watching her as her body fragmented, died and was reborn.

"That is what I want," he breathed. "Beautiful. *I* gave that to you. Your lifemate. Aleksei. I gave that to you."

His cock continued to drive deep into her body on the heels of the first violent orgasm and another, taking her over, ripping through her, tearing a low, wild keening from her that she couldn't stop. She swore her vision darkened as the firestorm rushed through her, consuming every cell in her body.

7

Aleksei needed to see the look on her face as he gave her that gift, that beauty. He knew he was far too rough. Too wild. But his lifemate was made for him. The other half of his soul, and even though she didn't know it—didn't recognize it—she was a wildcat and was a true match for his savage nature.

He didn't want to stop. It was pure heaven being buried deep in her body. Streaks of lightning forked through his body, drawing up from his toes to sizzle through his body straight to his brain. Around his cock her body spasmed and convulsed, bathing him in hot, rich honey. The intense strangling sensation added to the friction, as if a hot, wet silken fist gripped and milked him.

A third orgasm ripped through her and he felt his cock swell. Glorious. Impossible. Perfection. Her tight sheath pulsed around him, clamped down and pulsed again. Pulse after pulse. That rich honey scorched and burned and felt so good as with each spasm she poured more around his swollen, hard, *aching* flesh.

He stared down into her shocked eyes. She looked dazed. Her lips were swollen, her hair everywhere. She looked thoroughly taken. Claimed. His. He emptied himself into her, blasting his seed deep inside her.

Fighting for breath, he allowed himself to collapse over her, forcing her to take his weight while he buried his face in her neck. Her heart beat in that pulse point right by his ear.

He could hear the frantic rhythm. Feel her fighting for air. He turned his head and sank his teeth deep.

She cried out, arched her neck, her arms coming up to cradle his head even as a rush of hot liquid enveloped his cock. He held her down, letting her breathe shallowly as he blanketed her, his body connected to hers. Still hard. Still a thick spike that refused to relax while he took her blood. While he sated himself on her.

He began to glide. Slow. Easy. His hands slid to her breasts, kneading. Massaging. Taking possession of her nipples, rough. Gentle. Never setting a pattern. Each tug or roll rewarded him with a surge of liquid heat. Her hands were in his hair, and he loved the feel of her fingers there, moving through the strands. He loved the way she cradled him as he fed.

With a languid laziness, he swept his tongue over the twin pinpricks and then set his mouth there, marking her further. She would have his mark all over her body. Everywhere. And she would feel him everywhere. On her skin. Under her skin. In her blood. In her bones. Deep inside her most feminine core. He would be there with every breath she drew. Every step she took. Every move she made. He would be inside of her.

He lifted his head slowly, continuing to move in her. She still wore a dazed look, as if she couldn't quite believe what had happened. He felt alive. Exhilarated. Complete. He should have been sated, but he knew that if that were ever the case, it would be short-lived and very temporary with her close to him. He wanted to live inside her.

"I wasn't fighting you," she whispered, almost shyly. "I'm sorry I made you think that I was."

Her hips moved gently, rising to meet him. She was every bit as insatiable as he was. His match. He took his weight from her, planting a hand on either side of her so he could continue gliding in and out of her hot, welcoming haven.

"It was too much. Too fast. I couldn't process what was happening to my body."

"Did I hurt you?" He bent his head to the temptation of

her breast, capturing a nipple and drawing it into the heat of his mouth. His teeth tugged and his tongue laved before he let his prize go.

She gasped, and there was his instant reward, all that hot, slick honey bathing his cock while her body clamped down around his. Yes. She was definitely his lifemate. She liked it rough. She came apart for rough. He wasn't civilized and he doubted he ever would be. He'd been too long living on the brink of darkness, part animal, part savage and part demon. He was never going to be tame.

Gabrielle shook her head. "It was intense and it scared me."

He didn't let her gaze slide away from his. Waiting.

She bit her lip. "Sometimes it bordered on pain, but then . . ." She trailed off, a soft rose creeping into her face.

"You liked it," he encouraged. "*Kessake*, in this, in all things, you have to be honest with me. We are going to spend eternity together. There is going to be a lot of this." He took a moment to savor the feeling of her body surrounding his while he moved inside of her. "I need to know what pleases you. You need to know what pleases me."

"I don't understand this. Any of this." Tears suddenly swam in her eyes.

"*Kessake*." He whispered it. His name for her. Little cat. She'd scratched the hell out of him with her nails. Marking him. Scoring his chest and back. Loving what he was doing to her. Now she had tears in her eyes.

Her hands tightened around him and she circled his hips with her legs, hooking her ankles, wrapping herself around him. He knew she was unconsciously seeking assurance from him. He slid one arm around her back, half lifting her. Holding her to him. "Talk to me," he ordered softly.

Her body trembled. He picked up his pace, moving deeper into her. Filling her. He was talking to her with his body. Trying to tell her she was safe. They both were. They had completed the bond and there was no danger that he would lose his soul to darkness.

"Gabrielle."

"What does *kessake* mean?"

Her breath had turned ragged. Her eyes stayed on his and he liked the look there. He had put that there. Soft. Dazed. The tears still close, but he held them at bay with the easy, loving glide of his body. He gave that to her because she needed care. He'd been rough. He could see the evidence of his hands and mouth on her silky skin. He could see a trickle of blood mixed with his seed on her thighs. She needed gentle.

"It means 'little cat.'" He could see the tension coiling in her right there in her eyes. He heard it in her breathing.

"You call me little cat?"

He didn't want to talk anymore. He wanted to concentrate on feeling. Pure feeling. "Hold tight," he ordered abruptly.

Gabrielle obediently tightened her arms and legs around him. He liked that she kept to her word and obeyed when he told her to do something. It was necessary that she learn obedience right away. He wouldn't tolerate his woman looking at other men, and clearly she had something wrong with her that she had allowed herself to become involved with another Carpathian male. He would keep her away from other men until she learned her place was at his side. In any case, no one had argued with him, not in a thousand years. He was too much the predator, and one look at him was enough to convince even the dullest dolt of the fact.

Still, he wanted a woman who would speak her mind. Just not until he was certain she wasn't going to try to run off with another man. She had a fiery temper. That might actually be fun when he was feeling tolerant. After sex. He was feeling pretty damned tolerant right at that moment.

Shifting his hands to the carpet, he began to move in her the way he wanted. Deeper. Finding that sweet spot that took her breath completely and had her making those little noises in her throat he was certain she didn't notice, but he did. He wanted to hear those sounds for the rest of his life. And he wanted it to be a long life with her.

"You are so *peje* hot, so *peje* tight I can barely stand it." His voice sounded harsh, a groan more than words. He felt the shiver that went through her body. She was very receptive to him. His voice. His touch. His kiss. His cock. He had no idea a lifemate could be such a miracle.

He allowed himself to get lost in her body. Finding the perfect rhythm, building the tension in her so that he felt it coiling tighter and tighter. Switching from hard and deep to slow and easy just when she was close and he could feel her body gathering itself. Her soft cries sounded like music to him.

He loved the way her cries vibrated right through his cock. Her ragged breathing played counterpoint to the little keening and purring that came from her throat with each thrust. He knew this woman was worth having. Worth keeping. No matter that she didn't understand duty, he could teach her that. She was afraid of him. She didn't seem to know anything about lifemates and she wouldn't know that he wouldn't really hurt her. She'd learn loyalty from a strict master.

He kissed her again, this time more gently, taking his time, feeling her response. She followed his lead. She gave him more when he demanded it and she was good, feeding the fire storming through his body. Aleksei knew he was going to enjoy teaching her, training her, instructing her on what a lifemate should be.

He was a little shocked he had any gentleness in him, any tenderness, but he felt both toward her, in spite of the fact that she'd betrayed him with another man. She'd come to him, terrified. He didn't have to be in her mind to feel the terror coming off her in waves, but she had done it, not knowing if he would kill her or not. He had that right. No Carpathian woman should have done what she did. At the very gates. In front of the other ancients. Honorable men who were hanging on by a thread. She could very well have tipped him and all of them right over the edge.

He felt her hands pushing at his chest and his eyes jumped to her face, blazed down at her, took in the stark fear on her face. He realized he had growled and his hands had gone to her body, hard, holding her still while his body took hers roughly. He hadn't realized he was still angry with her. Not just angry, a kind of fury riding him hard. He needed to lose that if he was going to work this out with her—and he needed to work it out before the next rising so she would know what he expected of her.

He eased his glide to slow. To easy. He eased his grip on her hips. "Relax, *kessake*, you are safe. No matter what, I will see to your pleasure."

Her eyes searched his. She bit her lip. Every *peje* time she did that, he wanted to bite her lower lip himself. His hand found one breast. Her nipple, so hard and inviting, made his mouth water. He slowed his movements to a lazy, torturous glide, making certain his cock rasped over her sensitive little bud while he bent his head to take her other breast into his mouth. Deep. Sucking hard. Using tongue and teeth until she was squirming under him and crying out.

"Aleksei, harder. I need harder."

She couldn't stop her body from writhing under his. There was intense satisfaction in knowing he gave that to her. He did that for her. Not her other man. Him. She'd used his name just as he'd ordered, and she'd asked sweetly. Panting. Showing him need. Putting herself out there.

He drove deep. Hard. Giving her what she wanted. Giving himself that gift. That beauty. He had seen so much in his centuries. He had watched. Listened. Learned. He knew the things he wanted. Things he wanted to do to her. To have her do to him. Still, he didn't expect this. This absolute *peje* beauty.

He felt her body tighten, strangling him in that hot, wet, silken fist, milking and gripping. "Wait," he bit out. "Wait for me."

Her hands flew to his shoulders, nails digging deep. He felt her instant struggle to accommodate him, but her body was close. Very close. Demanding she let go. That she fly. "Not. Without. Me." He made it a decree. He wanted that. He even needed it.

"Hurry," she whispered. "Aleksei, please hurry."

It was her voice, that soft little plea. The sound of his name whispered in a panicky voice that sent him over the edge. He groaned and thrust to the hilt. Deep. So deep while she convulsed around him. He buried his face in her neck, letting her take his weight again. She was so soft. Her breasts were full and felt astonishing against his bare chest. This time, his cock was sated, at least for a short while, relaxing slowly in the haven of her body. He enjoyed the aftershocks shaking her, sending little shudders of pleasure through her body and bathing his cock with her honeyed liquid.

Aleksei knew he would forever crave the taste of her. Forever crave her body. He wasn't about to share that with another man, and she needed to know that right now. He was safe. There was no danger of him turning vampire, but if she thought to save him and then walk away, she needed to know immediately that wouldn't work. They were tied together for eternity. There was no Gabrielle without Aleksei. No Aleksei without Gabrielle.

He moved slowly, pushing himself up on one arm to brush his mouth over hers. He felt her retreating from him, withdrawing into her mind. He wasn't certain he was ready to follow her there. His anger still smoldered beneath the surface, and she deserved punishment. He didn't quite trust himself to find this man in her mind and see the extent of her betrayal.

He rolled off of her, automatically cleaning himself, although there was great satisfaction in seeing the evidence of his possession on his cock and thighs. He liked seeing it on her.

"We are going to set a few ground rules, Gabrielle," he said.

She rolled to her side and curled into a little ball, drawing up her knees in the fetal position. He caught the sheen of tears in her eyes before she curled into herself.

For some reason, the sight of tears swimming in her dove-gray eyes caused a curious jerk in the region of his heart. He didn't like that. He didn't want to be affected by her emotions. Not yet. Not until he knew what parts of her were real and what was manipulation.

"Did I hurt you?" It was the second time he'd asked her that question.

She shook her head, keeping her back to him.

"Gabrielle. Do not hide from me. I do not like it." He didn't. If she was going to cry, she could do it in his arms. He tugged her back into a sitting position. She resisted for just a moment, until his fingers settled around her arms like a vise in warning. "We are going to talk and you are going to do it looking at me."

She swallowed hard, pushed her hand against her mouth and nodded. It took a moment for her to settle, drawing up her knees, circling them with her arms, holding herself still and closed off even while she lifted her chin, her eyes reluctantly finding his. Her hands trembled. Her hair fell in waves down her back and pooled on the carpet around her buttocks. There it was. Him. Glistening on her thighs. She hadn't cleaned up. She'd left him there. Inside her. On her.

She cleared her throat. "I would like to put clothes on."

He knew she felt vulnerable. She was naked, and he liked her that way. He liked that he could just reach out and sink his fingers into her. That he could put his mouth on her. Taste her. Have her. He decided on strict honesty, although he was fairly certain she would be more afraid of him than ever.

"You need to get used to this. I like you naked. I like to look at your body and touch you. I like your skin touching mine." He wanted access to her body whenever he wanted her—however he wanted her. She was going to have to get used to the fact that his cock wasn't letting up. Not after having her twice. "You are safe right here. Just talk to me. If I did not hurt you, why are you crying these tears?"

She moistened her lips and made an effort to stop the tears. "I'm afraid of you."

"I know. You will learn, in time, you are safe. In the meantime it will not hurt you to fear me a little. You can be assured I can keep you protected from any harm that comes your way."

She swallowed. "I don't want to make you angry. You want honesty from me and I really want to give you that, Aleksei, but there are things I can't talk about."

"This man."

She bit her lip hard.

He caught her chin and turned her face up to his. "Stop that." He leaned down and licked at the small wound there. "Your body belongs to me. I do not want you injuring it, especially that beautiful mouth. That lower lip is tempting, and one of these times when you bite it, I will take over and do that for you."

Her body shivered, responding to his low, sensual tone. She started to bite her lip again and hastily stopped herself.

"Tell me what you are feeling."

She took a breath. Let it out. Her fingers twisted together and her gaze found his again and dropped away. "None of this makes any sense to me. I don't understand how I can have feel—" She broke off abruptly with a small sob before catching herself.

"Feelings for him and yet you responded to me." He kept his gaze steady on hers.

She nodded. "What does that say about me? I must be a terrible person. I want you. Your body. Your voice. Everything you do or say makes me respond to you, but my feelings, my heart . . ."

He swept back her hair and studied her face. Her expression. Her eyes. She wasn't making it up. In fact, she was finding it difficult to tell him. This wasn't a bid for sympathy. She looked miserable. Horrified even. Totally confused. And that confused him. She really didn't know what was happening to her. How could a Carpathian woman not understand the powerful ties between lifemates?

She shook her head, choking back a sob, rocking back and forth. "What's wrong with me? How can my own body betray me like that?"

His teeth snapped together in a hard bite. His sympathy was gone that fast. Her body *betrayed* her? "I. Do. *Not*. Think. So." His voice was pitched low. But it thundered through her body as it was meant to do. She winced back and bit her lip hard. Even that wasn't going to get her out of trouble.

His hand whipped out and he bunched that long hair in his fist, pulling her head back before she could hide her face from him.

"You understand something, Gabrielle. Get this straight. *You* betrayed *me*. Your body belongs to *me*. Not him. Your body knows what it is doing. You, however, do not, but you had better learn fast or you are going to find that your life is miserable until you do. You owe me allegiance. I gave you every chance to live your life without me, but you chose. You *chose*. I told you there would be no going back. You cannot survive without me now, nor I you. So learn this now. You belong to me. Your body. Your heart. Your soul and that treacherous, betraying mind of yours."

Gabrielle flinched with every blow he dealt her. It felt as if he'd punched her repeatedly over and over, right in her gut. She was grateful her knees were drawn up tightly or she would have doubled over. As it was, she felt bile rise. Her body had betrayed her. At the same time he was right. He was *right* about her. She wasn't worth anything at all. She was disloyal to Gary. Her beloved Gary. Gary, who represented all things human. He represented kindness and security. She wasn't ready to throw that comfort away and embrace this wild, rough man who demanded not only her allegiance, but her body, soul, heart and mind. Everything. He would take everything away from her.

She was already stripped bare. He despised her. She was terrified of him and the life they would lead together. There was nowhere to go. Nowhere to run. She knew she was tied to him, and not just through their blood-bond and their soul-bond. She knew she wouldn't be able to go long without feeling his body inside of her. His mouth on her. She would burn for him. She was addicted to his taste. To his touch. To his cock.

She covered her face with her hands and wept, uncaring if he saw her or not. She was lost. So incredibly lost. Was it possible for her to meet the dawn without harming him? For a moment, that seemed the only answer.

His hands pulled hers down and he looked at her face. She knew the moment his green eyes went dark that he saw what she was thinking. He didn't enter her mind, and she was grateful for that, but he looked more terrifying than ever.

"You will not even consider such a thing."

There was no trying to look innocent, and she'd promised him the truth. So let him hear it. "I don't know what I'm supposed to do. I've never been with a man. I know nothing of lifemates . . ."

"What family would not teach their daughter about lifemates?" Skepticism was in his voice.

"I *told* you. I am *human*. *Was* human," she corrected. Hadn't she told him? He had been so frightening. So out of control. It was possible he hadn't heard her. She couldn't remember what had been said or not said. "I was stabbed repeatedly by members of a human society who hunt vampires and I nearly died. I guess I did die and was reborn Carpathian. I don't know why they targeted me. But Mikhail, the prince of the Carpathian people, converted me."

Aleksei looked at her, his eyes burning right through her, but she couldn't tell from his expression if he believed her. Still, she plowed on.

"I'm psychic, from a family of psychics, and in case it is news to you, psychics can be converted without fear they will go mad. My sister is lifemate to a Carpathian. I don't know what I'm doing. I can't take blood by myself. I can't sleep in the ground, and I don't know anything at all about lifemates."

She lifted her chin and glared at him defiantly. "You got yourself a real bargain. I don't know the first thing about being your lifemate. I don't know how to be Carpathian, and I've loved Gary for a very long time. So not only did I inadvertently betray you, I betrayed him and I betrayed myself. So don't think you're all alone in this mess I've made. I pretty much screwed everyone."

There. She'd told him her sad tale and hoped he believed her because she wasn't going to repeat herself *again*. He might as well know the worst about her.

Aleksei stared at her for so long she was afraid she might just scream. There was absolute silence inside the four walls. Not even a whisper of movement. He was that still. A predator watching her, wholly focused on her. A cold chill crept down her spine. Her heart slammed hard and began to accelerate. Her blood went cold.

"This man you say you love. He is a Daratrazanoff. *He* knew better."

She knew in that moment that he would hunt down Gary and kill him. It was there in his eyes. That dark green that glittered with menace and ruthless intent. Aleksei really was part savage, as untamed as any of the wildest predatory animals roaming the earth. He was going to kill Gary, and she was certain he had the knowledge and skill to do it in spite of all the knowledge Gary had acquired when they converted him.

Gabrielle shook her head. "He wasn't. He was human, too. He became friends with Gregori Daratrazanoff." She swept a hand through her hair, suddenly exhausted, so tired she could barely lift her hand. She didn't want to do this. "This isn't Gary's fault. We had feelings for each other before we were converted. I had no comprehension of being someone's lifemate or what that would entail."

"Your sister is a lifemate to someone and she was human like you." The words were a low accusation.

She was intelligent. She had known. She hadn't wanted to know, but deep down, where she was good at hiding from herself, she had known there was the possibility. She'd just convinced herself it wouldn't happen because she was too afraid. She didn't want someone to consume her. She didn't want that side of her nature she kept hidden, repressed and pushed away ever coming out—like he had brought out in her.

She moaned softly in despair. There was no going back. He wouldn't let her. She knew that, she knew by his implacable expression and the hardness in his green gaze. He had said she was wild. That she matched him. She didn't want that. She was afraid of who she was. What lengths would she go to? He would rule her life if she allowed it and she was very, very afraid she would if she didn't find the courage to fight him.

"You will forget this man, Gabrielle. If you do not, I will kill him. You do not know me, so you cannot know I do not make idle threats. He has no right to any part of you, and I refuse to share you with him."

"I would hate you forever if you killed him," she whispered.

His hand tightened in her hair, forcing her to stare into his eyes. "If this man is in your mind and heart, there is no room for me," he said. "You gave yourself to me. *All* of you. Are you a woman of your word?"

She wanted to be. She moistened her lips. She knew he was telling her she had to let go of Gary, but he didn't understand it was so much more than that.

"Say it," he snapped, his fingers tightening in warning. "If you are not honest with me, I will take your mind and see to every corner of it and sweep this man away myself. I am giving you this concession. Talk to me honestly even if you know it will make me angry. If you do not, I will not ask again."

"I know I did something wrong," she said, unable to contain her rising temper. "I tried to make up for it. Punish me if that makes you feel any better. I don't know what else I can do. If I give him up completely, I've lost everything I was. Everything I am. Everything human. I'll be so lost I won't know how to get back to me." The stark truth burst out of her before she could sort through her desperate thoughts.

Again he just watched her. Forever. For what seemed an eternity. Abruptly, still holding her hair, he pulled her head back farther and leaned into her, taking her mouth. She kept her mouth closed. She was determined that he wouldn't have any more of her right then. She was too vulnerable. Too exposed. Too fragile. One more blow and she might not survive. She didn't want to know that her body was already his. She just wanted to be numb and not think about anything at all. Not ever again.

She turned her face to the side but he clamped his hand around her jaw, holding her face toward his.

"*Kessake*, you cannot be afraid you will lose yourself. I can always find you. I will always find you no matter how lost you are. You put yourself into my keeping, and I may be rough and half savage, but you do not have to fear these things. I will see to your happiness. I will cherish you and protect you."

His lips brushed over hers gently, almost tenderly, and her eyes burned with tears all over again. How could he be so sweet one moment and so frightening the next? She was just so tired.

"I will teach you the things you fear. You are intelligent, Gabrielle. You know information is power. You fear what you do not know. You will grow powerful and skilled in the ways of our people. That will not lessen who you are or who you were, only enhance it."

She pressed her forehead to his. "You're making sense, and that scares me a little," she admitted. She lifted her head. "How? How do I do what you ask?"

"You have no choice, *kessake*, because I have no choice. I cannot share you with another man. I will not. No other man touches you."

"I know that," she said. "I wouldn't betray you like that. Not even with him." And she wouldn't. She'd given her word, and truthfully, she wasn't certain any other man would ever satisfy her. Worse, she wasn't certain she could allow another man to touch her, not even Gary.

"I want all of you."

It was a demand, and it said everything about him. He was ruthless. Arrogant. He would kill. He had killed. He was hard and scary and everything that Gary was not. She let her breath out slowly and closed her eyes.

Gary. She breathed his name with regret. With sorrow. *I'm so sorry*. She was sorry. For everything, but mostly because she already belonged to Aleksei. Maybe not her heart, but she had chosen and she would stick with that choice, no matter how terrified she was.

She didn't know how to let Gary go, but she was going to try. Gary wouldn't feel the sorrow she did. She knew the love he had for her would barely be a memory to him if Gregori and Mikhail had managed to save him—and she was certain they had. She would have known if he was gone.

She breathed her good-bye and took another breath. When she opened her eyes, she found herself staring into Aleksei's brilliant green eyes. He didn't blink. He refused to release her gaze.

"Are you letting him go?"

She nodded her head slowly.

"Kiss me."

She pulled back a little, or tried to. She'd forgotten his hand in her hair. That said how gentle he'd been with her, but now she felt the bite of demand on her scalp. She licked her lips with the tip of her tongue. She wasn't ready for this. "Aleksei." She whispered his name, asking for mercy. Willing him to understand.

His hold slid from her hair to wrap around the nape of her neck. "*Kessake*, you need to trust your lifemate. I want you to kiss me."

She wrapped her arms tighter around her knees, holding herself together when she was afraid she would come apart.

"Lean into me. Put your hands on my shoulders and kiss me."

His voice was gentle. Patient. For some reason that turned her heart over and made her want to weep. She never knew what to expect from him and it kept her feeling off balance. She forced her body to uncurl a little, just enough to take her hands from her legs and put them on his broad shoulders. At once heat soaked into her. She hadn't even known she was cold or shivering. His skin was hot and warmed her entire body just by having her hands on him.

"That is a start, but you forgot the part where you lean into me. I want your breasts pressed against my chest and your mouth on mine."

Her eyes searched his. She didn't know what to make of his instructions, but she felt her body react at the suggestion. Her breasts were suddenly tender and sensitive, achy and in need of his touch. A throb began deep in her core. She leaned into him, letting his thick, heavily muscled chest take her weight.

His hand remained at the nape of her neck, while his other

arm swept around her back and locked her to him. She had to tilt her head up so she could see his mouth. She could fixate on his mouth, especially because she knew his taste. Knew the way he kissed.

She slid her arms around his neck, pressing even closer, letting him hold her. Comfort her. Care for her. That's what it felt like. At the same time, she felt a little like his prisoner. Surrounded by him. Taken by him. Branded by him.

Ignoring everything else that came into her mind, she concentrated on his mouth. His lips were full and sensual, his teeth very white and strong. There was nothing at all feminine about him; in fact, he looked fiercely male. She found her heart accelerating. Her stomach somersaulting. Her sex pulsed.

To block out her reaction to him, she moved the scant inches and brushed a kiss over his mouth. Then a second one. Her tongue touched the seam of his mouth and he opened to her. She was shy. She didn't really know what she was doing, but she had the experience of kissing him and she followed his example. He let her take the initiative for a few mind-stopping seconds. She explored the heat of his mouth, teasing his tongue, tracing his teeth, kissing him because now she had to, not because he demanded it.

Then he took over. Completely. Sweeping her away to another dimension. His kisses did that to her. He drove out every thought. Good or bad. Every other person until there was only Aleksei. Only the man holding her to him. Kissing the breath from her body. Starting fires with just his mouth alone.

Her body moved restlessly against his. His cock was suddenly hard and hot and resting against her thigh. Without thinking, she dropped one hand down to cover him, feeling him jerk beneath her. He felt like velvet over steel. Thick. So thick. So long. How could that fit inside of her? But it did and felt so good.

"Wrap your fist around my cock, Gabrielle."

He whispered the command against her mouth and then he was kissing her again. Long. Wet. Hard. So delicious. His mouth growing rougher. She couldn't resist the temptation and she wrapped her fingers around the heavy girth. He pulsed in her palm. So hot. Velvet soft. Iron hard. She didn't stop herself from exploring. From running her palm up the shaft and sliding up and over the broad crown.

"Yours," he said softly. "All yours."

One arm went to her back, the other beneath her knees. "Dawn is creeping upon us. We will go to ground and continue this next rising. And, *kessake*." He licked just behind her ear and then bit gently down on the skin between her shoulder and neck, sending a thousand flames dancing over her skin. "You did not think about him once, did you? I told you to trust me. I can help you. When you need help, you ask."

His eyes stayed on hers and she nodded slowly, her breath still caught in her lungs. He opened the earth, and she closed her eyes. "I've never gone to ground unless I was already asleep," she confided.

"You will lay with me, the ground open until we have to close it, and I will tell you how to do this. I can help you. And always know, you are safe with me. If you can conquer your fear, tell me and I will help you."

"I am not cleaned up yet."

"I want you to go to ground with me inside you. When you wake next rising, I promise you will be clean."

She wasn't certain what to think about that, but she did know one thing—she knew *exactly* why he wanted her to kiss him. Gary was gone from her mind just as he'd been when Aleksei had taken her body the first two times. Kissing Aleksei did that, and she didn't want to think too much about what that said about her.

8

Trixie Joanes was in trouble. Not a little bit of trouble, but a *lot*. The kind of trouble that could get one dead very fast if they didn't make smart decisions. She was fairly certain the mountains were probably hiding like a million vampires, but her vampire-hunting kit—the one she'd gotten off the Internet—was really difficult to lug around.

The entire box was large and weighed a ton. It was awkward and, when hiking up in the mountains—which was tough enough—impossible to carry. So really, what good was it? A big wooden box, with all kinds of contents, that when sitting at home in her living room looked really cool, but when she was trying to haul it around with her, hiking up a seriously high mountain, well, whupping vampire ass was out.

She'd been hiking for hours, running when she could, which, truthfully, wasn't very often. She was going uphill. She wasn't built for speed. She was a woman with a woman's body. In shape, but still, she had *curves*. Real womanly curves, not some stick figure that was all the rage.

"Seriously." She muttered the word under her breath as she avoided a field full of rocks and tried to find a place that was safe to sit down and rest. She really needed to rest. She'd gone up the mountain instead of down for a variety of reasons, none of which, at that particular moment, when she was sucking in air to try to give her burning lungs a break, seemed logical.

She spotted a smallish boulder back in the shadow of the mountain that rose behind it like a specter. She could just sit there for a few minutes. She didn't want to be out in the open where her traveling companions might spot her. They would have found her missing the moment they got up. She could only hope they thought she'd gone back to the village instead of up the mountain, but she was fairly certain Denny Jashari could track anything in the mountains.

Trixie had no business in a foreign country running with a pack of hyenas pretending to be good people when they clearly weren't. If any of her girls had made such poor decisions she would have boxed their ears and brought them home for a good ass whuppin'.

She sank down on the rock and dropped her back to the ground, considering for the millionth time whether or not to dump her vampire-hunting kit. It wasn't that she didn't believe in vampires anymore—she'd been convinced that monsters actually existed, she *knew* she wasn't two steps away from the loony bin—but quite frankly, she just couldn't conjure up enough energy to care. She didn't have to worry about monsters there on the mountain; she had to worry about them maniacs.

She didn't like to travel and yet she found herself in the Carpathian Mountains, somewhere near Poland, or the Ukraine, or one of those countries where she didn't understand a word anyone said. The *only* reason she would leave her home and her own neighborhood was her beloved granddaughter—Teagan.

Teagan *did* like to travel and she was always getting herself into scrapes. Mostly, she got out of them because she was extremely smart, but this time . . . Well, she needed her grandmother whether she thought so or not. Teagan was in love. With a foreigner. Trixie knew all about the human trafficking and sex trade going on with young, beautiful, *susceptible* girls like Teagan. She had to stop her from making a terrible mistake. Well, now her first priority was to save herself, and if she did, it would take a lot of luck. She should have known better than to get mixed up with a bunch of fanatics.

Trixie looked cautiously around her, trying to get her

bearings. She'd snuck out of the camping area on the pretext of gathering wood for a fire. She'd just kept going. Her traveling companions were totally whacked. Bonkers. As in *insane*. They might as well have been bible thumpers who spouted everything but the bible. Seriously whacked.

Teagan was Trixie's. Her special girl. Her sun in the morning and stars at night. No one was going to harm Teagan. Not some horrible stranger who charmed a young, inexperienced girl and was probably trying to marry her to get into the United States, and not the whacked-out vampire hunters who didn't know the difference between a vampire and a human being.

Totally bloodthirsty. Trixie didn't mind whupping ass when it was warranted, but she was discerning. Her traveling companions were *not* discerning. She scrubbed her hand down her face, trying to fight exhaustion. She'd been hiking most of the day, and the sun was about to set. She'd gone up the mountain, not down, because something compelled her to go toward the highest peak and the mist, rather than go back down.

The mist coiled just above her, thick and dense. Things seemed to move in the mist, and she could hear dark voices on the wind. Was Teagan up there? In that? If so, she needed rescuing, and Trixie was there to do just that. She could hear the music of the night. The wind, the trees shifting subtly, the rocks, some gently trickling down the mountainside, even the wolves, all blended together in harmony to make beautiful, breathtaking notes.

She heard music in people. Sometimes soft. Sometimes loud. Joyous. Sad. The music was always there, from the time she could remember as a young child. A part of her. As she'd gotten older she began to discern that the musical notes in people tipped her off to the type of person they were. Meeting her traveling companions at the bottom of the mountain convinced her she was in deep trouble. The notes she heard coming off them as they hiked the trail, as well as the conversations about staking people, made her physically ill.

She looked up at the fog again. Swirling into patterns. Unnatural. She didn't know how she knew it was unnatural, because the music it made was part of the night's song, the notes in the dense veil of gray not jangling, or jarring, but still, the swirling mass of gray vapor was definitely not normal.

Again she felt anxiety pulling at her center. Her feet wanted to follow the path right into the fog and go higher still. She hoped she was tuned to Teagan. She'd always known where her girls were because she felt their music. The path she took held faint notes that were Teagan's but they seemed just out of reach, as if she couldn't quite catch up with her. *And what was Teagan doing running around the mountains at night in a foreign country?* The moment there was trouble, she should have been on a plane back to the States. And she was in trouble all right. Huge trouble this time. That girl was going to experience a little whup-ass herself.

Trixie was in good shape. She still had her figure. She had curves and none of them were sagging. She looked fine in her really sweet ass-hugging cargo pants that shaped her booty and tucked nicely into her hiking boots. She still had the little tucked-in waist she'd been given from heaven and her hair was as full and as shiny as ever. She liked it long, with tons of braids so she could fix it in intricate dos that made her feel like a woman, not a robot.

Secretly, she had a thing for really nice—and sexy— underwear; of course no one knew about that little vice and she wasn't going to let her traveling companions find out her secret, either. They would if they killed her, and she had the feeling they would kill her when they caught up with her. If you weren't with them, then you were against them. They sounded like bigots—racists—and being black, she'd had enough of that to last more than one lifetime.

She sighed. The mountain path was steep and led straight into the fog. She might be in shape, but she was no spring chicken, and she'd been following those faint musical notes all night and now most of the day and she was tired. Very tired. Worse. The *very* worst was the fact that these men she had set out with were hunting her granddaughter and the man Teagan was with.

Trixie and her traveling companions had met up with a man in the village just below the mountain—a man by the name of Denny Jashari. He claimed that a couple—a man and a woman—had killed his son and nephews up on the mountain. *Four* of his nephews and his son. So five men. He described Teagan.

Teagan. Her beloved Teagan. As if Teagan could hurt a fly. Trixie had gotten the call from Teagan telling her that she'd met a man and was going to marry him. She'd also said her guide was a serial killer. And a rapist. That guide had been Armend Jashari, Denny Jashari's son. Yep. Trixie was in trouble, but so was Teagan. She had to find her granddaughter first and fast, before the others did, and get her home where she would be safe.

"I'm too old for this crap," Trixie muttered, and pushed off the rock. Her backpack felt like it weighed a ton and again she was tempted to throw out her vampire-hunting kit, but she might have to use it against human nutcases. Jashari had whipped the men she was with into a killing frenzy, convincing them that Teagan and her man were vampires.

She set her burning feet right back on the path and started up it toward the strange fog. The fog bank looked close, but although she had traveled an hour, it was still a good distance away. She really, really was too old for this. She should have pulled out her stake-gun thingie the moment they described Teagan and just shot them all right there in the old crumbling building where they'd held their meeting.

Fred Wilson had been her contact in the United States. It had been his wife, Esmeralda, who had first become friends with Trixie. Trixie shook her head. She'd been fooled by that old hag. They'd laughed together and had been snarky online—something they both enjoyed—meeting in chat rooms and becoming fast friends. She'd been such a fool.

She kept moving, picking up speed as she went over the way Esmeralda had pulled her into a web of deceit so smoothly. Trixie knew she was intelligent and she counted on that knowledge, sometimes feeling a little superior when others misjudged her because she didn't have a formal education. She'd educated herself and she'd done very well in the world of business. She'd raised her own daughter and four granddaughters, all of whom were college graduates. She'd done good. Still, she'd been played by Esmeralda.

The woman wasn't her friend. Not at all. She'd somehow known about Trixie's ability to tune to people. No one outside the family knew about it. Well . . . once a few years back she'd gone for psychic testing just for the fun of it. But that was confidential. Or so they had said. Esmeralda had known. She'd made the initial contact online at a site where readers of vampire novels came together to discuss the books. They'd had fun together. Then it wasn't so fun anymore, and it definitely wasn't fun now, not with Esmeralda's husband believing psycho man Jashari about Teagan. Of course they didn't know Teagan was her granddaughter or they probably would have killed her on the spot.

She'd heard them whispering in their tent together. How they would use her to find the vampires and then they'd have to get rid of her because she knew too much and didn't believe in their cause. As if her presence wasn't enough for them. She was fairly certain it was Jashari who wanted her dead. He'd led the discussions and the others deferred to him in all things. She had the feeling he was fairly high up in their organization.

Finally. *Finally.* She reached the fog bank. Or more correctly, a wall of fog. It appeared solid and impenetrable. Studying it from several different angles, she decided she needed to find a way in. The faint notes she followed were calling to her from *inside* that cover of thick, gray vapor— so she had to get inside.

Trixie was a lot of things, but patient was not one of them. She flung her pack to the ground, grateful to get it off her back, but not so grateful that she would have to sit on the ground and get her very fine pants dirty. They were cute and she really liked them. It wasn't that easy to find pants that showed off her curves to their full advantage. If she was going to get murdered up there on that mountain, at least they'd find her dead body looking extremely fine.

She tried to dust off the dirt and vegetation from around the spot before she sank down gingerly right there in the dirt, staring straight ahead into the fog. The vapor moved, swirling, almost mesmerizing, making patterns, but there was no wind that moved it. An unseen hand maybe, but not the wind. She could feel wind, but it wasn't moving the fog. She closed her eyes, refusing to look into the swirling mist. Instead, she listened carefully, hearing the music inside the fog. The notes of silver and gold sang softly to her.

The notes weren't discordant at all, not like the notes Denny Jashari and his friends gave off. These were warning notes, broadcasting to others to stay away, but rather than being out of tune with nature, they fit perfectly. Harmonious. Definitely a part of the wilderness.

The notes appealed to her as nothing else in her lifetime ever had. Something inside of her responded, matching the rhythm, almost like a heartbeat. She felt her body tune to the notes. Embrace them. Her own symphony played counterpoint and then sang harmony. Whoever or whatever had put those notes in the fog fit with her. Belonged.

In spite of the danger to her granddaughter, in spite of the very real danger to herself, for the first time in her life, she relaxed completely. She couldn't remember ever feeling relaxed. She was too busy. She had too much responsibility. She worked nonstop. She took care of children and their educations. She made a home for them. She didn't take time out to see to her own needs. Her family was her life. Everything. She didn't relax.

She found herself simply breathing, letting the notes fill her up. Revive her when she'd been so exhausted. She wanted to laugh. To cry. She felt safe wrapped up in that song. It was wild. Untamed. At the same time there was elegance there. Refinement. Things just out of her reach. She'd given them to her granddaughters, but she'd never had them for herself.

Sitting there in the dirt, she sang back to the notes, feeling, for the first time in her life, elegance and refinement. Feeling safe.

It took a few minutes—or maybe it was hours—to realize she was wrapped up in the fog. She hadn't seen it move, but then she wasn't looking. She was feeling. She felt for her pack because the fog was too dense for sight to penetrate. It was there, right beside her, so *she* hadn't moved. Just the fog had.

Still, she wasn't afraid. It was impossible to feel fear when everything inside you felt transformed. Golden. Perfect. She'd never had that before, and she wasn't going to give it up. She was tempted to sit right in that exact spot forever, but she knew she had to find Teagan. She still wasn't certain she was on Teagan's trail. Clearly, she'd been in the same fog. Trixie heard echoes of Teagan's song, but the notes were still very faint, as if she wasn't any closer to her.

Strangely it was the notes in the fog that called to her. They grew stronger, more insistent, and everything she was responded to the mysterious and beautiful notes. She stood up and caught up her backpack, shrugging into it, almost not even feeling the weight of it because the notes were so consuming, they made her light.

She followed the notes, uncaring that she couldn't see into the fog. She could have been blindfolded for all she cared. It wouldn't have mattered. The musical notes simply grew louder as she followed them. Her feet naturally found the path, if there truly was one. She didn't run into a single obstacle. Not one. She knew the sun was close to setting, and she should try to find shelter. The fog was wet and when she touched it, or turned her face up to it, she felt the cool dampness, like tiny drops of water on her skin, yet as she walked through it, she didn't get wet at all. She felt wrapped in a shawl of protection.

Trixie halted when tall, thick gates loomed over her. Her breath caught in her throat. She'd dreamt of a monastery at the very top of a mountain. Now it was all familiar to her. In her dreams the monastery was always enshrouded in fog and mystery. She sometimes saw things in her dreams, and they turned out to be real, but this was frightening. In her dream, *inside* the monastery, behind those gates, was something so terrifying to her, she'd never been able to face it. She'd forced herself to wake up. She'd been certain it was a vampire waiting to drain her dry of blood.

Her heart pounded. Hard. Urgently. Still, in spite of her fear, her hand went to the gate, her palm touching gently. Like a caress. The moment she touched the gate, she felt the notes there. Much louder. Summoning her. Reaching inside her to a place that had always, *always*, been alone. The-middle-of-the-night alone, when her girls were safely sleeping in the beds she'd provided for them. The best money could buy. Inside the home she'd bought for them. She'd been alone.

She'd pushed her own needs down in order to care for those she loved. And she did it happily, with no regrets. None. She would choose the same path every time, but that didn't mean, in the middle of the night, loneliness didn't call, and she lay awake keeping her mind blank so she wouldn't feel an aching hole that would never be filled inside of her. She knew she'd made that choice, and what she got in return was wonderful. Her girls filled her life with laughter and love. She didn't need anything more. Still, that emptiness rose up at times to haunt her.

The golden notes meshed with the notes inside of her. Sang to her. Called to her notes, so she sang back. She harmonized, and the emptiness in her filled with beautiful music. Music she'd never expected. There in the gate, she heard the notes swelling in volume, singing a soft, whispery song that beckoned her forward. She could see the notes now, dancing in the air, and her notes joined those, silver and gold, twining around one another.

There was a click and the gate swung inward, the notes sliding inside the open gate. Trixie didn't hesitate to follow. She stepped around the barely opened gate, following the dancing music into a courtyard. Behind her, the gate swung closed. She glanced over her shoulder at it, mainly because it sounded loud, and heavy, and final.

With the fog so thick, she couldn't tell if the sun was

setting, but it felt cold all of a sudden. She shivered and half turned. She couldn't see how to open the gate. As far as she could make out, there were several small buildings scattered inside a very high fence. The barricade surrounding the buildings was high and thick and took in a good deal of space. In fact, it was clearly a fortress.

Looking around, she was fairly certain it was a deserted fortress. There was nothing to indicate anyone lived there, and if they had once lived there, it was a very long time ago. She couldn't see anything that would indicate the existence of a human being. She took two steps toward the center of the fortress.

The buildings were old, but they were solid and made of great stones. The musical notes drew her attention back to them. The notes danced in the air all around the building closest to the gates. It was a beautiful sight, and she moved closer. The music increased in volume. Not Teagan's music, but much more masculine. Wild. Sexy. Elegant. Over-the-top masculine. How the song could be all of those things, Trixie didn't know, but it was and it was beautiful.

She went right up to the building, her heart pounding hard in her chest. Her mouth went dry. She didn't know what to expect, but the beautiful, perfect song surrounded her and filled in the missing notes of her song. She felt compelled to move forward and knew if she tried to stop herself she wouldn't be able to. She *had* to find the owner of that song.

Her fingers wrapped around the crudely carved door handle. There was no lock. The door was heavy but it swung open easily when she jerked on it, stepped inside and stopped. She let go of the door in shock, and behind her, it swung closed. The musical notes filled the room, dancing, playing all around her, but there was nothing inside those four walls but dirt. A dirt floor. An undisturbed dirt floor.

She didn't know why she wanted to cry, but she did. She was tired. Exhausted. She'd been like a child hunting the pot of gold at the end of the rainbow, and she felt cheated. She dropped her pack to the floor and sank down. Her legs were trembling so much she couldn't stand.

Trixie shook her head, refusing to let the sudden tears in her eyes fall. What had she been thinking? She was well past her prime. She'd lost her shot at any kind of . . . *what*? She didn't want a man. She was set in her ways. Snarky. She spoke her mind and was often sarcastic and nasty when she was crossed. Men liked sweet, and that wasn't her. Life had been good to her, bringing her granddaughters to her, but it had also taken a lot. She had her life the way she liked it now. She wouldn't give one moment of it up for a man.

She straightened her shoulders because, really, she had been in some kind of mesmerizing spell and maybe, just maybe, that teenage girl who had gotten pregnant and thought her man loved her and would stand by her had come to the front out of nowhere, dreaming again. She had to find her steel spine and her sense of humor, no matter that she was alone. She couldn't afford to dream. She'd given up on dreams for herself a good fifty years earlier. Her dreams were for her girls. And they were living the dream, and that was good enough for her.

Trixie looked around her. At least she had shelter. She was tired and needed to sleep. She was fairly certain the men who would be chasing her couldn't make their way through the dense fog. In any case, they couldn't see to track her once they hit the fog. She'd had the musical notes to guide her, and they didn't.

She opened her pack and pulled out her sleeping bag. She'd sleep right there in the empty building with the musical notes playing all around her. And she wouldn't dream. She wouldn't be lonely. She would just go to sleep. Being a careful type of woman and always believing in being prepared, she pulled her vampire-hunting box out of her pack and set it beside her.

Looking at it, she felt a little better. There was a vial of holy water and a bible. There were all kinds of other things as well, but she really liked the little gun that shot the small, sharpened stakes. They weren't as big as she would have liked. Not at all. She frowned as she examined them. If she had designed a kit, she would have gotten rid of most of the junk in it and would have concentrated on making some big-ass stakes. The kind that would make a serious hole in a vampire's heart so he'd never rise again. It was a point-and-shoot kind of gun, and she liked that about it. She put it beside her sleeping bag with the little board of extra stakes.

"Not that you're real stakes," she whispered aloud, because really, they looked silly. They looked like tips of stakes. She liked things big. Bold. Larger than life. Solid. Especially a stake that stood between her and a vampire.

Trixie lay back on top of the sleeping bag, looking up at the dancing notes, hearing the beautiful song, the one that made her dream when she didn't want to. When she knew better. "I never wanted a man of my own, not after learning they were lying, cheating, lazy bums. He never even spoke one word to our daughter. Not one. Our beautiful girl." Her hand closed convulsively around the little gun. Had her daughter's father been standing in front of her right at that moment, she would have staked him on the spot.

She was quiet for a long time, occasionally reaching up to wipe at the wet on her face. She didn't cry, so the tracks weren't tears, just maybe leftover residue from the fog. Still, her eyes were a bit watery and out of focus when she first noticed the disturbance in the dirt floor. Right in the middle. The dirt spewed into the air, small at first and then like a geyser.

Trixie scrambled to her feet and jumped to the side. She stood over the hole in the ground, staring in shock. The hole was deep and long. It was long because it had to accommodate a very large man. He lay down in the open grave—and it was an open grave—looking up at her. His eyes were *open.*

Trixie screamed. She wasn't the screaming type, and her scream scared her. Most likely it scared the angels in heaven. She lifted her hand and pointed at him. An honest-to-God vampire. Staring at her. It took a moment to realize the little gun was in her hand, and she convulsively pulled the trigger.

The tiny little stake flew out of the gun and hit him high in the shoulder.

He winced. His eyes, a gorgeous blue—and they were gorgeous, she'd noted that—darkened. Became twin storm clouds. More, he'd been entirely naked. As in *naked*. All of him. Even the best parts, and although it was truly her worst nightmare, she'd still noted his best parts were really the *best*. Holy cripes.

Her stupid little stake hadn't done the trick. She backed up, tripped and went down on her butt, hand trying to find the other stakes. She was loading the gun when he rose. Floated. In the air. Floated. Feet not on the ground. Holy cripes all over again. She shoved the stake in the gun and let fly a second time.

The stake nailed him in his arm. It really wasn't a point-and-aim kind of weapon like it was advertised, and it didn't seem to be killing him. At all. He looked really alive and really big. Lots of muscle. Lots of . . . um . . . *everything*.

She caught up the holy water and flung the glass vial at him, forgetting to take out the stopper. He caught the vial in midair. He was fast. Very fast.

"*Köd alte hän, emni,*" he snapped.

His voice was like music, even when he was cursing. The sound made her stomach curl, something that hadn't happened since she was fifteen years old. And he definitely was swearing at her.

"Stay back, vampire," she hissed, holding out the big silver cross. So far her very expensive vampire-hunting kit wasn't working. Hopefully the cross was real silver. "And for God's sake, put some clothes on."

Because *really*. How could she keep her mind on killing him when he was right there in all his glory? And he had glory.

A slow smile pulled at the hard edges of his mouth. He looked all man. Not those skinny, prissy boys they put on the covers of the books she liked to read. No, he was definitely a man. Hard edges and lots and lots of muscle. He might be a bloodsucking vampire, but he was a really hot, manly one. If she was going to die, at least the vampire killing her was scorching hot. She could take that to her grave and perv on it for a very long time in the hereafter.

"Lady, put that silly cross down and tell me what you are doing, because so far, you have shot your lifemate with two darts and thrown a glass vial at him. All of which can be considered disrespectful."

Her eyebrows shot up. *"Disrespectful?"* Oh, no, he was not going to pretend she wasn't a worthy opponent. "Those are not darts. They are *stakes*. And I've got more where they came from so don't think you're going to take a bite out of me."

His smile warmed his eyes, and seriously, there it was again, that stomach curl. This time it was accompanied by a curious flutter in the region of days gone by. *Long* gone by. As in forgotten. As in *seriously* cobwebby. He was dangerous, and he just had to put on clothes because she couldn't stop looking.

"You are trying to kill me?"

"Well, of course." She put her hands on her hips. "You're a vampire and I'm huntin' you. So yes. You're going to have to die, which is very sad, and I don't like being the one to have to dispatch you because your music is beautiful, but I'm up to the task, so don't come any closer." She glared at him. *"And put some clothes on."*

It had been a long while since she'd seen a naked man and she didn't remember them looking like him. The artists, the ones famous for their sculptures, didn't get it right. They should have tried sculpting him—before he became a vampire, anyway.

"You're distracting me and I've got a job to do," she announced, before she could stop the words tumbling out of her mouth. Now she knew where her granddaughter got her compulsion for blurting out things when she was nervous.

"And your job is to kill me?" he asked.

His voice was gentle, almost a caress. She felt the notes stroke over her skin like the touch of fingers. She shivered. She couldn't help it. She wanted to listen to his voice while she slept. In her dreams. All night. The tone was beautiful, like his song.

"*Someone* has to do it, and I don't shirk. You're a gorgeous hunk of male, but that doesn't matter. I won't have you biting me and bringing me to the dark side."

His smile widened. He had white perfect teeth. Not, she noted, vampire teeth.

"I appreciate that you think I am a gorgeous hunk of male."

She wanted to close her eyes to savor his voice, his accent, but it was just too dangerous. Everything about him was dangerous. His hair was very long and very black but salted with streaks of fine silvery gray. She always thought men with long hair looked a bit silly, but on him, his hair didn't detract for one moment from his ultramasculine features. She was fairly certain he had a tattoo that crawled up his back and moved over his shoulders and down his arms, but it wasn't like any tattoo she'd ever seen, and in the faint light streaming in through the windows she couldn't be certain.

"It will make you happy to know that I am no vampire. I hunted vampires for centuries, but stopped a very long time ago."

She blinked. Her gaze dropped to his thick, heavily muscled chest. Then to his flat—like, twelve-pack—abdomen. Serious muscle there. She swallowed, trying to school her gaze to keep from looking any farther down his body, but there was no stopping her wandering eyes. Damn. The man was fine. She was fairly certain he had a fine ass, too. He just hadn't turned enough yet.

"If you aren't a vampire, how can you float in the air and sleep in the ground?" she demanded. Her mouth was watering a little looking at the man's body.

His gaze drifted over her face. Then her body. She felt the touch right through her clothes to her core. The core that gave a convulsive spasm. He was waking up things best left alone. There was possession in his gaze. Interest. Not just any interest, but sexual interest, and she *so* wasn't going there, no matter how fine he was.

His feet touched the ground just in front of her. He waved his hand, a graceful movement that sent a myriad of notes dancing in the air between them. Immediately he was dressed. A thin shirt stretched across his amazing chest. His trousers fit him snugly. He wore sandals on his feet.

He looked pretty darn fine in clothes. *Really* darn fine. This killing-him thing wasn't going so well. And now he was close. So close she could feel his heat. She was cold so his heat felt good. Too good.

"I am Fane. Keeper and guardian of the monastery."

In her life, Trixie was rarely at a loss for words, but she could barely breathe. Up close he smelled good and his music blended with hers. She could hear the song and knew it was beautiful and it was right. How could he be a vampire when he had a song so perfect? It didn't make sense. The notes made their way inside of her, just as they had before. They settled, all silver and gold, in those lonely places, and this time they didn't retreat. They stayed. And they brought him with them. Her body began to tremble and she stepped back, tripped on the vampire-hunting box and started to fall.

Fane caught her, gripping her forearms to steady her, bringing her in close to his body. To his heat. Holy cripes. He was hot. He had to notice she was shaking like a silly teenager. She was an old lady, *well* past her prime. He had to stop looking at her with those hungry eyes. If they were just hungry for her blood, well, she could take that. She could fight for her life. She had the feeling he was hungry for something altogether different and she didn't know how to process that.

She put up a hand to ward him off. She wasn't tall and she wasn't short. She was a woman with curves, but he made her feel small. Her hand looked a little silly there, a slim defense against him. He stepped even closer so that her hand rested against his chest. She could feel those delicious muscles there. She felt his heart beat, part of the rhythm of his song. Did vampires have hearts that beat? She thought they were dead.

"Lady. Tell me your name."

He gave the command in a low, deep voice. Husky. Raspy.

Caressing. She had to find a way to pull herself together and stop her body from responding to just the sound of his voice. She was no teenager to get lost in a man. He was weaving a spell. Because. He. Was. A. Vampire.

"If I give you my name, doesn't that give you power over me?"

His smile flashed again and he shook his head. "*Sívamet*, you do embody the meaning of the word *cute*. I never much liked that word until this moment because I did not get the meaning. The meaning is a woman who thinks I am a vampire but still asks me questions thinking I would help her out. A vampire would kill you immediately. Or he would nearly drain you dry and then torture you before finishing you off. He is wholly evil. There is no conversation with a vampire. And these things you have brought with you are useless against him."

Well. That wasn't good at all. Not. At. All. She sighed. "I'm tired and I'm going to sit down, so if you aren't really a vampire, just give me a few minutes to rest. I've been hiking all day and most of the night and I'm not so young anymore." She thought it best to point that out to him so he'd get that really hungry look off his face. She was a dried-up old prune and had no idea what to do with a man as fine as he was. Well, she'd read enough books to know what to do with him, but since she didn't have any practical experience, she knew that wasn't going to happen.

Suiting action to words, she sank down onto her sleeping bag and began gathering up her vampire-hunting tools. At least she wouldn't have to carry the stupid heavy box around with her anymore, because none of it worked on him. Not one single thing. A waste of money, and if she ever got home she was putting up a one-star review and blasting the seller. That was for certain.

9

Fane studied his woman's features as she sank to the ground. She looked exhausted and was hiding scared. She had beautiful skin. That had been the first thing he'd noticed. Soft as a rose petal. A beautiful, dark, almost chocolate color that made him want to run his fingers over her skin. She had a *lot* of hair. It was long, reaching her waist, and was in small braids that wrapped around the sides of her scalp to the back, where it was gathered by a tie of some sort and the braids fell in a thick stream down her back. Beautiful. Unusual.

He hadn't seen in color in well over a thousand years. More. He hadn't felt anything at all. At first, it was difficult to assimilate just what he was feeling, but he was a patient man and elation was at the forefront. She was human, and she clearly had ideas about what was and what wasn't going to happen between them. He didn't bother to disabuse her of any of her very wrong ideas. She was his lifemate. His reward after so many centuries of keeping the world a safe place.

He was still able, after so many centuries, to keep a cloak of civility around him, and that had landed him the position of keeping the other ancients there in the monastery in check. He wasn't a man who argued or lost his temper. Looking at his lifemate, he was fairly certain he was going to need those traits.

He crouched down beside her, his fingers catching her chin so she was forced to look up at him. "Your name, my lady."

She scowled at him and for a moment he thought she might

defy him. He would be forced to take the information from her and he didn't want to frighten her any further. She was holding it together by a thread.

"Trixie. Trixie Joanes. I'm from the United States, and I've come here looking for my granddaughter Teagan."

Teagan. He should have known. Fane had felt a strong connection to Teagan, Andre's lifemate, from the moment he'd first met her. She was related to his woman.

"I have met Teagan. She is safe."

Her eyes lit up. She reached out and caught his wrist. "Are you sure it was her? When did you see her?"

"Last rising."

She frowned, and he realized she was of the modern world and human. "Last night," he corrected. "She is with Andre and he will keep her safe."

Trixie drew in her breath and shook her head, dropping her hand to look around for her pack. "I have to go, to get to her. She doesn't know the danger she's in and neither does this Andre."

"Tell me."

"I came up the mountain with a group of crazy men. Fanatics. I left them in the middle of the night. They're with a man from the local village, a man by the name of Denny Jashari. I overheard him describe Teagan and a man she's traveling with. He persuaded the men I was with to hunt and kill her. They have all kinds of strange weapons with them, and I knew they planned on killing me after I led them up to this monastery and to my granddaughter. Fortunately, they didn't realize Teagan is related to me."

"They know," Fane said. "There is a society of humans who hunt those they consider vampires indiscriminately. They have killed several of my people over the years, but I doubt if they have ever come across and successfully killed a vampire. Evil feels and smells different. They wouldn't recognize that stench because . . ."

"They smell and feel the same way," she finished for him. She looked down at her hands. "I'm sorry I tried to kill you.

I should have known you weren't like them." Her gaze jumped back to his face. "But you were in the ground." She was very confused. His song confused her. That and the fact that he rose out of the ground and was looking so fine when he should have been a really ugly, scary corpse, and that he seemed to make sense when really, he didn't.

"How did you get through the safeguards?" he asked.

She tried to pull her gaze from his, but his eyes held hers captive. His voice was gentle, but instinctively she knew there was nothing gentle about the question. It was a demand. He wanted to know. He was just a little bit scary, and that kind of set her temper on edge. She was too old to be scared by a man.

Now that she had a good chance to really look at his face—without the distraction of his naked body—he looked hard-edged and beautiful, but very bossy. She didn't do bossy. She *was* the boss. Just to be on the safe side she took a better grip on her stake gun.

"Would you mind giving me back my holy water and the two stakes I fired at you?" She was proud that she had managed to sound matter-of-fact and maybe a little snippy as well. After all, he had her things. She'd bought and paid for them.

"You want them back?"

She scowled at him and narrowed her eyes to show him she wasn't a woman to be trifled with. "I feel very strongly about this. They're mine."

He looked at the vial of holy water and then reached up to his arm and casually removed the dart. Blood dripped down his shoulder. She bit her lip. She hadn't thought the little stakes were still in him and that they'd actually hurt him. She felt bad about that. He seemed too invincible for her tiny little stake gun to do much damage. Secretly, she was just a teensy bit elated. Her money wasn't a complete waste.

Fane's gaze never left hers as he removed the second dart and more blood appeared, dotting his immaculate shirt. That didn't look good.

"I've got a first aid kit," she volunteered, although she wasn't certain she wanted to touch his muscles again. Just touching his chest made her go weak at the knees, and for a dried-up old prune, she had responded in areas of her body she had given up all hope on too many years earlier. "I could let you use it."

His steady, focused, *unblinking* stare made her nervous. It was the way he looked at her, as if he might devour her.

"You're actually bleeding a lot," she pointed out. "We aren't anywhere close to a hospital and if you don't stop the bleeding . . ." She trailed off.

"You will supply the blood necessary. You are my lifemate. And put that silly weapon down. You are liable to shoot me again by accident."

She tried her sternest look, the one that made her girls quake and run to their rooms. It always worked. "It wouldn't be an accident. Don't try bossing me around. I am not intimidated by you."

A slow smile curved his mouth and softened his features. Did he have to be so beautiful? She had never been able to stand seeing anyone hurt. And she'd been the one to do it. Still. He came out of the ground. Naked. And he floated. And put clothes on without actually getting dressed.

Her fingers closed harder around the gun. It wasn't loaded and she needed to try to get to the other stakes. When she put up her one-star review she was going to mention how the gun really needed to carry a full six rounds. You obviously couldn't bring down a real vampire with one or two mini stakes. You needed a big gun.

"I am reading your mind," he announced softly.

"I don't believe you. No one can do that."

"A bigger gun? Are you thinking of staking me again?"

The amusement in his voice annoyed her. "You need to take me seriously," she snapped. "I've got the gun, not you. And I'm not afraid to use it."

"You closed your eyes when you shot it. Your hand jerked and that sent you off target twice," he pointed out. "And then you forgot to take the stopper off the vial of holy water."

She glared at him. "It isn't very nice to sound arrogant and amused when you're pointing out a couple of minor mistakes. I'm certain I'll improve with practice."

"Lifemate. You have enough attitude for ten women."

"Exactly." She was more than pleased he saw that. That should send him screaming for the hills and respecting her vampire-hunting kit, even though it was kind of lame and needed a few improvements, which she intended to see to.

He was standing close one moment and the next he was there. Right there. In her space. The gun was in his hand and he tossed it away. She hadn't even seen him move. She'd blinked and there he was. All gorgeous, a hot, hunky mass of muscle in her space. Touching her. She raised both hands to ward him off. Her palms landed on his chest and she closed her eyes, feeling the muscle definition there.

"I like attitude," he whispered, his mouth against her ear.

She felt the brush of his lips on her ear and a multitude of tingles moved through her body on a real rampage. There was no controlling that reaction. Pushing against the wall of his chest wasn't an option, not when his mouth moved against her ear and his tongue touched just behind it in a small, delicious swipe that sent a little tremor through her body. Waking her up. She couldn't be woken. She'd tamed that monster a long time ago. She wouldn't know what to do with a man like him.

"Don't." One word. That was all she could get out. Her mind was sort of fraying around the edges. His mouth was hot on her skin. Seductive. She thought to resist. She knew better than to play with fire, but her body suddenly wasn't her own anymore. She felt too weak to move.

Are you saying no to your lifemate?

She heard the words in her mind, not aloud. She thought she heard them. But his mouth was at her neck, his tongue sliding over her skin, over her pulse, and she didn't want him to stop. She *needed* him to stop, but she didn't want him to.

Te avio päläfertiilam. You are my lifemate.

She had no idea what he meant by *lifemate*, but he sounded serious. She tried to concentrate, but his mouth was on her neck, teeth scraping back and forth, and it felt erotic. *Very* erotic. She loved the way it felt, although her brain continued to try to function properly and protest.

Éntölam kuulua, avio päläfertiilam. I claim you as my lifemate.

His voice was so sexy, with a deep timbre. She loved his voice. But she loved his mouth on her neck more. She even turned her head to give him better access. Whatever the lifemate business was, just this once she might put up with it just to feel his mouth on her.

Ted kuuluak, kacad, kojed. I belong to you.

She liked that he belonged to her. Just for that moment, of course. She was no young girl with dreams of a future. She knew men didn't stick around, especially not at her age. Especially when they looked like him. She was beginning to think she was caught in some kind of dream. If so, she was quite willing to stay asleep a little longer.

Élidamet andam. I offer my life to you. Pesämet andam. I give you my protection. Uskolfertiilamet andam. I give you my allegiance.

Oh my. She had never had anyone offer their life, their protection or their allegiance. She felt the honesty of his words and her eyes stung with tears. Truly, this was some kind of weird dream. Gorgeous men didn't rise up from under the ground and proclaim they would offer their life for you.

His mouth burned at her neck. Right over her pulse. Her *pounding* pulse. Her heart had accelerated until she was afraid it would burst out of her chest. Her breasts actually ached. She didn't know what to do with that.

His teeth sank into her pulse and her head fell back. Her body arched in his arms, and she heard a soft moan escaping her throat as a bite of pain gave way to pleasure. No. More than mere pleasure. Fire rushed through her veins straight to her core. She felt as if she might be sleeping beauty, asleep for decades and now awakened by the bite of a master.

Sívamet andam. I give you my heart.

His voice. That voice. Sexy. Tempting. Raspy. Perfect. She could listen to it forever. And she didn't want his mouth to ever stop working against her neck.

Sielamet andam. I give you my soul.

That was so beautiful, the tears in her eyes trickled down her cheeks. She had thought she couldn't be moved by anything anymore. She was past her time to dream, but here she was, caught in a dream, and it was more beautiful than she could ever have hoped. She found it rather creative and amazing of her that she could dream up a man as gorgeous as Fane. His name. His accent. His looks. And he wasn't even a brother. How weird was that? After her daughter's experience she *never* let her gaze stray. Okay, maybe that wasn't altogether true. Some men just looked good in a fine pair of jeans cupping their ass just so perfectly.

Lifemate. You do not look at other men's asses, and not when we are saying our vows. You pay attention to your man.

Whoa. *She* wasn't saying vows. No way. She was remaining silent and just letting the dream unfold. He was bossy and arrogant and liked to use that tone. So okay. The tone was all right, even though he did sound bossy and arrogant. It was hot. And in her dream, she was okay with hot.

You do not want me to stop saying our vows.

There it was again. Bossy. Arrogant. So freakin' sexy a woman couldn't help but get all fired up, even when the engine hadn't worked for ages. So no. She didn't want the dream to end. His mouth on her neck was so amazing, sending streaks of pure fire spreading through her body like the blood in her veins.

"No. Don't stop," she murmured.

Ainamet andam. I give you my body.

She sincerely appreciated that gift, although she didn't have the first clue what to do with it. It had been too long. Decades too long. She was an all work, no play kind of girl, as much as she didn't want to admit that to her dream man.

His mouth took one last pull and he reluctantly lifted his head, his tongue swiping over the spot so that she shivered.

"You taste exquisite, lady. You are like a drug in my system. Addicting. I will never get the taste of you out of my mouth, nor do I want to."

His shirt seemed to have disappeared and her hands were against pure steely muscle and hot skin. She turned her head and nuzzled him closely. There was a part of herself that seemed separated from her, looking on, a little shocked at the gesture. That wasn't at all like her. Still, he smelled delicious. He felt even better. And she liked that he called her *lady* when no one else ever had and she'd tried to make herself into one for her granddaughters.

He murmured something she didn't understand, something in that language he uttered before telling her what it meant. This time there was no explanation, but she found herself licking along his chest, right over his heart. She tasted his skin. Tasted his pulse. Then she tasted him. Hot. Spicy. Addicting, just as he'd said she'd been. His hand cupped the back of her head, holding her to his chest, her mouth moving against him, drawing out the perfect blend that acted on her like an aphrodisiac.

Her body moved restlessly against his. His free hand moved down her back, into her hair, over her hips. Every place he touched went liquid so that she felt as if her bones melted right into him.

Sívamet kuuluak kaik että a ted. I take into my keeping the same that is yours.

Oh. Wow. He was taking her body into his keeping. She liked the sound of that. In her dreams, of course. In reality, she would run screaming for the hills, or try to shoot him again with her vampire-stake gun. Because . . . really . . . he couldn't know she was practically a virgin at her age. How utterly humiliating.

Hän sívamak.

His voice was so sensual, when he whispered the words into her mind she felt beautiful and sexy. She felt *his*. She didn't even know what it meant, but she knew it was something he called her and it was an endearment of some kind.

You are avio päläfertiilam, my lifemate. There is no need ever for embarrassment or humiliation. I will always take care of you. Ainaak olenszal sívambin. Your life will be cherished by me for all my time. Te élidet ainaak pide minan. Your life will be placed above my own for all time.

Tears burned her eyes. He took the breath from her lungs with the beauty of his vows to her. No one had ever cherished her or placed her life above their own. He was a stranger to her, a dream man, but still, he said all the things a woman would want to hear.

Te avio päläfertiilam. You are my lifemate. Ainaak sívamet jutta oleny. You are bound to me for all eternity. Ainaak terád vigyázak. You are always in my care.

Fane's hand came up to slip between her mouth and his chest. She was reluctant to allow him to stop her from drinking the very essence of him. He was so perfect in every way. He tasted delicious. Still, he tipped her chin up toward his face and brought his mouth down to hers.

Her heart jumped. Jerked hard in her chest. Her feminine channel convulsed in utter shock. His kiss was hot. Hard. Wet. Sexy as hell. It went on forever. He kissed her over and over and she thought she wouldn't remember how to kiss, but she just melted into him and he was so fine, her mouth opened for him and their tongues tangled and danced and he filled her with red-hot urgency and a terrible need that sank straight between her legs and clawed at her stomach.

"*Susu,*" he whispered into her mouth. "I am home."

Home. He said he was home. Home was . . . her. She knew what he was saying to her. She knew what his kisses were saying. He wanted her. She wasn't young. She wasn't beautiful. She wasn't even a stick, like the accepted norm. Her time had long since passed even for this to happen in a dream. It felt all too real.

His body was hard and hot and she couldn't stop her hands from roaming over his skin. She found the ridges on his back, and she wanted to see what the tattoo was like. Her fingers traced the artwork. It was large, flowing across his back and up over his shoulders and arms. Not ink. At least not any ink she had ever seen. Characters. Letters. All woven into the tattoo.

She almost asked him to turn around, to let her see it, but she knew if she did, she would know too much. She would go too far with this man and not be able to pull back. Trixie had a secret that she kept strictly to herself. She wouldn't have given it up to anyone. Ever. She had great confidence in her abilities to raise her granddaughters. To work long hard hours and provide a home. She could gossip with the best of them and she had turned sarcasm and snark into an art form. People were afraid to cross her. She exuded confidence when she confronted others. She fought for her girls in every respect and never backed down.

Truthfully, she had absolutely zero confidence in her ability to be a sexy woman. She had given up on that dream too long ago, and she had no skills and even less desire. She'd fought too hard to stop needing a man. To stop needing sex. To stop needing comfort and protection.

"You don't understand," she whispered. "It's too late for me. You're too late. You can be in my dreams, but you can't be real."

She was shy. She'd always been shy around men she found attractive. She got tongue-tied and she felt like a silly teenager. She didn't know how to handle a man's attention, and she usually ran him off fast with her sarcasm and attitude. She had a special prop she called up. Her sea hag. No one could do sea hag like she could. She was going to have to find her fast, because she couldn't get any deeper with Fane. Not if he was real, and he felt all too real when he kissed her.

She couldn't allow herself to feel this urgent hunger clawing at her. She had sacrificed being a woman for her family. She couldn't go back on that. She wouldn't know how.

"Hän sívamak," he said softly, right into her mouth. He poured the endearment down her throat. Into her lungs so that she breathed—him. The word found her veins and crawled inside, to spread through her body like hot lava, burning her from the inside out.

"I don't understand," she whispered. She couldn't find her voice or her attitude. Her sea hag had disappeared completely. She just refused to come out around this man.

"My lifemate is my home and she is *hän sívamak*— beloved."

Beloved. She couldn't be anyone's beloved. "I'm a grand-mother," she blurted out. "I'm a great-grandmother. I'm probably old enough to be *your* grandmother. I am not your beloved. You have to stop kissing me because I think there's some kind of law against it. And if there's not, there should be."

"I am centuries old. An ancient among my people. I am locked in this monastery away from all humans. Away from my own people, those I have protected all of my existence, because it is not safe to be among them. Or it was not. Now, with you, it is. You will bring hope to my brethren here. My beautiful, beloved lifemate."

She was horrified. Hor-rif-ied. "Now you're talking crazy. Seriously crazy. Centuries, in case your English isn't so good, means hundreds of years. People don't live that long."

He had to stop stroking her skin. His fingers had gone to the nape of her neck and just stayed there. She squirmed a little to remind him she was half lying on a sleeping bag and he was half lying over the top of her and this wasn't going to happen. Even if he could kiss like sin. Even if he looked like sin. Even if he *was* sin.

"Humans do not live that long," he corrected gently, and leaned in to brush his mouth over hers. "There is no need to tremble. I could never harm you, but we are tied together now and the ritual must be completed. I am far too close to dark-ness to wait. You want me. I want you."

She pushed at his chest again, giving it some muscle this time. He didn't rock back so much as an inch. In fact, he didn't appear to notice.

"I have news for you, Fane. Any woman would want you. But it isn't going to happen. Not with me. There's really pretty women down in the village and you just have to waltz right in and any number of them will oblige you." It hurt to say the words. In fact they tasted bitter in her mouth. She was encouraging this gorgeous man who wanted *her* to find someone else. Better now than later, when he realized she wasn't the only woman available to him, and once he saw the others he would throw her away. Just like before. And that hurt. Bad. She wasn't going there again. Not ever.

"Lady, you think I do not see your mind? I *see* you. The one you hide away from everyone else. That is *my* woman. The woman belonging to me. And I know what the English word *centuries* means."

For one horrible moment she couldn't breathe. She didn't know why she believed him, but she did. He was centuries old. He had perfect skin and perfect teeth. He had the body of a man who was a warrior and maybe in his late thirties. She was not going there with him just for that alone. Sheesh. Was he crazy?

"I need my gun back. If you're centuries old and you sleep underground, you have to be a vampire, and I'm obligated to kill you."

He moved. Just inches. That was all—a few inches—but she found herself on her back, staring up at his beautiful face. That mouth. Those eyes. Her heart pounded in anticipation, not fear. That in itself was scary. He was scary. Everything about him was scary because she couldn't seem to find the strength to shove him off her and make a mad scramble for the gun.

He brushed back her hair and framed her face with his hands. "You are obsessed with that silly gun. *Hän sívamak*, it will not kill me. It will not kill a vampire. You are clinging to it because you are afraid to face being my lifemate."

"You aren't human," she pointed out. Again her voice refused to go above a whisper and there wasn't a single note of snark. Or attitude. She felt exposed and vulnerable, afraid he could really read her mind, and that would be *so* embarrassing.

"Would you kill me because I am not human?" His eyes stayed on hers, holding her captive while the pad of his thumb traced her lips. "Would you, Trixie? Would you kill me simply because I am not human?"

There was no way she could kill him. Not really. She had closed her eyes when she fired the stake gun, but it was rather jerky of him to point it out. "No." His song was too beautiful. His music was already wrapped around hers. She heard their song, their harmony, the way they belonged.

He smiled down at her and brushed his mouth over hers. "I told you, lady, you can trust me to take care of you."

"See, that's the thing," she said, determined not to get lost in his gaze. That was hard. She was falling fast into all that beautiful blue. The odds were stacking up very quickly against her. This couldn't happen. But his hands moved down her body, and he had great hands. She felt the peculiar lethargy that had overtaken her before. Her body lay under his, *wanting* him. Even her brain betrayed her, whispering, *Just this once. You're alone with him. Just this once let yourself feel beautiful. Sexy. Like a woman.*

"I don't need taking care of," she informed him.

His hand slid under her shirt and moved up her side, fingers taking in her skin. Skin that was hot. Needy. Skin that longed for his touch. His hand reached the sides of her breasts and stroked. Her breath hitched in her throat. Left her lungs in a rush. She should have screamed and pushed him away. That was the only sane thing to do.

Once she had this beautiful memory, it would haunt her forever. She wasn't stupid. She knew she felt things too deeply. She had to protect herself or she would be scarred by him for life. Until the day she died. She would feel beautiful. Sexy. A woman. And then he would be gone and she would be alone.

"You live too much in your mind."

He took her mouth. Not gentle. Not coaxing. He took it. As in claiming it. As in making her mouth—*his*. She could never kiss another man. Not ever. Not without tasting him and thinking of him and comparing. There would be no comparison. Every other man would come up short.

She tried to keep her sanity. She tried to chant in her mind who she was. Who she would always be. But his kisses swept through her like a drug. So hot. So tempting. So demanding. She gave herself up to have more. So many more. He had to exchange breath with her to keep her from passing out. Still he kissed her, and then his hands were on her breast and she heard herself cry out. Soft. Exposed. Needing him. Needing more.

Somehow, after all the years of emptiness, he poured himself into her, filling every empty place. Giving her something she was terrified of taking. Waking her body up when it had gone to sleep so long ago. She felt like a virgin. A terrified virgin. That was totally humiliating considering her age and that she should be a woman, not a teenager unable to control herself.

She had no idea what to do, but she needed more. She kissed him like a woman starved, and she had been starved. She kissed him like a woman possessed, and she was fairly certain he'd possessed her. At the very least she was under some spell he'd ensnared her with.

His hands were on her bare skin, whispering over the swell of her breasts, sliding down to her nipples, thumbs doing delicious things that sent fiery streaks straight toward her most feminine core. Then his mouth was there. At her breasts. Alternating between them, sucking them deep and then flicking with his tongue, using the edge of his teeth until she was crying out in desperate hunger.

There was no holding on to sanity. Her mind slipped right past every coherent thought and she could only feel when his fingers moved down her body, his mouth following. His fingers found the heat and wet silk between her legs and dipped. Her head thrashed wildly and she dug her fingers into his shoulders to anchor herself when she was fairly certain she was going to fly apart and never come back together. It didn't matter.

This was worth her sanity. Right here. Right now. His hands. His mouth. His hard, hot body. She'd forgotten what a man's body felt like. No, she'd never had a man's body. She'd been a teenager fumbling in the dark with another teenager. This man knew exactly what he was doing, finding her song. Her music. Playing her body like a master would play an instrument.

Her breath came in ragged gasps. Her body was burning up, the tension coiling so tight she thought she might die. She couldn't get enough of touching him, and twice she tried desperately to roll over, to be on top, to attack him to get what she wanted because he was going too slow and she was nearly sobbing with her need.

"Shh," he whispered. "I have you. You are in my care, *hän sívamak*, and I will give you everything."

She tried to be calm. She tried to get her brain working, but her body had taken over. There was no going back and she didn't even want to. He had to be inside of her before that empty, hollow hole consumed her. He had to be inside of her until the horrible, unrelenting emptiness was filled by him, just as he'd flooded her mind with him, filling every lonely spot.

Then he was there. Kneeling over her, between her legs. She felt him at her entrance. She heard him let his breath out as he slipped just an inch inside of her. Burning. Stretching. He had to fight her tight, hot tunnel. One small inch at a time. Retreat. Come back. She thrashed under him, her hips bucking. Trying to take him. Needing him.

He felt far too big. He'd looked far too big. She didn't think her body could ever accommodate his size, but his soft murmurings and gentle but insistent hands told her he was going to possess her.

"Relax, *hän sívamak*, do this for me. Trust me. This will be good for you. You are so tight, and scalding hot. Heaven. Nirvana. Lady, give yourself to me."

His voice was a rough growl. He slid in farther, pushing against her tight muscles that didn't want to give way, not even when she was so slick with need. So hungry for him. Her hands went to his broad shoulders, the only part of him she could reach. When he retreated, she sobbed, trying to get him back.

"Trixie," he whispered softly, "look at me."

Her gaze jumped to his face. He was beautiful. His hunger was every bit as deep as her own. She saw the clawing need there. For her. For her body. For Trixie—no other woman— and she wanted to weep. She saw herself in his mind. He thought she was beautiful. In the same way she saw him. Her eyes burned. Stung. No one had ever looked at her the way he was. Not one single person. As if she were his everything. His reason for getting up and going to bed. His reason for breathing. She saw that, in his eyes. On his face. In his mind.

"Give yourself to me. Let yourself fly."

"Too high. Too much," she said. But she wanted. *Wanted.* Everything he could give her. But then after . . . After she would lose such beauty. Could she live with that?

"I will always catch you, no matter how high. Give yourself to me."

How could she resist his voice? His voice was so rough with hunger. Rough with need. Sensual. He pushed deeper into her, connecting them. She took a breath and let herself take the plunge. Eyes on his, she forced her body to relax.

"Thank you, *hän sívamak*. Beloved," he whispered. "You are so tight and scorching hot. I had no idea it would be like this. Did you? Did you know?"

He slid in another couple of inches, stretching her past bearable, but it was so good. So unbelievably good. She hadn't known. How could she? Tears leaked out of her eyes. She couldn't stop them. She couldn't believe he was inside of her. Filling her. Taking her. Wanting her.

What's more, the way he looked at her filled that hollow space, the one she had never been able to fill with her love of her family. The one that haunted her every night when she went to bed. He was there. Fane. A man she didn't know, yet she knew him better than she knew herself.

"Hold on, beloved. Take a breath. I am going to take you all the way."

She didn't know if she could stand so much pleasure. She took a breath and kept her gaze steady on his. Wanting him. Needing him. Welcoming him. He drew back and surged forward, tunneling through her tight channel. The slide of his cock, the stretch and burn coupled with the friction, sent her tumbling over the edge into some other dimension. She heard herself scream. She felt the tide take her, throwing her out into space. He kept moving in her, driving deep, over and over, prolonging the massive wave rippling through her.

No. She hadn't known anything could be like this. She couldn't catch her breath, but she never wanted him to stop. And he didn't. Fane was already building the next wave in her, taking her right back up, his rough voice turning more sensual as he encouraged.

"That is my lady," he said. "Again. For me. Again, Trixie. Give yourself to me again."

She was going to keep giving herself to him as long and as many times as she could all night.

IO

Aleksei woke to the sound of choking. Beside him, Gabrielle's body was hot, covered in sweat, and she was gasping for breath, clawing at the dirt surrounding them, fighting for air. His first thought was to open the earth for her. He didn't. He wrapped his arms around her and pulled her body over the top of his, his mouth finding hers, breathing for her. Into her. Filling her lungs with air.

Kessake. Do not panic. You are safe with me. You are fully Carpathian. Not human. You are not buried alive.

Her hands clutched at him, fists finding his hair, gripping hard. Holding on to him. Her heart beat so hard he feared it would explode, but she held on to him and let his mouth take hers. He was gentle. Calm. Willing her to be so.

Your heart beats too fast. Feel mine. Hear mine. Follow the rhythm of my heart and slow yours, little cat.

He actually felt her make the effort to follow his instructions and he moved one hand down her spine, following the delicate curve to the smooth slope of her buttocks. As he did, he cleaned her body and provided a slight cushion of air above them. He let his hand stay on her bottom while she slowed her heart until it matched the rhythm of his.

Aleksei continued to breathe for her. Slow. Easy. Intimately. Her body felt wonderful draped over his, her soft breasts pressing deep into his chest. He could wake up every rising just like this, although he might prefer to find his cock buried in her or her mouth wrapped around him. Just the thought had his body stirring with need.

That is what I wanted exactly. You are doing good. Now open your eyes and look at me.

Her heart lurched. Her fists tightened in his hair and he felt her body stiffen. *No. No, I can't do it, Aleksei.*

What did I tell you about saying no to me? There is no reason not to open your eyes and look at your man. I have you in my arms. In my care. Do as I say.

Please. Please. Please, don't ask me to do that.

He felt her mounting terror. She still had the idea that she was buried alive in her mind. He didn't touch her mind, but he knew. He knew because she was so terrified and her body showed that terror to him.

He stopped breathing for her and kissed her. Gently. Very gently. He hadn't known he could be gentle, but that was what she needed. Coaxing. *Kislány.* He whispered the word in her mind. Little girl. Baby. His. *You are safe with me. Now open your eyes and see me. See that you are safe with me.*

She struggled with obeying his command. He felt her struggle and was proud of her that she tried when clearly she was so afraid. He stroked one hand through her hair; the other smoothed over the curve of her bottom.

Finally her long lashes lifted and she looked at him. Straight into his eyes. He smiled at her. *There you are. Can you see that I would never allow any harm to come to you? I may be more demon than man, but you are my woman and in my care. Kiss me, Gabrielle. Do not worry about breathing. Feel the earth. The soil. It strokes over you, feeding your body. Healing and rejuvenating you. Nourishing you.*

Her lashes fluttered. He kept his mouth on hers because he knew if he moved even a breath away from her, panic would come back. She was barely keeping it at bay, but she trusted him enough to follow his instructions. She didn't realize she was giving him that gift—her trust. But he did. And he knew how precious a gift it was.

Her eyes clung to his, but he felt some of the tension ease from her body. He rewarded her, kneading the firm muscle of her buttocks and then slipping his hand between their bodies to find her core. The moment his finger slid over her soft velvety folds, he felt the welcoming dampness. He loved that. He loved that she was scared, clinging to him, relying on him, and yet still got wet when he touched her. So ready for him. She was his lifemate without a doubt. She just had to believe it.

Do you see you have nothing to fear? The earth belongs to us. We belong to the earth. You can wake and not need air until you surface. You can open the earth above our heads with a thought. Visualize the earth open. Do it now, Gabrielle.

It was a command, but he kept his finger moving gently in her folds, slipping into her for a moment and then back to making small, lazy circles. His own body stirred. Filled. Became engorged and hot and needy. He wanted her mouth there. He *needed* it there, but this was more important. Letting her feel her own power.

She didn't take her gaze from his, but he felt the surge of energy, and the soil around them moved. Lifted. Pulled apart. Cool air found them. He smiled against her mouth. *You did it, kessake. There is no need to fear. When you do not know something, simply ask me and I will teach you.*

He floated them out of the earth and closed the opening after them. All the while he kept her body sprawled over his. They lay on the same carpet. It mattered little what was beneath them. Her hunger beat at him. She didn't know how to feed properly and he would teach her that as well. But not yet. Not until he taught her other things. Not until he gave her other things.

"I was so afraid," she confided, lifting her head, her eyes still on his. "I feel like I've been afraid for so long I don't know how not to be anymore."

"You will learn." He kept his fist bunched in her hair. "You are the kind of woman who needs to know what she's doing to feel comfortable. I will give you that."

Her tongue touched her lower lip, drawing his immediate attention. She was sexy and she didn't have the slightest clue. He was amazed at the combination of innocent and sexy and just what it could do to his blood.

"Tell me what to do now," she whispered. "I want you, Aleksei, but I don't know what to do to get you."

Her whispered confession yanked at his heart. Hard. Punched him in the gut. Harder. His body went tight. Painful. His cock swelled, thickened, lengthened. Burned like an out-of-control fire. The blood in his veins rushed like a firestorm.

"I dreamt of you," she confided. "I dreamt you were inside me and I was flying free and I wasn't afraid anymore."

"Carpathians do not dream." He growled his response, because first, lifemates didn't lie to each other. Second, she was killing him, taking him to the very edge of his control again, and he'd promised himself he would be gentle with her.

"I do. I have nightmares of that night when he stabbed me over and over. I can feel the blade going into me over and over. It hurt so bad. Sometimes I can't get the sound of it out of my head. But I didn't have that nightmare. You chased it away." She kissed his chin. Then his throat.

He closed his eyes and savored the feel of her body, all soft skin and lush curves moving over him. She might not think she knew what she was doing, but she could drive a man out of his mind with the soft whisper of her lips on his body.

He believed her. Her voice had the ring of truth, and he had been looking into her eyes. She meant every word. He had taken away her nightmare. It bothered him that she had nightmares when Carpathians didn't dream. Shouldn't dream. She had to be clinging so hard to her human ways that even the blood of the prince hadn't removed those needs from her. But he would. He would take away those nightmares and replace them with beautiful dreams.

"Keep going," he advised. "Do not stop there. Your body belongs to me, Gabrielle, but mine belongs to you. You want it, you take it. When I have had enough, I will take over."

She lifted her head to look at him. She actually licked her lips. "Tell me about your tattoo. On your back and shoulders. I feel it when I . . ." She broke off.

He smiled. "When you turn into my little cat and rake my back with your nails?"

She blushed, the color stealing up her body, turning her skin a beautiful rose. "I'm sorry. I couldn't help myself."

"I like it. Just like you like rough, so do I."

She ducked her head toward his chest, but not before he caught her biting her lip hard. It embarrassed her that she liked rough.

"Gabrielle." He waited.

There was a short silence. His hand smoothed over her bare bottom. Once. Twice. A silent warning, but he didn't think she understood.

"Look at me."

She took a breath. Her breasts pushed against his chest, and feeling that silken slide sent a rush of heat straight to his cock. She lifted her head again.

He held her gaze because it was important she understood. He never wanted her to feel ashamed or embarrassed by anything they did together. "You are my lifemate. The other half of my soul. You were created for me. Me for you. You were born to meet my needs. I was born to meet yours. Do you understand what I am saying to you?"

She took a breath and then nodded. "I have to get used to this, that's all."

His smile widened. "You have to get used to a lot, then. I intend to get very creative, and living as many centuries as I have, I have acquired a great deal of knowledge I would like to try out."

A little shiver went through her body. Heat flared in her eyes. "I think I would like that."

The shyness in her voice and eyes, so at odds with the daring of her answers, sent more flames rushing through his blood, straight to his cock.

"I need your mouth on me." He gave her the stark, raw truth. "Give me that mouth, *kessake*, and I will attend to your every need."

"Will you tell me about the tattoo?"

Her mouth moved down his chest, lingering on his hard nipples, her hair brushing over his skin like so much silk. He closed his eyes and let her have his body. One hand found its way to her hair because he couldn't help himself. He needed to feel it bunched in his hand. He liked giving her this. It was power, but she hadn't realized that yet. Power over his body. Over him. He felt her mouth nuzzling him. Felt her hunger.

"Not yet," he denied her. "Wait. Waiting makes it better. Sharper. I want you to claim me the way I claimed you."

She didn't hesitate. Her hands moved over his body. He brought both his hands behind his head and looked down at her. She was beautiful. Far more beautiful than he had ever imagined a woman could be.

"When a Carpathian male has killed too often, has seen too much violence, and has lived in darkness, the whisper of temptation to feel, just for a moment, becomes overwhelming. One only needs to kill while feeding. To make that choice. After a thousand years of darkness and no emotion, that temptation, perversely, becomes the only thing left to us."

She made a soft sound of distress, as if she'd never considered how difficult an ancient's life could be. Her mouth smoothed over his flat belly, her tongue tracing the muscles so defined there in his abdomen. Her hands went to his hips, tracing the bones, the contours. Taking her time. Killing him.

He tried to concentrate. To give her something of himself. "Still, that is not the worst. When more centuries pass, even that is gone. There is only darkness and the demon inside us embracing that darkness. So close. We can no longer afford to hunt the vampire and kill because that kill would send us into a realm we dare not go, not after acquiring the skills and knowledge we have."

Her teeth scraped along his hip bone. The air left his lungs in a rush. *Kessake.* He couldn't help breathing his endearment into her mind. She had to get serious soon or he wouldn't be able to give her this. Need crawled through him until he wanted to pound his body into hers. To just stay there in that exquisite paradise he had claimed the last rising.

"Tell me more," she whispered against his thigh. Her breath was warm. Her hands stroked. One cupped his heavy sac and simply held him.

"We came here. Nine of us. We could not meet the dawn because it felt wrong. We had lived honorably. We fought. We needed to go out fighting, but the cost was too high to risk that. So we made this place our home. Fane guards the gates and brings blood when we need more than what we give one another. He is dark, but nowhere near the rest of us. It is his duty to make certain we stay strong. Should one of us fall, he will be the one to destroy the fallen."

She made a sound and, at the same time, wrapped her fist around the base of his cock. The sound vibrated straight through his body. Every single *peje* cell.

"Use your mouth to get me wet and slick, Gabrielle," he instructed, trying not to clench his teeth. Her hand rolled the velvet sac gently. He felt the brush of her tongue. A barely there sweep that made his cock jump. He forced himself to keep talking to her. "We came up with the idea of etching our vows into our bodies. Something tangible. Something we could see and feel on one another."

Her tongue tasted him. A tentative lick. It curled around the underside of the sensitive crown. His hips nearly came off the ground.

"*O jelä peje teräd, emni*. In case, Gabrielle, you do not understand the ancient language," he bit out, his hands fisting in her silken hair, "that means, 'sun scorch you, woman.' Get on with it."

For some insane reason, when she'd been so terrified of him, she didn't seem in the least bit afraid of his outburst. He actually felt her smile as her tongue worked up and down his shaft. "I take it you like this."

"Woman." He made it a threat, and tugged on her hair to force her head exactly where he needed it.

Her mouth engulfed him. Took him into heat and fire. Wrapped him up in a place he knew he would need for all time. She could use her mouth, and she did. Instincts kicked in, but it was more than that. She wanted this for him. She gave him this. She did it for him, not for herself. He felt the difference, and he knew it was a gift with no strings.

His lifemate. The woman he had come close to killing. He knew he couldn't have done it, but the thought had been there. Now she was giving him such beauty, such perfection, taking him to a place he'd never been. His wildcat. He let her set the pace. Let her take him close. So close he skated on the very edge of his control. So close his hips thrust into her mouth. So close he ground himself deep and held himself there for a few moments of absolute bliss.

"Come here."

She didn't stop. She kept working him. He reached down and caught her under her arms, so close to losing control he was afraid he would fill her mouth when he wanted to fill her body.

"I said, come here," he snapped, dragging her up his body.

He rolled her under him, caught her thighs and jerked them apart. He took one moment to lean down and take a taste. Her body bucked. She was delicious. His. All of that was his. He shoved her legs over his shoulders, braced himself on his hands and thrust into her. Hard. Deep. Rough.

She was tight, as if he hadn't already stretched and opened her. He could barely force his cock inside her narrow tunnel. He groaned with the effort. With how good the scorching heat was. How great the friction was. Her little mewling cries and ragged breathing added to the fire engulfing him. He withdrew and her tight muscles grasped and clung, clamped down around him in a stranglehold that felt like heaven.

He looked at her face, the beauty there, all feminine. Soft, perfect skin. Her large eyes, framed with far too long and thick black lashes. Like the silk of her hair. All that hair that he loved feeling against his body.

"This dawn, *kessake*, I want to lie with you in the earth,

your head in my lap. Your hair falling across my hips, my cock and my thighs. I want to wake up feeling that, feeling what is mine surrounding me."

The moment he began speaking, her gaze had jumped to his and clung there. His admitted need fed the fire in her. He knew because he felt the sudden rush of fiery liquid bathing his cock, and saw the hunger in her eyes build all the more.

"You are going to give that to me." He made it a statement, an order, because he could see that she would. She took his breath. His mind. She was taking his heart. Stealing it a little piece at a time. He didn't want that, not with her, not until he knew she would be faithful to him. Loyal to him.

"Don't," she said softly. "Please don't. You said not to bring him here with us and you're doing it."

He realized his hold on her had gone from rough to brutal. His hips had gone savage, driving deep and hard, over and over like a piston. She hadn't fought him or tried to escape; instead, she lifted her hips to meet each thrust, helping him to go even deeper. Her hand touched his face, fingers smoothing the fury from his features.

"Tell me who you belong to," he bit out between his teeth. She didn't hesitate. "You, Aleksei. I belong to you."

"Who do I belong to?" he demanded, his body jolting hers with every deep stroke.

Her eyes softened. Moved over his face. There was a hint of possession in her soft features. A hint that liked where she belonged, even if she didn't know it yet. Again she didn't hesitate. "Me. Aleksei, you belong to me."

His woman was mixed up, but she was willing to be straightened out. He had to let it go. He wasn't the kind of man to let another poaching on his territory go, but it had to be done. He just hadn't figured out how yet. He wanted to kill Gary Daratrazanoff. He wanted to have a few words with the reigning prince about what he should have done and what his mistake had cost all of them. Most of all he wanted to believe the woman he had his cock buried in so deeply. Surrounding him with heaven.

He took her up fast and hard, keeping his eyes on her face, wanting to watch the helpless pleasure as she came apart. He loved that dazed look in her eyes and he kept moving in her, not allowing her to come down, feeding that fire so one orgasm ran into the next and she turned into his little cat. Writhing. Claws raking, her body demanding. Her hips rising to meet his, her need and hunger etched into her beautiful face. He loved that. *Loved* it.

She gave him her surrender three times, and he watched each time. Feeling it. Satisfaction. Knowing he gave that to her. Knowing the addiction was every bit as strong in her as it was in him. The fourth time he took her up he went with her, allowing the tidal wave consuming her to sweep him along with her. He took her mouth, groaning down her throat, pouring himself into her, feeding his own hunger.

Take my blood. Feed from me. He needed her mouth on him. More, he wanted her to know she could do that without aid. The hunger was in her. He felt it beating at him. She needed. He provided.

She didn't move. Aleksei lifted his head and looked down at her, his body still hard in hers. Still feeling every after-quake. Every ripple.

Her gaze moved over his face, assessing his mood. "I can't." She whispered the denial. "I'm sorry. I can't."

He kissed her. Hard. Wet. Demanding. He kept kissing her until she melted into him again. Until her body clamped down on his and she was kissing him back. He kissed his way down her chin to her throat.

Remember how I tasted? Taste me now, Gabrielle. He whispered the temptation in her ear, sent it into her mind. Into her body.

Gabrielle closed her eyes against the power in Aleksei's voice. Her body clenched hard around his. He was sin. Pure sin. She could taste him in her mouth.

I belong to you. That taste, kessake, that is all yours. Just yours.

For the first time, she felt the slide of teeth, the sharpness there. She cried out, closing her eyes, shaking her head.

There is no need to be afraid. Give this to me, Gabrielle. I need this from you.

She could hear her heart pounding. She wanted to give him anything he wanted. She didn't have any other way of pleasing him. Of giving back to him what she'd taken away, but if she did this . . . If she gave this to him she would be giving more of her humanity away. Piece by piece they were taking her until she didn't know who she was anymore. Tears burned behind her eyes. She was so lost. Fear choked her. She needed to scream. To run. To fight. For self-preservation.

"Stop."

The one word spoken aloud shocked her. His voice was a whip of an order and she realized she was fighting him. She was choking on her own screams. The tears did fall even though she was so certain she had controlled them. Her hands were pinned to the carpet on either side of her head. His body was on hers, covering her, allowing her to feel his full weight and his immense strength. His cock was still buried deep and she felt him like a steel spike, growing even thicker and longer, the dominant in him responding to the fight.

"I'm sorry."

"Talk to me. Right now, Gabrielle. Give me truth."

Ohgodohgodohgod. She had sworn she would tell him the truth. She had *sworn* it. To him. To herself. How could she possibly put this into words he'd understand? She licked her lips. Swallowed hard.

"Give me your eyes and give me the truth." It was a demand.

"Aleksei." She whispered his name, a plea, needing to touch him. Needing an anchor. He held her hands down and his face was implacable. His eyes burned into her. Seeing her. Seeing the mess that was her.

"Give me you."

She shook her head. "You don't understand. There is no more me. I'm so lost I don't know who or what I am anymore.

I woke and I was buried in the ground. Like death. You said Carpathians don't dream, but I do. I have that horrible nightmare over and over and I can't get out of it. Humans don't take blood. They don't crave it or need it and yet I do. But if I do this for you, on my own, without your help, there is another piece of me gone, and there are already so many pieces gone, I can't find me."

She felt the tears on her face. She hated admitting to him how truly screwed up she was, but then again, he had the right to know. He knew he wasn't getting a bargain with her. He knew she had forced him so close to becoming the very thing he'd hunted for centuries. She could barely look at him; her gaze kept sliding away because she was ashamed. She was humiliated. Embarrassed. She wanted him, but she didn't. She loved his body, but she didn't know how to give him anything more than sex, and he deserved so much more.

"Keep your eyes on mine."

"I'm trying." She gave him that.

"Kislány." He released her hands and rolled so that she was on top, sprawled over him, still connected. He brushed at her tears very gently with his thumb. The movement forced his cock deeper into her and she felt her sheath spasm around him.

Her heart turned over at the gentleness from him. At the sound of his voice. That wasn't his *little cat* endearment. She knew it was more like the human form of *baby.* Or *little girl.* Whatever it was, it caught at her heart.

"No matter how lost you are, I will find you. No matter how many pieces are scattered or lost, I will find them for you and give them back to you one at a time. I am your lifemate. You are safe now, Gabrielle. You will always be safe with me."

She shook her head. "How can you find me when I don't even know who I am?"

"It does not matter, little one. I have you. You can shatter into a million pieces. You can feel torn apart and lost. I will hold you safe. You cannot go anywhere that I cannot find you. Let go, Gabrielle. Let go of what you cling to. Your body trusts me or you would not be able to fly so high. You ignite for me. When I touch you. When I kiss you. When I take you so hard, so rough, you still trust me. Let go. Give all of you to me, not just your body. I will keep you safe."

"I don't know if I can, Aleksei," she whispered, more tears spilling over. "I want to give you everything. I do. I'm not being stubborn. I'm so terrified. I have been my entire life."

"Tell me the earliest memory of being afraid."

His voice was too gentle for her to stand. Her heart melted. She didn't want that. She didn't want a connection other than sex. He was too . . . *everything*. He was too dominant. Too scary. Too capable of losing his temper.

She moistened her lips. Her mother had a terrible temper and she threw tantrums. "I was very young." She tried to pull up the memory. When had it first started? She had never thought to go back and figure that out. "My mother was very over the top emotionally. She would fly into a rage, kicking, hitting, throwing things, and then five minutes later be laughing and kissing us."

That was so true. She never knew what mood her mother was going to be in. "Her tantrums never bothered my brother or sister or my father." She fell silent.

"But they upset you, and that made you feel as if you were wrong to feel afraid."

She nodded slowly. "When I was really little she got mad at me for breaking one of her favorite vases. I didn't mean to. I was running and I bumped it and one of the pieces cut me. It hurt and I started crying. She was furious and she started throwing things. Breaking them all around me. Glass rained down. I couldn't move. I was so afraid, and I got cut on my arms and my legs and feet. She suddenly snatched me up and ran into the bathroom with me and then my dad was there. I didn't tell him what she did, because he would have smiled, shrugged and said, 'That's your mother, the drama queen.'"

"*O köd belső,*" Aleksei swore. "Your father does not want to meet me. What kind of man allows his woman to behave in such a way? It is no wonder you are afraid of becoming what you are."

"And you," she whispered. "You have no problems expressing your anger."

He stroked his hand over her hair. "Do you think that I
would ever harm you? We are fully bonded. I am beyond the
temptation of darkness."

"You're very scary, Aleksei. And you have a temper." That
seemed a mild way to express the fury that could overtake him.

"That is so," he agreed calmly. "I will definitely get angry
over things, and you will learn to be all right with that. What
I will *not* do is throw things at you or our children. If you are
punished for something, I will make certain in the end, you
are all right with your punishment and with me."

She couldn't help the shiver that went through her body.
"Punishment? I'm a grown woman. Men do not punish women
anymore. That went out a century or two ago." She was a little
wrong with her math, but she didn't care. She wasn't going
to have this man think he could treat her like a child.

He lifted his head toward her ear. His tongue stroked and
his teeth caught her earlobe and tugged. "But then I am not a
modern man. My lifemate does not run wild, nor does she run
over me. You are my woman and you have given yourself to
me. You will live in my world with me. There will be no more
mistakes, such as betraying me with another man."

Gabrielle winced when he delivered the full body blow.
She'd tried to make up for her mistake. She had done everything she knew how to do and even forced herself to do things
she had no clue about, just to make this man realize she hadn't
betrayed him on purpose. She wasn't that kind of person. She
tried to sit up, to pull away from him, but his arms locked her
to him, preventing movement.

She turned her face away from him. She had no idea what
she was doing there. With him. Clearly she didn't belong
there, either. She wasn't human. She wasn't Carpathian. She
wasn't even fully in her own family—the one she'd been born
into. She didn't fit anywhere. The dawn was looking better
and better.

He growled. His hand spanned her throat. "Do. Not. Even.

Think. That. Not ever." He bit out each word. Snarled it. His eyes held a kind of fury. "You will fight for our relationship. You gave me your word. Is your word no good? Tell me now. Tell me now and I will end this for both of us."

She knew she should never have tried to give even a part of herself away to him. If she'd just kept it to sex, she could handle it. She loved sex with him. Not her brain, but her body. She couldn't help it. She melted when he touched or kissed her. But this, this other, she didn't have the strength anymore to keep losing bits and pieces of herself.

Aleksei's fingers tightened around Gabrielle's throat. Her pulse beat into his palm. "Look at me," he hissed.

She would *not* harm herself. He didn't care about himself, but she was his lifemate and would have his protection from everything. Everybody. Even herself. He would go into her mind if she didn't back down. He had been careful of her wishes, giving her the time to purge the other man from her mind, but he would have to go back on his word if she continued thinking such blasphemy. They were fully bonded. She was his. Body. Mind. Soul. And heart. She just hadn't accepted it yet. But she would.

"Gabrielle," he hissed again.

She might have been more afraid when he used the word *punishment*. She might have been genuinely indignant, but at the same time, he was buried deep in her body and he felt the scorching liquid heat of her body's reaction to his dominance. She was made for him. She needed to learn to trust him and relax in his care. He wouldn't let anything hurt her, but she had to come to terms with being a Carpathian. Being a lifemate. Being the lifemate of an ancient who had skated too close to the edge of madness and was left with demons.

She did the most unexpected thing. She brought her hands down and framed his face. Her fingers moved, featherlight, over his rough features. She traced his eyebrows, his eyes, his bone structure, down his jaw, over his nose, and settled on his mouth.

"I won't go back on my word, Aleksei," she said. "But no

matter how angry you get, no matter how many times you throw what I did in my face, I can't change it. I did it. I betrayed you. I didn't mean to do it, but I still did. I accept that. And I accept who you are. I have lived a certain way and I'm going to make more mistakes because I don't know the rules of your world. But I won't go back on my word."

He hadn't realized his belly was tied into a thousand knots until he heard her affirmation. He believed her. She was confused. Afraid. And miserable. But she wouldn't leave him. Not by seeking the dawn.

He had hurt her. He had felt her flinch when he brought up her betrayal. He hadn't meant to be so petty as to fling that in her face. Not again. He'd tasted fear when he read her features. She was not adept at hiding her thoughts and clearly she contemplated meeting the dawn. He hadn't known fear for so long he hadn't even recognized the emotion when it first crept into his body and then took over.

"A relationship is about trust, Gabrielle," he said softly, his lips moving against the pads of her fingers. He curled his tongue around one and sucked it into the heat of his mouth. He began to glide gently in and out of her. "We will start small. One thing at a time. Let me inside you a bit at a time so you understand I am not taking you over. You take pieces of me when you want or need them. When you feel you can process them without panicking. Do you think you can do that?"

She moistened her lips, her gaze clinging to him. Already her body moved to ride his, her hips rising and falling with the rhythm he set. He could see the beauty of her pleasure already pushing the fear from her eyes.

He caught her hair in both hands, fists tightening. "Taste me, *kislány*, remember how good it was. Your hunger is beating at me, and I want this for you. This small step. I do not want to take the triumph from you. Take what belongs to you, Gabrielle."

She swallowed, ran her tongue around the inside of her mouth, and he knew she felt her teeth slide into place. His voice was a sinful temptation—he'd made certain of that—

but there was no compulsion. He wanted her to see that she could do this. Be Carpathian. Open the earth. Feed herself. Be a woman who could be self-sufficient. She wouldn't need anyone—not even him—to do those things for her. She needed to feel powerful in her own right. He wanted that for her, and this small thing—a huge obstacle to her—would start her on that path.

You can do this, kislány, I know you can. Kiss your way down to my chest. Ride me while you taste my skin. While you feel my heart beat. While you hear my blood calling to yours.

She looked at him for a long time, her eyes searching his. Her legs drew up on either side of his body so she straddled him completely. Holding his gaze, she nodded slowly, still moving her hips. Riding him. Slowly. Leisurely. Scorching hot.

His hands went to her hips, fingers digging into her flesh while she leaned down and kissed his mouth, just a brush of her lips over his. She kissed his chin. His throat. His cock nearly burst. Suddenly the leisurely ride wasn't enough. Still, he needed to give her this. He wanted it for her. If he took control, she wouldn't feel her own power, and that was essential.

Her mouth moved down his chest. He felt her tongue and a groan escaped. She needed to hurry. He simply *needed*. His breath came in ragged gasps and already he was changing the rhythm, rocking her body with each jolting stroke, his hands lifting her and pulling her down hard as he surged up to bury himself in her hot, silken depths.

He felt the scrape of her teeth. Her tongue swirled and then she did it. Her teeth, without his help, bit deep. Found his vein. Hooked in. Connected them intimately. The erotic pain gave way instantly to pleasure. Such pleasure. His woman. His lifemate, feeding on her own. Taking what was hers. Taking her lifemate's blood for the first time without assistance.

He had that from her. He alone had her body. He was the first. He was the first she took blood from all on her own. He gave her that gift of power. Her mouth moved. His hips took her over and over. When she drank her fill and stroked her tongue over the pinpricks, he caught her up and rolled her, taking her hard. Taking her the way he needed. The way she needed. They both went over the edge together, his face buried in her throat.

So proud of you, kislány. You took control and you did it. Aleksei lifted his head when he could breathe properly and kissed her thoroughly. *I have to help Fane feed the others. We may have to leave to keep from growing too weak and find blood in the village. Do not enter any of the buildings while I am gone. You can walk around the grounds and you will be safe enough. Do you understand?*

He waited for her to nod her head and then he kissed her again before he left her. She rolled over and drew her knees to her chest, curling into the fetal position. He didn't like it, but he could feel the combined hunger of the ancients rising and knew he didn't dare delay ensuring they had their fill of blood.

II

Ohmygod. *Ohmygod. Ohmygod.* She'd just had sex with a gorgeous man. A total stranger. On the ground. On her sleeping bag. She was a grandmother for heaven's sake. No. She was a *great*-grandmother. Worse. She hadn't had sex since she was fifteen years old so she was practically a virgin, and she'd acted like a whacked-out slut.

Trixie stared up at the handsome, *gorgeous* face and thought about turning the stake gun on herself. She'd lost her freaking mind. Totally. What was she going to tell her grand-daughters? Absolutely nothing. Nada. Nothing at all. "We are going to our graves with this," she hissed at his smirking, all-too-satisfied face. "I mean it. To. Our. Graves."

She looked around her. Where were her clothes? Her *panties. Ohmygod.* She was naked. *Naked.* Without panties. On a sleeping bag. With a stranger. He had to be a vampire. He had to have cast a spell over her. She was so far above this nonsense, but her body refused to move. Refused to stop quaking and rippling and feeling his *magnificent* . . . um . . . Her mind refused to do anything but give her a picture. That was burned in her brain. And she swore she had skid marks deep inside. He'd branded her there.

"We are going to our graves with what?" Fane asked.

He'd better not be smiling. She looked up at him, narrowing her eyes. "You'd better not be smiling. I mean it. Wipe that self-satisfied male smirk right off your face. You will not tell a single soul that this happened. And it is never going to happen again. I'm dressing and going down the mountain and getting on a plane."

She took a deep breath. He hadn't moved. He was still locked inside her and she could feel him. So big. Stretching her almost painfully, but in a good way. He should be letting her go. He got what he wanted. Surely he was finished with her. He could have any woman he wanted, whether he was centuries old or not. After all those years, she was certain to have *cobwebs* in her . . . um . . . That was it. He was stuck because cobwebs were sticky.

"Lifemate. You are just a little crazy," he said. "I think I am going to have to stop your mouth and your mind in very creative ways."

There was amusement in his voice. *Laughter.* He didn't seem in the least afraid of her lecture, her snarky voice or her narrowed eyes. He bent his gorgeous head to hers and took her mouth, his tongue moving right past her parted lips to sweep in and claim her. To shut her up. That's what he meant. To shut her up.

She tried to hold on to her tizzy fit, but her body melted and her mouth caught fire and she lost her train of thought completely. He kissed her thoroughly, his body moving gently in hers before he finally pulled out. He lifted his head. "You can walk around the grounds, but do not enter any of the buildings. I mean it, Trixie. They are dangerous. Other ancients reside here. I have to see to them."

He did *not* just say that. He really was going to give her the slam, bam, thank-you-ma'am treatment? He wasn't going to hold her? Or talk to her? Or reassure her that she wasn't the complete idiot she knew she was? Of course he was. Men did that. Sixteen-year-old boys did it—of course grown men did. They got what they wanted and they left.

"Trixie. Stop." Fane said it gently. His hands framed her face. "I will return as quickly as I can. You are exhausted. Go to sleep and wait for me. When I return we can talk."

She hated his voice because she loved it. She felt it under

her skin. Inside of her. She was afraid she'd never get him out. Mostly she hated herself for being such a fool. "Go do whatever it is you have to do." She wanted him *gone*. She'd been a fool at fifteen, and clearly she was still a fool. There was a reason she didn't have anything to do with men.

Fane sighed. "Do not think you are going to leave the moment I am taking care of business. You would endanger all of us by opening the gates."

She glared at him. Gave him the *killing* glare. He didn't go up in smoke like he should have. "I have the right to leave."

"Actually, you do not. You entered the monastery of your own free will. You walked right through the safeguards and you left a trail behind for others to follow."

She looked around for the vial of holy water. She probably needed to douse herself with it. His sexy voice was beginning to have a "tone" to it, one she didn't like. She wasn't a child to be scolded, although lying there buck naked made her feel vulnerable. She caught up her shirt and pulled it over her head without even looking for her bra.

"There is no need to talk to me in that tone. I warn you right now, I'm not a child you can boss around just because we had great sex. I haven't had sex in so long, it's possible anything could have been called great sex." Of course there was the outstanding kissing, but she wasn't going to mention that. Instead, she wiped her mouth with the back of her hand as she sat up to wiggle the shirt over her back.

"Lifemate, you are a child to me. Your age is just about the time we are considered adults. Clearly you are feeling shame." There was an edge to his voice now and his eyes had gone hard. Smoky. "You are my lifemate. My lifemate should want to be with me, not feel shame because we expressed our joy in being together."

"Joy in being together?" she echoed. She looked around for her stake gun. And she wasn't subtle about it. "I haven't been with a man in *decades*," she hissed. She snagged her panties and her cargo pants and dragged them close. "You seduce me and then decide you have to go to work and I can stay here and sleep. Then you accuse me of leaving a trail for the others to follow right through your safeguards. In a *tone*."

She knew something about tone. She was the *queen* of tone. She didn't care how old he was, or even what he was, no one could beat her tone. It was sheer perfection. She gave it to him full blast. "You are a hound dog, just like every other man I have ever run across."

"Lifemate." He growled the word at her. His strong white teeth snapped together as if he might take a bite out of her. "You do not ever want to throw your sexual exploits at me. I will overlook the fact that you did not wait for your lifemate, but I will not have them flung in my face."

She stared at him. Shocked. Unable to move for a moment, her mouth hanging open. "My sexual exploits?" she finally managed to sputter. "You're overlooking my sexual exploits?"

He shifted away from her, standing with a fluid motion that sent a thrill right down her spine. He was fully clothed. She blinked and dragged her pants and underwear into her lap, wishing she could just stand up fully clothed instead of sitting on her sleeping bag feeling his seed trickling down her thigh. There wasn't even a bathroom to clean up. He seemed to be implying she was some kind of a slut—having just had wild sex with a total stranger probably put her in that category, but she was going to shoot him and bury his body right there in that weird building.

"I see you do not intend to be reasonable, Trixie. I told you we would talk when I returned. I would prefer to stay with you and clear these matters up, but my brethren call to me and it is dangerous here. For you. For Aleksei's lifemate, and now for me and Aleksei."

"I didn't bring the others here," she snapped. She used her panties to clean off her thighs, trying not to die of shame and embarrassment.

He waved his hand, and not only was she perfectly clean but she was fully clothed. Her breath caught in her throat as she realized just how powerful Fane really was. She had no idea how he'd talked her into having sex with him. She just knew that looking at him was a terrible mistake, because she wanted to have sex with him again.

He stepped close, took her hand and drew her up, his arm locking around her back, drawing her into him. She wouldn't have let him—at least she lied to herself, telling herself that—but he had to hold her up. Her legs felt weak around him, her knees giving out.

"Trixie." He murmured her name softly. "Why are you ashamed of being with me? I do not understand. I know you felt the same pleasure I did. Explain this to me. Please."

Was there hurt in his voice? In his beautiful eyes? She was hurt. Shocked at herself and angry with herself. She was old enough to know better. With any other man she might have just taken the time as an unexpected gift, but she knew she would forever feel this man inside of her. That wasn't his fault. That was hers.

"In spite of my age, I'm not exactly experienced. I don't have sexual exploits and it's a little embarrassing to have sex with a man I don't know." There. That was all he was going to get.

She wasn't going to tell him he somehow had wormed his way inside of her and she would never be able to get him out. Or that she was ashamed because at fifteen she'd had a baby because she'd let a boy touch her nine months earlier. Now she'd done the same thing all over again. There had been no dates. No courting. No sweet words. Just sex. It didn't matter that the sex was amazing, it was still her acting like an idiot. She hadn't learned one single lesson in her sixty-odd years of being on earth.

"What is this thing you called me? This 'hound dog.' It did not sound like a compliment."

She moved to put a little space between them. His arm locked around her back and his other hand came up to her hair. She had a lot of hair, and no man had put his hands in her hair, ever. The sensation sent a small answering spasm deep in her core. This man was lethal to her. She brought both hands up to push against his chest. The moment her palms encountered his muscles beneath his thin shirt, heat hit her. He was like a drug, rushing through her veins and spreading through her body with incredible heat. She wanted him all over again.

"I don't understand any of this," she whispered, wanting to be alone so she could have a good cry. In private. She wasn't sharing that. She never cried in front of anyone.

He put a little more pressure on her so that her body was tight against his. Very tight. She sighed and gave in, relaxing against him, allowing him to hold her. She recognized that he was trying to comfort her.

"I know for you it is difficult. I will explain everything when I return. I will not be gone long. Please do me the courtesy of staying within the gates. I am aware you have some kind of gift that allows you to walk through my safeguards, but it is not safe. I will return as fast as possible, and we will clear things up between us."

She bit her lip, allowing herself a moment to slide her arms around him and just hold him. Feel him. All that masculine strength. She wouldn't ever have this again, but she had it now. She inclined her head, as if agreeing with him.

"Trixie." There was amusement in his voice. "I can read your mind."

She blinked. Pulled back. If that was true, it wasn't a good thing. Her mind was a place no one else should ever be. She censored a lot.

"You leave me no choice. I will add to the safeguards at the gate. One I doubt you will be able to get around. If you go out the gates, lifemate, you will do so without a stitch of clothing on."

She shoved at him. Hard. "You can't do that. There's no way you can do that."

He didn't even rock away from her, not so much as an inch, and she put a lot of power in that shove. "Of course I can. I am Carpathian. You will stay here and wait for me as you should. I enjoy your attitude, but open defiance or putting yourself in danger will not be tolerated."

Her eyebrows shot up. This time she smacked his chest hard. "You did not just say that to me. You did not."

"I did. Heed my warning, *sívamet*. You walk out of the monastery, you will be doing it naked."

She had clothes in her backpack. She'd walk out all right, naked or not, and she would . . .

"Trixie. You are going to be difficult." He waved his hand.

She spun around. He let her by loosening his arm at her back. The moment she was fully facing away from him, he locked her in place again, his arm around her stomach. Her backpack was gone. The only thing left was her vampire-hunting kit—which did not contain a change of clothes—and her sleeping bag.

Trixie sighed and laid her head back against the solid wall of his chest, trying to keep her mind blank so he couldn't read her next move. Since she had no clue what she was going to do, but it probably involved murder and mayhem, she was certain he wouldn't get anything more out of her mind.

"Mayhem and murder?"

The male amusement in his voice, so soft and gentle, coupled with his hand at the nape of her neck was nearly her undoing. He sounded affectionate. Like he cared. Like she mattered to him and he found her cute, not annoying.

"My murder?" he prompted, turning her back in his arms so that she once again faced him, her body tight against his.

She nodded, her breasts aching and sensitive. There wasn't much else to do besides nod when he was reading her mind. That stupid, stupid stake gun wasn't going to do the trick. It was *so* getting a blistering one-star review when she got back home.

He laughed softly and framed her face with his hands, tipping her mouth toward his. "I will have to work much harder to convince you I am worth far more to you alive than dead. I am certain, given time, you will see just what I can do for you."

He brought his head down slowly. Very slowly. She should have turned her face away. He was holding her there, but his hands were gentle and she could have escaped. But no. His mouth was too tempting. The look in his eyes was warm, moving right on to hot, and she knew the taste of him.

He took her mouth gently. Well. It started out that way, and then he was kissing her hard and deep, sending her entire body into some kind of weird meltdown. She melted from the inside out due to the firestorm rushing through her. When he lifted his head she heard, to her everlasting shame, a moan of protest escape her throat. She blinked up at him, feeling dazed. Weak. Her hands were fisted in his shirt and she clung to him.

"Trixie. *Hän sívamak.* You have to let go. I cannot wait any longer. I am needed, but I will return as quickly as possible."

She nodded, looking at him. Tasting him. The fire not even tamping down a little bit. Not. One. Little. Bit.

"Hän sívamak," he repeated, his tone tender, turning her heart over. His hands came up to hers and he gently removed her fingers from where they clenched his shirt.

She blinked some more, trying to come out of her fog. Out from under his spell. Where was Trixie? The woman she knew. The woman who handled any situation without so much as batting an eyelash. She was so far out of her depth she had no clue how to react.

"Say you will wait for me," he prompted.

At that precise moment she would have given him anything. She would have stripped naked and wound her body around his. She would have . . .

"Trixie." It was his turn to groan. "I am reading your mind, woman, and you are not making this easy for me."

She felt exactly how she wasn't making it easy. He was pressed up against her, tightly, his body hard. Hot. Deliciously hard. Without thinking, her hand slid down to the bulge there, wrapped around as much as she could get so that he pressed into her palm. She felt the answering jerk and found herself smiling. And happy. He wanted her. Again. She didn't have one lick of experience. She was old. Cobwebby. A dried-up prune, and he still wanted her. This gorgeous man.

She stepped back to give him room to leave, but her hand didn't leave his cock. She felt him, scorching hot, burning through the material of his trousers. If he wanted to leave, he was going to have to step away from her.

"I am going to make you beg me," he warned softly. "When I come back, I will have you again, and this time you will beg for release and I will not give it to you for a long, long time."

She raised an eyebrow and gave him the haughty look she'd perfected on schoolteachers and principals at the schools where her granddaughters went. The teachers assumed— rightly—her lack of education, but one haughty look and they stopped being so judgmental.

"There will be no more sex until we're in a proper bed with nice sheets. A bed I can go to sleep in afterward. Because camping is not my thing and I'm too old to be having sex on the ground. I've got enough aches and pains without adding to them." Of course, she was fairly certain she *deserved* a good time after so many years of absolute nothing. This gorgeous man wanted her again, dirt floor or not, she was *there*. But she preferred a bed.

Fane hooked his hand around her neck, laughing softly. "I will take care of the aches and pains and see to any of your requests on my return."

He leaned close, brushed his lips over hers and just like that he was gone. As in *gone*. The magician kind of gone. As in vanishing in thin air, which was a little disconcerting to say the least. What was he? If he was a vampire, wouldn't he feel evil even if he didn't look evil? Frankly, she didn't care. She was in a foreign country. No one, not even Teagan, knew where she was. Well. Not precisely. She was going to take as much as she could get from Mr. Gorgeous and then carry it home with her. A wonderful secret.

He'd woken her body after so many years of emptiness. Of being alone. When she was with him, she didn't feel alone.

She felt alive and incredibly happy. She loved her girls and her great-grandchildren, but for the first time in her life, she felt beautiful and special to someone.

"Although," she murmured aloud, "I'd feel a lot more special if he had a bed."

She went to the door and opened it, looking out into the night. Fog swirled above the monastery. It was dense and dark, like a veil pulled over the entire fortress. She heard voices, muted, but male. They didn't sound happy, and she shivered and stepped out of the building. She was exhausted and nothing that had happened to her since she'd entered the monastery seemed real, but she knew it was. She wasn't caught in a dream or a hallucination. She couldn't conjure up a Mr. Gorgeous, not like him—she didn't have that kind of imagination.

Her granddaughters thought she was going insane when she made the mistake of telling them about vampires. Esmeralda had shown her video recordings and at first she thought they were faked, but eventually she became certain they were real. The idea of those monsters living anywhere near her grandchildren made her crazy. She'd protected them all her life, and Esmeralda admitted that Teagan would be a prime candidate for a vampire's victim. He would be drawn by her gifts. Everyone knew Teagan had gifts.

She'd been just as susceptible to Esmeralda's bullshit as she had been to Fane's touch. She was fairly certain her loneliness had made her susceptible. She didn't have that many friends, and she found herself on the Internet in the chat rooms with Esmeralda as often as she could, just because they laughed so much together. She loved having a friend.

Another sound reached her ears. Not male this time. Distinctly female, and whoever the woman was, she was crying. Muted. But definitely weeping. Like her heart was broken and there was no fixing it. Trixie tried to appear tough and mean, but she'd raised five girls and she was just as susceptible to a girl's genuine tears as she was to Esmeralda's bullshit and Fane's touch.

The sound was coming from inside a building. Fane had told her not to go into any of them, but she couldn't bear the sound of those heartbroken sobs. She made her way across the yard barefoot, because when Fane had clothed her, he had remembered underwear but forgotten shoes. She frowned. She didn't think Fane was the type of man to forget too much, and she couldn't get very far on the mountain, hiking around barefoot. Maybe it wasn't a mistake after all.

The dirt was soft under her feet, not at all rocky like she expected, almost like a thick carpet. She could see it was rich in minerals and somehow, although she wasn't a barefoot sort of woman outside, she liked the connection to the earth. The soles of her feet seemed to absorb the minerals, and the spots where she was aching from the hours of hiking in her boots just seemed to heal. No blisters. No pain at all. She curled her toes into the dirt while she stood at the door, staring at it, listening to the sound of sobs. She raised her hand and knocked.

The sobbing didn't stop. She was fairly certain whoever was inside hadn't heard. She dropped her hand to the carved handle and pushed the door open easily. Just as Fane's house was only four walls and a roof, with a dirt floor, so was this one. In the middle of the floor was a young woman lying curled up on a thick carpet. A blanket lay over her, but it was clear she was naked underneath it.

Moving closer to the crying woman, Trixie could see marks on her skin. Bruises. Love bites. Smudges that looked like fingerprints. Her heart turned over. What if this had been Teagan or one of her other girls? She couldn't leave her like this. In fact, she needed to come up with another weapon or two and help this child escape.

Trixie crouched down beside the girl and laid a gentle hand on her forehead. "Honey-child, you're going to make yourself sick."

The woman lifted her tear-soaked lashes, now long and spiky, her gaze startled, her dove-gray eyes swimming with tears. "I'm sorry," she whispered. "Did I disturb you? You could hear me?" She sounded frightened, and she sat up, pulling the blanket around her.

At least the woman had a carpet to sit on, much better than Trixie's sleeping bag. Trixie sat on the edge, close to the woman without waiting for an invitation. "I'm Trixie. Trixie Joanes."

"Gabrielle Sanders," the woman introduced herself. "You must be related to Teagan."

"I'm her grandmother." Trixie smiled her encouragement. "Do you know her?"

Gabrielle shook her head. "I know her lifemate, Andre."

There was that word again. *Lifemate*. Clearly it meant something, and no one took it lightly. Still, she'd come back to that. She touched Gabrielle's shoulder gently. "Did someone hurt you?"

Fresh tears flooded Gabrielle's eyes. She shook her head and pushed back her hair. "Not like you're thinking. No one hit me. I'm just a . . . a mess. It's me. Not him. I screwed up so badly there's no fixing it."

"Honey-child, there is always a way to fix something. I raised five girls. I've seen and heard it all. Just talking to someone else helps sometimes."

Gabrielle pressed her lips together. "How are you inside the monastery? No one is supposed to be here."

Trixie waved her hand airily. "Fane is my lifemate." She had absolutely no idea what that meant, but Fane had said it and she was going to put this child at ease by using that as an excuse for her presence.

Gabrielle's eyes widened. "That's amazing. And good. No, great. I'm Aleksei's lifemate." She burst into a fresh storm of tears.

Trixie gathered her into her arms, blanket and all, holding her like she had her daughter and granddaughters when life had been cruel—and she was fairly certain life had been cruel to this woman. She looked young, very young, to be all alone, lying on a carpet naked, covered in bruises and up in the mountains inside a hut with four walls, a roof and dirt floor.

"Talk to me, Gabrielle. I've seen a lot of life." And tasted bitterness and cruelty. She knew those things. She knew about giving up dreams. She knew about loss.

Gabrielle looked up into Trixie's face. The woman was beautiful. She had exquisite skin and incredible hair. Gabrielle wasn't certain how old she was; she seemed elegant and timeless, even in her cargo pants and bare feet. Still, she'd been attacked by a man who wanted to kill vampires, and she couldn't allow herself to be deceived.

She chewed on her lower lip. She had never pushed her way into another's mind. Not once. Not for any reason. She could talk telepathically to her sister and brother. She could use the common path of the Carpathians, but actually invading someone else's mind, or having them in hers, seemed far too intimate. She had planned to give that to Gary. At the thought, tears welled up again.

Trixie put her hand over Gabrielle's. "I raised five girls, and I can't have you lying in this empty shell of a house crying your heart out. Talk to me. Let me help. If nothing else, use me for a sounding board."

Gabrielle looked into Trixie's eyes. More than anything else, it was the kindness in her eyes that allowed a very private and distrusting Gabrielle to blurt out her sins to Trixie.

She confessed everything to this total stranger, but Trixie actually seemed to care. She actually seemed sympathetic. Gabrielle needed someone she wasn't afraid of to talk to. How could she just stop loving Gary? It wasn't possible. She couldn't let Aleksei into her mind, but she knew sooner or later he would just stop giving her that and take it. He would know how she felt about Gary. She had sworn her allegiance to Aleksei, and she craved him. He did fill her mind and her thoughts. He owned her body. But the betrayal was there now on either side. She betrayed Gary with Aleksei and Aleksei with her feelings for Gary.

Throughout her entire confession, Trixie remained silent, intently listening, her hand rubbing Gabrielle's back gently.

"You can't have your Gary?"

Gabrielle shook her head. "Worse, he won't be able to feel anything for me. Well, that's worse for me, but thankfully not for him."

"If you could have him, would you leave Aleksei for him?"

"It isn't possible. I'm Aleksei's lifemate. We're bound together."

Trixie frowned, looked as if she might question that and then shook her head. "That isn't what I asked you. If you could, right now, after all that's happened, after spending time with Aleksei, would you leave him and go to Gary?"

Gabrielle opened her mouth to explain she couldn't—that Aleksei wouldn't let her leave and Gary might not want her even if he could feel because she'd been with Aleksei—but she closed her mouth. Trixie asked a legitimate question, and why wasn't her answer a firm and resounding yes? She should have jumped at that. She should have immediately, without thought, said yes. Why didn't she?

She blinked several times, veiling her eyes from Trixie's penetrating gaze. "I don't know," she finally confessed in a low, shocked voice. Not shocked. Horrified. Aleksei was terrifying. He had a temper. He was her worst nightmare. Gary was sweet and kind. Everything she ever wanted. "I don't know if I could." The admission brought a fresh flood of tears.

Gabrielle looked up at Trixie. "What is wrong with me? What kind of a person am I? I know that I love Gary. I *know* it. But Aleksei has taken me over so that I'm obsessed with him. I crave him. I don't know how I could go from having the kind of sex I have with Aleksei to being with anyone else. He makes me feel . . ." She stopped, biting her lip hard. "He just makes me feel," she added lamely. "I don't know how to describe it, but . . ." She broke off, throwing her hands in the air. "I'm such a slut. How could I even consider trading a man I'm certain I love for sex?"

"You want to make it work with Aleksei?" Trixie asked gently, ignoring her drama.

Gabrielle was fairly certain she had lots of practice ignoring drama, what with raising five girls. She nodded slowly, trying to be as honest as possible. She was mixed up and confused, but still, there had to be honesty. "Aleksei scares me. He's the scariest man I've ever met, and I've met a *lot* of them. Male Carpathians are dangerous. It shows in everything they say or do. But Aleksei, he's a little different. Something inside him that is so dark . . ." She trailed off again, because saying that felt like another betrayal. She didn't want to say anything bad about him behind his back. "I want it to work," she whispered firmly, meaning it.

"But you're feeling guilty because you feel loving Gary has betrayed Aleksei. In fact, still is betraying him? Have I got that right?" Trixie asked.

Gabrielle wiped at her tears with the edge of the blanket. "That's about it," she admitted. "And making the decision that I know is the right one makes me feel guilty about letting Gary go. And it makes me feel slutty and selfish. How could I betray Aleksei?"

"You didn't know him."

Gabrielle sighed. She shoved both hands through her hair, keeping the blanket in place with her elbows. "But then I turned around and now I'm betraying Gary."

Trixie smiled at her. "Child, loving someone is never wrong. Never. There are all kinds of love in the world. Gary was sweet and kind to you when you needed it. You didn't have anyone and you didn't have any experience. He was the first man you fell in love with. In essence, your teenage love. Think about it. He had work in common with you and he made you laugh, but you didn't have sex with him. You didn't take every minute you could to be alone with him, sneaking off because you couldn't keep your hands off each other."

Gabrielle frowned at her. "I don't know what you mean."

"Can you keep your hands off this Aleksei of yours?"

"Well." Gabrielle thought about it. Not when she was with him. She wanted him touching her. Kissing her. She mostly wanted him inside of her. "No. But that's just sex. We don't make love. He isn't gentle."

"But you like what he does."

"Yes. A lot." Gabrielle was honest. She had to be if she was going to sort this out. And she needed to sort it out fast. Before he came back.

"There are all kinds of ways to make love. If it's good, that's what you need. But going back to your Gary. You clung to him because he made you feel grounded. Everything around you was so different and you didn't know how to handle it. I think you do love him, Gabrielle, but I don't think you're *in* love with him. If you were in love with him, you wouldn't feel as if all your loyalty should belong to Aleksei."

"I know that I love him and he loved me."

"Yes," Trixie agreed. "But I doubt if either of you were *in* love. Not a soul-destroying kind of love. If you had been, you would have been like you and Aleksei, all over each other. You love each other because you both are intelligent, have a lot in common, make each other laugh, all those things. But, child. Where was the passion?"

Gabrielle closed her eyes. Trixie was making sense, and that only seemed to make her feel worse.

"Gabrielle. Think about it. This man, Aleksei, frightens you. He doesn't give you one single thing you thought you wanted or needed. But you're reluctant to say anything that might put him in a bad light. You refuse to say one bad thing about him, and looking at you, seeing your misery, I think there are a few lessons that man needs to learn about women and he needs to learn them fast."

"You don't understand the enormity of what I did," Gabrielle said. "You can't possibly understand yet. You're still human. You don't even really know about Carpathians. The betrayal went so deep." She frowned and waved her hand. The moment she did, she was fully clothed, although, like Trixie, she'd left her shoes off.

"How do you *do* that?" Trixie demanded.

Gabrielle blinked as if coming out of a deep fog. "It's because he's my lifemate."

"That's another thing. Maybe you should explain Carpathians and lifemates to me, because I don't quite get that, either."

Gabrielle turned her head, sweeping her long hair over her shoulder to stare at Trixie in shock. Clearly shocked. "You told me you're Fane's lifemate." Her heart began to pound. Hard. What if she'd made a mistake? She couldn't trust her own judgment anymore. If she was talking to this woman, taking her at face value, and she was there hunting them, she had just helped convince the hunter to kill them.

"That's what he told me," Trixie said. "But I don't understand exactly what that means."

Gabrielle bit her lip hard. Hard enough that her teeth drew a small drop of blood. Trixie winced for her, but Gabrielle didn't really do more than register that small movement. She didn't know what to do.

There was one moment when she felt something stirring in her mind. And then he was there. Pouring into her. Warm. Intimate. It didn't feel at all like an invasion. She felt complete. Safe.

Kessake. What is it? What has you upset?

Didn't he mean *more* upset? If he knew she was worried about something, he had to have known she had been crying her eyes out. How? If he hadn't been in her mind . . . Had he lied to her?

I cannot lie to you. I will not lie to you. Your soul is tied to my soul. I feel your emotions, just as you can feel mine should you try. I entered your mind because you are very troubled. I am your lifemate and if you have need of me, I will come to you. Tell me. Now.

12

Gabrielle knew Aleksei had just given her an order. If she didn't tell him what he wanted to know, he would take the information from her mind. She took a deep breath. Submitting. Not because she was afraid of him, but because she was afraid for him. She was afraid for all the residents of the monastery.

There is a woman with me. Her name is Trixie Joanes. She said she's Teagan's grandmother and lifemate to Fane. I've . . . God. God. Why was she so gullible and stupid? Why didn't she think before she acted? Now she had this hanging over her head as well. *I've told her things that revealed a lot about what you are. She could be an enemy. I didn't think, but I could have put everyone here at risk.*

What we are.

She swallowed hard at the tone he used. Velvet over steel. A rasp she felt inside her body like a caressing stroke, but something else that set her heart pounding. *I don't understand.*

We are. You. Me. We. We are both Carpathians. If you put me at risk, then you have put yourself at risk as well. And. I. Am. Not. There.

Uh. Oh. She got that. She got that right away. He was not happy with her at all.

What should I do?

Fane says the woman is his lifemate. What is she doing with you?

This was getting worse by the moment. Still, there was something in his tone that compelled her to answer. *I need to sort myself out. She's someone I can talk to. Maybe she can help me.*

Fury. Hot. Wild. Intense. It poured into her. Filled her mind. *O jelä peje terád, emni. Sun scorch you, woman. Get rid of her. You talk to me. We sort you out together. Not an outsider. You. Me. Together.*

She held herself very still. She knew she'd gone pale, she could feel the blood leaving her face. *You swore at me. In Carpathian. That's considered swearing, isn't it? And you keep saying the word peje to me.*

Scorch. Scorching. Like the more modern fuck.

She winced. Not only did he get angry with her, over-the-top, crazy angry, but he swore at her. She was trying to sort herself out, for him. Okay, she'd screwed up royally, but she was trying. She wasn't at all certain he was.

Well, I don't like it. She would have settled for *scorch* or *scorching* if he hadn't compared the word to *fuck*. Scorch didn't sound half as bad. And she got the implication. Sun scorching a Carpathian was burning him to death or sending him to hell, or in this case, saying fuck you.

Not fuck you.

I still don't like it.

Get used to it. Get rid of her. Now.

Gabrielle gritted her teeth. *Trixie is no threat to us. Clearly. You can't dictate to me who I can see or talk to or be friends with.*

Are you my woman?

Her breath hissed out between her teeth. *I didn't say I would obey.*

Are you my peje woman?

"Gabrielle?" Trixie said, drawing her attention. "Are you all right?"

Gabrielle nodded. *Yes, I am. But I'm the biggest mess in the world right now and I need to sort things out. You just make me crazy. I can't talk to you about what I'm feeling because my feelings make you crazy. Both of us can't be crazy.*

Get. Rid. Of. Her. This is between us. I warn you,

Gabrielle. You do not want to test me over this. Abruptly he was gone.

Gabrielle took a deep breath and let it out. Okay. That was scary. Beyond scary. But he wasn't going to dictate friendships to her. Trixie was making sense. Helping her. Listening to her when she needed it.

"I'm okay, Trixie. I'm trying to figure out how to explain what a lifemate is to you. It's rather complicated. Fane isn't human. He's a Carpathian. Just as Andre is and Aleksei. They live very long lives. *Very* long," Gabrielle emphasized.

Trixie took a deep breath and stared into Gabrielle's eyes. She believed every word she was saying. Knots began to gather in Trixie's stomach. Fane had used the word *centuries* more than once. She'd overlooked it because, quite frankly, he was gorgeous and she was already so far under his spell she didn't want to hear anything that might bring her out of it. But if that was true along with sleeping in the ground . . .

"He's a vampire," she whispered.

"No." Gabrielle said it sharply. "Absolutely not. He *hunts* vampires. He's devoted his life to hunting them. Carpathian males live very difficult lives, Trixie. They lose their ability to feel emotion or see in color after so many years have gone by. There is only one woman for them. One. She can restore those things to him. Without her, he has only two choices. He can give in to the darkness, lose his honor and become vampire, or he can walk out into the sun and die a hideous death. His lifemate is everything to him. He binds her soul to his and he is safe."

Trixie was beginning to get a really bad feeling. "How does he do that?"

Gabrielle hesitated.

Trixie shook her head. "That doesn't bode well, you looking at me like that. You know something I need to know."

"You have a psychic gift, don't you?" Gabrielle said softly. "Like Teagan. Like me. You have a gift."

Trixie couldn't deny that. She heard songs in people.

Gabrielle's song was sad. Fearful. Fane's song was beautiful, and every single cell in her body responded to it. "Yes. Why?"

"The Carpathians are nearly extinct. They began to have fewer and fewer female children born. And then those children died before they were much more than toddlers, or the women miscarried. Soon, there were too few women and a child that lived was rare. I was helping to research along with Gary in order to help them. Their prince discovered that a human woman with psychic abilities could not only be a lifemate to a Carpathian, but she could become Carpathian. She could be converted."

Trixie didn't like the sound of that. "Is that what happened to you? Is that why you didn't realize you have a lifemate? You weren't Carpathian? You were human?"

"I was human. I was nearly killed, and the Carpathians saved me by converting me. That didn't stop me from thinking like a human or clinging to human ways. I didn't want to consider that because I had psychic gifts, a male Carpathian who had suffered centuries of darkness might be looking for me to save him."

Trixie tasted fear in her mouth. Whatever was happening here was much bigger than she'd expected. She was prepared to have a short fling with a very hot man. One she knew would eventually burn her, but she thought it would be worth it. No. She *knew* it would be worth it in the end. He had already replaced those terrible memories of that scared, innocent fifteen-year-old girl.

Fane had made her feel beautiful and sexy. He'd made her feel like a desirable woman. She wasn't a woman to kid herself. She was too old. She lived far away, a completely different life, but she could hold Fane in her memories. She didn't have to share those memories with anyone else. She'd given and given her entire life. So many pieces of her had gone missing along the way. No dreams. She knew better than to dream for herself, but she'd dreamt big for her girls and seen to it that they had the chance to make those dreams come true. She had no regrets. None. But Fane would be hers alone, and she deserved every memory she could make with him.

She took a deep breath. Now she feared the price was far, far higher than she ever thought possible.

"Trixie." Gabrielle whispered her name. "I shouldn't be the one explaining this to you. Fane should be. Or Teagan and Andre. Teagan's happy. I'm too confused and mixed up to be a good example of how wonderful it is to find a lifemate. And my lifemate is different. Very different."

"Does he have a tattoo on his back?" Trixie guessed.

Gabrielle's eyes widened. Her lashes fluttered. She nodded slowly.

"So does Fane. If your man is different, then Fane must be like him. How is he different?"

Gabrielle shook her head. "I'm absolutely not doing this with you. It's scary to find out you're a lifemate, but my sister is so happy. You have no idea how happy she is. You will be, too."

Gabrielle didn't look happy at all to Trixie. She was certainly anxious, her gaze sliding toward the door over and over again as if she expected something terrible to happen at any moment.

"I'm in my sixties, Gabrielle. I've lived my entire life without a man. Making my decisions. Expressing my opinions. Doing what I wanted to do. I've worked hard, and I have a family I love above all else. I am well past child-bearing years if they're looking to repopulate. I would never put up with any nonsense from a man, and I can tell you right now, any man who is a man would find me a pain. We would clash every minute. You're sweet and you want to find a way to please your man. Me, I'd just as soon hit him over the head with a frying pan."

That earned her a smile from Gabrielle. A first. When Gabrielle smiled, her beautiful face nearly glowed.

"You are breathtaking, child. Like my Teagan. No wonder these men both had their eyes on you. Your Aleksei is lucky to have you. You think about that when he's with you. He should make you feel beautiful and special. Not undermine your confidence in yourself."

"He does make me feel beautiful," Gabrielle admitted. "The way he looks at me, as if he would never see another woman the way he sees me."

Trixie closed her eyes briefly. She knew that look. Fane's entire focus had been on her. She'd felt that exact way. As if he would never see another woman like he saw her. This was getting more and more complicated by the minute.

"I've got me a stake gun. It fires little tiny stakes. It didn't do me much good when I shot at Fane and hit him. He just laughed and pulled them out. But you're welcome to it if you think it would do you any good," she offered. Because she wasn't going to need it. She was leaving. Right now. Fast.

She scrambled to her feet. "I'm heading down the mountain, Gabrielle. I would invite you to come along, although I might have to hike out in my altogether. I have to find my pack because I have extra clothes in it and I can put them on when these disappear. He hid it, but I can find it."

"Fane threatened to take your clothes?" Gabrielle guessed.

"He did. I didn't think he could really do it, but he's done quite a few things that looked impossible, so I'm not taking any chances."

Gabrielle felt a smile rising. That was two smiles Trixie had given her in the space of a couple of minutes when she had believed she'd never smile again. She really liked the older woman. *Really* liked her. She stood up as well.

The door didn't open. Not at all. The hinges didn't creak. But he was there. Filling the room until it vibrated with fury. The air was so heavy Gabrielle choked. Coughed. She froze, afraid to move in any direction. Her gaze slid to Trixie. The woman had frozen as well. Gabrielle wasn't the only one who felt that anger like a blow.

He materialized close to her. So close Gabrielle felt his heat. He smelled of forest. Of the mountains. Of rain. His hair was a wild fall around his face, and his eyes blazed a pure green at her. His jaw was set. His mouth as well. He looked so menacing, Trixie instinctively took a step toward her, as if she might put her body between Gabrielle and Aleksei.

He didn't look at Trixie, his fury-filled gaze focused completely on Gabrielle. He waved a casual hand toward Trixie and she stopped moving, her body going still, her mouth partway open, but no sound emerged. Gabrielle knew instantly Aleksei had frozen her there, and that was even scarier than the four walls filled with his wrath.

"Would you like to explain yourself to me?" He bit each word out between strong white teeth.

Gabrielle straightened her spine. Tears still clung to her lashes, she could feel them, making her lashes wet and spiky. Fat lot of sympathy she was getting from her lifemate. She moistened her lips, her heart pounding like a drum. "Not really, no."

His head jerked up. If it was possible, his eyes went pure green, no other color. Glittering green. Like a green flame. He took her breath away. She was terrified, but he was still the hottest man she'd ever seen in her life. She bit her lip and tilted her head to one side, sweeping her hair over one shoulder, a nervous gesture she hoped Aleksei didn't interpret that way.

"Not. Really. No." He repeated each word as if he couldn't believe what had just come out of her mouth.

Gabrielle bit harder at her lower lip and once more shoved at her long, flowing hair, getting it off her neck because she was suddenly very hot.

Aleksei stared at his woman with unblinking eyes. That small gesture, that sweep of her hair, revealed her delicate neck, her throat, revealed her vulnerability. Looking at her neck made him want to sink his teeth deep, to taste her. Claim her. Her hair was everywhere, cascading around her like a waterfall. So much of it, wild and untamed and so *peje* soft he could barely breathe when he buried his fingers in it, just as she was when he touched her. She always withdrew from him after, but he knew, one touch, and he could ignite that fire. Turn her into the wildcat he knew she was.

"Aleksei," Fane hissed, striding through the door. He didn't slow down, moving swiftly into Aleksei's dwelling.

Aleksei waved his hand to free the other woman—the one who had dared to invade his space and interfere in his relationship. "Your lifemate had no right to enter my resting place." There was a definite threat in those words—and rightly so. To enter any of the ancients' space was a violation of the monastery rules.

"I take back every single thing I said, Gabrielle," Trixie snapped. She drew in a deep, shuddering breath, glared at Aleksei and opened her mouth again, clearly outraged at his behavior. Fane was there instantly, standing solidly between her and Aleksei. He grabbed her arm in a viselike grip.

"I am certain my lifemate, out of respect for you and for me, will apologize to you later, Aleksei. We will leave you to your lifemate."

A single sound of protest escaped Trixie's throat, but it was muffled and cut off as Fane marched her out of Aleksei's designated resting place, leaving him alone with his very disobedient woman.

Gabrielle looked very pale, the heavy fall of her dark, gleaming hair emphasizing her soft skin. The sweep of her very dark lashes did the same with her soft gray eyes. He resisted reaching out and curling his fingers around the nape of her neck as he wanted to do. He waited until he was certain they were alone and then his raw fury vibrated through the dwelling.

"Repeat what you just said to me," he snapped, making it clear that if she did, there would be hell to pay.

Her gaze jumped to his. Held there. He could see the trepidation. Her hands shook. Her body trembled. She leaned close to him, not away, surprising him. Her gaze remained steady on his.

"I've had enough, and I don't really care much what you do to me. I was *trying*—working through things for *you*. It wasn't easy and I was terrified, but I was trying to find my way to you."

He waited. Holding himself still. Locking his gaze with hers. Using a predatory, possessive stare he knew intimidated her. Still, she leaned even closer.

"I have a suggestion for you, Aleksei," she bit out softly, her mouth inches from his.

"Be very careful," he warned her. "You're already in trouble."

Her eyebrow shot up. "Then it won't matter when I give you my honest suggestion one way or the other. So here it is. Why don't you go to one of the cemeteries, you know, the really old ones, like say from the sixteenth century or even earlier. Dig yourself up another lifemate. There should be a lot of women to choose from. Breathe some life into her, or hey, maybe not. Maybe you should just prop her up in the middle of the carpet where she can't give you any lip. In any case, dead or alive, she might actually obey you like a trained idiot far better than the lifemate you've got now, because I can assure you, I will *not*."

Before she could pull back, he curled his hand around the nape of her neck and held her in place. Through his palm he could feel the tremors running through her body. She totally intrigued him. Terrified, she still stood up to him. And she was terrified. She was also a natural submissive, which was a good thing given his dominant nature. She didn't even try to look away. She meant what she said. She'd hit a wall.

She more than intrigued him. Amused him. *Amused.* He had forgotten there was such an emotion. He fought the impulse to pull her close, but truthfully, her small rebellion captivated him. She knew he was powerful, far more powerful than she would ever become, even as his lifemate. He was enormously strong. Yet she stood up to him, giving him attitude in the face of his anger.

The blood rushed hotly through his veins. The dominant in him rose fast. Along with all of that, he wanted to smile. Dig up a dead body? Really? She wasn't nearly as afraid of him as she thought she was.

"I think I will forgo the dead body," he said softly, his

mouth against hers, "and put in a little time with the lifemate standing in front of me, seeing as how she is the *only* one."

He moved with blinding speed, one arm sliding behind her back, the other behind her knees; before she could protest or try to fight him, he was in the air, taking her away from the monastery, away from any possible interference.

You want to sort things out, Gabrielle, you sort them out with me, not some stranger. A stranger, by the way, who was leading a group of assassins straight to our monastery. Those men all have weapons and the intention to kill us. All of us. You included.

She gave a little shocked gasp and clung to him, her arms circling his neck as he took her into the mist. Her body shivered against his and he automatically regulated her temperature for her.

They travel with a puppet of a vampire. The vampire calls himself Aron Mazur and he is an ancient, very dangerous. Andre is tracking Aron. The puppet is capable of walking in the sun and was created to aid Aron in finding and destroying us.

Gabrielle pushed her face against his throat, burying it there.

Fane and I met up with Andre. We destroyed the camp using natural means, but we were not able to kill the four hunters because Aron sent his pawns after us. There was a battle . . .

Her breath left her in a gasp and she raised her eyes to his. He read anxiety there. Her hands went to his shoulders, his arms, smoothed down his chest, looking for evidence of wounds. He nearly stopped her, but then it hit him. She was *worried* about him. That anxiety was for him. The concern was for him. He'd never had that. At least if he did, he didn't remember it.

I am fine. A few lacerations easily healed. Do not be upset.

He *liked* that she was concerned about him—maybe a little too much. He dropped his head over hers and nuzzled the top of her head with his chin as he took her a good distance away from vampires and hunters, to a place he had marked a hundred years earlier. It was high enough in the mountains and deep enough in the forest that he knew it would still be there, in spite of all the changes.

He was a dinosaur from ancient times caught in a modern world. He knew that. He knew he would have to come to terms with that now that he had a lifemate and couldn't lock himself away from the encroaching modern values and changes. He knew those changes started with the woman in his arms. Still, he couldn't change his nature. He was a predator and he was a dominant. He was filled with darkness. He battled demons, and even with the finding of his lifemate, those demons still haunted him, haunted his soul.

He dropped down into the deeper forest, finding the cave he'd closed so many years earlier. It had everything for a perfect lair and he'd marked it well. He moved the large boulder away, took her inside and repositioned the boulder, adding both cover and safeguards to ensure Aron Mazur or his underlings wouldn't be able to accidently stumble across them.

In spite of the fact that he could see perfectly in the dark, he waved his hand to send sconces blazing along the narrow hall leading to the deep chamber. He had been in his woman's mind, if briefly, and she wasn't in the least bit as used to the sterile environment as he was.

Before they reached the chamber, he fixed that as well. The ceiling was high, the room long with a series of pools toward the back. One was large, the other two small, all of them hot and natural. He added a wide bed, one he had plans for, one just the right height. He hadn't taken her in a bed, but he knew humans used them, and she had been human.

Overhead he scattered stars across the ceiling, and he sent a light breeze to clear the air so that the sconces on the walls inside the chamber danced and flickered as they entered. He added two chairs and a small fire as well. He'd seen rooms in houses and he created one similar to one he'd liked.

As he set her on her feet, Gabrielle looked around her. He

caught a glimpse of her face and knew he'd done the right thing. She looked as if she could hardly believe her eyes.

"What is this place?"

"Our home for the moment. A safe one. We cannot leave the others too long. I will have to help Fane defend the ancients from the assassins, but there is no way those hunting us will be able to recover from our attack tonight. So, *kessake*, we have this night to continue our discussion without interruption." Deliberately he kept his voice low. Neutral.

She raised her chin and went to step away from him. His hand snaked out and his fingers shackled her wrist, preventing movement.

"Dig up an old grave?" he repeated.

Her large gray eyes softened and he caught a hint of amusement. "Seemed like a good idea at the time. Maybe not so much now. I think the corpse would have been really happy with that carpet in your old place. I like this." She looked around her again.

"Gabrielle." He said her name in a low voice. Softly.

She turned back to him, her gaze a little wary. Finally. He was getting somewhere. He wanted her to see him. Just him.

He bent his head and took her mouth. There was no thought. His body just reacted, just needed, and he dragged her to him, his tongue stabbing deep, his mouth hot and urgent. She didn't hesitate. She opened for him. Went wild for him. Her mouth as ravenous as his.

It took restraint and discipline not to keep kissing her. His body was already hot and hard and aching. He knew he could have her. She would give herself to him without hesitation, just as she'd kissed him. Holding nothing back. Her body was his. She'd given him that, committed herself that far. He thought that would be enough for a while, but he found he wanted more. It was that little rebellion. The "dig up a grave" that got under his skin.

He lifted his head, his gaze searching hers. "Tell me what else you need tonight. Look around. Clothes? Anything at all to make you feel more comfortable."

"I actually did ask my sister how to do the clothes thing," Gabrielle admitted. "I like nice clothes. Although in the evenings when I was by myself, before I was Carpathian, I would sit in my comfy sweats and sip a glass of merlot. It was nice to wind down after dealing with hot viruses."

"What else did you ask your sister to teach you?" He took her hand and tugged her across the room to the chairs in front of the crackling fire.

"The first thing I wanted to learn was shapeshifting. I loved the idea of flying. It seemed like it would be pure freedom."

He had never thought of it that way. Not once. Shifting and flying were things he took for granted. The ability had never been a gift to him, but seeing it through her eyes, shapeshifting and soaring through the sky took on an entirely new meaning.

"When did you learn?"

She bit her lip and ducked her head so that clouds of gleaming black hair fell around her face, hiding her expression from him. She waved her hand and instantly she was wearing soft drawstring pants that clung to her hips and shaped her legs. Her top was short, barely covering her midriff, exposing a small strip of intriguing skin.

"Gabrielle," he prompted. "We made a pact to talk to each other. You do not like me in your mind. I have tried to be cognizant of your privacy, even when I did touch your mind."

"Would you change these chairs to the picture I have in my mind?"

It was the first time she'd invited him to share her mind. It was simply the image of a chair, but she'd *invited* him. That, along with the clothes that showed more skin than he'd ever seen a woman expose, sent a rush of hot blood coursing through his veins.

"Is that outfit considered decent in the modern world? I am not complaining, but do women wear such clothes?"

She looked at him from under her long lashes. Her face was soft, her eyes gentle, turning his heart over. "Yes. Some women wear a lot less. I like these clothes when I'm just relaxing. This outfit would be considered casual."

"These are not clothes of seduction?"

She shook her head slowly, and the expression creeping into her eyes and onto her face sent another wave of heat through him.

"Later I'll show you clothes designed to seduce a man."

His cock reacted in spite of his resolve to keep his body under control. He wanted to give her a chance to settle with him. Intense sex every time they got together was great, but it wasn't getting him her heart—and he wanted her heart.

He sent her a slow smile. "I will look forward to that. Show me this chair you desire."

He poured into her mind slowly. Easily. She had dropped her shields. He took care not to look around, not to pry. He wanted her to get used to giving him full access to all of her Everything was his, and he wanted it. He wasn't going to accept limitations in their relationship. The chair she wanted looked very comfortable. Deep. Wide. Overstuffed. He switched out both chairs immediately, aware she hadn't answered his question about when she'd learned to shapeshift. She had avoided it. He didn't make the mistake of looking in her memories.

"Is this right?" he asked, putting his hand on the back of the chair nearest the fire.

She flashed a pleased smile and sank down. "It's perfect."

He took the one beside hers. He had to admit, it was a very comfortable chair, almost decadent.

"Do you like it?"

Her voice was shy. Hesitant. He reached over and took her hand, bringing it to his mouth, kissing her knuckles before letting her go. Immediately both her hands went to her lap, her fingers twisting together.

"Very much. When did your sister teach you about shapeshifting?" He kept his voice gentle, knowing he usually sounded as if he were making demands or giving orders.

She moistened her lips and looked up at him, still nervous, still not relaxing the way she did when he held her.

He tipped her face up to his. "Settle, Gabrielle. You are safe with me."

She started to reply, bit it back and took a deep breath.

"You have to be able to talk to me. We are just talking, getting to know each other. I respect the fact that you prefer me to wait to share your mind. If that would be easier for you . . ."

She shook her head. "Not yet. I'm not there yet."

"I see that, *kislány*. We are just talking."

She nodded. "I know. I do know that. It's just that . . ." She raised her eyes to his. "You said you were going to punish me. Well. Maybe not in those words, but you were angry with me and said if I didn't do what you said . . ." She trailed off again.

"And you're nervous about that?"

She nodded. Bit her lip. Twisted her fingers in her lap. He laid his hand gently over hers, stilling her fingers.

"*O jelä sielamak*, even if I do punish you for putting yourself in danger, I would never hurt you."

"How was I in danger?"

He heard the little bite in her voice. He should have known. She couldn't light on fire for him the way she did if she didn't have passion in her. If she didn't have a backbone. He had misread her. She wasn't nearly as submissive as he thought. She had wanted to please him. She had wanted to make up for her earlier betrayal that, now, knowing the facts, wasn't as much of a betrayal as he'd first thought.

He liked that she wanted to please him. He liked that a great deal. "That woman traveled with assassins. I was not there to protect you. Already, these people turned your life upside down. You told me you were attacked by them and had to be converted by the prince. Not by your lifemate, but by another. Because I was not there to watch over you."

She blinked at him, and he knew he had revealed something important to her and she got it. His anger was directed more at himself than at her. He detested that he had left her in order to help feed the ancients and make certain they were safely contained in the ground again before returning to her. He had been delayed by the battle with the master vampire's lesser vampires, and during that time, someone had penetrated his resting place when he considered her safe. He hadn't even set up safeguards to protect her. That was on him. That would always be on him.

"Aleksei."

Just his name. His heart turned over at her tone. He knew she had forgiven him everything just by the tone she used saying his name. Like music.

"It is my privilege and my duty to protect you from all harm," he said.

"I'll take more care," she promised. "You couldn't know she was going to be there. She heard me crying and just came in," she admitted. "I didn't even hear her."

That didn't make him feel any better. "Why were you crying?"

She swallowed. He knew answering him honestly was going to be difficult for her, but she was determined to give him truth. His respect and admiration for her rose a little more. She'd promised him truth, and no matter what, she was giving him that.

"I felt like a slut. I like having sex with you." Her eyes avoided his. She gazed unseeing into the fire while she made her confession. "A lot, Aleksei. I like it a lot. I wanted more. When I'm with you, I'm only thinking of you, and that felt like a betrayal of Gary." Her gaze jumped to his face and then she corrected herself. "Of him."

Clearly she was afraid of saying his name aloud to him. He'd done that. He'd made it so she couldn't discuss her feelings with him. That was why she'd turned to a stranger. Again. Totally on his shoulders.

"Then when you left and I thought that, it felt like a betrayal of you."

"Gabrielle, you have not betrayed me. I was wrong to make you think that. I did not know you had been human. You were not guided as you should have been. These mistakes are mine, not yours. I had not felt emotion in hundreds of years. I was so far gone I had to lock myself away to protect my own kind. Even now, there are darkness and demons inside of me."

"That isn't necessarily a bad thing, Aleksei," she said, her voice shy.

He loved the sound of her voice when she talked to him in that tone.

"I like you a little scary. It's exciting."

"Do you know what is truly exciting?" he asked.

Her eyes darkened. Smoldered. Sexy as sin.

"The thought of seeing the clothes meant to seduce a man."

13

Aleksei stayed very still, willing Gabrielle to comply. He wanted her to make a move, to show him she wanted him as much as he wanted her. He was beginning to need her. Not the allegiance of a lifemate, but the vow, the promise of a true lifemate. He wanted her to want him. To see him. He had to admit, he hadn't given her much. He intended to change that.

"Sometimes it takes me a couple of times to get the clothes right and inevitably I forget something," Gabrielle admitted.

He liked that she told him that. It was a small thing, but still, it was something she was giving him, a piece of herself.

"And the shapeshifting? Do you make mistakes with that?" That would be worrisome. If Gabrielle's clothes weren't perfect, that would still be fine, but shapeshifting was dangerous if one didn't know what they were doing. He didn't like that she was so reluctant to discuss that with him.

She took a breath. "I shifted for the first time the night I came here to confront Gary." She bit her lip. "Um. Him," she corrected.

"Kislány." He called her *baby* gently in his language. "You can say his name to me. It is not just you who needs to come to terms with this. I do as well. And I am." Slowly. Very slowly. He wanted to rip the man's heart out, but she didn't need to hear that. "Tell me about shifting. If you were converted some time ago, why did your sister wait so long to teach you anything?"

"It was my fault," Gabrielle said hastily. "Joie is very busy. She's gone a lot. I was busy doing a lot of research."

He touched her mind. He couldn't stop himself. Gabrielle was clearly choosing her words carefully because she didn't want him to think less of her sister. He inhaled sharply.

"Where did you get the idea that you were less than your sister? Or your brother?" It came out before he could censor. Before he *wanted* to censor. Her mind was more than just confused. She really believed that ridiculous notion.

He saw the instant retreat. Felt it. He reached out and caught her face, turning it back toward him. "You are not less than anyone. She was not doing work that was needed more than what you were doing."

"As soon as I asked her, she showed me," Gabrielle said in a small voice, a whisper of sound.

His heart turned over. Her mother had done this to her. Made her feel small and powerless. She didn't have the personality to deal with the temper tantrums. And she'd been too young. Too sensitive. Too intelligent. She'd buried herself in the acquisition of knowledge and no one had noticed she'd retreated—gone into her own mind and lived there. She was too young for the crowd around her in school, and again, she simply disappeared into studies and into her own mind.

He realized that had become a pattern with Gabrielle. When she'd been traumatized, stabbed repeatedly by the assassins who hunted Carpathians on the pretense that they were vampires, she had retreated into her own mind. No one had noticed. *Not even her sister.* Not the prince who was responsible for her. No one had taken care of her. They hadn't taught her the very fundamentals of being a Carpathian. To feed. To sleep in the soil where she would be rejuvenated and protected. Safeguards. Shapeshifting. They had given her nothing. It was no wonder she thought herself less than others. To them, it seemed she had no value.

Gary had noticed her. He had realized she needed friendship. Help. Someone to talk to, to share her work and laugh with her. To pay attention. It was no wonder she thought herself in love with the man. He was the only one who really showed her any interest or kindness.

Aleksei shifted out of the chair, opened her thighs and wedged himself between them, kneeling on the floor there between her legs. He framed her face with his hands. "Without you, Gabrielle, I would be either vampire or gone from this world. Without you, the thought of you every single rising, I would have succumbed to the darkness growing in me. I took a vow, for you, that I would never dishonor you. You kept me sane. You did that."

Her breath caught in her lungs. She shook her head. "No, Aleksei, that was you. You're an honorable man. You stood fast against the darkness."

He held her gaze captive. "I made that vow to you, Gabrielle. That vow for my lifemate flows in letters across my back. For you. To you. Whether I found you or not, I knew you. I saw you, there in my mind. In my heart. I knew you would be passionate and sweet. That you would give me whatever I asked for. And that is you. You always give me what I ask for."

"I disobeyed you," she whispered.

"I am not talking about obedience. When I asked you if you would wear your hair down for me when we were alone, you said yes. You gave that to me. Every time I have asked you for something, you have said yes. You give it to me. I had no idea you would be this beautiful, but I knew you. I talked to you. Each rising, before I went hunting, I told you I would be there for you. I would give you everything you wanted or needed. That I would keep you safe. I would protect you. I would love and cherish you. I meant those things. You saved me. You did that, no one else."

She shook her head. "This is why you were so angry. I understand it better now. I betrayed you when you needed me most."

He stilled her face. "No, *o jelä sielamak*, which means 'light of my soul,' because that is what you are to me. The light of my soul when I had none. When I was nothing but darkness."

"Aleksei." She whispered his name. A denial.

"You are the most important person in my world. I know you are afraid of me. I have demons. The darkness resides in me. I control my world. I want my woman to myself. I want her devoted to me. None of those things is easy to live with, and when you combine them, it makes it particularly difficult. It is no easy task to take me on, but always, *always* know that you are the most important person in my life."

"You scare me most of the time, Aleksei," she admitted.

He smoothed his hand over her dark hair. "I know I do, *kislány*, but fearing me makes you come alive."

She took a breath and let it out, nodding. Giving him that. She was reluctant and embarrassed to admit it, but still, she gave the admission to him.

"I cannot stop being who I am, Gabrielle. I will always be controlling. I will do my best to try to remember you are modern, but I have had centuries of being a predator with no one challenging me. When you challenge me, it makes me crazy. It makes me need to dominate you. To show you who you belong to. I need you to give in to me."

She gave him a faint smile, her fingers trailing along his jaw. "It's kind of nice to have someone else making decisions, especially when I question every decision I'm making. I can't be any different, though, either, Aleksei, and I'm not all about obeying."

He laughed softly. "Then we will have to make certain both of us enjoy your disobedience."

"Is that possible?"

"Oh, yes, my innocent, it is *very* possible. You will learn that lesson this night. We have many lessons to enjoy together. We can practice shapeshifting so I will know you are safe, and then we will continue until you feel as if you were born Carpathian and are powerful in your own right. Does that sound like a plan?"

She nodded.

For the first time she relaxed completely, and she looked happy.

He ran his hand down her front, from her throat to her lap. Light. Possessive. Claiming her. "You can start by showing me these clothes of seduction."

"I don't think you need clothes of seduction to be seduced," she said, her long lashes veiling the sudden sultry expression in her eyes. "I think you get all revved up without them."

His eyebrows shot up. She was teasing him. He'd never been teased— or if he had, he didn't remember. It tasted wonderful on his tongue. Her smile. The sound of her voice. The teasing tasted like Gabrielle and filled his mouth with the exquisite flavor he was so addicted to, the one he craved and now needed so urgently.

"What's your favorite color, Aleksei?"

Her voice came out husky. Sensual. A whisper that had blood pounding in his cock.

"Color?" he repeated.

"You must have one color you like more than others."

He didn't understand where the conversation was going but he was willing to go along with it because her beautiful eyes promised him paradise.

"I like fire. Red."

"Of course you do." Gabrielle inhaled sharply, drawing Aleksei's masculine scent deep into her lungs. She should have known he would prefer red.

She kept her gaze burning deep into his, waved her hands slowly down her body, letting her fingertips skim the sides of her breasts, trace her tucked-in waist and the flare of her hips. Her touch continued down her thighs. All the while, she pictured the daring image in her head of the sexiest lingerie she'd seen.

The camisole was a deep red, made of stretch floral lace, revealing and concealing, but definitely showing off her abundant curves. The front had a mock corset detail, so that the ties were crisscrossed but showed an abundance of skin. The garters attached to red fishnet stockings that were topped with floral lace. The small, red thong was more stretchy lace, and she had made certain she was smooth and bare for him.

Aleksei sank back on his heels, his face going hard, lust fueling the fire in his gaze. "Stand up," he whispered, almost hoarsely.

A rush of heat flushed her body a deep rose. He hadn't moved back, so when she stood, the junction of her legs was level with his mouth. That sent a quiver through her body. She was fairly certain she had a mini orgasm just from the look on his face. Damp heat flooded the little thong, so she knew it would be soaked when he went to take it off.

"Walk. Slowly. Around the room."

She did as he directed. She knew how to walk and she wanted him to look. She loved seeing that look in his eyes. He made her feel beautiful and special when he looked at her like that. Like a starving wolf determined to devour her. A predator, and she was his only meal.

She knew he liked her breasts and her butt. She had curves, soft and full, and he paid a lot of attention to both. She made certain to turn and strut, showing him her bare buttocks with that little strip disappearing between her cheeks as she walked away.

His breath hissed out of him, a slow exhale that made her nipples tight. She was already aching for him. *Aching.* He hadn't touched her. Not physically. Not one hand. He knelt on the floor watching her, his eyes burning with lust. With such fire. All for her. She may have never felt beautiful before, or special, but she did now, walking slowly around the room, showing him her body.

"Mine," he corrected, showing her he was in her mind. "That body belongs to me. You gave it into my keeping."

She should have been upset that he was in her mind without her knowledge, but truthfully, she didn't mind. Not at that moment. She wanted him to know how much she wanted to please him. To give him this. To give this gift to herself.

"Stop."

She stopped right in the middle of the room, her back to him. She felt him. Close to her. Behind her. She shivered, but she stayed very still. Just standing there in the red lace and stockings made her feel sexy. His hand swept her hair from the back of her neck and around to her left shoulder. She felt his breath on her nape and she closed her eyes, drawing in a ragged breath.

She loved that he was so tall and strong. She loved that he exuded such power. Looking at him made her body come alive, but when he was like this, compelling, mesmerizing her, every cell went on alert. She was drenched in her own lust and need. He still hadn't touched her. She ached for him. Wanted to plead with him to put his hands on her breasts, to give her that, but she stayed silent. Waiting. Holding her breath. Needing him. Needing to give herself to him any way he wanted her.

His mouth moved against her neck. A touch. Light. She shivered. Her nipples peaked into twin hard pebbles. Her sex spasmed. A low moan escaped her throat. She couldn't help it. The sting of his teeth had her jumping. He was gone that fast. She bit her lip, upset with herself. She went very still, drawing in a breath. Waiting while her heart pounded and her body coiled tighter.

His mouth came back to the nape of her neck. She felt his tongue glide over the bite. His lips brushed her sensitive skin and then his teeth bit down a second time. She didn't move. Didn't cry out. She let the feeling wash over and through her. The hot fire. It was so beautiful. So perfect. She was afraid her heart might beat out of her chest.

My woman. You please me so much, Gabrielle.

Her entire body went into a meltdown at the intimacy of his praise inside her mind. She couldn't remember why she hadn't wanted him there before. Now it felt like he found every lonely place, every shadow and every memory that hurt, and he filled them with himself. With his strength. With his belief that she was beautiful and special. His hands went to her shoulders. Again, his touch was so light she shouldn't have been able to feel much, but instead it felt as if he were branding her.

I would have to kill any man who saw you in this outfit of seduction.

She swallowed. Hard. He wasn't joking and she knew he was powerful enough to kill a man in many, many ways. She moistened her lips. Prayed for his touch. She needed him.

Would you wear this for any other man?

His fingertips moved down the curve of her back. She felt the heat through the stretchy lace. His palm smoothed over the bare skin of her buttocks, sending another spasm straight through her sex. She knew her thong was soaked. Her legs began to shake, growing weak just from his light touches.

She shook her head. *Only for you. I wanted to give you this.* She realized that was the truth. She loved standing in the room that had been created for her, knowing his eyes were on her. His. Aleksei. She wanted to belong to him. Somewhere along the line, she had taken in the truth of Trixie's wisdom. She had clung to the familiar. She had needed someone to notice her. To share with her. She would always love Gary, but she had to let him go in order to find her lifemate. In order to be a lifemate.

She was putting herself in Aleksei's hands. All the way. Giving him all of her trust. She realized, standing in front of Aleksei, in her sexy, daring lingerie, waiting for whatever he had in store for her, that he had been demanding her trust. Now he was asking her for it and she handed it over to him without a single thought of survival.

His palm stroked her bare skin, shaping the firm, rounded cheek of her buttocks, sending more shivers down her spine. Her knees threatened to give out. Without warning, the flat of his hand landed hard. It stung. It sent heat spiraling through her body, straight to her core. She whimpered. She couldn't stop the helpless little sound.

Do not move, he whispered into her mind.

Her channel clutched emptily. In need. She felt like a moth drawn to a flame. A very hot flame she clearly couldn't resist. He pushed her comfort zone, but she went willingly. Trusting him. She knew a great part of that was the lifemate bond, but more, it was the way he made her feel safe. A contradiction when he scared her as well.

She stayed very still, wanting more. Needing more. His

hand caressed the heat on her bare cheek. His hand slipped down and around, following the tiny strip of material nestled between the globes of her buttocks. He found her wetness. The extent of her need.

My woman wants me.

Very much.

His large hand smacked her bottom, this time with a little more force. Heat burst through her, every nerve ending alive. Four more rapid, hard smacks sent fire racing through her buttocks, straight to her sex. She cried out, pushing her body back, wanting more fire. More heat. Wanting him.

His hand caressed first one burning cheek and then the other. She held her breath. Needing. Her breath caught in her lungs as she waited. Two more rapid smacks and then he plunged two fingers inside of her and her slick heat drenched him, her sheath clenched tight, trying to pull his fingers deeper. She pushed down against his hand. Grinding. Needing. Instantly he withdrew his fingers. She nearly sobbed.

Aleksei.

His mouth was back at her neck. Just his mouth. His palm had gone back to caressing the bare skin of her buttocks. She closed her eyes, holding herself utterly still, not wanting to lose anything else. Not his touch. Not his mouth. Another smack sent hot flames spiraling through her. Once again his hand was there, smoothing away the heat, rubbing caresses in small circles, sending so many sensations crashing through her mind she moaned aloud again.

I don't think I can stand up anymore, Aleksei, she admitted, afraid she would fall at his feet.

Then go to the bed, but walk slowly so I can watch you. Kneel up on it, all fours. Hands and knees, facing me.

She moved, because she knew if she didn't, she would have to crawl. Her legs just wouldn't support her anymore. Shaking with anticipation, with need, she made her way to the bed. Slowly. Loving that he watched her. The burn had gone from smoldering to full-blown heat. She could barely keep from begging for him to take her.

She positioned herself exactly as he'd told her, facing him.
She could see him finally. He was completely naked, his body
hard, his erection full. His hand loosely circled his cock and
it was the sexiest thing she'd ever seen, the casual way he slid
his fist over his thick shaft. The lines in his face were deep,
his eyes hot with desire—for her. He looked sensual, focused
wholly on her. Hungry. Possessive.

Her entire body went hot. She felt the cool air of the room
against her scorching channel, and even that felt sexy. Her
bottom still felt the heat of his hand, stroking, caressing,
smacking, bringing every nerve ending alive.

You look so beautiful.

Her hair hung down in a long fall around her, the ends
pooling on the sheets. Her breasts stretched the lacy fabric,
feeling full and aching almost painfully. The lace teased her
nipples, rubbing at the tight pebbles so that she wanted to
squirm, adding to the sensation, but his look held her in place.
Her gaze dropped to his hand as it fisted his shaft. She knew
what he was going to do and she wanted it. Her mouth watered
for the taste of him. Her feminine sheath pulsed and wept.

He stepped closer to her, caught her hair in one hand and
used it to lift her head. She could see pearly beads on the
broad, flared head of his cock. Her tongue came out, she
couldn't stop it. She moistened her lips, her gaze on her prize.

He rubbed those pearly drops along the seam of her mouth
and then over her face, a slow caress with his hot flesh. It felt
wanton and sexy. *Open your mouth for me. Look at me, kessake. I want to see your eyes.*

Her hands supported her on the sheets. She had to trust
him, and she knew that was his deliberate intent. He was
showing her she did trust him, that her body did. He was in
her mind. He would know how much she wanted this. He
would know the moment she didn't like something he did
to her.

She licked her lips again, raising her gaze to his. Oh. God.
That burn there. That intensity. His eyes were hooded, his
expression raw sensuality. He steadied her. Made her feel as

if she could do anything for him. Anything with him. She opened her mouth, her eyes on his.

Do you want this? It belongs to you. Tell me you want it. Tell me what you want to do with it.

He brought his cock close so that she could feel the heat of him, smell his masculine scent, the one that made her feel wild inside. The one that drove her insane. He was pushing her comfort zone. She could tell him she wanted it, but to say what she wanted to do with it was difficult. Still, she knew he was pushing those boundaries to break them down. To allow them complete intimacy. And she wanted that. To be able to make her own demands, to tell him aloud or intimately what she wanted or enjoyed, was important. She knew that.

I want your cock in my mouth, she said, knowing he could read her discomfort. But if he could read her discomfort, he could also read her eagerness. He would know that her body was on fire, dripping wet. Her slick, hot cream was beginning to touch the insides of her thighs. She couldn't imagine how wet the thong was.

What do you want to do, little cat?

I need your cock in my mouth. I want to lick you clean and suck you until I'm filled with the taste of you.

And then what?

Then I want you deep inside of me. Taking me.

Gentle or hard?

Both. Whatever you want. I love what you do to me.

She knew it was a good answer, because he put the broad head of his cock against her lips and then slowly fed it to her. If she was being entirely honest with herself, this was the part of sex she'd dreaded the most. She didn't know if she would like it. She didn't know what she was doing. For her husband, she'd always wanted to be good at this, to the point that she'd actually looked up how, but she really didn't think she'd be any good because she couldn't imagine liking it.

She hadn't counted on his taste. The fact that he was hers. And she wanted hers. She hadn't counted on the lifemate bond being so strong already. More, she hadn't realized how much she wanted to feel safe and secure, to have some direction in a world she hadn't wanted to live in. Aleksei was all those things, but even more. He was Aleksei. And she wanted to give him something special. Something to remember. She couldn't use her hands, but she found being at his mercy was sexy and exciting because she had to trust him.

He was gentle and that surprised her. Very gentle. She took him into her mouth and used her tongue to explore, to catch the drops that tasted like hot spice and cool forest. Like Aleksei. He was large and intimidating, so she couldn't do what all the books had said to do, but he didn't seem to mind.

Peje hot. You look so scorching hot. A tight wet fist wrapped around me. Just like that, kessake. Perfection. His hands gripped her hair and he pulled her just a little closer, so that he went a little deeper.

She loved that he was careful. She loved that his eyes burned into hers as she suckled and used her mouth and tongue to pleasure him. She mostly loved that *he* loved what she was doing to him. She could see that on his face. In his eyes. In his body. Feel it there in her mouth.

Enough, kessake, or I will not be responsible for what happens.

Her lips clung to him as he slowly slid out, his hand wrapped firmly around the heavy base of his shaft.

You're beautiful, Aleksei. I loved having you in my mouth. She wanted to tell him she wanted to continue, that she wanted to learn more, to be really, really good at giving him pleasure, but her body was already shaking with need.

He moved around her, until he was behind her, his hand on her back. He hooked an arm around her waist and pulled her back until she was kneeling on the edge of the bed. His hand went between her shoulder blades and began to apply pressure. She complied instantly. Her head and torso went to the mattress. She kept her butt in the air.

Higher. Push up with your hips.

Heart pounding, she did so. At this angle, he would be able

to really penetrate, to be deep inside her. Connecting them. She could barely breathe with anticipation. She waited. The cool air hit her hot entrance and she closed her eyes as the sensations swept through her. Waiting was so difficult. She couldn't see him. She couldn't hear him. She could only wait for him to touch her.

His hand came down on her left bare cheek, sharp, flat, unexpected, making her jump, flooding her body again with liquid heat. It didn't hurt, although it stung, but in an erotic way, and his palm was there, smoothing and rubbing caresses. Then she felt the jerk of her thong and it was gone, shredded. Leaving her completely exposed to him. She wore only the stretchy lacy camisole and her garters and stockings. His hands moved to the insides of her thighs, stroking until fingers of desire raced up and down.

She swallowed hard, trying to stay still for him. Trying not to plead and sob when she was becoming desperate. Then he started really torturing her. Light smacks all over, never in the same place, hard enough to send warmth spreading and to sensitize every nerve ending, not hard enough to hurt. She'd never felt anything so erotic in her life. She didn't know how to breathe through it. The tension in her wound tighter and tighter until she knew she was going to implode.

Aleksei. She tried to warn him. She was not going to be able to hang on, and she knew instinctively he didn't want her to orgasm. She was so close. So needy. It was too much. All that heat and fire. Building, constantly building with no relief.

No.

The single command vibrated through her body. Sent her even higher. She forced air through her lungs, determined to hang on for him. His fingers plunged deep and she screamed. Nearly shattered. Fought it back.

I can't.

You can. Not until I tell you.

He was in the mood to play. Her body shook with urgency as his fingers were replaced by his mouth. His tongue plunged

deep and she moaned and pushed back, grinding herself
against his mouth. Immediately he was gone and she cried
out in frustration.

*Patience, kessake. You are becoming my little kessa ku
toro, my wildcat.*

His voice steadied her as nothing else could. She drew in
another deep breath and waited. She didn't have to wait long.
His mouth came back and he proceeded to torment her over
and over, bringing her to the very brink, suckling her clit,
using the edge of his teeth and the flat of his tongue and then
backing off just before she tipped over the edge. Each time
he backed off, his hand was on her bare butt, a little harder
each time, sending fire through her body, pure flames licking
over her skin and pouring into her bloodstream.

Aleksei. She wailed his name.

What is it you want, kessa ku toro? Tell me.

*Your cock. Inside me. Please, baby. I need it now. I don't
think I'm going to survive this.*

His fingers dug into her hips and he surged into her. Like
a jackhammer. Driving straight through tight muscles, invading deep, forcing her body to accommodate his size. She was
slick with liquid heat, but still, the friction was too much—
too good—and she screamed, unable to contain the wealth
of sensations pouring through her.

You wait for me.

Ohgodohgodohgod. She repeated the mantra over and
over, trying to hold her fragmenting body together for him.

He pounded into her, sending more flames storming
through her. It felt like a takeover. A claiming. Pure possession. It felt like heaven. Perfection. Still, she didn't think she
could hold it together. She was so close. Right there—on the
edge—and he showed no signs of stopping. Of letting her
have her release and then going on.

I can't. Really, Aleksei. I'm too close.

He stopped. Held himself still. Buried all the way to the
hilt in her, so deep she was afraid he was lodged in her womb.

He felt huge, filling her and still pushing hard against her inner muscles.

No. Don't stop. You can't stop.

He rubbed her buttocks, smoothing soothing caresses over her warm cheeks and down her thighs.

You taste delicious. I am addicted to your taste. I could spend hours eating you.

Her feminine channel convulsed around his cock, tightening more until she was practically strangling him.

I love how you need me. How your body craves mine and tells me so. You are scorching hot, so tight, so perfect. A man could live in you and never get enough.

Please. Please. Please. She didn't care that she was begging.

So hungry for me. He bent forward and kissed the base of her spine, right at the curve there. His fingers tightened.

Gabrielle held her breath. He slammed deep. Once. Twice. She panted. So close. She wasn't going to be able to stop a tidal wave. It reached for her. Overtook her. Shaking her. Consuming her. She screamed. Sobbed. Her entire body seemed to convulse, the ripples racing up to her breasts and down her thighs. It didn't stop, going on and on, so intense she thought she might die. Just as she thought the monstrous orgasm was subsiding, Aleksei slammed deep again, over and over, pumping his seed into her, hot jets splashing, triggering a second wave every bit as strong as the first one.

He held her hips to him, one arm sliding around her waist as her body grasped and milked his greedily. Her knees would have collapsed, and she had no idea how he was still on his feet. He'd powered into her over and over, until she lost track of time, her mind moving into another place, another realm, but she knew he had spent a long time inside of her. She was deliciously sore.

He moved up onto the bed, guiding her around so that she crawled, still connected to him, around to face the headboard. With every movement she felt her body ripple around his, grip his tightly, reluctant to let him go. He was right, she craved him. She knew she always would.

Still kneeling behind her, he moved in her gently, bringing them both down from that floating space they occupied. His hands urged her to move back into him just as gently so that her body rippled and pulsed around him. He kissed the base of her spine, murmuring to her in his own language, his hands caressing her buttocks and smoothing over her thighs. Then he very gently slipped out of her. Gabrielle couldn't help the small cry of protest at the loss.

He helped her to lie down, keeping his hands on her, tucking her into his side as he turned his body into hers. He kissed her eyes. Her nose. Moved his mouth gently over hers and then kissed her chin.

"Are you all right?"

"That was perfect."

"So you enjoyed your punishment?" he asked, nuzzling her throat. She felt his smile against her pulse. "I certainly did. I liked seeing the way you look with such an intriguing color, my hand caressing all that heat."

"Uh-oh. You're in trouble, Aleksei, if that was my punishment. I'll end up being like the bad girl of the century."

His hand moved over the stretchy lace. Found her nipple and tugged. "This is a beautiful covering. I like to look at your body, but if you have to be covered, this is sexy. You are very sexy, Gabrielle."

She snuggled closer to his heat. "Thank you. I like that you know what you want, Aleksei. I don't have to worry. I'm a worrier. I never think I do anything right, and when you take charge like that, I love it."

He shifted just a little so he could nuzzle her breast. Her body pulsed. She really was hungry for him. He didn't seem to mind that she wanted his body so much.

"I like things a certain way, Gabrielle. You are my lifemate, my other half. It is natural that you would suit my needs and I would suit yours." His tongue lapped at her nipple through the lace as if the stretchy fabric intrigued him. She wished she'd thought to add taste to the texture. Maybe next time.

"I like them your way, then," she said. "If someone had ever told me I would like a spanking, I would have told them they were nuts, that I'm not a child."

He nuzzled her breast again. "*O jelä sielamak*, an erotic spanking is far different than a man slapping the hell out of his woman. If you did not enjoy it, we would not have done it."

"Even to punish me?"

"Of course not. I can think of far more creative ways to make you beg for forgiveness."

The sensual note in his voice made her shiver. She realized the "punishment" wasn't his hand on her bare bottom, but building the need in her until she begged him for mercy. She laughed softly. "You are very creative, Aleksei, and I appreciate that as well."

His mouth moved right over the lace and pulled her breast deep inside where it was hot and moist. She was still ultra-sensitive and the feel of his mouth through the lace fabric was sexy, exciting, and it sent streaks of fire straight to her feminine channel. She pulsed and throbbed. Needing. She had to get a handle on her cravings.

She liked how he fit her so close to his body. She loved his mouth suckling at her breast. She loved that she could wrap her arm around his waist and that his thigh was over hers and the other was in between hers. It felt safe. Sensual. Perfect. She suddenly wanted to know everything there was to know about him.

"When you thought about having a lifemate, what kind of world did you want for yourself? Where did you want to live?"

He moved his head slightly, unlatching from her nipple, his tongue broad and flat, stroking caresses there. "I thought only of making my lifemate happy. Of claiming her and being done with darkness. During those times, I imagined I would still hunt the undead. I did not have demons dwelling in me. Or such unrelenting darkness."

She rubbed her hand over his chest, smoothing over his

bare skin right down to his flat belly. She liked all the muscle. So much of it. Better than any six-pack she'd ever seen. She liked that he seemed to enjoy snuggling with her. She liked how strong he was. How in a world that seemed to be constantly shifting out from under her, Aleksei was a rock, a steady anchor. More, she just plain loved sex with him.

"What about you, Gabrielle. What do you want?"

She opened her mouth to tell him all about her dream home. The house. The gardens. The white picket fence. The children laughing and the all-important porch swing. She closed her mouth just as fast. Did she even know what she wanted anymore? That had been her human dream. What was her Carpathian dream?

"Kislány."

His word for *baby*. The soft way he said it turned her heart over. Melted her insides. He was in her mind. She felt him there. Filling her emptiness, those lonely places, just as his cock filled her sheath. Already he was becoming a part of her. In her mind, he was the best part.

"I buried myself in research because it was a way to hide from the world, Aleksei." She wanted to give him truth. To give both of them truth. "I thought if I became a wife and mother I wouldn't want to do that anymore, but the research I'm doing is important and I'm good at it."

"You mean the research you are doing with Gary?"

She winced at the mention of his name and then she realized it was the first time she'd thought about him since Aleksei had returned. She took in a deep breath and let it out. She'd let her dream go. She'd let go of Gary. She loved him. She would always love him. She would always feel as if she had a connection to him, but Trixie was right. She loved him, but she wasn't *in* love with him.

She was beginning to believe she had no idea what love was, but she wanted to wrap her life around Aleksei. She wanted to feel just like she did at this very moment. Part of him. Complete with him. Sated. Elated. She loved to see that look on his face. The total focus on her. The approval. The urgent need.

"He lost his emotions and his ability to see in color all at once. I saw his face. His eyes. He is lost to our research, and that makes it all the more important that I carry on," she said. "I think he knew, maybe had precognition. I never knew what exactly his psychic abilities were. We never talked about them."

She realized that was true as well. They had discussed research and Carpathians and problems with babies endlessly, but they didn't share details of their personal lives with each other.

"So are you telling me you would like to make your home in the Carpathian Mountains near the prince? Is that where you have set up your laboratory?"

His voice was strictly neutral. She had no idea if he was for or against the idea. She bit her lip, torn between telling him the truth and guessing at what he wanted.

"Gabrielle." This time his voice was commanding. Authoritative.

Her heart nearly exploded out of her chest. She *loved* that tone. She loved how he could go from looking so gentle, almost loving, to a dark, scary predator. She knew she was safe with him, so that only enhanced the sensual, very sexy attractiveness. His voice thrilled her, sent fingers of desire down her spine, up her thighs and pulsing through her sex.

"The truth is, Aleksei, I don't know. I want to be decisive, but I don't know where I want to live. I know I need to work. I know it's important to make certain our women can conceive, carry a baby, feed the baby naturally, and that we can produce female children who live more than a year. It wasn't just one problem to be fixed. There are many reasons why this happened to the Carpathian species. Xavier attacked from many angles and he was successful. It will take a lot of work to figure out all the various things he did and find a way to reverse them."

"And you can do that?" There was admiration in his voice. "I have myself a very smart lifemate."

She found herself glowing inside. She loved that he thought she was intelligent.

"I really believe I can help. I don't know about actually figuring out every thread and eradicating it, but I'd like to try."

"Fane told me his woman will need to return to the United States very soon, along with Andre and her granddaughter. I will be needed here until another can take over guarding the gate and the ancients within. If Teagan can actually do as she thinks she can and help those remaining be able to leave this place seeking their lifemates, we will be able to leave."

"That was why Gary was sent here. He was to find out if our healers could do the same for other hunters or if only Teagan could." She didn't realize she had used the term *our* until after she said the words. More and more she was beginning to accept that she was Carpathian, not human. "Josef, one of the younger Carpathians but very skilled in technology, has a database of psychic women and where they live. Carpathians are trying to get to them to protect them. The vampires as well as the human society of assassins are hunting them. If Teagan can give them the time, it's possible I can point them in the direction of their lifemates."

"How?" He sounded neutral again.

"I have this strange gift. It's never really been good for much, but I can be with someone and look at a map and know they should go to a certain spot, that if they do, something amazing will happen to them. I don't know if it would really help, but if I had the addresses on a map and the ancient standing in front of me, it might work."

His hand smoothed over her hair. "You are a miracle, Gabrielle."

"It might not work," she pointed out. "I always kind of considered the ability a silly parlor trick. I never thought about it before—putting an ancient in the general vicinity of a potential lifemate."

"If that is the case, we will go to the Carpathian Mountains, although I must warn you, *kislány*, I am beyond ancient. Darkness dwells in me, and I will never be fully rid of it. I have demons that I cannot always overcome. I am from very ancient times. That means, no man touches my woman. He does not put his hands or his mouth on her. He does not hug or kiss her in greeting. Your body is for me alone. All of you. I do not know how long I will be able to tolerate others in close proximity, but for you, I will try. I have seen the long hours and days you put in and, more recently, the nights you have been putting in working. When I tell you enough, there will be no arguing. You will come with me. To me. Do you understand this?"

She was a modern woman and why that would thrill her, she didn't know, but not only did it thrill her, she was damp immediately. She nodded. "Sometimes, when I'm working, I forget the time. You'll have to . . ."

He leaned over and bit her at the junction between her neck and shoulder. Hard. Sinking his teeth in just a little bit. "No. You will comply. I will give you time for your work, but your first duty is always to me. You will come to me when I call to you." His mouth moved against her skin, his tongue lapping at her, taking the sting away. "When I want your body, wherever you are, you will give yourself to me."

She loved that, too. "If I want your body?" she challenged. "Do I belong to you?"

She didn't hesitate. "Yes."

"My body belongs to you. That is not to say, if you need punishing, I will not prolong your wait."

He sounded far more sensual than threatening, and she shivered. "If that's the case, Aleksei, I want your body right now. I want your mouth back on my breast."

"My lifemate. She needs her man's cock often."

"She needs her man all the time. But yes. I'm very, very fond of your cock."

14

Trixie was absolutely furious. She was too old for this crap. Having men dictate what she could or couldn't do. Silencing her with a wave of their hands. A wave. What was up with that? She wasn't living with that kind of power in a man. No way. Not happening. She went with Fane because she had no choice, but the moment they were back in his ugly shell of a house and he released her, she broke away from him and stomped across the dirt floor to her backpack.

"I'm leaving. I'm going home," she announced, without looking at him. She couldn't look at him. Or be close enough to feel his body heat or inhale his scent. There was something about him that worked on her like a magnet and she wasn't taking any chances. "I will not be treated that way. That man is abusive to that girl and he was to me. You continued . . ." Her gaze fell on her pack, suddenly right there in front of her.

"Trixie."

Fane simply said her name. Gently. Softly. His voice so low she barely caught the thread of sound, yet it vibrated right through her body along with his song. She could hear that, too. She could even see the musical notes floating around the room. His. Hers. Her notes filled in the symphony and it was beautiful. Still, she wouldn't look. Wouldn't acknowledge it. She needed to go home. More, she was going home and no one was going to stop her. Not even the hottest man on earth who had given her mind-shattering orgasms for the first time in her life.

She grabbed the worthless vampire-hunting kit and started discarding the things that didn't do her a bit of good. She wasn't *about* to carry anything she couldn't use. She was keeping the gun and extra stakes because it was the only weapon available to her. While she stuffed the vials and stakes into her pack, she found a magazine and pulled that out. It looked harmless enough, but she'd learned one could use that innocent-looking item as a very good defense.

She knew she was panicking. She'd only panicked twice in her life. The first time had been when her parents threw her out onto the street because she was pregnant. It had taken three solid days of sobbing in the corner of an alley before she stood up, determined to make a life for herself and her child. The second time was when she stood over her daughter's body watching the life drain out of her while the doctors frantically tried to save her. Both times, she couldn't breathe.

Even as she stuffed her belongings back into her pack and tried to roll up the sleeping bag, she found she couldn't get enough air. She was a fool. Such a fool. How could she have been so stupid? She wasn't fifteen anymore. She knew one didn't risk their entire family, their life, for a brief fling. And that's all this would ever be. A fling. Because for one moment, this man—a total stranger—had made her feel beautiful and sexy. He'd made her feel like a woman, not an empty shell.

Stupid. Stupid. Stupid. She ducked her head to try to draw in deep breaths. Whatever these people were, no matter how beautiful their songs, how melancholy or sweet, they were powerful and dangerous. She wanted no part of that. She had a family. People she loved. People she protected. Whatever spell Fane had cast over her was gone. She was leaving. She'd sort out her head later. *Way* later, when she was on the long flight back to the United States.

Trixie felt heat at her back. Fane's masculine scent enveloped her. When she drew in air, she drew in him. His scent. His presence. His hand went to the nape of her neck, his fingers gentle but insistent, holding her head down.

"Breathe, *hän sívamak*," he said softly.

His voice wrapped her up in a cocoon of safety. A web of instant desire. His voice was low and so tender she could almost believe he cared. But she knew better. He had forced her silence. That wasn't a caring thing to do. She refused to cry. She'd shed enough tears when she was fifteen and abandoned by her parents and her boyfriend. They'd knocked her down hard, but she'd stood back up. She didn't understand why this blow felt as deep. As hurtful.

She drew in her breath. Even that was sharp and painful. She could taste him in her mouth. Feel him deep inside of her. She was such a fool. An *old* fool. She pressed her fingers to her eyes, trying to blink back the burn and ignore the way his fingers massaged her neck. He was so good at what he did. So practiced. She should have known better than to get played. To be seduced. How was she ever going to live with this memory without squirming in embarrassment?

"Stop it, Trixie," he admonished. "You have no reason to be embarrassed. I am your lifemate. Of course you responded to me."

She detested his voice. His touch. He managed to get inside her, pierce her every shield with those two things, and she wouldn't allow it to happen again. Taking a last deep breath, she forced her body to straighten. She still had the magazine in her hand and as she raised up, she dropped the sleeping bag, rolled the magazine, took a step away from him, turned and attacked.

She hit him repeatedly, hoping to drive him backward. He didn't move. Rock solid. He didn't flinch. He was tall and the magazine hit him in his belly. She went for every man's nightmare and her weapon bounced away from that area. So he was ready for her, protecting himself, trying to show his superiority by not moving. Big mistake. She jumped and went for his throat, jabbing.

He caught her wrist and twisted, drawing her close, easily removing the magazine from her hand and tossing it aside. She fought him. She was strong. He let her struggle, not doing much more than locking her to him, her back to his front. It was impossible to turn around, but she managed to strike a few blows with her heel right into his shin. The entire time she fought, she berated him, calling him the worst names she could think of, but he didn't react to that either, nor did he silence her. He didn't wince when her heel connected with his shin. He simply remained silent and stoic.

Eventually she wore herself out. Her breath came in ragged, shuddering gasps and she fought back tears, feeling helpless; she hung like a rag doll over his arm. The moment the fight went out of her, he drew her back against his body, one arm still locked around her waist. His free hand moved her hair from the back of her neck and he pressed his mouth there.

Trixie tried not to let his light touch affect her, but her body shivered. Fingers of desire crept slowly down her spine in a sneak assault.

"*Hän sívamak*, I know you are hurt and even afraid, but I could not allow you to place yourself in danger. Aleksei is incapable of harming his lifemate. They have already completed the ritual and he is safe. Still, he is extremely dangerous. We have worked hard to strike a balance here at the monastery. We do not engage in battle. Had Aleksei said or done anything against you that could be construed as an attack, I would have defended you and one of us would have been killed. Our lifemate would have been lost as well. It was simply easier to remove you from the situation in order to explain it to you when all parties were safe."

His mouth moved against her ear. "I am sorry you were upset that you could not speak your mind. With me, you can speak it as much as you like. I find your attitude endearing and sexy, but Aleksei would not. He is . . . fighting demons. Even with his lifemate to balance him, he still has that darkness prevailing. Most of those who live here do. I would shield you from that danger."

Trixie closed her eyes, trying not to hear him. Trying not to believe the sincerity in his voice. Trying not to let in the fact that she was so tight against him she could feel his large, very hard body imprinted against her. She didn't want to feel how hard he was all over, let alone how his erection was pressed so tightly against her. It was all she could do not to rub against him. She hated herself for that.

"Let me go. I want to go home."

"You know I cannot do that, Trixie."

She stiffened, her heart pounding so loudly she was certain it echoed throughout the four empty walls.

"We will return to your family," he said softly. "I promise you that. When the ritual is complete, we will call Teagan in to try to help heal the ancients enough to allow them to leave this place. If it does not work, I have already explained to Aleksei that you need to return home and I will go with you to the States."

She shook her head. She couldn't bring him home. Not to her granddaughters and their husbands. What would they think? They already believed she'd lost her mind. If she showed up with a man as gorgeous as Fane, one who looked far younger than her . . .

"You are beautiful, Trixie. Absolutely beautiful. We belong together. You already know that. I saw the conversation with Gabrielle in your mind. You know what a lifemate is."

"There's a mistake," she said in a low voice. She had to reach for her voice because there was a part of her that wanted to keep him. She didn't know why. She was an independent woman and common sense dictated that she didn't want to have a man around to share her life, to be bossy, and there was no doubt in her mind Fane could be bossy. *And he had the ability to silence her.* That was totally unacceptable. She would *not* be silenced. She fought too hard to get where she was. No man was going to take that away from her. "This is a terrible mistake. You recognized the wrong person."

His mouth moved over the nape of her neck, around to the side where her pulse pounded hard. "You know it is not a mistake. You feel it, too." His tongue tasted her skin. Swirled there. Her head fell back of its own volition, turning slightly to give him better access. An invitation.

Her pulse pounded and throbbed in that secret part of her. She felt her womb clench and her sex spasm. Her breath left her lungs in a hot rush. As hard as she tried, she couldn't stop her body's reaction. His mouth was hot. His tongue swirled and his teeth scraped erotically. Anticipation had her body growing hot, but anticipation of what, she couldn't say, only that she wanted . . . needed.

His teeth sank deep and she arched her back, crying out, reaching around behind her for his bent head, trying to circle it with her arm to hold him to her. She felt in a fog, a hazy, sinful dream that sent spears of desire shooting through her, straight to her core. Fire spread, down her thighs, up her belly, traveling to her breasts so that the material of her clothes hurt her skin.

She heard herself moan. Low. Needy. Hungry even. His mouth continued to work at her neck and she knew she would have a love bite there, just like a silly teenager. She thought to protest, but her body was too far gone, already belonging to him. She tasted him in her mouth. That was the odd thing. She knew his taste although she had no idea where it came from, but suddenly the craving was there.

She felt him moving in her mind, stroking caresses there, soothing her, whispering softly in his own language. She had no idea what he whispered to her, but it was soft and sexy and she knew it was beautiful. She knew because the notes around them blended into the most beautiful symphony she'd ever heard. Her own moans seemed to accompany the song playing around and through them.

Joŋesz éntölem, fél ku kuuluaak sívam belsö. Come to me, beloved. *Palj3 na éntölem.* Closer. *Aćke éntölem it.* Take another step toward me. *Ñůp@l mam.* Toward my world. *Söl olen engemal, sarna sívametak.* Dare to be with me, song of my heart.

His tongue swept across her neck and he turned her around to face him, still locking her body close to his.

Tödak pitäsz wäke bekimet mekesz kaiket, emni. He spoke again in his own language and then once again translated for her, the words in her mind, not spoken aloud. *I know you have the courage to face anything, my lady.*

His hand moved to his shirt, opening the front. Very gently he took her hand and smoothed her palm over the heavy muscles of his chest right over his heart. *Feel that. You are hän ku vigyáz sívamet és sielamet.* Once again he whispered the words into her mind, filling her with him. With his strength. With his need. He translated into her language and it was poetry. *Keeper of my heart and soul.*

She leaned forward to press her mouth over his heated skin. She felt his pulse accelerate. Call to her. She heard the swelling notes of their song.

Joŋesz éntölem, fél ku kuuluaak sívam belsö. Come to me, beloved, he repeated. *Come closer to me, Trixie. I need you.*

His finger slid across his chest, right over his pulse, and she followed that path instinctively. He cupped the back of her head and threw back his own, his breath leaving his lungs in a harsh stream. She tasted that exquisite ambrosia in her mouth. It was familiar to her, and immediately she couldn't get enough. She lapped at the tiny beads there and then, at his urging, began to suckle, drawing more and more into her mouth. The taste burst through her like champagne bubbles.

Fane knew he was taking unfair advantage of his lifemate, but right then, it didn't matter. She wanted to leave him. She had a life far from the Carpathian Mountains, one she wasn't willing to give up. He could live with that. She had no intention of incorporating him into her world. He couldn't live with that. He had thought to give her time, to allow her to get used to the idea of Carpathians in the world, and then she would become one and live with him.

Andre chased the master vampire. That meant the human assassins, the puppet traveling among them and any lesser vampires would be trying to reach the monastery. Fane had the other ancients to protect. He couldn't allow them to battle. A single kill could send them over the edge. He knew Aleksei would stand with him, but although Aleksei had a lifemate and had completed the bond, he wasn't certain how far the darkness in the man had spread, or if it would continue to spread with each new kill.

There was no living without this woman. She didn't see herself as he did. She saw herself in human terms. She considered herself old. She was a mere child by Carpathian standards, barely out of her teens. He knew she thought herself too old for him, but that was more amusing than anything else.

Standing so close to her, her mouth moving over his skin, drinking his essence, his body went hard. Aching. He wanted her again. They needed to talk, to sort things out, but his body wasn't going to wait for that to happen. She was so beautiful. He especially loved her skin. The color. The feel. The way her muscles moved under all that softness. The way her lush curves invited his body to paradise.

Her second exchange. So close. Only one more and she walked fully in his world. She would not be able to be comfortable without him close, but he was in her mind and she had determination. Absolute determination. His lady wouldn't hesitate to place herself in an uncomfortable situation, or sacrifice herself for someone she loved. She loved her family and she didn't consider Fane a part of that—yet.

Enough, he said softly, and inserted his hand between her mouth and the laceration he had made over his pulse.

To distract her as his body healed, and because there was nothing else he wanted more, he tipped her face up to his and took her mouth. Her tongue tangled with his and hot spikes of desire pierced deep. Her hand slid under his shirt to find warm skin. The feel of her palms moving over him, her body pressing close, was every bit as amazing and wonderful as the first time he'd touched her. Kissed her. Felt her skin and the silk of her hair. He would always have this sense of wonder that she could be real. That she would catch fire from his kiss and burn hotter than he had ever imagined a woman would do.

Behind her, he waved a hand. She had said she wouldn't have sex with him again without a decent bed. He provided her with one, all the while kissing her. Her mouth was sheer magic. He could kiss her for hours and never get enough.

Fane walked her backward until the back of her knees hit the mattress. "Your bed, *hän sívamak*, just as you requested. You have only to ask and it is yours."

Trixie blinked at him, confused. Dazed. Coming out from under the dark veil he'd woven around her. His mouth found hers again before she could make it all the way to the surface. He loved the bemused look on her face. In her eyes. The innocence there. He'd given his woman her first orgasm. He intended to try for many. He wanted that for her.

She deserved more than she'd ever allowed herself, and it was up to him to give her everything she'd ever dreamt about. The trouble was, Trixie didn't dream for herself. She had had big dreams for her daughter and she'd worked day and night sweeping floors and cleaning offices and eventually toilets in bars in order to get off the street before her baby was born. She had worked until she had the money for a small room in a boardinghouse and then worked harder to get them out of that and into an apartment.

The more Fane looked into her mind and her memories, the more he admired and respected her. This woman had a will of steel. She had likely passed that legacy on to her daughter and granddaughters. She made her own way in the world and didn't ask anything of anyone. And she was *his*. This amazing woman who loved her family and made her way in the world without her own dreams. Saving them for her girls.

Fane kissed her again. Long. Hard. Over and over. Wanting her to get what was building so strong in him. That respect. That admiration. The fact that he was going to uncover every secret dream, the ones she didn't even know she had, and give them to her because his lady deserved them.

"A bed?" she murmured into his mouth, her dark eyes looking around her.

As Fane took her down he removed their clothes, needing to be skin to skin. She didn't protest; in fact, her hands swept over him, stroking caresses.

"I like your body," she confessed. Blurted it out and then looked shocked.

He lifted his head and looked down at her. Smiling. Because how could he not smile when she said things like that to him? When she obviously meant them? He liked the way her gaze moved over him. Over his face. His body. Her hands smoothed over his chest and then began to journey down toward his groin. His entire body tightened.

"Thank you, beloved. I am more than pleased that you like the way I look."

"I do. A lot. I have to remind myself you're real. I don't think I could dream up a man as gorgeous as you are."

She moved under him, clearly trying to squirm away from his scrutiny. He caught her thoughts. She was old. Too curvy in a world where curves on a woman weren't appreciated anymore. Although she'd always made certain to take care of herself, to stay fit and to look her best, she didn't want him to see her body.

Fane was going to change that. Right now. "You are truly beautiful, Trixie, such a beautiful woman." He caught both of her wrists and lifted them up above her head, stretching her arms out, pinning both wrists to the mattress easily with one hand. The action lifted her breasts perfectly, tempting him. He stared down at her. Hungry. He let her see that hunger. Possessive. He let her see that, too.

"Fane." She whispered his name on a protest, her eyes sliding from his. Shaking her head. "I can't."

"You can. For me." He bent down and took her mouth again. Letting her taste the need in him. "I cannot convince you with words, *hän sívamak*, so let me show you with my body. Let me show you my need of you. My hunger for you. Only you. There is no other woman in my world and there never will be. Only you."

Trixie closed her eyes, trying to shut out the honesty on his face. In his eyes. That stark, raw hunger had been her undoing earlier. He'd taken her body and then he'd left her. And then . . .

"Beloved. Stop." He bent his head again and pressed kisses to each eyelid and then trailed more down her face. "Open your eyes and look at me so you know I speak the truth. I cannot lie to my lifemate."

She couldn't stop herself. His voice was so compelling to her that she *had* to open her eyes. His eyes were so beautiful. Like twin sapphires. She had never considered that she would find a man like him so attractive. He was just so big. Scary big. She'd never let men frighten her, because she was her girls' protection, but if she was being strictly honest with herself, Fane was a very scary man. Not in the demonic, terrifying way that Aleksei was, but she had learned over the years to read people, and her Fane was definitely a man you wouldn't want to cross.

She moistened her lips. Swallowed hard. She didn't protest but just looked him straight in the eye, her heart beating fast. She hadn't realized she was genuinely hurt over the way he'd left her so abruptly. She had wanted something different. She *needed* something different. She wasn't certain what that was, but she'd felt abandoned by him. She couldn't move her hands because he had pinned her wrists above her head, leaving her exposed and vulnerable. She'd *felt* exposed and vulnerable earlier, so raw, and he'd cut her deeply.

Fane groaned softly. "I have to explain to you. I did not want to leave you, Trixie. I had no choice. I could not allow the hunger of the ancients to escalate. They had to be fed. They were dangerous. Far too dangerous. They are predators, and they grow even more so as each rising passes and they are caught in this endless nightmare. I am what stands between them and the world. Now, because he has completed his bond with his lifemate, I have Aleksei to aid me. I could not take any chances, not even for you, as much as I wanted to stay and comfort you."

She squirmed a little at that. She didn't need comfort. She was a grown woman, capable of taking care of herself. It didn't help that she felt tears burning behind her eyelids. She had wept in an alley when she was a child. She had wept in a hospital room when she'd lost her daughter. She refused—*refused*—to weep for a man who had used her body and left her.

"You are not listening to what I am saying to you."

She winced at the mild rebuke in his voice. She was listening, she just didn't want to hear. She didn't want to take that chance. She couldn't have him. Couldn't take him home and keep him. She had no idea what to do with him and she hated that she was lying there in her sixty-year-old body, exposed and vulnerable, and he was so fit and perfect. It wasn't right. She couldn't be anyone's lifemate. She couldn't be his entire world. She needed to go home and close her doors and shut out the world.

Fane made a sound deep in his throat, a growling rumble that vibrated through her body, sending damp heat between her legs. His gaze, so hot as it moved over her body, sent a spasm to her sex and blood rushing hotly straight to that same, special place. It shouldn't be so difficult to resist him. She was strong. She had a will of iron. She knew she did, but she couldn't stop the way her body melted and needed and *craved* him.

Before she could protest, he dipped his head to slide his face along hers. It was such a benign movement, and yet at the feeling of his shadowed jaw sliding along her cheek, her heart accelerated and she felt a melting sensation in the pit of her stomach. He licked her ear, tracing the shell and then dipping along the path to her throat. The burn between her legs grew hotter.

Fane kissed her throat, a mere brushing of his lips, but it felt as if he were worshiping her. He pressed another kiss into the little indentation at her sternum. Butterflies took flight in her stomach. His hand stroked over her, claiming her body.

"I am going to let go of you, but I want you to keep your hands right here. I am in the mood to do some exploring. I would very much like to know every inch of you intimately." He kissed the sweet curve of her breast. "Will you do that for me? I need this, Trixie."

His voice had gone raw. Pure sex. Sinful sex. A temptation she knew she should avoid, but she couldn't resist. Keeping her eyes on his, she nodded.

"Watch my hands. My mouth. See the beauty I see. Your body is the most beautiful thing in the world. Mine. A treasure I will cherish for all time."

He said things she was fairly certain most men would never say to a woman, and his words matched their song. He kissed his way across the soft upper curves of her breasts, and she couldn't help herself, she writhed, arching her back, needing his mouth on her. The need was so great it overcame everything. His eyes, staring down at her breasts, so focused, so hungry, were so hot she thought she might spontaneously combust.

He lifted his gaze from her breasts to her eyes. "Look at you. Already panting. Breathing ragged. Your body soft and melting. I love that you do that for me." He swept a possessive hand from the valley between her breasts to the vee at the junction of her legs, watching the shiver that followed his palm. "I bet you are already wet and welcoming for me. Are you, *hän sívamak*? Are you that ready for me?"

She was. To her everlasting embarrassment she was. He made it sound like a good thing. A *great* thing. As if she were the sexiest woman in the world. More. Just the way he said it to her made her even hotter for him.

His hand continued to trail down her middle, between her breasts, across her belly—which was softer than she would have liked—and lower until his hand hovered just above her mound. More liquid heat spilled out. His mouth moved close to her left breast just above her taut nipple, so close she could feel his warm breath. Her hips bucked and she arched toward his mouth again, unable to stop herself. Needing. Even a moan escaped, a soft little pleading moan.

She moistened her lips with the tip of her tongue under the heat of his gaze. His eyes went from desire to lust, but there was something else there. Something she was afraid to name because it was too close to an emotion she knew she couldn't have from him. Still . . . he waited. She knew what he was waiting for. She swallowed and nodded. She was ready for him. She would always be ready for him, no matter where the future took them. She'd never belonged to a man, and right now, for this time, she was wholly his.

Fane smiled, his teeth very white and strong, the smile so tender she could barely breathe as he bent his head to brush a series of light kisses around her breast. Up over the swelling curve, down along the side, underneath and then up the other side. Worshiping her—claiming her—it felt just like that, and again she felt the burn of tears behind her eyes. No one had ever touched her like he did. No one had ever taken the time to bring her body to such life.

"I knew my lady would welcome me. Thank you, beloved. You cannot know how much your welcome means to me. I love that you have done as I asked, keeping your arms above your head. Thank you for that as well."

Clearly he knew how difficult it was for her to lie still under his heated gaze, giving her body to him when she had to struggle not to cover up. She was inexplicably pleased that he cared enough to notice.

His hand closed over her left breast and he pulled her right one deep into his mouth and suckled strongly. She cried out as fire streaked through her body, from her breast straight to her sex. Her channel rippled. Shuddered. She nearly had an orgasm just from his mouth.

So sensitive. So responsive. What man could ever expect such a gift?

He took his time, savoring the feast of her breasts. There was no other word for it. He savored while she gasped and clutched her fingers into the sheet above her head, through sheer willpower, when she wanted to bury her fingers in his hair and hold him to her. Her body felt feverish. Empty. Desperate. His hands were everywhere, kneading her breasts, tugging at her nipple, sliding down to cup her mound possessively. He added his tongue and teeth until she began pleading with him.

"Fane. I have to touch you. I can't just lie here. It's too good."

He lifted his head. "Just another few minutes, *hän sívamak*, let me have this for another few minutes."

She might die of a heart attack. Or heatstroke. Or another mini orgasm that came out of nowhere, but she would give him anything when he looked at her like that. Once again, because he seemed to need an answer, she nodded. He smiled again, so beautiful. So perfect. All hers. She would never, *ever*, forget that smile or the way he looked at her as if she were the only woman in the world. She would take that vision home, burned into her mind, and whenever she was alone, she would dream again. She would allow herself that. She would dream of him.

His mouth left her breasts and moved down her rib cage to her tummy. She squirmed a little, and it took a *huge* effort not to cover herself up. He had a twelve-pack, or maybe even a twenty-four-pack. Not a single ounce of fat. She was soft all over, especially her tummy. She was no young girl, but a woman . . .

Stop, Trixie. You are my lady.

Fane whispered the words into her mind. So intimate. She shivered at the intimacy, almost as intimate as when he was inside her body, maybe even more so. She loved that he called her his lady. *Loved it.*

My lady is beautiful and sexy. Everything about her is. I love your curves and your lush body. I love the way you feel against me. For me, you are perfect. I do not care about the rest of the world, nor will I ever care what their opinions or standards of beauty are. For me, you will always be the epitome of beauty in a woman.

Now the tears really did form. She couldn't stop them so she closed her eyes. There was no mistaking the sincerity in his voice. She heard truth from him. He really felt that way about her body. About her as a woman.

She felt his kiss like a brand on her belly button. A trail of kisses led down to her hip, first one, and then the other. He kissed her mound and the breath left her lungs. He smoothed his hands over first one thigh, and then the other, his mouth following. He pressed kisses to her legs and down to her feet.

He lifted her legs and wrapped them around him as he moved up and into her, using his body to open her legs for him.

Her sex throbbed. Her channel pulsed. Hot blood rushed through her veins, calling to him. And then his mouth was there. Gentle. Not ravenous. Not crazy. Gentle. Light almost. Driving her crazy. He sipped at her as he might at the finest wine. He savored each drop of her honey. He used his tongue in a languid exploration of her body. An unhurried claiming. She thought she might go out of her mind.

Her body shuddered with anticipation at that first touch of his mouth, but then settled into a joyous, easy bliss. But he didn't pick up the pace. He didn't stop. He just kept on, using his mouth and fingers so that it became torturous, glorious but torturous. She began to think she might actually go crazy.

There was no keeping her hands where he wanted them. She had to touch him. Her body couldn't keep still. Her hips bucked against his mouth, ground deep, trying to reach that explosive end, but his tongue circled her clit, flicked hard so that she gasped, reached, and then it was gone.

She caught his hair in both fists to tug him closer. "Fane." She could only gasp his name. He really was driving her mad. He stabbed his tongue deep and used his thumb on her clit. She came close. So close. Then it was gone and he was sipping at her. Eating her as if she were a leisurely meal. Before she could settle into that, his teeth scraped and his mouth suckled and she screamed and begged.

"Fane. *Please.* I need you." Her voice said it all. Ragged pants. Gasps. She could barely plead with him, unable to find enough air.

The moment she said that, he was up and over her. Blanketing her with his weight. With his heat. He caught her legs on his arms, planted his hands on the mattress and surged into her. Not slowly. Not leisurely. Hard. Deep. Fast. Perfection. Exactly what she needed. The wave took her on that first stroke. She fragmented. Dissolved. All the while, he stared down into her face as if she were the most beautiful thing he'd ever seen.

He didn't stop moving, taking her while her body squeezed and strangled and pulsed, scorching hot around his cock. Already, the first orgasm was building into a second, not flowing easily, but building sharply. So hot. On fire. He leaned his weight into her, catching her bottom in his hands and urging her hips to meet his harder. Stronger. Deeper. Another wave took her. Shaking her. Consuming her.

She screamed his name, clutching his shoulders hard as he kept going, surging faster into her. Not stopping. Not allowing her to catch her breath. Already the third wave was building. Higher. Stronger. Coiling so tight she feared she might not hold herself together when it came.

She felt him swelling—impossible, but he stretched her even more. He had watched her through two orgasms, now he took her mouth. Hot. On fire. Then his face was buried in her neck and she felt his teeth bite down over her pulse. That erotic sting sent her careening over the edge, taking him with her. He thrust several times and then buried himself deep, staying still, his mouth still on her neck.

Her arms went around him and she held him to her. Strangely, she could hear their hearts beating in perfect mad synchronization. The drumbeats added to the perfection of their song. The musical notes exploded all around them, like silver and gold stars bursting in the air as their song crescendoed. It was beautiful. It was perfect. And she let the blinding tears track down her face. She had never known being with a man—the right man—could be so good.

15

Fane was a big man and his weight was entirely on her. Trixie found it a little difficult to breathe. Still, she didn't want him to move. She could feel him in her, his shaft pulsing, sending ripples spreading throughout her body. So good. So amazing. He swept his tongue over her pulse and pressed kisses into the junction of her neck before lifting his head. At once his gaze swept her face, noting the tears sparkling on her lashes and the fresh tracks on her face.

"Hän sívamak."

Just that. In his voice. She knew what that meant now. *Beloved.* He called her beloved. She'd never had a man give her an affectionate or loving nickname. He'd given her two. She'd never had a man hold her as if he never wanted to let go or look at her with a mixture of tenderness and reprimand.

He bent his head and tasted her tears. Her body clutched his harder. His every movement sent more ripples throughout her body. She loved that they were still connected. She traced lazy patterns with her fingertips on his back.

"Tell me why you are crying."

She couldn't look away from the compelling blue of his eyes. "You're so beautiful, Fane. This is beautiful. I wish I could—" She broke off. "I have to go home. Back to my life there. It's a beautiful dream, but I don't think you could really live with someone like me, my attitude and my very strong opinions. I doubt I could live with a man. What you've given me is more than I've ever had in my life and . . ."

He kissed her. Instantly her thoughts scattered. She

couldn't think with his mouth on hers and his body gently moving in and out of hers. So gentle. Soothing. And then he slid out and rolled off of her, but retained possession so that she was tucked close to his side, facing him. One knee slid between her thighs. One leg went over the top of hers to pin her there. His arm circled her waist.

Trixie looked up at him, afraid he might be upset. She was. She almost hoped he would be, but he looked down at her with something close to amusement.

"You are my lifemate. Your soul is bound to mine. We cannot be apart."

She frowned. He said it as if being lifemates was an everyday occurrence and she should know she couldn't be apart from him. She knew the idea of leaving him made her want to weep, but still, she had a life she had to get back to. At the same time, she couldn't make herself move. He held her close to him. So close, his hands smoothing over her body, rubbing and kneading, a gentle massage. Trixie had never thought, after all those years alone in a bed, she would like to snuggle, but she did—so much so that she stayed and listened when she should have run.

"You and Gabrielle both use the word *lifemate* as if I would know all it meant. She explained a little about you. That you can live in darkness until you find the right woman . . ."

He nuzzled the top of her head with his chin. His hand was smoothing the curve of her breast, his thumb sliding over her nipple, causing a shiver through her body and a distinct quiver in her feminine channel.

"There is only one woman or one man for a Carpathian, Trixie. We cannot make mistakes. The ritual words binding our souls together are imprinted on the male before he is born. Once those vows are spoken and the two are tied together, they cannot be apart for very long. Those ties enable them to speak telepathically on an intimate path."

Trixie took a breath and opened her mouth, but she had no idea what to say.

"Darkness does not describe the hell we live in waiting for

our lifemates. The world is bleak, and we have only our honor to keep us from turning to the wrong path. Vampires are Carpathians who choose to give up their souls for the chance to feel a rush when they kill. That is how desperate it becomes, living in that raw, ugly world." He brushed kisses over her ear and down to her neck.

Her heart accelerated. His hand was at her waist now, back to stroking soothing caresses over her skin, splaying his fingers wide to take in as much of her as he could.

"You have to have made a mistake, Fane. I'm not that woman."

"We lose our ability to see in color and to feel emotion. Both fade slowly so we do not succumb to the madness of our lives being slowly taken from us, but it is wearing after so many years. Each kill we make in the name of justice adds to the darkness. The longer we live, the more difficult it can become. When we find the one woman, our woman, our lifemate, she restores colors and emotions to us. We can feel how perfect and beautiful making love is. We can see her amazing silky skin and feel her hair sliding over our skin. When we kiss it's a kind of ecstasy, because every feeling is appreciated and felt intensely."

Trixie moistened her lips. She felt languid, so relaxed she couldn't move, but at the same time, unease had crept in. This would never be her home. At her age, she couldn't just drop everything and follow a man, no matter how much she might want to. And more, how much the thought of leaving him made her crumble inside. "Fane, are you saying I've done that for you? I gave you back your ability to see in color and feel emotion?"

"That is exactly what you did for me."

She closed her eyes, sorrow sweeping through her at the enormity of his simple statement. She had always been intelligent, able to grasp a concept immediately, and she knew that what he'd just said meant they were tied together. Soul to soul. She might have scoffed at the notion or made light fun of someone believing such nonsense if she weren't lying next to him, naked and sated from amazing sex. She didn't do this kind of thing. Ever.

"I'm so glad I did, Fane. You're a good man." She took a breath. "But I am human, not Carpathian, and I have an entire life in another place."

"I am aware of that, Trixie. I am in your mind. I have seen your life and your lack of dreams for yourself. You have given pieces of yourself to everyone you love all of your life and you held back nothing for yourself." He brushed another kiss along her temple, and now his hand moved lower, between her legs. "I was born to give you everything. To keep you safe and make you happy. Truly happy."

"I am happy, Fane."

"I know you love your family, but I found the emptiness in you. That place that feels just as alone as I was. You hold it away from everyone, deep inside where it only belongs to you. Now it is mine to fill."

She closed her eyes. Wanting him. Knowing she couldn't have him. She'd gone nearly a lifetime without a man. It was impossible to incorporate one into her life. Fane was sweet to her, but she could see he was a scary man. Dangerous. He wore that look in the lines of his face and the set of his shoulders. The way he moved. He was a man, meaning totally masculine. He would be bossy. She was bossy.

"Fane, I've lived alone for a very long time, making my own decisions, not only for myself but for my children. I have attitude. Sass. I wouldn't suit you. Eventually we'd fight all the time because you wouldn't be able to live with me."

His hand smoothed over her hair. She'd never liked anyone touching her hair. It took forever to put those cornrows in and then braid the entire mass. Somehow, she didn't mind when Fane stroked caresses and massaged her scalp. His touch felt good. *So* good. She could get lost in his touch. Forget all her objections and just want to stay right there with him forever.

Forever. The word reverberated through her mind. These people slept in the ground. They lived for a very long time. What else did they do?

She moistened suddenly dry lips, trying not to stiffen, but she must have because his fingers stopped moving along her skin and instead bit deep, as if he were holding her to him. "When you said you had to feed the ancients, what did that mean?"

"It is not safe for them to leave this monastery and go hunting."

She felt everything in her go still. In her mind, as erotic as it was, she knew just how often Fane's mouth had been on her neck and she'd felt the bite of his teeth.

"Blood? Like a vampire? Do you exist on blood?"

"Yes."

She closed her eyes again and held herself tight. Heart pounding. She'd asked, although she'd already guessed his answer. It was no wonder the humans who knew of vampires got Carpathians mixed up with them. "What is the difference?" she asked in a low, unfortunately shaky voice.

"We do not kill when we feed. We are respectful and we ensure it is not traumatic and not remembered."

"Teagan?" she asked softly. "She is with one of you?"

"She is Andre's lifemate." Fane framed her face with both hands and looked into her eyes. "He is totally devoted to her, as I am to you. He will never allow harm to come to her, and he will move heaven and earth to bring her happiness. He intends to relocate to the United States."

He brushed her mouth with his. Her lips were trembling. Her Teagan. Her beloved granddaughter. These men took her blood. She tried to roll away from Fane. She had to get to Teagan, somehow find a way to protect her.

"Hän sívamak."

Fane uttered the endearment in the voice that always tore her up inside. His arms locked her in place and she knew it was useless to fight him.

"I have taken your blood and you enjoyed it. You were never in any danger from me. Not ever. I could never harm you or see you come to harm. You hold my soul. You are light to my darkness and you light the way for me. You are *susu*. Home. Mine at last."

She shook her head. "Teagan . . ."

"Is happy. We will see them soon. Very soon. It takes three full blood exchanges for a conversion to take place. We have exchanged blood twice."

She didn't like the sound of that. "I really need to sit up. To put some clothes on." She needed armor. She needed space. *Two* blood *exchanges?* What did that mean? The word *exchange* inferred that she had taken his blood. Images rose, hazy, but there, of her mouth on his chest, of the taste she couldn't get out of her mind. The moment she thought of it, the craving began all over again.

Once again she fought for breath, gasping and choking. He leaned down and took her mouth, breathing for her. Breathing for both of them. He forced air into her lungs, his hands strong and sure, holding her close, comforting her even as he tore apart her world.

When he lifted his head, his eyes blazing down at her, moving possessively over her face, she shook her head. "I can't have this. I can't, Fane. It's not right."

"Do you hear yourself, *sívamet*? You are saying 'cannot.' You want this. You know it is right. We are right. You feel it, I know you do because I am with you. You are afraid you will lose your family, but you will not. I will see to your happiness, Trixie, and the thing that makes you who you are, the one thing that makes you happiest is your family."

Why did he sound so confident? Why did he make sense when none of what was happening to her made sense?

"Gabrielle told me that few women have children and that is why everyone is working to allow that possibility. My child-bearing days are long over. I'm too old. I wouldn't be of any use." Even as she admitted the truth to push him away, she felt like she'd shredded her own heart. Children were important to Carpathians. She'd gotten that from Gabrielle, but because Fane was sharing her mind, she picked up things about him. And children meant a lot.

"Of course you can have children. When you are converted, a woman of your age is just coming out of her teens.

Our children mature at around fifty years. You are the perfect age."

With a surge of adrenaline, Trixie shot up, dragging herself away from Fane, rolling out of the bed, clutching at the pillow. When he sat up, she bashed him with it. "I. Will. Not. Be. Having. Children." She bit out each word from between her teeth. She smacked him with the pillow again for emphasis.

He made a muffled gurgling sound, and she pulled the pillow up in order to make certain she hadn't done permanent damage. In any case, she was smacking the wrong portion of his anatomy. His blue eyes dancing, he burst out laughing.

"Woman, you have a penchant for violence." He caught the pillow, preventing the next blow.

She loved the sound of his laughter. He sat up as she tried to wrestle the pillow away from him. His laughter caught at her insides, making her heart melt and her stomach turn over in a slow somersault. She found herself trapped between his muscular thighs. They were like twin oak trees. Strong. Very defined muscles. Her gaze dropped to his groin. The smile faded from her face. He looked . . . delicious.

"You really are beautiful, Fane," she whispered, holding the pillow for protection. How could she walk away from him? From his need? His hunger? From everything he was offering to her? Without thinking, she wrapped her fist around his thick, silken shaft. So hot. Scorching hot. His cock jerked in her hand. Pulsing. Alive. So thick and long she wondered how he could have managed to get inside her.

"Trixie. I will take care of you. I will cherish and protect you. Your attitude is a trait I very much enjoy. When I have had enough you will know. The thing you need to remember about lifemates is that both parties need to make the other happy. It is a need."

She licked her lips, her hand sliding up slowly to the crown of his cock. He fascinated her. When she did that, keeping her fist tight, but gliding so slowly, the muscles in his abdomen rippled in response.

"Gabrielle was crying her eyes out. When her lifemate

came in he looked as if he might murder her," she pointed out. "He was the scariest man I've ever seen, and his look didn't change when he saw his woman's tearstained face."

"Aleksei will see to her happiness, Trixie," Fane said gently. He wrapped his hand around hers and moved her fist into a deeper rhythm. His breath turned ragged. "He cannot abuse her. They have things to work out, but they will do it because there is no other alternative. Their bond is strong. I can feel it when I am with them both."

He reached up and caught her braid, tugging until she sank to her knees on the ground. He had carpeted the floor in a deep sheepskin so the position was comfortable. She was beginning to forget what they were talking about. It had been important, but right now, there was his hunger beating at her. His desire. His need. She found he was right, she wanted— no, needed—to satisfy him.

His hand in her hair urged her head forward. She licked her lips. Touched the crown right where there were two droplets beading and instantly the taste of him burst through her mouth. Swamping her with that craving.

We can have babies fifty years from now, a hundred, he said softly, intimately, pushing the thought into her mind. *We need time to explore each other.*

I raised my family. I did that already. He had to know. And yet when she made the protest, mind to mind, and knew he heard, something in her flinched away from making that a deal breaker. She had never raised children with a man. A strong man. A man who would stick with her and help her. She'd never had that. She'd wanted it in a long forgotten dream, but she had accepted that she would never have it.

She licked at the soft—hard—beautiful crown, savoring the taste of him. *I've never done this.*

You do not have to do this now.

His hand remained in her hair, his fist surrounding hers while she glided her hand up and down, watching and *feeling* the shudders of pleasure whipping through him. She loved that she was doing that to him. She loved that she could. He was powerful and large. He was beautiful. And yet it was her making him feel this way. The deeper she was in his mind, the more she knew how he felt.

He let her in. Not in a small way; all the way. She saw the darkness in him. She saw his ability to battle. To kill. She saw the cost to him—the bleak loneliness—and she identified with him. He'd done his duty. He'd *chosen* to do his duty—just as she had.

He needed her. She bent her head and took him in her mouth, feeling the rush through her bloodstream and unable to tell whether it was his rush or hers. He wanted her. Her. Trixie Joanes. At her age. He wanted her with every single cell in his body. All of her. He *saw* inside of her. He admired her. Respected her. He liked her attitude and even her outrageous attacks on him. He didn't just like them. He *loved* them. She made him laugh. She made him think. More, she did this for him—created fire. Created paradise.

Want me back, Trixie. He breathed the invitation into her mind.

She felt his tone, that mesmerizing voice, like the touch of his fingers on her skin. She liked what she was doing to him, liked the way his body shuddered with pleasure and his mind was consumed with it. She knew, as she experimented with her tongue, just what he liked the most. Being in his mind was an amazing gift. She knew what to do. She could follow his mind, the erotic images and the pleasure streaking through him. His taste was so familiar, so perfect, and she wanted more. She wanted it all.

Want me back, Trixie.

She looked up at him as she took him deeper, as she rolled her tongue beneath the crown and felt his response. Watching his eyes. Those beautiful sapphire eyes.

Say it. Say you will come into my world with me and allow me into yours. Say it. Tell me you want me that much, hän sívamak. My beloved.

She couldn't give him up. She knew she couldn't. He was a gift. He thought she was a miracle and she knew he always would, but what he didn't get was that he filled her. That empty place where she'd been hollow for so long. For all her life. A place where she knew no man loved her or ever would. He did. He would. This beautiful, amazing man.

I want you that much.

The moment she gave him that, he reached for her, tugged her up and over him, so that she straddled his lap. His hand went between her legs to assure himself she was ready for him and he all but slammed her down over his cock. The breath left her lungs and she cried out, shocked at the streaks of fire racing through her. Then his mouth was once again at her neck, and this time, there was no haze, no veil. Just his mouth and his teeth, biting down right over her pounding pulse.

She cried out at the blistering pleasure surging through her. At the feel of his mouth pulling strongly, taking her blood. It didn't feel gross. It wasn't in the least frightening. It was entirely sensual, and all the while, his body moved in hers. His hips rose while his hands guided her to a faster rhythm.

Ride me, sívamet. Just like this.

She wrapped her arms around his body, lifting herself up and gliding down, a tight, hot spiral that sent flames racing through her. Through both of them. His pleasure was so acute, she could barely breathe with it. She wanted to give him more.

He lifted his head just enough to swirl his tongue over the pinpricks on her neck. He kissed her neck, her shoulder, and then kissed her mouth. She tasted that nectar, an ambrosia she couldn't get anywhere else. She loved the taste.

Give me more. Give me all of you.

He sounded like pure temptation. Sinful. Beautiful. Heaven. He brought her mouth to his chest.

There, beloved. Take all of me. There is no part of me that is not yours.

She felt the beads bubbling up, those deep crimson drops, better than any wine she'd ever tasted. Him. All Fane. Hers. She drank. Deeply. All the while, his hands dug into her hips and he took over the pace, filling her. Filling the hollow spot deep in her soul. Filling her mind where all that loneliness resided. Taking it all away.

I will cherish you for all time, Trixie, he whispered into her mind. *When you are ready for another family, you have only to tell me and we will do that together. Anything you want and I can provide, it is yours.*

His hand moved in her hair, tugging, telling her she'd had enough, and she did just as he had done—swirled her tongue over the small laceration as if she could close it, or as if she needed one last taste.

Fane rolled them, keeping them connected, her under him so that he could watch her face as he moved in her. She was so beautiful. He loved that she had lived life. That she'd known sorrow and happiness. That she'd lived her life as fully as possible and taught those she loved to do the same. She understood loneliness. She needed him in the same way he needed her.

He took her over the edge and went with her, and then stayed there, deep inside his lady. Feeling her beauty. Feeling her contentment. Loving that she relaxed beneath him, trusting him.

He kissed her over and over before he rolled to his side, tucking her close, his hand splayed over her soft belly. "This will not be easy. Andre told me the conversion is difficult, but I will get you through it, *hän sívamak*, trust me to get you through it."

She made a lazy circle with her fingertips on his abdomen. "Conversion?"

"From your world to mine. We cannot be apart. During the day, I cannot be in the sun. A paralysis overcomes me. It is getting close to dawn and we will need to be in the ground."

Trixie blinked at him. She went very still. "I can't sleep in the ground with you, Fane. I would suffocate."

"Not if you go through the conversion first," he pointed out. "You will become as I am. You will be able to see your family, Trixie, have no fears of that. We can make adjustments . . ."

"I want to be with you, Fane. I agreed to that," she said,

"and I don't go back on my word. But I'm not going to have to take people's blood to survive or sleep in the ground like a vampire. For one thing, I'm just too old for that nonsense. Seriously. You had better listen to me because I'm laying down the law here. I mean this. I'll sleep on a mattress next to you even if you look and act dead in your paralysis, but *not* in the ground. I don't even like camping."

She was "laying down the law." He liked that. It was completely preposterous of course, but he liked that she thought she could. A lot. His lady had courage and attitude; he was fairly certain she would try to face down a vampire if the situation warranted it.

"I can see I am going to have to watch you if I go hunting vampires. Clearly you are the type of woman to grab your silly vampire-hunting kit and try to help."

"My vampire-hunting kit is *not* silly," she denied. Then she ruined her adamant tone by snickering. "Okay, so it's a little bit silly. Most of the stuff is absolutely useless."

"I hate to tell you this, *sívamet*, but all of that junk is absolutely useless."

Beneath his hand he felt her stomach tighten in a long wave. She gasped and clutched his wrist. Her eyes widened in alarm. He immersed himself in her mind to steady and monitor her.

"I'm right here," he reminded gently.

She breathed through the pain, like a woman might when giving birth. In a way, he could see that. This was the death of a human and the birth of a Carpathian. Still, even with Andre telling him the procedure was difficult, he didn't expect such pain. It burned through her. Agony. She didn't make a sound. Not a single sound. Not a scream, not a cry, not even a moan.

She kept her eyes on his, and the one time he reached to get a cool cloth, her hands tightened on him and he brought his gaze back to hers. He heard her protest in his mind and knew she was trusting him to get her through and that meant his eyes were on hers at all times.

She was sick, a wrenching terrible cost as her body rid

itself of all toxins, and the vomiting seemed to last for far too long. It was brutal and ugly and she still never protested. Her body convulsed and she held on to him tightly, to his hand, and when she couldn't hold him anymore, he held her.

Hän sívamak, you are so brave. So very brave. We are almost done.

Fane talked to her using a mixture of his ancient language and her English, holding her to him all the while. Rocking her. Telling her of his life. Of the nights he'd held on to his dream of a lifemate. Of the woman who would be his someday. He explained Carpathian life to her. The pros. The cons. He kept his voice low and soothing, but mostly, he wanted her to know he was there with her. In her mind. Feeling the brutality of the conversion with her.

When he realized the terrible waves of pain had begun to lessen and he was certain he could do it, he leaned close, his mouth against her ear, even though he spoke in her mind. He wanted her to feel the brush of a kiss there when he spoke.

I will send you to sleep, Trixie. You no longer have to bear this burden. I can do so for you.

She shook her head, her fingers tightening around his. *Did Teagan go through this? Was Andre as good with her as you have been with me?*

Fane didn't feel as if he was good with her. *She* was the one who had suffered. He'd tried to bear the brunt of the pain, but it had been impossible. He couldn't send her to sleep until it was safe to do so. Now she didn't want to sleep. He could see and feel her exhaustion and already another wave of pain rushed through her body. Just like in the beginning, she breathed her way through it.

"Yes, beloved," he murmured aloud, "Teagan was converted by Andre. It is a painful process. We cannot take the pain away as much as we would like to do so. I am certain he was good to her. For Andre, the moon rises and sets with her."

She was silent, waiting for the pain to ebb away. "You do know this wasn't just painful; it was also humiliating for you to see me this way."

Her gaze still clung to his. He forced a reassuring smile, when he really wanted to weep for the agony he'd put her through. "If you go through something so painful and life altering, I will go through it with you. You will never be alone again."

Another ripple of pain caught at her. Clearly the worst wasn't over. He smoothed back her hair, and with a wave of his hand, cleaned her, the bed and the floor.

"That will come in handy." She managed a smile. Her hands clung to his. Her eyes hadn't moved from his. "I never did like housekeeping much."

"You trusted me," Fane murmured softly, his hand splayed across her stomach where he knew it felt much like a blow-torch had been taken to her insides. Her grip on him didn't waver. He leaned down to sip at the tears leaking from her eyes. She didn't need to know they were bloodred.

"You said you would get me through it, and I felt you there with me. I listened to our song."

"Our song?"

She nodded. "Your song and my song have blended together and I can't tell where yours starts because mine is so completely embedded in yours."

He still wasn't certain what she was saying. He could see the musical notes in her mind, silver and gold, moving around them in the air, sometimes close, sometimes spreading out. He couldn't see them without looking in her mind.

"That's how I found this place." She gasped and shuddered, her hands tightening on his wrists while she breathed deeply, breathed her way through the rippling pain.

Fane breathed with her, staring into her eyes. Inside her mind, he could see the musical notes turn to crimson and ruby. The notes blazed brightly, so brightly it hurt his eyes. Intermingled with the crimson and ruby notes were others in purple and black. Sorrow. Pain. He knew her song had merged with his.

"You take my breath away," he said softly. "Even in this,

when pain surrounds you, there is such beauty. Your song is amazing, Trixie. It's all about love and acceptance."

She moistened her lips. "So is yours."

"We fit."

She nodded. "I will not be so easy to live with."

He heard the warning in her voice. She thought herself so tough. She had no idea of the dangerous man he was. He would never be dangerous to her, but he would guard her fiercely. He wanted her to have her life—the one a young girl had dreamt of. He was the man who would be at her back and catch her every time she might fall. He didn't mind her little penchant for violence—he found it amused him, and most things didn't amuse him.

"I won't be, Fane," she warned again. "I think this is one of those cases where you should be very careful of what you wished for."

He brought her hands to his mouth, kissing her knuckles, an intimate gesture he hoped told her how he felt. "You trusted me, Trixie. You gave that to me."

"I believe in you, Fane. I don't know when it happened, because I've never believed in any man, but I knew you would see me through it, no matter how bad it got. More, I needed to know what my Teagan had gone through for her lifemate. I wondered if she had done so willingly, or if he forced her."

Fane winced. He knew she felt that wince in his mind. Through his body and the connection of their hands.

"I would say we have no choice, *hän sívamak*, but of course there is always a choice. I would not have survived without you. Andre would never have survived without Teagan, and Aleksei . . ." He leaned close to her. "Aleksei would have been difficult for any of us to kill. He is skilled beyond imagining. All of the ancients secluded here in the monastery are."

Her eyes moved over his face. Drifted. Her eyelashes fluttered. She was exhausted. Still, he didn't send her to sleep. He'd asked enough of her and she had stepped into his world willingly. She hadn't expected the agony of the conversion, but she'd handled it stoically. His lady. *His*. He had never believed, after so long, so many centuries of darkness, that he would ever find his lifemate. He had given up hope. The others in the monastery had given up hope as well.

"You needed me, didn't you?" she whispered.

"I needed you more than I needed air to breathe. I always will. You will never have to worry that I would look elsewhere for my happiness. You are home to me. You are my miracle, and having gone centuries without you, believe me, I know how precious you are."

"Fane."

She just said his name. A reprimand. She was reprimanding him because he was trying to reassure her. She thought he would be happy with a young, immature woman, but she had seen life and she was accepting of difficulties. She put family first. She was loyal and generous in her giving, which meant she would be in her lovemaking. She had every trait he could possibly want in a woman.

"Let me say this, Trixie. You deserve to hear it. You are my world. Do not ever be afraid of speaking your mind. Telling me what you think. If there comes a time when your outspoken opinions put you in danger, trust me to handle that."

She gave him a faint smile. "You mean by shutting me up?"

"If need be. But I do not foresee a lot of that happening in the future."

"Just so you know, if you silence me I will retaliate."

He laughed softly. "I have no doubt of that, beloved." He smoothed his hand over her hair. "You need to go to sleep, Trixie. When you wake, you will be completely healed."

She cleared her throat and, for the first time, looked frightened. "Do I have to sleep in the ground?"

He wasn't going to lie to her, but he wished he could soften the blow. For humans, that was one of the most difficult obstacles to overcome. Sleeping in the ground, for them, was like being buried alive. He picked that thought from her mind. For her, it was worse than taking blood. She liked the taste of him.

"You will go to sleep and I will put us there together. The soil will heal your body. You will not wake until I bring you back to the surface."

"How can you be certain?"

"I am extremely powerful, Trixie. You have no need to worry. I will be with you, and eventually I will teach you to open the earth on your own."

Her gaze clung to his for a long time. Searching. Finally she nodded. Relief swept through him. He needed for her to stop hurting. He gave her the command and she slipped into a deep sleep. Only then did he open the earth and call the rich minerals to him to aid in her healing process.

16

The room at the inn was very small and crowded. Gabrielle tasted fear in her mouth but she had to try. Natalya would kill this man. This human being. Brent Barstow. He was so mixed up. One moment she was talking about stem cell research with Natalya and the next, Barstow was in the room, a gun to the innkeeper's head. The innkeeper's family was downstairs, kidnapped.

So fast. Life changed in an instant like that. She couldn't get enough air. Natalya was already losing it, so close to the edge, so ready to tear Barstow to pieces. Gabrielle tried her best to calm down the situation. That had always been her role, the peacemaker, the one who stepped between combatants and tried for sanity in an insane situation. Even after Barstow was disarmed, Natalya was ready to rip him to pieces.

Gabrielle did what she always did—she stepped between the two of them. She knew what was coming. She'd relived this moment a thousand times and still, she couldn't prevent herself from stepping in front of Barstow. In one more second she would feel the first slice of his knife into her kidney. Three. Four. Then he would stab her chest repeatedly. Over and over. The agony would begin all over again.

She felt heat at her back and she swung around because that had never happened. She'd always been ice-cold. It was her nightmare, reliving the attack over and over, and the scenario never deviated because it had happened. Now, when she turned, there was Aleksei standing between her and the knife. She knew he took the blade, those repeated slices into his body. His eyes were on her face. His hand came up and he gently swept the hair back from her face.

She could feel pain radiating through him, but he didn't flinch. He didn't look away from her. She felt him then, in her mind, filling her with his strength. He gathered her into his arms and lifted her, cradling her against his chest, and he took her right out of there, out of the horrible little room where she couldn't breathe. Where she couldn't stop the stupid, *stupid* action of stepping in front of a killer. Of the terrible agony of the knife going into her flesh.

You are safe, Gabrielle. Open your eyes. You are here with me and I will never allow harm to come to you.

She took a breath of fresh air. Still, she didn't open her eyes. She wanted to feel his arms around her. He made her feel safe. She'd never felt safer than when she was with him, which was insane, because he could terrify her with one look. Still, she snuggled closer to him. To his rock-solid chest and his arms of steel. She wanted to stay right there and just dream sweet dreams of him.

She felt his mouth brush her temple. *I have a mind to turn sweet to erotic.*

That made her smile. She couldn't help it. *Why am I not surprised?* Still, she lifted her long lashes and stared into his brilliant green eyes. So piercing. So beautiful. So expressive. Right now, he looked at her almost tenderly, and she'd never seen that particular look on his face. Her stomach did a slow somersault and her heart shifted in her chest.

"How did you do that? How did you stop the nightmare?" She reached up to touch his face. It was daring; she'd never touched him on her own unless they were being fiercely intimate, and she couldn't help herself. Now she wanted to shape his face with her hands, to push the stubborn silky strand of hair falling around his face back.

"I told you, *kessake*, my woman cannot have nightmares. Not now. Not ever. Whatever upsets you must go away immediately."

She swept his hair back, loving the feel of the silken

strands against her fingers. "Thank you. I know you felt the blade of the knife." She shuddered and snuggled closer to him. "I didn't want that for you."

"I know, but I am your lifemate, Gabrielle, and you are always in my care. No harm touches you, not even in your dreams." He turned his head and pulled her finger into his mouth. His eyes held hers. "No one makes you afraid, not ever again, not even your own mother. I will always stand between you and anything that makes you uncomfortable."

Her heart beat wildly. Everything he said held a ring of truth, a stark, raw honesty that couldn't be denied. He meant what he said. She made a mental note to keep him away from her mother. Gabrielle loved her mother, but there was no doubt she was the queen of drama and tantrums. Her family had always allowed her to get away with it, but Gabrielle knew immediately, Aleksei wouldn't.

Looking into his eyes, her breasts suddenly ached and she felt a damp heat between her legs. His eyes were hooded. Sexy. Filled with hunger for her. She loved that. Everything he did seemed entirely sensual. Erotic just came natural to him. She touched her tongue to her lips.

Hunger beat at her. She wanted to lean forward and sink her teeth right into the pulse that beat so strongly in his neck. More, she wanted to crawl over him and taste every inch of his body. She wished she were brave enough to do it, but she could only look at him a little helplessly.

His hand stroked down the length of her hair. His fingers sifted through the strands. He scraped his teeth against the pad of her finger, sending little sparks shooting through her bloodstream.

"Gabrielle, do you have any idea how much you please me? I have claimed you, every single inch of you, for my own. When I want to kiss you, or touch you, or eat you, or be inside you, however, whenever I want that, I expect to have it. Why should your needs be any less than mine? I belong to you. That means you claim every single inch of me for your own. Not just my body, *kessake*, but my mind and heart and soul. If I expect you to give me those things, you should have those same expectations."

She liked that a lot. She liked that he wanted that for her. She was going slowly with him, feeling her way because she'd screwed up so badly when she'd realized she had a lifemate. She was shy with him, mostly because he was smoldering hot and she didn't know what to do with that. Mostly because he was dangerous and his temper burned as fiercely hot as his sexual needs.

"Did I not tell you I could have handled things better? We will look forward, not backward. You are not to blame for anything. I should have looked into your mind. I would have seen what happened, and I would have known you were an innocent. If there is forgiveness that must be had, you need to do the forgiving of my sins."

She didn't like that at all. Aleksei was an ancient and he had more than paid his dues. He had fought for centuries in darkness. She might not have known him, but once she was Carpathian and the possibility that he was out there somewhere was a reality, she should have taken better care.

"I have nothing to forgive you for, Aleksei," she stated firmly. "Nothing at all, and please, for me, don't ever say that again. I see you. What's inside you. You're not only a good man, you're an exceptionally great man. You deserve the best."

She saw that he would have protested, frowning, so she leaned close and took his mouth. It was daring. Scary. Thrilling. She pressed her lips to his, running her tongue along the seam there, just as he often did to her. At once he opened his mouth to her and she slipped her tongue inside, stroking caresses, building the heat. Even with her initiating the kiss, it was hot and a little wild.

Aleksei took over and the kiss went from hot and a little wild to totally out of control and scorching. She poured herself into him, uncaring how much she was giving away. She had to let Gary go, let go of being human and give herself totally to this man. In doing that, she accepted what he gave her. Accepted him. He wasn't perfect, but then neither was she. He made mistakes; so did she. They fit. She didn't know why, when he was so terrifying, she felt safe with him, but she did.

This was her way of telling him she was fully committed. Fully in his world. Fully trusting him. She kissed him over and over, her tongue matching his every stroke, her heart matching the rhythm of his—and it was perfect. She loved his mouth and the way he could use it. She loved his hands, cupping her breasts, caressing her nipples and then unexpectedly rolling and tugging, even pinching so that fire shot through her.

He seemed to know what her body craved and he gave her that. Still, she wanted to be the aggressor, to have him her way. She knew he wouldn't give her a lot of time. He took charge when it came to sex, but she liked that and he knew it. He'd given her every indication that he was willing for her to take the lead, and she wanted it. She used the flat of her palms to push him down, realizing for the first time that she was in a bed with him—the bed he'd given her—in their beautiful room—the room he'd created for her.

She lifted her head just inches, framing his face, sprawled out over him, her body pinning his beneath her. She felt his cock, thick and hard against her stomach, and part of her wanted to go there immediately, but not yet. Not before she took every inch of him for her own.

She brushed kisses over each of his eyes. They had gone dark, a deep green that filled with hunger. With lust. With something she didn't dare name, but that set her heart pounding and the pulse between her legs throbbing. She kissed his nose, that straight, aristocratic nose that was strong and fit perfectly in his masculine, very manly face. She kissed either side of his oh-so-talented mouth.

"I love your mouth," she whispered into it. "I love the way you kiss me and the way it feels between my legs when you're devouring me. So ravenous. I love the sound of your voice. You're mine, Aleksei, and I'm claiming you for myself. Every inch of you." She felt very daring. His eyes went even darker. Sexier. Pure sensuality.

She kissed her way along his jaw—that stubborn, very masculine jaw, always shadowed in a way she thought was sexy. "I love this short, dark shadow feeling so sexy on the insides of my thighs, the brush of it over my belly and grinding into my sex. It's the most amazing, sensual, *sinful* thing I've ever felt in my life and it's pure you."

She gave him that. He deserved that. He could make her come apart just by looking at her, but when he got down to business, there was nothing to compare. She wanted to make her exploration good for him, sexy for him, in the way he made it for her. She whispered her confessions to him, trusting that he understood what she was giving him and that he'd hold it precious.

She blazed a trail of kisses down his throat and across his neck to spend a few moments on his ear, and then his pulse where it beat so strongly in his neck. "I like that your heartbeat is always so strong and steady. I can rely on that—rely on your strength. Even when you scare me to death, I feel safe with you. I don't know why and I don't even care. You make me feel that way. I need that. I love it, and I love that you give that to me."

She kissed her way across his shoulders. She loved how broad they were, like a huge axe handle, his arms powerful and roped with muscle. She loved the tattoo, although it was so different, etched into his very skin, not with ink, but with something razor sharp.

She moved down, over his chest, ignoring her growing hunger. She wanted to taste him, to fill herself with his essence, but she had a plan and she was sticking to it. She would have all of him today. She would let him know he was hers in a way that could never be taken back.

"I love your chest, the muscle here and your abs that go on forever." She used her tongue to trace them, sliding down his hips, closing her eyes when her legs straddled his and she was so open. He could smell her welcoming scent, but she refused to be embarrassed. Not this time. Maybe never again. He was hers, and she was taking what was hers. She had the courage to do that much.

Her hands slid over his hot skin, noting how hard he was. There was no real give to his body, but she liked that, too. She felt his hands in her hair, and loved the way he seemed to like the way it fell over his body in sheets. She loved the way his muscles rippled as she got close to his cock.

She lifted up more so she could look at him. At what was hers. For her. Only for her. She would never have to worry about him finding another woman attractive. He belonged to her and he was wholly focused on her. She was in his mind now, and she knew the truth of that.

The knowledge made her feel beautiful and special in a way she never thought she could. He was big. Powerful. Thick. Long. She couldn't believe he could fit inside her, but he did and he was perfect. She stroked her hands down the thick column of his thighs. Trailed fingers inside, pushing his legs apart.

Aleksei accommodated her and when she glanced up to look at him, her stomach curled into a hot wave and blood rushed through her, pounding right in her clit. His eyes were pure sensuality. Erotic. Hot. Filled with lust. His fingers remained gentle in her hair, but she could feel the growing hunger in him. She needed to speed things up or she wouldn't get her way.

Her hands cupped his heavy sac. Velvet soft. She rolled her fingers gently and then bent to press kisses over him. She heard his gasp and she smiled. She was definitely making a statement. She sucked him into her mouth, her tongue teasing and her hands exploring. He nearly came off the mattress, but he didn't. He gave her that. But he growled.

"*Kessake*, whatever you are going to do, you'd best be doing it," he warned.

"You like this. I knew you would," she said. She licked up his shaft, all the way, curling her tongue around it, flicking at the underside of the crown.

His fingers tightened into fists in her hair. "You are killing me, Gabrielle."

He never shortened her name, and she liked that, too. She

liked the bite of his fingers in her scalp. She liked the rough in his voice. Mostly she liked what she was doing. She hadn't thought she would so much, but the moment her tongue swirled around the crown and she tasted him, that addicting masculine taste that was pure Aleksei, she knew she wanted more. All of it. And she was going to have it.

She took her time. He wanted her to hurry, she could feel the urgency building in him. He growled more than once when she pulled him deep into her mouth, taking in as much as she could, even though he stretched her mouth, just as he did her feminine sheath, but it was so good. So perfect. His hips bucking gently, his hand suddenly clamping down around hers, making her fist even tighter as she worked him.

"That is enough, Gabrielle," he bit out, between his clenched teeth. "You have to stop before it is too late."

She wanted it to be too late. She suckled deep and strong, using her tongue, flicking at the spot that made him go so crazy. She worked him with her fist, gliding up and down just as she did with her mouth. Tight. Hot. Wet. So hard. Velvet over steel. She loved that.

You said I could have whatever I wanted. I want this.

There was silence. She glanced up to meet his gaze and her heart nearly stopped at what she saw there, although her mouth didn't. His eyes glittered, so dark now with lust she felt the tension coiling tighter and tighter in her own body. His expression was nearly savage and she knew she was pushing his control, but she wanted this. Really, really wanted this.

Please, Aleksei. Give this to me.

She saw the sudden capitulation.

Turn around. Get your ass up here. I want my mouth between your legs. That is the only way you get this.

Her sex spasmed. Hard. Without taking him from her mouth, she turned her body, slowly straddling his chest, then his face, giving him what he wanted. At the first flick of his tongue her entire body shuddered and then came apart. That was how much she liked what she had been doing.

She had to pause and pant a little with her body fragmenting. He didn't stop, he lapped at her, suckled and flicked with his tongue, inspiring her. She focused on him, on his taste and following the heightening pleasure she felt in his mind. She wanted this for him. She wanted to give him this. Her idea. Her gift. Although she was beginning to realize she was being a little selfish because she liked it so much.

She moaned, the sound vibrating through his cock. His breath hissed out of him right through his clenched teeth, a long, slow rush of raw desire.

"Right there, *kislány*, that is perfection."

She liked the power, but more, she liked bringing him pleasure. He made her feel whole. Complete. When she was with him like this, no matter how bad things were in her mind, she wasn't alone, she wasn't afraid, and she was happy. Alive. He made her feel so alive and vibrant.

His hips began to move, turning aggressive. She kept her fist around the base of his cock but took him as deep as she could, feeling the fire spread through him. The streaks of lightning *she* gave to him. That was all Gabrielle. The feel of him moving in her mouth, one hand fisting in her hair, was exhilarating.

I love this, Aleksei. I love that you feel so good and I make you feel that way.

His mouth moved from between her legs and he caught her head in hard hands. He pushed in deeply almost before she could grab a deep breath. She relaxed, taking him deep as he thrust. He swelled, jerked, pulsed. Filled her throat with the aphrodisiac that was exclusively Aleksei. He pulsed over and over and she kept up with him with difficulty but determination.

"My turn, *kessake*," he hissed from between his teeth. "I get you the way I want you now. You have had your fun."

She liked that rough velvet in his voice, the one that said she'd brought him to the end of his control and he was taking over. She lapped at him, stripping him of every drop, taking her time in spite of the urgency of his tone. In spite of the fact that his fingers dug into her hips and he was once again rumbling with deep growls.

She felt his body shudder and knew he wasn't going to move her until she was finished. And she wouldn't be finished until she had all of him and knew he was completely clean and there was nothing semihard about him. Until he was all hard. Like a rock. Just for her.

"Satisfied?" he growled when she lifted her head just a little.

She smiled, breathing warm air over him. Loving that she had taken what belonged to her. "Very."

"You are done?"

She ran her tongue over her lips, leaned forward and kissed the crown of his cock, allowing herself one last taste. "*Now* I'm done." There was both satisfaction and a little mischief in her tone. Definitely triumph.

Aleksei didn't waste another moment on commentary. Decisive. She loved that. He caught her hips in hard hands, yanking her back toward him as he came up onto his knees, one hand pushing her head toward the mattress so that her bottom jutted up for him. He slammed his cock home, pushing through her tight, slick, scorching-hot folds, invading deep, driving inside to fill her full of him.

The beauty of it took her breath away. He was so large, stretching her beyond her imagining, the fiery friction so good she felt the fire already beginning to consume her. He'd just come and come hard, yet he was already thick and full and desperate for her all over again. The feeling, so exquisite, held so much pleasure it bordered on pain. She already skated so close to the edge from his mouth and fingers.

"Aleksei." She tried panting, trying to hold off the rising tsunami. "I can't hold it back. I can't . . ."

"Let go for me, *kessake*. Give me everything. Give me you."

Her entire body tightened at his words, and just like that she shattered. He kept moving in her. Relentless. Insistent. Her body gripped and pulsed around his. The ripples spread through her body along with the rush of hot blood. He picked up the pace, one hand sliding around to find her breast. His fingers shaped the soft, full mound and then found her nipple.

"Again," he demanded. "Now, Gabrielle. Again."

Gabrielle gasped when he tugged hard on her nipple and fire shot through her, sending a series of quakes through her body. Her third orgasm rolled straight into a fourth one. She sobbed his name, pushing back into him as he continued to thrust hard. So deep. She was afraid he would lodge in her womb and just stay there. It felt like paradise, and yet she needed to catch her breath. She needed to stop for just a moment, regroup, but there was no letup. He took her up again, hard and fast, his hips like a savage jackhammer, almost brutal in his possession of her.

"Again, *kislány*, give that to me again." His voice was rough. Raw. Pure sex.

"I can't. I can't, Aleksei." It would kill her. She was too high now, coiled too tight, her body already shattered.

She knew she belonged to him. She *knew* it. He showed that to her. Her body wasn't her own, and no one else would ever make her feel like this. His teeth suddenly sank into her neck, his fingers tugged hard on her nipple again and his other hand went between her legs, his thumb unerringly finding her clit.

"*Now*, Gabrielle. I want it again now." That was pure Aleksei, all command, one she didn't dare disobey. One she *couldn't* disobey. He made it impossible with his earth-shattering mouth, hands and cock.

She screamed. Her entire body shook. He thrust again, burying himself all the way while her sheath convulsed around him, gripping his cock in a strangulation hold.

So hot. Peje hot, little cat. I love how you come to pieces for me. How you give that to me. You are tight and hot and just plain peje paradise.

She would have collapsed, falling forward because there was no way to keep herself up, but his arm was an iron band around her waist. He eased her to the mattress, sliding out of her, his hands moving over her back and buttocks in a soothing pattern as her body rippled and shuddered for what seemed like hours.

Listen to my heartbeat, Gabrielle. Let your heart follow mine.

She realized her lungs burned for air. Her throat felt raw. So did her sex. Sated, but raw. She turned her head to look at him, smiling. *I think I have skid marks. Inside.* She touched her throat. Her hand drifted down her hip to disappear beneath her body. He got the idea immediately.

Aleksei instantly leaned into her, turning her body until she was on her back and he was over her, his expression concerned. He wrapped one palm around her throat and the other cupped her mound. She felt him moving inside of her, a white-hot energy, pure spirit, healing her in the Carpathian way. She hadn't expected that of him, not for something so minor as discomfort. A *delicious* discomfort.

At once the raw feeling was gone so there was only the delicious part. She found herself looking into his green eyes. Where there had always been possession, there was now something else, something she loved. She could see affection there. Maybe the beginnings of something more.

She touched his mouth with her fingertips. She knew he was already inside of her, in her soul. Deep. He'd claimed her body. "Thank you for taking away my nightmare. I've had that every single night since it happened."

"You stepped between them. The Carpathian woman and the human. Why?"

Aleksei scooped her up, cradling her against his body protectively. At least, to Gabrielle, the way he held her felt protective. Her heart fluttered in reaction. She slipped her arms around his neck while he carried her to a shallow steaming pool. When he sank down, he kept her on his lap.

"I don't know why I did it. When I was a child growing up, I did the same thing once I stopped hiding under my bed. Mom would lose her mind over something and throw a tantrum, which meant throwing objects. I would get between her and my sister so she couldn't hurt her. Not that she ever meant to, she didn't. She just had these blind, very destructive temper tantrums. They were over fast and then she'd be all smiles and comfort and 'let's get ice cream.' I think it's kind of automatic for me to do that sort of thing."

Gabrielle turned her face into his throat and licked at his skin. He always tasted so good. His hand came up to cup the back of her head, holding her close to him.

"Take what you need, *kislány*, your hunger beats at me. Then we will go hunting and I will teach you how to get food for yourself. I do not want you to, but you can practice in case of an emergency."

"You don't want me to hunt for myself?"

"The thought of you seducing a man with your voice to call him to you does not sit well with me. Still, you need the skill."

"Why?" She clutched at his shoulder, suddenly afraid of the reason, but needing to know.

"I will hunt the vampire again, and in doing so, there is the possibility of injury. You may need to bring blood back for me."

She took a breath and let it out slowly. She thought it would be an aversion to hunting humans that would upset her, but it was the thought of him injured. She stroked her fingertips over his pulse. So strong. So steady. Her rock.

"Why do you have to go back to hunting vampires?"

She could have bitten her tongue. It just slipped out. She felt like a child whining instead of a grown woman accepting the fact that Aleksei had been in thousands of dangerous situations and knew what he was doing. She was being selfish. Afraid for him. Afraid for herself. She knew Carpathian hunters battled vampires. They hunted killers and stopped them. They were necessary.

"*Kislány.*"

His voice was so gentle her heart turned over.

"You are Carpathian and you know the danger we face.

Both from humans and from vampires. I have certain skills and now that I am safe from the darkness . . ."

"Don't." She shook her head, keeping close to him, nestling her face in his throat, letting his pulse beat beneath her ear. "I see inside you, Aleksei. I see you fighting your demons. I see the darkness there."

"It is not the same, Gabrielle. There is no danger of me turning vampire. I will always have to watch myself around others. You are the only person on this earth who I know for absolute certain is safe. Any other . . ." He shook his head. "As for my demons, I think you are very good at handling them." He caught her face in his hands and tipped it up toward his, forcing her gaze to meet his. "My sweet woman. So ready to give me whatever I need when I need it. You face my demons, Gabrielle, on every rising, and you never flinch."

Gabrielle stared into his green eyes and let herself fall into them and drown there. He was a beautiful man whether he knew it or not. She knew it. She recognized the way he was far before he ever showed it to her. She had nearly destroyed this man. At first she thought she deserved to feel his demons raging, but then she realized he would never hurt her. He would push her limits of comfort, but he would also bring her so much pleasure sometimes she thought she might die of it.

"I'm afraid in your world," she admitted. "All the time." She knew it was why she clung to the familiar. She had chosen Gary because he shared that human world with her in such an unfamiliar and dangerous place.

His fingers sifted through her hair with infinite gentleness. "Gabrielle. This is your world, too. You are with me now. You will never have to be afraid again. I have centuries of skill in battle. *Centuries.* There is little the vampire or his puppets can bring to me that I have not seen. You will always be protected. You can live your life, however you want to live it. We can have the house you want, or we can go back to the mountains where the prince resides and you can continue your work. Regardless, you can do so without fear. You trust your body into my keeping, trust that I will protect you at all times."

She searched his expression. His eyes. She had seen Aleksei in a rage, a full-blown fury that turned her blood to ice water, but this was new. This was gentle. And sweet. Tears stung. Burned. She had to blink rapidly to keep from making a fool of herself. She nodded slowly.

"Take my blood, before I decide I need you again."

She liked the gruff in his voice. She knew he wanted her again, the evidence was tight against her buttocks where she sat on his lap, but he was determined to show her how to hunt, and although she wanted him as well, she liked the idea of getting out into the open.

She moved her face back to his neck and inhaled his masculine scent. Already his taste was on her tongue and the fierce, gnawing hunger beat at her, overcoming her inhibitions. At least, she told herself it was the hunger, but when she was being strictly honest, it was Aleksei. She wanted him, all of him. Including this. He had made the act of feeding erotic.

She licked over his pulse and felt it jump beneath her tongue. Her arms went around his neck and she settled close to him, pushing her breasts into his side while she brought his head closer to her. Deliberately she used her teeth to scrape gently back and forth, building the tension. He was a master at that with his touch. With his mouth. She was a quick study. She always had been.

She felt his body tighten. His muscles lock in place. Beneath her buttocks, his cock jerked. Hard. She kissed his pulse, just a brush, a barely there kiss. He groaned and his hand tightened in her hair.

"You are playing with fire, *kislány*. If you do not want to spend the entire rising flat on your back with me playing for a long, long time before I allow you release, keep this up. I do not have endless control."

She smiled against his pulse, liking that she could make him lose control. His "punishments" weren't very scary, and in fact, they mostly made her not want to be so "good." Still, she did want to get out a little bit. She couldn't help herself, even while she obeyed him, she slipped into his mind as she bit down with her teeth, just to feel what that sensual bite did to him.

The taste of him burst through her—through him. She felt the intensity of his pleasure as she fed at his neck, taking what he so freely offered—more—what he'd all but ordered her to take. His essence. Rich. An ancient's blood was different, she realized. Aleksei's tasted and felt like him. Dangerous. Hot. Rich. Masculine. Very, very powerful. Aleksei, who could drive away nightmares, standing between her and her past. If he could do that . . . She closed her eyes and savored his taste, her fingers moving in the silk of his hair.

Aleksei held her tightly, nearly crushing her to him, his hand moving over her body, shaping her breasts, sliding his palm down her side to her hip. Over her back. He touched and held her as if she meant everything to him. Tears burned close at the beauty of it. At the beauty of being his entire focus. His only. The one.

Gabrielle swept her tongue over the pinpricks in his neck and rested her head against his shoulder. "You're really beautiful, Aleksei," she whispered. "So much so, sometimes you take my breath away."

He was silent a moment. Tense. She felt the way his body had gone hard and tight. His hand went to her chin. She didn't want him to see her ridiculous tears so she stubbornly tried to keep her face buried against his shoulder. She should have known better. Aleksei didn't take no for an answer. Not about anything. His hand moved to her jaw and he turned her face to him, tipping it up so his eyes could drift over her.

"Kessake."

Her heart beat faster. There was possession there. But there was so much more. His eyes burned over her. Marked her. His brand sinking deep. The sound of his voice, calling her *little cat* in his own language.

"I almost destroyed you, Aleksei. I could have lost you. The world could have lost you, all because I was so foolish and didn't understand the gift I was given."

His thumb moved through the trail of tears. "I want you to stop this. Right now, Gabrielle."

His tone was velvet soft, but still commanding. Firm. Gentle. She had no idea how anyone could manage that, but he did.

The pad of his thumb followed the track of her tears right down her face, erasing them. His mouth moved close and he sipped the tears from her lashes and then used his tongue to wipe every evidence of them away. His hands went to her hips, fingers digging deep, and he turned her, right there in the pool.

"Straddle my lap, *kessake*, we are not nearly finished before we go hunting."

He really gave her no choice, not that she wanted one, but the moment she turned, her legs over his hips, her breasts tight against his chest, his cock buried deep, his mouth was on hers, and everything fell away but him—everything but Aleksei and the feel of his hard body and the pleasure he brought to her.

17

Men are stronger and you can take a little more from them, especially if they are big. If you can avoid it, do not go into a house, even if invited. And you must be invited in if you plan on taking blood. That is a protection measurement for all as well as showing respect. It will not be difficult for you to get an invitation, you will simply use your voice to enthrall, but still, the risks are greater. Children. Family members. Not a good thing, *kessake*."

Gabrielle stood in the shadows with Aleksei just outside a bar. The sky drizzled silver drops but he kept the rain off her, his arms locked around her waist, keeping her body tucked close to him, sheltering her. She leaned back into him, liking the way he surrounded her with his protection. He made her feel safe. Her body was trembling, but she didn't know if it was from nerves or excitement.

No one had ever bothered to teach her these skills. Aleksei wanted her to learn to be self-sufficient. She loved that. She wasn't certain she could actually lure someone to her and take their blood, but she wanted to try.

"Do you understand, Gabrielle? It is important. You can get into a house if you cannot find adequate prey elsewhere and only in an emergency."

"I understand," she said softly, reaching back to touch his face with her hand. "I'm listening. And I'm grateful you're taking the time to teach me."

He nuzzled her hand with the slightly rough scruff on his

jaw and then turned his face to press a kiss right into the
center of her palm.

"I am enjoying our time." He moved the long slide of hair
off the nape of her neck, pushing it around her left shoulder
as she dropped her hand. That gave his mouth access to bare
skin and her right ear, unhindered by her thick hair. "It is
always better to find a place such as this one where there are
numerous patrons to choose from. Always choose one entering if possible. They have not had anything to drink and so
they are untainted. Those coming out can be used in an emergency, but their blood is not that good."

She moistened her lips, more aware of him, of his strength,
of his hunger, of his power. When he moved he was fluid, a
flowing of muscle and bone; when he stopped, he was utterly
still. It was impossible to conceal the power in him, and he
didn't try. When he didn't want to be seen, he veiled his presence, rather than trying to blend in.

She sensed a sudden change in him, in his focus, and a
shiver of trepidation and excitement went down her spine.
She'd never felt more alive.

Aleksei's mouth moved over her ear, causing a slow roll in
the pit of her stomach. "This one, *kislány*, take this one. Use
your voice. Draw him to you. Bring him into the shadows. I
am here, watching over you. I will ensure nothing goes wrong."

She licked her lips again, hearing her heart pound. Could
she really do it? Walk up to a man and enthrall him with her
voice alone? Draw him back into the shadows with her and
leave him with the vague impression he'd had a conversation
and nothing else had happened?

She studied the man approaching the pub. He was young,
in his early twenties, and he looked strong. She felt Aleksei's
arms drop away from her and she took a step out of the shadows, on a path to intercept the young male. His eyes came to
her immediately and he instantly smiled, slowing his purpose-
ful stride.

Gabrielle smiled in return, and his head jerked up. She
stopped where she was and allowed him to come to her, one

hand going to her hair, sliding her fingers through the silky mass as she waited. His gaze dropped to her breasts as they lifted beneath her blouse with the action, and then moved back up to her face.

"Come with me," she said softly, using a mesmerizing tone. "Come with me now." She held out her hand to him. "I have need of you."

She couldn't believe the way her voice was so sensual. She knew Aleksei had given her that   the confidence she'd never had in herself as a seductress. He made her feel beautiful and sexy.

You are beautiful and sexy. Reach for his mind, kislány. You need to know you have complete control, not just that he's seduced.

Not only was Aleksei's voice gentle, but she could feel his pride in her. That made her want to glow, and it surprised her at the same time. He was a man who would be jealous and not want another man touching her. This was truly the last thing she expected him to help her with. She admired him all the more for it.

The man took her hand, moving in close to her. She didn't like it. He didn't feel like Aleksei felt. The burn of his sexual desire felt wrong. She could barely stand the touch of his skin against hers. She almost pulled away, but Aleksei was there, in her mind, supportive and strong.

I like that you do not like his touch, Gabrielle. You are doing very well. Reach for his mind. Take control of it so he cannot weave fantasies of you.

She hadn't considered that he might do that and again was grateful for Aleksei's guidance. She took a breath and forced past the barriers in the male's mind. For a moment she felt sick, her stomach protesting the invasive act.

You are not hurting him in any way. You are protecting him. Do not worry so much. We will remain to ensure he is well after. If possible, always do that. You never want to inadvertently take too much blood and leave them unprotected. Aleksei's voice stroked her mind. Gentle. Supportive. Persuasive.

She knew if she backed off, told him she couldn't do it, he wouldn't be upset with her, but she *wanted* his approval. She wanted him to have reason to be proud of her. More, if he was ever in trouble and needed her to get blood to feed or help heal him, she was determined to know how.

The man's mind was filled with all kinds of images of the two of them writhing on the ground together. She ignored that and took control, soothing him, planting a brief conversation about directions. She walked him right up to Aleksei.

Aleksei reached for her, his hand curling around the nape of her neck, pulling her to his other side and away from the man who docilely stood in front of them, keeping her close to him as he reached for the man. Gabrielle watched as, without preamble, Aleksei took over, pushing into the man's mind, calming and soothing him, as he sank his teeth deep and drank. All the while he reaffirmed the idea that the young man had had a conversation with a pretty tourist asking for directions.

Gabrielle stayed in the man's mind, to assure herself that he wasn't afraid or that he didn't know what was happening. She couldn't help but see that he was a good man, hoping to find the "right" woman to settle down with, but he knew all the available women in the village and they weren't for him. He was a hard worker, loved his parents and was well educated. He was wrestling with the idea of staying and helping his father in his business, or getting out so he had a chance of finding a woman to love. She liked him all the more for that and found herself feeling protective of him.

Aleksei's hold tightened on her. He clamped her firmly to his side as he finally raised his head. With one hand he lowered the man to the ground and allowed him to rest against the crude wooden bench there.

"You cannot get attached, *kislány*. It is not healthy. Nor would I like it. I prefer that you allow me to hunt for you and feed you. I will take you on the hunt with me to help hone your skills, but you do not need to collect other men."

She winced. Honestly, it felt as if he'd delivered a hard

body blow. She almost wished it were physical, because, really, it hurt like hell when he reminded her of her indiscretion. She tried to pull away, but his arm locked her in place. He caught her chin and forced her to meet his eyes.

"I was teasing you, Gabrielle, not chastising you. I did not have Gary in my mind at all. I understand what happened between you and I do not blame you for it. I misread the situation and handled it wrong. I have told this to you and I expect you to hear me this time and let it go."

That was both sweet and infuriating. He could be so arrogant, ordering her to just let it go when she'd caused so much damage, like she could just forget everything because he told her to.

A faint smile lit his face for a brief moment and then, just that fast, was gone. "When you are angry with me, little cat, your eyes blaze fire. I like that." He took her hand and brought it to the front of his trousers so that her palm covered the thick bulge there right through the material. "You make me as hard as a rock when you get that fire in your eyes. Mostly because it reminds me of how you catch flame when I touch you."

She didn't know what to do with that, so she ignored it. "You cannot just order me to forget something and expect it to happen."

She should have moved her hand, they were right out in the open, but his hand had clamped hard over hers and she knew if she tried there would be a struggle. The man he'd used for food stirred and groaned softly. She wiggled her palm to try to warn Aleksei his prey was coming out of the enthrallment. More, she could hear two other men approaching with heavy footsteps.

Aleksei refused to relinquish her hand but moved them both back farther into the shadows. His free hand tipped her chin up to his. *I would not ever embarrass you or allow another man to see what is mine and only for me. Still, when I want your touch, or to touch you, I will have it. You will have to trust me to protect us.*

It feels . . . She wanted to say *like exhibitionism,* because it did, even though now she believed him when he said others could not see them. And he'd implied he would do far more than press her palm over his material-covered cock.

It feels like heaven, Gabrielle. When you touch me, it always feels like that. No one can see us. It is always just the two of us.

Deliberately he slipped his hand inside her blouse and caressed her breast through the lace of her bra. And then her bra was gone and her breast was being cupped in both hands, his thumb sliding across her nipple. The breath left her lungs as whips of lightning streaked straight to her sex. Aleksei's mouth came down on hers, and the world fell away. Her brain malfunctioned. Melted. Sanity was gone and there was only him and his mouth and his hands.

Abruptly he was gone. His head had turned toward the two men now parallel with them. His breath hissed out, a long dangerous signal, as he thrust her behind him. She realized her bra was back in place and her clothes were in complete order. She blinked rapidly, trying to regain her ability to think. To understand what was happening.

Aleksei? The air around them had gone from fresh and clean to a murky, disturbing, very heavy feel. She pressed a hand to her stomach and tried to peer around his large frame.

Aleksei swept Gabrielle back again with one hand, this time using force. *Stay.* He bit the word out, snapping the command in her mind, her only warning. *If you do not obey, I will force your obedience.* He let her see he meant that as well. She caught at the back of his shirt for support, her hand fisting in the material. She didn't pull. She didn't fight him. She didn't protest or even act, in her mind, angry with him in spite of his very real threat to her.

He studied the two men approaching the man he had used for feeding. Both were tainted. Both stank of vampire. Both stank of conspiracy. They had clearly been headed to the pub, and when he lightly touched their minds, he knew there was someone inside waiting for them. He feared he knew what that someone was. Not human.

He shared his knowledge with Gabrielle. Her fingers

twisted tighter in his shirt, but she remained very still, and
he felt her there in his mind.

Can you control them?

He realized she was afraid for the young man they were
helping off the ground and onto the bench.

*If necessary, but they are connected to what is inside and
the pub is full tonight. If he knows there is a hunter out here,
he will not leave peacefully. There will be a bloodbath.*

"Izaak? What is wrong? Have you had too much to drink?"

The language was Polish, not English, but Aleksei interpreted in his mind so Gabrielle could better understand.

The one holding Izaak's collar stiffened. "He has been
tainted."

Gabrielle's fingers dug into Aleksei's back. *I thought you
said no one could tell. Did you leave a mark?*

Aleksei's breath hissed out again in a long rush of annoy-
ance. His woman thought he would make such a mistake? *I
will not chastise you for that insult as you are very distraught,
but I do not leave evidence or marks. There is something else
here. Something I have yet to understand. I rarely run across
a puzzle I have not seen before.* He very carefully slid into
Izaak's mind, staying very quiet and unmoving, so as not to
draw the attention of either of the puppets.

Are they vampire?

*Human, but a vampire controls them. They do not realize
that, of course. They believe they are hunting the vampire.
The vampire is using them to hunt the Carpathian people.*

*If they see me in Izaak's mind, will they know what hap-
pened? Is that how they knew? Can they get into his mind?*

Aleksei was careful in looking around. Ordinarily, a puppet was simply that—a body for a vampire to use any way he
saw fit. He could use the eyes to see what the puppet saw. He
could use his mind to move in another's. He was fairly certain
the puppet had discovered Izaak had been used for blood all
on his own and would report to his master. And that just might
draw the master out to them. He would want to examine Izaak
himself to see what he was dealing with.

"Kill him, Denny," one said. "Kill him before he turns into one of them."

"Not yet, Vaugn. We need to take him to the cabin and force him to tell us everything. You got the drug on you?"

It was telling that Denny had switched to English. Vaugn had to be one of the hunters who had come from out of the country.

Denny is Denny Jashari, a local whose son was a serial killer along with his nephews. They tried to kill Andre's life-mate, Teagan. Andre took care of them, but Jashari is clearly the head of the local vampire-hunting society. They operate in secret, but mostly target people they do not like. They accuse them of being vampire and then they kill them. Andre told us they were hunting Teagan. Aleksei gave Gabrielle the information.

He continued to stay in Izaak's mind, waiting to see what Denny and Vaugn would do next.

Vaugn slipped his arms around Izaak. "Get up, boy. Let's walk it off."

Izaak cooperated, trying to find his feet when he was dizzy. Denny suddenly straightened and looked around warily. He actually looked right through Aleksei. "Drop him, Vaugn," he ordered. "Drop him right now."

Vaugn let go of Izaak, and Izaak swayed and tried to reach for Vaugn so he wouldn't fall. Vaugn shoved him away, looking around, too, his face revealing anxiety. Aleksei smelled their fear. He pressed Gabrielle back. He knew what was coming.

The door to the pub opened. Music and laughter poured out into the night. The rain hissed as it fell on the man striding out. He was tall and confident-looking. Handsome to the extreme. He seemed ageless, and moved with ease. He turned his gaze on Denny and Vaugn and both men froze.

"Good evening." He sent both a smile. The smile did nothing to light his eyes or illuminate his face. Instead, he actually appeared menacing. He stopped very close to them. "You did not inform me you were taking a prisoner."

"He has been used," Denny said, his voice higher pitched. Strangled. As if he couldn't get enough air.

"And you knew this how?"

"You taught me how to know, Master Aron. I touched him, and he was cold, and his blood volume was low enough to make him dizzy." Denny cleared his throat repeatedly and his hand crept up protectively, as if he might pry strangling fingers away.

"And still, with me giving you that gift to aid your cause, you did not think to inform me of this man?" The vampire spoke quietly. Calmly. His tone was deadly.

Aleksei recognized him from his youth. He went by the name of Aron Mazur. Andre was on his trail, so he knew the Carpathian hunter most referred to as "the Ghost" could be close.

"I thought I wouldn't bother you unless he had important information," Denny stammered. Wheezed. Tried to suck in air. "Vaugn has the drug on him and we thought we would use it, extract the information and then bring it to you."

Aron's eyes, flat and cold, entirely without emotion, stared at his puppet. "Do you think I do not know what is in your mind, Denny? I could split open your head and see the rotten debris there. You know what I am. Vaugn is a pawn, nothing more. A pawn to both of us, but you wanted to show him your power. You wanted him to fear you. Your ego once again has gotten the better of you." His eyes began to glow a dark red. "I thought we were past that. Do you need another lesson?"

Aleksei felt Gabrielle's forehead against his back. He reached behind him and found her free hand, threading his fingers through hers and bringing her hand to his thigh. The bracelet on her delicate wrist glowed with fiery flames in protest of the evil in the air, but the links were cool to the touch.

He knew they couldn't be seen, but still, he was careful no air was displaced. He realized Gabrielle had never been in the presence of such evil. The vampire had chosen to give up his soul, deliberately torturing his prey before he killed it, so he could get the adrenaline high. He was wholly evil, and he had found a human counterpart in Denny Jashari.

Gabrielle had been stabbed multiple times by a man infected with fanaticism, poisoned by one such as Jashari. The Jashari family was clearly twisted, producing men who raped, tortured and killed women. It wasn't a huge step to see how Aron Mazur had found Denny and enlisted his help rather than killing him. Still, Mazur would want to keep him cowed and bowing before him.

He knew Gabrielle was frightened. He could feel her body trembling and her nightmares were very close, but when he took her hand and pressed it against his thigh, she quieted, her breathing following his. Her heart as steady as his. She gave him that gift. Trust. In the face of extreme danger, she gave him that.

He bent slowly, bringing her hand to his mouth, gently kissing her knuckles and rubbing the pad of his thumb over the links of her bracelet. It was a weapon, one he knew would come to her aid if she was in trouble. He liked seeing it on her wrist, especially when she was naked. He liked knowing it was there just in case. Knowing he had to show her he had absolute confidence no matter the odds against them, he returned their joined hands to his thigh.

Denny staggered back, away from the master vampire, clearly terrified, his hand still at his throat. His face was red and swollen-looking. It was difficult to listen to him gasping for air. Vaugn looked from one to the other, clearly uneasy and not knowing what to do. He didn't like being called a pawn, but he didn't want to challenge the man he knew as Aron Mazur. He didn't try to help Denny. He moved away from both men.

Aron smiled, revealing sharp, very white teeth. "I thought you would get my point, Denny." He waved his hand and Denny's body sagged as he drew in a deep, gasping breath. With that, the vampire turned toward Izaak.

Aleksei squeezed Gabrielle's hand and then let go of it. *Step back slowly. Give me room, and do not reveal yourself for any reason, even if you think I am in trouble.* He pushed the order into her mind. *Do not disobey me, Gabrielle.*

She stepped back. He wasn't satisfied. She had shown courage on several occasions. She had thrown herself on him in order to protect Gary. She had come to him in the courtyard, although he had shown her both his darkness and his demons and she had known she was taking her life in her hands. He had no doubt, should she think he was losing the battle, she would try to enter in spite of her great fear.

I need you to give me your word you will remain hidden throughout, or I will have no choice but to bind you.

Aleksei. What if . . . She trailed off when he lifted his hand toward her.

Now. He nearly spat the word. They were running out of time. Any moment now, Mazur would give up his little show to take possession of Izaak's mind and all hell would break loose.

For you, but it's the most difficult thing you've asked me to do.

He knew that. He also wasn't positive she would be able to keep her word should she believe he was in trouble.

Andre is close by. I do not know how close. Should there be trouble, reach out on the common path and call to him. He will come for you.

He said no more. He let go of Gabrielle and reached for the darkness in him. The demons that drove him. They settled into him like old friends, familiar cloaks that covered every bit of humanity, leaving only the warrior, the predator.

He waited. Crouched. Calm. His heart rock steady. His breathing unchanged. Still, the monster was there, close to the surface, stretching, ready. Waiting with him.

He felt Mazur invade Izaak's mind. The vampire struck, a piercing spear of pain, deliberately cruel. Izaak cried out. Screamed in pain. Went to his knees clasping his head in his hands. Vaugn leapt back, looking scared, as if he wanted to run. Denny smirked and moved closer, obviously enjoying the torture of Izaak, a man he had known since the man had been a boy.

Aleksei didn't wait. He struck at Mazur, a hard blow, meant to end the battle before it really began. He used the trap of Izaak's mind to gain control, pushing hard into the master vampire's rotten mind, breaking through every barrier so the rot was exposed. So that his every pawn and puppet were at Aleksei's command. Mazur had no real choice; he turned to flee, desperate to save himself as his brain began to fragment.

There was no holding on to his ability to keep his human image. The rot and decay was so severe, he stood, his flesh sloughing from his bony skeletal frame. His teeth were all filed to points, stained black and red. His nose was no more than a hole in his face and his eyes were sunken and red. He screeched his fury and fear as his thick head of hair disappeared to be replaced by nothing but patches of long dull strands of gray that looked and smelled filthy.

Aleksei hit him hard in the chest, his fist driving deep, impaling Mazur, lifting him into the air so his body weight added to the blow, helping to embed Aleksei's fist and arm deep into the chest cavity. The blow was so strong his fist traveled through muscle and bone, straight to the shriveled, blackened heart.

Gabrielle gasped as black blood poured down over Aleksei's arm and his skin actually smoked and burned, as if the substance were acid. Aleksei didn't so much as wince. Denny crawled away toward the darker shadows of the mountains. Vaugn whipped out a knife and rushed Aleksei.

It took every ounce of discipline she possessed to remain where she was. *Aleksei!* She tried to warn him, but she *felt* the blade sliding into his back. Ice-cold. Fiery hot. She could see Vaugn behind him, but she couldn't see what he was doing, not from where she was. She could only see Aleksei's arm being charred to the bone, the smell of burning flesh filling her lungs.

She pulled in a ragged, gasping breath, and gave up fighting her instincts. She couldn't help him with the master vampire, but she could with Vaugn. She tried to move and nothing happened. Nothing. Her feet were planted firmly, as if they'd taken root. She couldn't move at all. Her heart contracted with fear. Her stomach knotted. She might have to stand right there and watch Aleksei be slaughtered.

He whirled around, still holding the master vampire straight up in the air, his fist and forearm buried deep in the vampire's chest. Mazur shrieked horribly, the sound reverberating up and down the streets of the village, a hideous noise that hurt ears. He sounded like a wounded animal, and yet he raked and clawed at Aleksei's face. Somehow Aleksei avoided the wicked talons much of the time, although several times they scored deep furrows not only in his face, but also in his shoulder. Clearly the vampire was trying to gouge out Aleksei's eyes and rip open his neck.

Aleksei swung around to face Vaugn, who was still stabbing at his back, and as he did, he threw the master vampire into the man with the knife. The blade went into the vampire, straight into his back. The force of the throw buried the knife to the hilt and sent both vampire and Vaugn tumbling together several feet away from Aleksei.

Aleksei's arm emerged from the chest wall. In his fist was the blackened heart of the vampire. Immediately he dropped it and held his burned arm toward the sky. Lightning sizzled. Forked. Streaked down to slam into the heart, incinerating it. Even as he did so, Aron Mazur was up on his feet, rushing Aleksei, slamming into him, his monstrous teeth driving into Aleksei's shoulder, ripping and tearing.

The vampire suddenly stiffened, his mouth stretched wide in another scream, although this one was silent. He crumbled to the ground and the whip of lightning struck his body, turning it to ash. Aleksei casually bathed his body in the white-hot energy and then looked toward Vaugn.

Gabrielle went to her knees and was sick, over and over again. Dry heaving, gagging, her stomach protesting what her mind couldn't deal with. She still couldn't move her feet and she was fairly certain Aleksei would be furious with her, but at that moment she didn't care. Her world crumbled around her. She had thought she could do this, live with him in his world, be what he needed her to be, what she *wanted* and needed herself, but she knew she couldn't. She could never, ever be a true lifemate to an ancient warrior like Aleksei—and clearly he knew that.

Vaugn stared in horror at the ashes on the ground, at the whip of lightning and Aleksei, who hadn't even changed expression. He tried to push himself up off the ground to run, but he couldn't move, somehow frozen to the spot. He watched in absolute horror as the lightning burned bright. Thunder rolled. He couldn't stop looking as the whips of white-hot energy took on renewed life, forking out, reaching with burning greed right toward him. He didn't scream. He didn't have time. His hand had gone up in protest. He opened his mouth, but the whip had already reached him. He didn't even feel the burn. He was simply gone as if he'd never been.

Immediately, Aleksei turned to Gabrielle, his eyes still burning with a kind of menacing fury. She knew the instant he released her, but she didn't move. She was still heaving. Still gagging. The smell of burnt flesh permeated the air. She watched as Aleksei went to Izaak and gently put his hands on the sides of the man's head. She saw him leave his own body, making himself completely vulnerable as he went into Izaak's mind to heal it and remove all memory of what had taken place.

Aleksei gently laid the man down on the bench and planted memories of a great night with friends at the pub in him. As soon as he was certain the man would be fine, he waved his hand to clear the air of all scent of battle as well as clean the ground of all evidence. Only then did he lift the barrier between the pub and the outside world he had hastily erected so no sounds of the battle could be heard inside.

He turned to Gabrielle. His lifemate. She was still down on her knees and now there were tears in her eyes and tracking down her face. He pushed down his temper, knowing his reaction came out of fear for her. Had she managed to move before he could stop her, she would have drawn the attention of the vampire and Vaugn. Denny was long since gone in the woods, hiding like the coward he was, but she could have been harmed. Still, he didn't have the heart to chastise her, not when she was looking like her heart was breaking.

"Come here to me," he said softly.

She shook her head and his heart clenched in his chest. She shook her head hard. Adamantly. He knew immediately her head was in a space that didn't bode well. He didn't bother to argue. He went to her, gathered her up and streaked across the night sky, allowing the rain to hit both of them, drenching them, washing his own blood from his body.

He felt her move, even with the tears in her eyes, reaching up to his shoulder where the ragged tears were, her tongue instinctively lapping to use the healing saliva in her mouth to close those lacerations. Then she was holding his face between her hands, doing the same thing, ignoring that they were in the air, air that grew steadily colder as he went up the mountain to his chosen lair. All the while she wept while she healed his face, and then sought out every other place on his body, examining his back for evidence of the knife wound, eventually finding even the smallest cuts to heal.

By the time he reached the safety of his cave, set the safeguards and had her on the bed, her head in his lap while he tried to comfort her, he honestly didn't know who was more upset—Gabrielle or him.

"That is enough, *kislány*. You are going to make yourself sick and there is no need for these tears. I am just fine. So are you. Nothing happened."

Her fingers balled into a fist and she thumped his thigh. "Something happened," she declared through her sobs. "I have to go. I have to leave you. I can't stay here with you."

He tensed. Huge knots formed in his belly. His hands tightened convulsively in the thick mass of her hair. He made himself breathe. In. Out. Waiting for the fury to pass. Waiting for his demons to quiet.

"Gabrielle, you are my lifemate. We do not leave each other. Talk to me. Tell me what is going on in that head of yours. I am being polite and allowing you your space, but if you cannot stop, I will have no choice but to take this information from you so I can stop you from making yourself sick. Talk to me."

"I can't do this. I should never have been converted." She covered her face with her hands and sobbed, great wrenching, heartbreaking sobs.

Aleksei's fingers sifted through her hair, keeping her head on his lap, breathing in and out to keep his demons at bay. His woman was hurting. *Hurting.* That was unacceptable to him. "My little cat, you are my lifemate. You were born my lifemate. You belong in my world with me. What makes you think you do not?"

She wrapped her arms tighter around his legs. "I didn't help you. I should have been able to help you when you needed it. Joie, my sister, would have jumped right in."

Aleksei stroked caresses through that mass of dark silk. *"Kislány."* He whispered the endearment softly. "You *did* try to jump right in. I prevented it."

"The difference . . ." She tried to sit up, to pull away from him.

Aleksei refused to allow it. He kept his hand on her head, preventing her from moving. He applied pressure until she subsided, collapsing against his thighs with another sob, as if even her inability to fight his strength was a sin.

"The difference," she repeated, "is you would have *allowed* my sister to help because she would know how. She wouldn't throw up. She wouldn't be a disadvantage to you—she would be an asset."

Another storm of weeping ensued. This time Aleksei pulled her up so that her face was pressed into his chest. He wrapped her up tightly. "That is enough. I allowed all those tears because you needed the release. You were shocked by the violence and afraid for me, but now you are just going to make yourself sick. Stop. I mean it, Gabrielle."

Her fingers curled into a fist and she thumped his chest. "You can't tell me to stop crying and expect me to obey."

"Yes I can, *kislány*. Stop right now. You obviously do not understand the concept of lifemates, and we need to be very clear on this. I need you to look at me, not hide your face. I do not want tears in your eyes when I talk to you about this. I need to be able to see that you are getting it."

She pressed her face deeper into his shirt. He felt the wetness of her tears, and he gave her time to obey him. The seconds seemed like hours before she finally took several deep, hiccuping breaths and lifted her face, drawing in the air to try to obey him. His fingers came up under that heavy fall of silk to curl around the nape of her neck. She was beautiful, even with her tear-drenched face. Her large eyes met his and he felt that impact in the pit of his stomach. His body stirred as it always did when she looked at him. When she was close to him. Anytime.

He stroked a caress down her cheek with his free hand, as if he could wipe away every tear. "*This* is why you are my lifemate, Gabrielle. Not your sister. Your sister would never suit me. We would not ever fit. *You* fit with me. When I tell you to do something, no matter how difficult, you do your best for me. Did you think I did not feel your struggle to stay still when I was in battle? You tried hard for me. Your nature, whether you know what you are doing or not, is to aid others. But you tried to do as I asked."

"Ordered," she corrected, sounding a little miffed.

He didn't smile, although he wanted to. "Ordered," he agreed. "I am a man who will order his woman and expect obedience. I will also take great care of her, always. In every way. I will see to her happiness because, *kislány*, by giving me that, by giving me her obedience when I need it, she is making me happy."

"I told you I'm not certain I can do obedience."

He did laugh then. Softly. Gently. So that she would know she meant everything to him and he wasn't laughing at her. "I get that, Gabrielle. But you *try*. That is what makes it such a gift. If it were easy for you, if it did not matter to you that I was in trouble and you stayed on the sidelines because obedience was easy, it would mean nothing. You needed to help me and yet you fought to do as I asked."

"But in the end, I disobeyed."

"I am certain you will disobey me often. It is the gift that it is difficult and you try that matters to me, not the actual doing. Although, in a battle, I will never allow you to aid me. I am not that kind of lifemate, nor will I ever be. My woman stays safe where I put her. There is no discussion about that. There never will be. Your sister would never suit me, Gabrielle. Not in a million years. I would not want a woman who could battle at my side. I am too much of a . . ."

"Chauvinist?"

He laughed and brushed a kiss on her mouth. Her sweet mouth that always tempted him. "I was going to say 'protector,' but chauvinist will do."

"I hated that. I hated knowing you could be killed, that you were being burned to the bone by the vampire's blood. That Vaugn was repeatedly stabbing that knife into your back." She shuddered, her hand moving over his face, gently touching the lacerations that were no longer open, but still raw.

There was tenderness in her touch. In her eyes. His heart shifted in his chest. She'd never looked at him with that particular expression. Soft. Loving even. He didn't want to think that word. He didn't know if he could take the disappointment of her not feeling that emotion, so he stayed out of her mind. Giving her space. Giving her time.

18

Gabrielle shifted positions, climbing onto Aleksei's lap. Straddling him. Fitting her body tightly to his. He seemed to always be hard for her. Ready for her. She leaned into him, grinding her mound against his hard bulge while she gently kissed each scratch and tear on his face. She didn't know what she was feeling, only that she felt full. Completed. Whole. And he made her feel that way.

"Do you mean it, Aleksei? You aren't disappointed that you didn't get a woman who could fight by your side?"

"It is impossible to be disappointed in you, *kislány*."

Aleksei slid his hands down her body, from beneath her arms to her hips, taking her clothing with it. He bent his head to capture her mouth. "We do not have a lot of time, little cat, and there are things I want to do to you. Things I need from you, so this time, you will give that to me." He murmured the command against her lips, his hands spanning her waist.

"I already gave you obedience," she pointed out, her mouth seeking his.

He lifted her easily and deposited her on the bed, following her down, his mouth on hers, his much heavier body pinning hers. *I see the allure of beds for humans.*

Nice, right? She lost herself in his mouth. In all that heat and fire. She couldn't believe anyone could kiss like him. When he kissed her, if he asked her for the moon, she would have tried to find a way to give it to him.

Very nice.

Aleksei kissed his way down to her throat. *Put your hands*

*above your head, kislány, I like the way it lifts your breasts,
like a wonderful offering. I intend to take my time, what time
we have before we have to return to the monastery, worshiping your body. I want your eyes on me at all times. Do not
look away.*

Gabrielle stared into his eyes. So green. So filled with
desire. Desire so intense, she felt her body instantly dampen
in response. Not taking her eyes from his, she slowly complied, lifting her arms above her head.

She had no idea how much time had passed or how many
times her body gave him exactly what he demanded. His
mouth, his teeth, his tongue and his fingers were everywhere,
claiming her, pushing her up over and over, until one climax
ran into another. Until she thought she might die before he
actually took her. Until she was writhing on the bed, sobbing
his name, pleading with him.

Tell me who your lifemate is, he demanded, dragging her
down the bed, kneeling as he threw her legs over his shoulders, putting her in a vulnerable position. He guided the head
of his cock to her dripping entrance. *Leave your hands where
I told you, Gabrielle.* His voice was a whip, hard and authoritative after he had pushed her so far from her comfort zone
and she'd gone there with him.

"I can't," she said, her head whipping back and forth. "I
have to hold on to you."

She reached for him, or tried to. She couldn't move her
wrists from the mattress. Her gaze jumped back to his face.
"Aleksei." She breathed his name. Ragged. Panting. Writhing.
He just held her there, suspended, his body against hers, and
she tried to impale herself on him, but he refused to allow it.

She fought for control, her breasts heaving, her lungs burning. "Please, Aleksei. Tell me what you want."

"I want you to tell me who your lifemate is. And know it,
Gabrielle. I am entering your mind when I enter your body.
You had better know who you belong to."

She licked her lips to moisten them. He was asking for
more than her body. She knew that. She didn't care. She might

be the most fickle person on the face of the earth, but this man had found his way inside her. Soul to soul. She would always love Gary. She knew that and accepted it, but she would love him differently, as the man who saw her and saved her when no one else could see her.

"You're my lifemate, Aleksei," she whispered. She gave him truth. She opened her mind to him. Let him see her. Let him see how she loved Gary and how, already, her love for her lifemate was so intense, so beyond anything she could have imagined, that she knew he wouldn't be worried about her feelings for Gary.

"He is lost to you," Aleksei said softly. "Beyond any emotion now. Perhaps his memories of you will keep him safe on whatever path fate has for him. But you are mine. Fully and completely mine."

She nodded. She knew that. "Yours, Aleksei, and I'm burning up. I need you right now."

He answered her the only way Aleksei ever answered—his way. He took her hard and fast and deep. Somewhere in the middle of her body coming apart again and again, she realized he'd given her back her hands, and she used them well, holding on to him, digging her nails into him every time he took her over the edge and continued pounding into her until she was screaming, her cries echoing through the chamber.

She felt him stretching her more. Impossibly. Her breath caught so she couldn't cry out, but her eyes never left his. She saw it moving over him, through him. She felt it, the crushing wave of pleasure, of bliss, that swept upward from his toes and downward from his head, to come together in a crashing wave so huge, it swept both of them away.

He buried his face in her neck, letting her take his full weight, holding her there for several long minutes before lifting his head to look down at her. He framed her face with his hands, using his elbows to prop him up. His green eyes blazed down into hers.

"You are good, *kislány*?" he asked.

Her heart turned over at the gentleness in his voice. "How

could I not be good?" Her body was still rippling. She felt sated and loved and wrapped up completely in him.

"With us. Are you good? Do you understand the concept of a lifemate? Not just anyone would suit my personality, or yours. We fit. We belong. You to me. Me to you. Most women couldn't possibly live with me."

Gabrielle shook her head. "That's not true."

"*Kislány.* It is. I am from ancient times, when a man protected his woman and was expected to go out hunting while she waited at home, protecting the family. More, the man expected his woman to see to his needs and be happy doing it. You see to my needs and you are happy doing it."

"You make that easy for me, Aleksei."

"And when we live near others? Will it be easy for you then, when your family and your friends expect you to challenge me at every turn? When I refuse to allow your mother to throw her tantrums around you? When I will not back down and make certain not one single thing hurts or harms you in any way? Not just physically? Because, Gabrielle, that is what you can expect from me."

"I know that. I've thought a lot about you and the way you are." She had, too. She rubbed her hands up and down his arms, feeling the defined muscles there. He was a beautiful man, and once she'd gotten over being worried about what everyone else might think of her relationship, she began to think about what she could live with, what would make *her* happy, given her nature.

"The thing is, at first your arrogant bossiness made me crazy . . ."

"*Arrogant* bossiness?" There was humor in his voice.

"You know you're arrogant, Aleksei, and you're definitely bossy."

The smile faded from his face. "I want you to know what you are getting into, Gabrielle. I am not the kind of man to carry on idle conversation with others. I have never associated with humans and I do not have tolerance for people and the way they think they are entitled."

She studied his face. He was very serious, but he wasn't telling her anything she didn't already know. "What are you trying to tell me, Aleksei?"

"I do not like that you think you are not a worthy lifemate for me. I will never put up with your mother, or anyone else, for that matter, intimidating you by throwing tantrums. Your father and your brother should have protected you. They did not. I will. If this woman, whom I know you love, picks up an object and throws it at you or one of our children, I will take care of the problem once and for all. Do you understand? I do not want you to start our relationship thinking you got yourself someone nice."

She touched his mouth with two fingers. "I would never describe you as nice, Aleksei. You can be sweet, though. I realized you taking charge made me feel safe for the first time in my life. I love my father and my brother. I do. I adore my sister. But in my home, growing up, I never felt safe. I never felt as if any of them would stand up for me against my mother. I might be wrong, because I never, ever challenged her, but I *know* you would. I know you wouldn't let her throw things and maybe hit one of our children with whatever she throws. I know if I were upset by her behavior, you would definitely stop her. So I know, for you, for that kind of protection, for leaning so heavily on your strength, doing what you asked would never be a burden."

His green eyes blazed down at her. Flared with heat. She felt his cock, deep inside her, jerk, stretch the tight walls of her channel, and it felt delicious. Perfect. So right.

"So you know I am not going to try to make people like me, even your family or friends. I do not care if anyone likes me." His face softened and he bit her chin gently, sending another ripple of fire through her. "With the exception of you. I would much prefer it if you liked me."

Gabrielle couldn't help it, she laughed softly. "I think you're safe, Aleksei. I'm pretty certain I like you."

"That is good." His body began a slow glide in hers. "I was worried."

"You weren't in the least worried. If you thought I didn't like you, you'd just order me to get over it." Her fingers dug into him. "You can't possibly start all over again."

"I think you are wrong, *kislány*. I am fairly certain I can."

Gabrielle burst out laughing, the sound ringing through the chamber. Her laughter was genuine, and she realized she was happy. Really happy. She wasn't in a house with a white picket fence and a swing on the porch, she was in a cave high up in the Carpathian Mountains, and she was happier than she could ever remember.

She circled Aleksei's neck with her arms and pulled his head down to hers, her mouth finding his. He made it easy, and his kisses lit up her world. And she loved that, too. She gave herself up to him. To the fire he created. To the way he made her feel, safe and cherished. In a million years, she would never have believed Aleksei would have been the man to make her feel so happy.

She didn't know how much time had passed. She was lost in his body, in the things he did to hers, but she felt it was all too soon before they were dressed and heading out of the cave. She paused at the entrance, looking back, knowing they were returning to the monastery, to that place of four walls and nothing else.

"Gabrielle?"

She turned back. Aleksei stood there, tall and wholly masculine, his long hair unbound, the wind moving through it just as she liked to sift her fingers through it. He held out his hand to her. She looked at it for a long moment. He had big hands, strong. So strong. She took a deep breath and put her hand in his. Aleksei pulled her to his side. Close. She liked how he always did that. He liked contact with her. A lot of contact. She slipped her arm around his waist.

"What is it?"

"I like it here. I don't like the monastery as well." Honesty was the only way to go with Aleksei. She knew if she tried to avoid answering him, he would stand there forever until either she told him or he lost patience and looked in her mind for the answer.

"We will not be there forever. I know your work is important. As soon as possible, we will make a home closer to where you do your research." He brought her hand up to his mouth, his lips skimming her knuckles. "We will have a beautiful home, Gabrielle. Anything you want."

"Will you be gone a lot?" She couldn't keep the trepidation out of her voice.

He frowned. "Gone where? Where do you think I will go?"

"You hunt vampires."

"I do not leave you. If I go somewhere, Gabrielle, you will be going with me." There was a hard authority in his voice, as if he thought she was trying to get rid of him.

She leaned into him, circling his waist with her arm and tipping her head up to look at his face. "I'm glad. I don't want you going anywhere without me."

"You know that Gary will not be working with you." He made that a decree.

"He didn't want Gregori to convert him, even though he was so close to death. He knew. I don't know how he did, but he said he was worth far more to the Carpathians as a human than as a Carpathian. He's a genius. His mind is incredible, Aleksei." For a moment she forgot what Gary meant to Aleksei and that he might not like her being so enthusiastic about him. She clapped a hand over her mouth. "I'm sorry." She whispered it. "I wasn't thinking."

He gently pulled her hand from her mouth and held it tightly over his heart. "That is the first time you spoke of him as if he were a colleague you admired and not the man you wanted to spend your life with. After seeing your childhood, and how your life has been since, especially after you were converted, I am grateful you had his friendship. To know you had someone who cared about you makes me happy, Gabrielle, not upset. This man will not be able to feel, but he will remember you, and if he is the man I see in your mind, if that is his character, he will check on you to make certain you are happy. He will stay in contact, even if from a distance."

"Will you be okay with that?" She didn't want Aleksei to be angry with her, or worse, fight with Gary.

"I have you. You gave yourself to me. A precious gift that I know you will never take back. I have you. He does not. And he never will. I know what it is like to love you, Gabrielle. He may not feel it, but he remembers it. That will always be very difficult for him."

She swallowed hard. "You love me?" She couldn't believe that. How could he possibly have fallen in love with her when she'd . . .

Aleksei tightened his hand over Gabrielle's, pressing her palm hard into his chest. "Do not, *kislány*," he warned. He was not going to have her keep blaming herself for something he did not feel was her fault. "We have put that subject to rest. How could I not fall in love with you?"

She didn't see herself as he did. She was highly intelligent. Gentle. Sweet. Vulnerable. She needed care, and he was a man who needed to care for a woman. He had enough darkness, enough demons, for more than one man. He needed a woman who was all light to bring him back from that edge when it got too close, not one who wanted to fight. He needed her to know he was often at that edge, that his demons didn't stand down, and when he reached for her, to lose himself in her, she was welcoming, she reached back, knowing that was more important to him than fighting at his side.

Gabrielle was that woman. She abhorred violence. It made her sick. He was thankful for that. He would teach her to protect herself, because she needed to know how. For her. For their children. And for him. He had to know that when he wasn't right with her—which would be rare—she would be able to defend herself if the need arose. Other than that, he wanted his Gabrielle. Vulnerable. Sweet. With enough attitude and a lot of intelligence to keep him very happy. Even more, she was scorching hot in his bed.

Gabrielle buried her face against his side. "I want you to

love me, Aleksei. I swear, I will do whatever it takes to make you happy."

He smiled down at her. She didn't have a choice in the matter, because he wasn't going to give her one. He thought it might be prudent to keep silent about that. "Andre and Teagan are headed up to the monastery. We need to meet them there. Fane has gotten the ancients to agree to let Teagan try to heal them enough for them to get out and look for their lifemates. Andre has access to the database of psychic women through a boy called Josef. If you can connect with each of the ancients and try to be a compass with this parlor trick you spoke of, we may be able to give them hope of a future."

"If Teagan fails?"

He took a breath. Let it out. She was too intelligent not to know what would happen. He would have no choice but to remain at the monastery, becoming the gatekeeper as Fane had been. Fane had to be released from his duties so he and his lifemate could travel with Teagan and Andre back to the United States.

"I am sorry, little cat, I would have to stay and protect the ancients. We would remain here. I have seen your dream of a house and yard and children playing . . ."

"Dreams change, Aleksei," Gabrielle said, pressing her fingertips to his lips. "That was a child's dream. You are home to me. You. Not a house and a yard. We can turn wherever we are into a home because we're together. My work is important, though. I really feel we've made a tremendous amount of progress. Shea's a great doctor and she has a way of putting us on the right track when we're all throwing out ideas, but with Gary gone, I'm needed."

"Then if we stay, we will have to get together a laboratory for you to do your research in at the monastery."

"You would do that?"

He smiled down at her, shaking his head. "*Kislány.* I am a selfish man and want you all to myself. I will not ever apologize for that, but I am not so selfish that I would not want you to do important work that only you can do for our people. If we return to the Carpathian Mountains, I might even offer my services to the prince. I have not sworn my allegiance to him nor did I think I ever would, but I have a family to think of now."

She burst out laughing. "Such a chore. Swearing allegiance to your prince."

He gave her a mock scowl when her laughter was the most beautiful music in the world. "Woman. I have been on my own for centuries. I take no orders from any man."

"You could just beat your chest," she suggested, still laughing.

He wrapped his arms around her. "We are heading up the mountain, back to the monastery. Just for that crack, you can regulate your own body temperature."

Gabrielle snuggled into Aleksei's arms, realizing immediately that almost from the moment she had gone to him to give her allegiance to him, he had been ensuring she remained warm and comfortable. She hadn't thought about it. She'd struggled with the whole temperature-control thing, as well as keeping the volume down. It took practice, and her head was always filled with her work. Until Aleksei. Now it was filled with him. She also realized he was a puzzle her mind tried to work out and she would probably never find an entire solution to him, but that was okay with her. She *loved* that he'd regulated her body temperature.

She didn't say a word, but as they moved through the cold air, farther up into the mountains where the thick mist swirled ominously, she deliberately didn't keep herself warm. She waited. Shivered. Instantly, she was warm. She smiled to herself. Aleksei. Taking care of her even when he threatened not to. She loved that even more.

The mist was disorienting and felt heavy against her skin. She heard voices whispering, warning, and she recognized the power of strong safeguards. She remembered moving through that mass on her own, seeking Gary. She'd been so afraid. Now, with Aleksei holding her, she wasn't afraid at all. She realized he hadn't had her shapeshift to go through the mist. He had noticed it bothered her and held her close to him, once again making her feel safe.

She had never considered that Aleksei could be so thoughtful. *I'm falling in love with you.* She had to give him that. He'd told her he loved her. He'd put himself on the line and he'd handled her with care once he knew she hadn't been born Carpathian. How could she not have intense feelings for him? She wasn't all the way there; she'd spent too long believing she was *in* love with Gary, not realizing how she loved him.

Trixie had been right all along. There was a difference. She had no doubt in her mind that had she and Gary never been converted, they would have lived a happy life together, but it wouldn't have been anything like what she had now. She wouldn't have missed what she didn't know, but still, she wouldn't have had Aleksei. She sent up a silent prayer that Gary would find his lifemate and, when he did, that he would be every bit as happy as she was now.

She felt the brush of Aleksei's lips in her hair.

Best not to tell me that when we are in the air, little cat. You giving that to me makes me hard. I suppose we could manage to have sex in flight, but keeping you warm, and making you shatter for me, it could be difficult keeping us from crashing.

She turned her face into his chest and laughed. *Everything makes you hard, and I have no doubt you would have no trouble making me shatter many times, keeping me warm and keeping us from crashing. You're just that talented.*

At last. Glad you recognize that.

Okay, that beginning-to-fall-in-love was heading toward definitely there. She loved that he had a sense of humor and could tease her and that when she teased him back, he was all right with it. More than all right. She felt his answering laughter. She loved the sound because she knew he hadn't laughed often—if ever—before he claimed her.

The monastery gates loomed ahead as they emerged from the mist. She twisted her fingers into Aleksei's shirt. "You weren't very nice to Trixie, Aleksei," she pointed out. "You might want to repair that damage."

Aleksei set her down right outside the gates. "And I should be worried about this because?"

She heard the challenge in his voice. He had laid it out for her earlier, letting her know in no uncertain terms he didn't care if people liked him or not. Not her family. Not her friends. Anyone. She had to handle this carefully. She ran her hand up his chest, staying close.

"Trixie helped me. A lot. I needed to talk to someone . . ." She broke off when his body hardened, every muscle locked down. "Aleksei, just listen to me for a moment. I know it's important to you that we work things out, you and me, together. I want that, too, but I was so frightened of you and so ashamed of myself and feeling guilty that I *couldn't* talk to you."

"You can always talk to me, Gabrielle. I am the person you *should* talk to."

His hand came up, sifting through her hair in the caressing way he had that always made her so aware of him as a man and her as a woman. "I know, I know," she said hastily. "But right then, I was grateful to her because she listened to me when I didn't think I was making sense and she told me had I been *in* love with Gary, and he with me, we wouldn't have been able to keep our hands off each other."

She risked a quick look at his stone face. He definitely looked as if he could have been carved from granite. She sighed. "I'm making things worse. I just wanted you to know she helped me. That's all, honey. I needed to sort through everything in my mind, and she helped me do that."

His hand slid to her face, cupping her cheek. "You called me 'honey.' You have never once used an endearment of any kind." His green eyes moved over her face and her stomach did a slow somersault. "I like that, *kessake*, I like it a lot."

He was so sexy. Everything he did. The way he touched her. The way he looked at her. The sound of his voice, caressing her, mesmerizing her.

She sent him a quick smile. "Maybe it isn't so important

that you get along with anyone else. I can live in the monastery and just stare at you all night and be happy." She bit her lip. Hard. Had she just blurted that out? Aloud? Faint color crept up her face.

His smile sent a minor quake to her sex, and her breasts actually tingled. He didn't have to do anything at all, not even open his mouth, and she just melted.

"In case I have not told you this rising, *kessake*, you are the most beautiful woman I have ever seen." He bent his head and brushed a kiss over her mouth. "Andre and his lifemate will be here in a couple of moments," he added in warning.

She felt it then, the disturbance in the mist. She didn't know if she was enough in Aleksei's mind that she felt his warning system, or if his lessons in being Carpathian were bringing out other things in her as well. She hoped so. She was in his world, and now she wanted to embrace it.

Seconds later, a great owl landed on the ground, a few feet from them. Aleksei instantly glided between her and the bird as it shapeshifted. He made the movement seem natural, as if he were stepping forward to greet Andre, gripping his forearms in the traditional way of Carpathian warriors, but Gabrielle knew it was more than that. He had once again used his body to shield her.

She waited while they spoke softly in their language, but when Aleksei made no move to let her greet Andre, she started to step forward on her own. She'd seen Andre on more than one occasion, although she hadn't talked to him. He had been there when she'd tried to persuade Gary to go away with her. She wasn't looking forward to facing him, but she figured now was a better time than later. No one else was around. She was completely unprepared for Aleksei to move again, cutting her off. Again, it was a subtle step, but she couldn't move around him.

Wait until his lifemate joins us.

She didn't understand that, either. Outwardly, Aleksei appeared calm and friendly, but she felt the tension coiled in him, like a snake, ready to strike. *I thought you two were friends.*

Yes. But I never risk you. Never. He can bring his lifemate out into the open before he has access to you.

Gabrielle reached up and bunched the back of his shirt into her fist. Connecting them. Holding on. Forcing herself to push down the natural peacemaker in her and stay where she knew Aleksei wanted her to be. In a way, it was easier. Knowing Andre had witnessed her betrayal of his friend—and Aleksei was his friend—having him know just how close she'd driven Aleksei to madness was beyond mortifying. She *hated* that he knew how she'd rejected Aleksei's legitimate claim on her.

We have put that subject to rest, Gabrielle.

Aleksei's voice was stern, yet soothing at the same time. She didn't know how he managed that.

You are not to be embarrassed about that anymore. Do you understand me? Let it go.

Gabrielle sighed. There it was again. His demand for her to let something go that ran through her head like a loop playing. Half the Carpathian world had to know by now. She knew Gary had been taken to the cave of warriors for healing by the prince and Gregori. Every Carpathian knew that; the news had gone out on the common path. She figured they were all talking about her betrayal on more common paths.

It isn't that easy, Aleksei. He was there.

He reached behind him and caught her free hand, pulling it down to his thigh, his hand pressing her palm into the hard muscle there. He'd done it before, and for some reason she felt that gesture so deep she had to drop her forehead against his back, drawing in a deep breath to keep the tears clogging her throat at bay. He was so sweet. Instinctively, she knew few people would ever see that side of him. He reserved that for her.

Sweet and bossy.

You like my bossy.

His tone implied all kinds of things, sexy, erotic things. Images filled her head because they were filling his head. Some of those images made her blush, so she was glad she was hiding behind his large body and Andre couldn't see her face.

Being tied down is not sexy. But it kind of was.

It will be when I do it to you.

She did a full-body shiver and decided it was prudent, due to the circumstances, to quit talking, but she realized she wasn't embarrassed anymore. She was too busy thinking about those images in Aleksei's head and wanting to try them all.

A heartbeat later, a smaller owl joined them, spiraling down to land beside Andre. Teagan was much lighter skinned than her grandmother, but both were beautiful. Gabrielle could see glimpses of Trixie in her. She had a *lot* of hair, tons of it, cascading down her back, and she wore the same intricate braids that Trixie did.

The moment Teagan arrived, Aleksei drew Gabrielle to his side, clamping her there with an arm around her waist. He introduced her immediately. Andre introduced Teagan. Aleksei turned on the charm and his high-voltage smile.

"Your grandmother came to Gabrielle's aid and I am indebted to her," he greeted. "She is a very wise woman."

Gabrielle's heart did another stutter. Aleksei did that for her. That was not something he would normally say, she knew that instinctively. He was being friendly toward Teagan because he intended to make amends with Trixie. For her. Because she asked him to and he knew Trixie mattered to her. She slid just a little bit more in love with him.

Teagan instantly beamed. "She is, isn't she? I can't wait for Andre to meet her, although I'm a little terrified she might try to use her vampire-hunting kit on him."

To Gabrielle's shock, Aleksei casually delivered information he hadn't even told Gabrielle. "Fane told me she used the gun on him, trying to stake him with ridiculous darts."

"Oh, dear," Teagan said.

Both women glanced up at Andre's impassive face. Andre's mouth didn't so much as twitch. Neither did Aleksei's. The two women looked at each other and then burst out laughing, and Gabrielle didn't know if they were laughing at Trixie's gutsy attack on Fane, who must have been shocked, or the two men who refused to laugh, but had to think it was funny.

"And she threw the vial of holy water at him, but she forgot to take out the stopper, not that it would have done much more than get him a little damp." Aleksei delivered that tidbit with the same expressionless face when they had sobered.

The two women dissolved into laughter again. Neither man laughed.

Gabrielle rolled her eyes at Aleksei. *I guess macho, arrogant, bossy men don't laugh in front of other macho, arrogant, bossy men? Because this is funny. Although not quite as funny as you and Andre pretending it isn't.*

If we laughed, we would lose the status of macho, arrogant, bossy men. Aleksei caught her chin and looked into her eyes. *You are giving me a hard-on right now, teasing me like that and rolling your eyes at me.*

You can't get a hard-on from being teased or having your lifemate roll her eyes at you.

I can when she is you and you are teasing me and rolling your eyes, because it means something.

Gabrielle stared into his piercing green eyes. Her heart stuttered. Her belly somersaulted. And he got an answering spasm in her sex. A direct shot. With his look. With his words and the intimate delivery straight into her mind.

His words echoed through her. *I can when she is you and you are teasing me and rolling your eyes, because it means something.*

She knew what he meant. Teasing and eye rolling meant she was comfortable with him. That she knew him enough now that he wouldn't be upset by her antics. That he even liked them. That love was growing, and she belonged. She had accepted fully that she belonged with Aleksei.

She moved into him, sliding her arms around his waist, uncaring that Andre and Teagan knew all about Gary. Uncaring that anyone knew. *Now I wish we were alone and I had your cock in my mouth. I would do my best to show you the care I intend to take of you, honey.*

His eyes narrowed. Against her stomach she felt the hard evidence of his response, growing even harder.

Kislány, you know better than to say things like that around me. And if you do not, you had better learn fast. I could take you right now, hard and fast right up against the monastery walls, and shield others from seeing us. You keep that up, it will happen.

Gabrielle laughed softly in her mind, all the while holding his gaze, letting him know his warning didn't scare her in the least. If he wanted her that way, she was ready and willing to oblige him. She let it show in her eyes. In her mind. She wasn't going to be intimidated by something that promised total pleasure. If no one could see, who cared where they were?

He shook his head. She felt his slow smile. He liked it that she was all right with his threats.

We will be taking care of this business fast, my little cat, because I like that you will have me in your mouth each time we play out one of those images you saw in my head.

She bit her lip. Hard. She liked that, and suddenly taking care of business didn't seem as important as it had. They went through the gates, Aleksei's hand on her back, guiding her, making her feel safe, his soft, intimate laughter in her mind.

19

Gabrielle watched the reunion between Trixie and her granddaughter. Trixie enfolded Teagan into her arms and kissed her on each cheek. Both women had tears in their eyes. It took their men stepping up, wrapping an arm around each of them, to bring out watery smiles while introductions were made. Andre was gallant, leaning down to brush a kiss on Trixie's forehead, while Fane kissed Teagan's hand. Gabrielle was happy to share that moment, even from a distance, because the ancients emerging from the ground or buildings were terrifying.

Even if Teagan can really give these men a little more time, Aleksei, I don't think it would be a good thing for them to be let loose in the modern world.

Gabrielle bit her lip hard, her fingers moving to the bracelet on her wrist. It felt warm and maybe a little comforting. She had no problem with Aleksei keeping his body between her and the seven men forming a semicircle around them—in fact she liked that he was there. Solid. Safe. She could tell Trixie had the same opinion she did. Trixie was plastered to Fane's side, her worried eyes on her granddaughter approaching the ancient called Dragomir. Andre was beside Teagan, his arm around her, his body very protective. Still, the ancients were both beautiful and terrible.

Tension was so thick one could cut it with a knife. The ancients were no longer men. They were mostly demon, so dangerous their own kind feared them—and Fane, Aleksei and Andre were powerful and dangerous in their own right.

Still, they approached the ancients carefully, without the women, persuading them to try Teagan's healing stone.

Now, with the ancients sitting tailor fashion on the ground, Gabrielle felt as if she were in a cage of tigers—tigers that hadn't been fed in months. Years even. The men were large, built like Aleksei, very muscular, with ropes of defined muscle. It was their faces that held a strange masculine beauty, almost as if each had been meticulously chiseled from the hardest, but most beautiful stone on earth. They all had the same tattoo covering their backs and reaching up over their shoulders and down their arms with their creed flowing in ancient letters. They each had long, flowing salt-and-pepper hair. Each had a few scars, showing the fatal battle wounds they had somehow managed to survive. That was where the similarity ended.

Dragomir's attention seemed wholly focused on Teagan as she came close to him, his golden eyes—and they were absolutely gold—boring right through her. His teeth were very white. Gabrielle could tell because he clenched them tightly, as if Teagan invading his space hurt him in some way. Since he couldn't feel, Gabrielle knew it was because he was holding himself back from harming her. He looked as if ice ran in his veins—the coldest arctic temperature ever recorded. He was more than terrifying.

Gabrielle gripped Aleksei's hand as Dragomir's body shuddered and a low, rumbling growl emerged. Andre halted Teagan's progress abruptly by stopping and clamping her to his side. Dragomir's rumble made it clear, the distance was as near as he could tolerate. Her bracelet had definitely gone warm, as if it had become watchful. She tried to block out the low hum emerging from it, but fortunately it was low enough that the ancients didn't do more than glance her way.

Teagan knelt in front of Dragomir, a stone in her hand. It was round and flat and unpolished. Still, it gleamed as gold as old and ancient as the gold of Dragomir's eyes. Gabrielle felt the instant connection, the pull. At the same time, she felt compelled toward the maps drawn in the soft, rich dirt. She moved away from Aleksei and crouched close to the ground, her hand hovering over the lines there. Trixie's swift indrawn breath told her that she was seeing what she called a song emerging from Dragomir.

Teagan began a soft chant, her eyes closing. To Gabrielle's complete shock, she could see Teagan's aura begin to expand from where she was kneeling in front of Dragomir to surround and encompass his aura. His aura was layer after layer of unrelenting dark. Teagan's aura was a cool, fresh green, like the springtime. As her aura stretched and enveloped his, a rainbow of colors began to infiltrate the darkness.

The sight was so amazing and unexpected that Gabrielle could barely pull her gaze away to observe the effect on the other ancients. They were staring impassively, but she could see their eyes beginning to go from dead to something else. They wouldn't be able to see the actual color, but they could see light moving in streaks through the gray.

The one called Sandu, the complete opposite of Dragomir, with fire in his eyes rather than ice, seemed to call up flames so that his black eyes burned a deep red. Isai, with his sapphire-blue eyes, leaned forward to watch more closely. Petru had eyes that were mercury in color, and right now they were an eerie liquid, as if deep inside of him a volcano had erupted and sent heat throughout to turn him fluid.

Gabrielle glanced at Aleksei, her fingers on her bracelet, that warmth there. He, like Andre and Fane, stared at Teagan as if she were a miracle. It was awesome. More colors were added into the layers of darkness, infusing Dragomir's unrelenting gray world with streaks of brightness. Gabrielle realized no one could live in that world for long without suffering the effects. To know that these men had done so for centuries made her respect them all the more.

Aleksei had done that. *Her* Aleksei had lived in that terrible, unrelenting gloom. A shadow world where he could never connect with anyone. And her Gary had been dropped abruptly into it with no slow conditioning. After having emotions and colors for his entire life, how could he experience the loss of emotion and color of every single warrior who had gone before him in the Daratrazanoff lineage and not go insane?

She wanted to weep. She was weeping. So was Trixie. They all felt it. The burden these men had carried for far too long. Aleksei's hand found her shoulder and slid to the nape of her neck, holding her steady.

Honey, she whispered softly into his mind. *You were like that. You endured that. And I . . .*

You were my personal miracle, and those colors she's pushing into that darkness have not penetrated beyond that first layer. Your colors streaked through the darkness in me all the way to the very core. You gave me that, Gabrielle. You.

He humbled her. His caressing voice. The tenderness in his eyes. She could barely look at him when he looked at her like that—as if he believed every word he said. And the thing was—he did believe it. She felt herself slipping further under his spell. Sliding from "falling" straight into "in" love. Not just "in" but wholly "in."

His eyes began to glitter. *You cannot look at me when we are in the middle of something this important. I need to be alone with you when you give that to me, kessake.*

Instantly the familiar reaction spread through her body like a firestorm. Her body tightened and a very pleasant spasm happened in her deepest core. She sent him a small smile and turned her attention back to what was happening.

Benedek, another ancient with the same etched tattoo, long salt-and-pepper hair and his own unique midnight-black eyes, actually flowed to his feet, stepping closer to Dragomir in order to try to ascertain what was happening. Gabrielle knew they didn't see the colors, but they were all sharing the same psychic path and they could feel the difference in Dragomir. The ancients saw the streaks of lighter gray moving through the darker gray of his aura.

Trixie moved a little closer and cocked her head to one side, listening. She was also using the same path, enabling the others to hear the mournful notes playing through her head. Not just mournful—Gabrielle grasped—but the notes of a feral predator searching for prey. She shivered, hearing those notes, knowing that was Dragomir's song. The notes sprang into the air above the map drawn on the ground. Notes that held no real color, only the same darkness that permeated through all the ancients.

Andor, an ancient with indigo eyes, inky blue-black, stood abruptly, reaching for one of the notes as if he could capture it in his hands. His hair, so long it hit his waist, moved with the slight breeze, and his muscles rippled beneath his skin, bringing his tattoo to life. Fane moved in closer to Trixie, stepping between Andor and Trixie without hesitation, a subtle warning that the women were trying to aid the ancients, but not to get too close.

The moment Fane moved in between his lifemate and the ancient, the seventh ancient, the one they had introduced as Ferro, came to his feet as well. His eyes were the most unusual of all. The color of iron, complete with the rust. Every bit as piercing as Aleksei's eyes, maybe more so. He was tall. His shoulders were wide—wider even than those of the other ancients. He was a very imposing figure in the midst of such powerful men. He glided across the ground, and Gabrielle held her breath as he neared Trixie. He wasn't looking at the woman, but rather at the notes and the way they surrounded Gabrielle.

She bit her lip hard. She didn't like attention. At all. She was used to being alone in her laboratory for nights on end, weeks, months even, staying alone. She didn't have the vivid personality of her mother—larger than life—or her sister and brother. She faded into the background, at least she did her best to, and having the focused attention of all seven ancients was disconcerting.

Still, it was her turn. She had to try to help them with her silly parlor trick. She shouldn't have mentioned it to Aleksei, that she might be able to do this. The small flames seemed to have come to light in her bracelet, the links dancing with fire, yet only warm and reassuring against her skin. She rubbed at them nervously.

Teagan had done her best for Dragomir. Trixie had found his unique, signature song and sent it to Gabrielle. Now it was up to her to try to find a location somewhere in the world where his lifemate might possibly be. Andre would contact Josef, who was standing by with the database, and he would look up any psychic women in the vicinity.

Gabrielle's heart pounded. Teagan had done amazing work. Astonishing. A miracle really. Trixie had given her a key. Now it was up to her to unlock the door so Dragomir had a chance to find his lifemate. Sitting in the monastery afforded him nearly a zero chance. She knew what she was doing wouldn't get an exact location. It didn't work that way. Countries were big. They covered a lot of ground.

You can do this.

Aleksei. He believed in her. His voice alone steadied her, but his fingers on the nape of her neck made her feel grounded. She took a deep breath and let go of her own ego, her own personality, all that she was, much in the way Carpathians healed one another. She didn't become white-hot healing energy, she simply expanded, her consciousness reaching out into the universe. She took Dragomir's song with her. As dark and dangerous as it was, as untamed and feral, as violent and mournful, as in need. She took it with her as the energy that was her moved over the map drawn into the dirt.

At first she felt nothing at all. She didn't let that discourage her. If she did, she would retreat back into her own body, and this wasn't about her. This was about a man of intense honor who had no hope. He deserved so much better than he'd got. She didn't know what kind of woman would be strong enough to handle these ancients, so far gone there was nothing civilized left in them. Nothing remotely human. She couldn't think about what it would be like for them to go out into the modern world, even with Andre giving them every scrap of information that he had accrued about that world, as well as

Aleksei and Fane adding what they had learned from their lifemates.

Then she felt it, a pull that came out of nowhere, slight at first, but she honed in on her target range. The United States. Somewhere in the northern part of California. California was a big state. Gabrielle tried to pinpoint the pull a little closer but she couldn't. She shook her head and drew a circle with her fingertip, keeping the strongest part of that pull inside the center of the circle.

"I'm sorry," she said. "That's the best I can do. I think she's somewhere in that range, but it's a big range."

There was a silence while the ancients stared down at the circle. Dragomir cleared his throat. When he spoke his voice was husky, as if he hadn't spoken aloud in ages. "You believe my lifemate exists and she is somewhere inside that location? That circle? On another continent?"

Gabrielle swallowed hard. She nodded. "I'm sorry I couldn't be more specific, but maybe Andre can help narrow it down."

The ancients exchanged long looks.

Kessake, they searched the world over several times. You are giving him back hope. You, Teagan and Trixie. Amazing.

I could be wrong. I have no way of knowing it is for certain. I've just always been able to locate things and people this way.

You never told anyone else about this ability? The prince? Gregori?

She shrugged. *It seemed more of a parlor trick than actually useful. It never occurred to me there might be a way to find lifemates. I needed Dragomir's song, and only Trixie could give that to me.*

"I have given that location to Josef. He is looking up any psychic women who might be in the database right now. Dragomir, that does not mean she will be one of these women. Not all psychic women went to the institute for testing. You will need to search the entire area," Andre said.

Dragomir nodded. He stood up, a fluid ripple of muscle,

much like a great jungle cat stretching. He bowed toward the three women, the gesture old-world and courtly. "I cannot repay you. Whether what you have given me to aid me in finding my lifemate actually brings her to me or not, I am indebted to you."

He looked around him at the other ancients who had shared the monastery with him for the last century or more. "Do not hesitate. *Arwa-arvo olen isäntä, ekämak.*"

Honor keep you my brothers, Aleksei interpreted for Gabrielle.

Andre clasped his forearms in the traditional way of the Carpathian warriors. "I will send you every location of psychic women in that area as they come in. Teagan and I will be following you soon to the United States. Tomas, Mathias and Lojos have gone ahead of us and I promised them I would join them. We will be there soon should you need aid."

Dragomir looked to Fane and Aleksei. He stepped close to them, reaching toward Fane. Fane caught his forearms in a firm clasp. *"Arwa-arvod mäne me ködak,"* Fane said.

May your honor hold back the dark, Aleksei whispered into Gabrielle's mind.

That's so beautiful, she whispered back. And it was. These men, so determined to help one another hold on.

Dragomir turned to Aleksei and clasped his forearms in a strong grip.

Aleksei returned the grip. *"Arwa-arvo olen gæidnod, ekäm.* Honor guide you, my brother," he repeated in English for Gabrielle.

With one more bow toward the three women, Dragomir was gone, leaving the monastery for the first time in over a hundred years. There was a long silence following his departure. A cool breeze slid through the courtyard. Teagan moved first, pulling out a different stone. This one was the color of indigo. She knelt in front of the ancient called Andor. Waited. Slowly, very slowly, almost as if he were a wild animal being pushed into a corner, the man sank to the ground and fixed his eyes on her.

They worked through most of the night, bringing a little relief to each of the ancients. Shockingly, each of their life-mates seemed to be somewhere in this century. Had Mikhail's father known when he'd chosen the ancients to leave? It was said Vlad had precognition, so it was possible.

Not one of them had any idea how long Teagan's infusion of color into their relentlessly dark auras would last. For some, like Andor and Ferro, the colors refused to penetrate even all the way through the first layer. Still, through Trixie's ability to see their songs, Gabrielle found a pull for each of them. The women were scattered across several continents, but she was able to point them in a direction.

The moment the last of the ancients had gone, the three women collapsed, exhausted. Pale. In need of blood. Aleksei gathered Gabrielle into his arms to hold her close to him, his body sheltering hers.

"Next rising, I will find Denny Jashari and bring a little justice into his life," he told the others.

"Two of Mazur's pawns were disposed of," Andre reported. "The third disappeared."

"He will likely move on," Fane said.

"And the other human hunters?" Aleksei asked.

"They were headed for the nearest airport," Andre said, as he wrapped his arms around a swaying Teagan.

Trixie gave a disgusted snort. "Cowards. Fred and Esmeralda Wilson recruited me. Esmeralda pretended to be my friend, but I heard her talking with her husband and the others that they needed to kill me as soon as I led them to all of you. They were already complaining about having to hike in the cold. Jay Benson was with them. He was with me on the plane, and we had coffee many times back in the States. He wanted me dead as well. I'll bet all of them are already on a plane heading back to the States." She sank to the ground and looked surprised that she was there.

"They will not escape," Fane said softly, reaching for her. "We will be going home as soon as Josef has all of our papers in order. That should be next rising."

Aleksei nodded. "Gabrielle and I will remove the monastery and ensure there is no evidence of it, and then we will go to the prince and let him know that the three women were able to help the ancients."

"He will want to send other ancients to them," Andre said. "Clearly what you three did for the ancients was successful, at least in giving them hope, time and a direction."

"Difficult if Gabrielle is working in her laboratory in the Carpathian Mountains and Trixie and Teagan are in the United States," Aleksei pointed out.

Andre nodded thoughtfully. "Is it necessary to have your lab here, Gabrielle? Could you work out of the United States?"

Gabrielle's heart jumped. She rubbed at her wrist, her fingers tracing the flames on the links of her bracelet absently as she considered Andre's inquiry. She hadn't been home in a very long while, but then her mother and father lived in the States. She stayed a distance from them because her mother still had the power to hurt her. She wasn't afraid of her anymore, but she still despised the tantrums, and age hadn't mellowed her mother's fiery nature.

This is something you would be interested in doing? Living in the United States close to Teagan and Trixie?

She liked Trixie. The woman wasn't just wise; she truly cared about people. Trixie might think she was as tough as nails, but she had a gentle heart, a gentle soul. If the three of them lived close they could support one another when needed.

I hadn't thought of living there, Gabrielle admitted, *and I know my research is important, so I wouldn't want to do anything that might jeopardize it. Still, I kind of like the idea now that it might be a possibility. What do you think?*

I think I will be happy anywhere that you are, Gabrielle. If we live there, you can have your dream house as long as the soil beneath it is rich in minerals.

Again her heart jerked hard. He had seen her long-ago dream and cared enough to remember. She didn't need it anymore, but still, she was very happy that it mattered to him. She slipped her hand into his. *Reality is far better than any dream, Aleksei. If we get the chance to move to the United States near Trixie and Teagan, I will love that, but I will love it just as much wherever we settle.*

"Gabrielle?" Andre prompted. "Can you take your work out of the Carpathian Mountains? Teagan and Trixie have family in the United States. They cannot leave. We could set up a state-of-the-art laboratory for you. No one can live as long as we have without accumulating wealth. We can get you anything you need."

Trixie nodded. "It would be nice to have you close, Gabrielle."

She loved the genuine character Trixie had. Clearly she was a woman who called things the way she saw them. She was still eyeing Aleksei with a distinct wariness.

"I don't honestly know. All the samples are here that I've been working on. The soil and the . . ." She trailed off. She'd been studying the biological makeup of the women who had suffered multiple miscarriages, looking for a common anomaly that might explain why they couldn't carry and couldn't breastfeed properly with the necessary nutrients. "Babies used to be able to go to ground with their mothers; now, they can't, not the first few months. In a couple of cases, not for several years. Many of the women can't properly feed their babies without supplements. There is a reason. It could be environmental, like the parasite that was a contributing factor, but . . ." She trailed off again, realizing they probably weren't that interested in what she did. They just wanted to know if she could do it anywhere.

She ducked her head. "I'd be willing to go to the States if Shea agreed to provide me with anything I needed from those living here."

Aleksei's fingers threaded through her hair. "If you would prefer to live in the United States, Gabrielle, I will have a word with the prince and we will make it work. What you are doing, the work you are doing, is too important to have you uncomfortable or unhappy. We will find a way."

Gabrielle looked at Trixie and Teagan. They could help

other ancients, but only if the three of them were together. Word would get out, as it did, on the common path of the Carpathian people, and the ancients would seek them out, especially if any of the seven ancients found their lifemate.

"I definitely would prefer to live in the United States near Trixie and Teagan if I can have a laboratory. We could help other ancients and . . ."

Maybe even Gary.

The thought was there before she could stop it. She glanced nervously up at Aleksei, meeting the brilliant green of his eyes. She lifted her chin. "I want to help Gary find his lifemate." She said it firmly. Meaning it. Wanting Aleksei to see she meant it.

Aleksei nodded, his eyes warm and soft with an emotion that sent her heart skittering in her chest. "Of course you would want to help him, *kislány*, I would expect nothing less of you."

His gaze continued to move over her face, and that slow drift of green held possession and something more. The *more* made her heart go from a fast flutter to a slow melt. Love. Pure and simple.

"You need to feed." The words were intimate. His tone mesmerizing.

Gabrielle stared up at him, feeling as if she were falling, tumbling straight into those deep green twin pools. So cool. So beautiful and compelling. She didn't notice that Andre had taken Teagan to the far corner of the courtyard, or that Fane was wrapped protectively around Trixie, clearly giving her blood. She had eyes only for Aleksei.

They were moving, floating across the courtyard until they were against that heavy wall. She felt secure. Safe. Sexy. The way he held her. The way he looked at her. She knew she would get far more than blood. She felt his body, hard and thick, pressed tightly against hers. She also knew he would conceal them, wrap them in a cocoon of silence where no prying eyes could see or hear them.

She loved that he took her when he wanted her—and that

he wanted her so often. He made her feel sexy and important to him.

Woman, you are sexy. More, there is nothing and no one in this world more important to me than you. I know your body is already welcoming to mine.

It was. He was absolutely correct. Hunger beat at her. Weakness. It didn't matter. Only that he was close. Hard. Hot. Delicious. She smoothed her hands over his broad shoulders, let her hands drift through his hair indulgently.

"I love the way you smell, Aleksei," she whispered, and nuzzled his neck. "Like a man. Like the forest and mountains. Fresh and clean and a little wild. You taste like that as well. I crave the way you taste. Sometimes, when I'm just thinking about you, I can taste you in my mouth." She made the confession a little shyly.

His hands were at her breasts, cupping the soft weight of them in his hands. She hadn't noticed her clothes were gone until that moment and that all she wore was her fiery bracelet. The cool mountain air felt decadent against her hot skin.

"Put your arms around my neck and hold on, *kislány*, you are going for a ride. Take my blood now. Take whatever you need. I will have enough time for the hunt and then get back to you, but not enough time to take you again before we rest."

She shivered, loving his demanding tone. Loving that he knew he wouldn't have enough time to bury himself in her before they had to go to ground if they didn't take the opportunity now, and it mattered to him.

His hands went to her bottom and he lifted her easily. She wrapped her legs around his hips, and her mouth found his. She loved kissing him. *Loved it.* She could kiss him forever. She took her time. She could feel the broad, flared crown of his cock press tight against her entrance, but he kissed her as if kissing her mattered as much to him as it did to her.

Little cat. You are my world.

She kissed him again. And again. He had somehow become her world and she didn't even know when. Only that he was. Only that she loved pleasing him. Making him happy. Seeing his face light up while they talked.

You're mine, she whispered back.

He didn't slam her down over him as she thought he might, but lowered her slowly, so that she felt every exquisite inch of him filling her with perfect slowness. She gasped, threw her head back and allowed the feeling to engulf her. Pure bliss. Aleksei. He gave her that every time.

Take my blood, kislány.

The need in his voice was almost as strong as the hunger driving her. She nuzzled his neck, listening to the ebb and flow of his blood. So hot. So strong and powerful. All hers. His heart was as steady as he was. Always her rock. Always to be counted on. She licked over his pulse. Caught his earlobe between her teeth to feel him shudder. To feel his cock swell, forcing her tight muscles to stretch. That bite of pain only added to the pleasure spreading through her like wildfire.

Gabrielle.

He hissed her name and she knew she was giving him the same pleasure as she moved her hips in a slow ride, up and then back down, the friction intense as her body gripped his so tightly.

She ignored the warning and ran a series of tiny bites from his ear to his shoulder. Nipping. Little stings her tongue soothed. She loved the way his cock swelled and jerked inside of her, pushing at her inner muscles, demanding she take all of him. She lifted up and slid back down, moving in tight little circles, listening to his breath hiss out and loving that, too. She felt the convulsive bite of his fingers on her butt, hard, meaning business, and she sank her teeth deep into his pounding pulse.

He dug his fingers deeper and roared. His unique taste burst through her mouth, and every nerve ending in her body grew even more aware, more sensitive, his essence acting like an aphrodisiac.

He took over, surging into her, leaning her back against the wall, bending so she wouldn't lose contact with his neck as he pounded into her. It felt so good. Great. Perfection. Utter bliss. Fire streaked through her from breast to core. She felt the familiar tension coiling tighter and tighter. She fisted his hair in her hands, holding on, loving the way he surrounded her, was in her, in her mouth, in her body.

She could feel strength pouring into every cell, giving her power. Filling her just as his cock made her feel full beyond bursting. At the same time, his mind poured into hers, filling every empty place, sweeping away the last remnants of loneliness. He had taken her body from the start, owning it. Then he'd claimed her soul and she'd given him that as well. Now, she knew, it was her heart he had. All of her. Every inch of her, inside and out, belonged to Aleksei.

She licked over his pulse, closing the twin holes she had placed there, and rested her head for a moment on his shoulder, savoring him. All of him. She kissed his throat, his neck, trailed kisses to his ear. Placing her lips close so he could feel the whisper right there, she told him what was in her heart. What was there in her soul—and had been almost from the start. What was in her mind and body.

"I love you, Aleksei. With everything in me. I love you. I belong to you. All of me, belongs to you."

His head jerked back. His green eyes met hers, a fierce, possessive burn that seemed to go right through her. His body took hers, hard and fast.

She cried out and then dropped her face to his shoulder, biting down to keep from screaming. *I have to let go.*

No. You wait for me.

It was impossible. She was flying too high. The coiled knot was wound so tightly, every nerve ending burning for release. *Aleksei.* She sobbed his name.

You wait. He was implacable.

He pounded into her, driving deep, driving her up higher than she ever thought she could go, but she hung on—for him—she would do anything for him, her arms tight, her fists in his hair, reaching with him.

"Now, *kessake*, my little cat. Give that to me. Come with me."

She had waited, holding the tidal wave back when she thought she couldn't, when she thought it was impossible, just because he wanted it. Colors burst behind her eyes and radiated through her mind. Her body flew apart, finding another dimension, a subspace where she floated, while her body rippled and quaked, milking his, her tight muscles strangling until she felt his bliss as well, until he groaned and his fingers dug so deep she knew she would have his marks on her and she loved that, too. Everything.

When she could breathe, she lifted her head. "Aleksei?"

"In a minute, *kessake*, give me a minute to let your admission sink in. To know it is real and I did not make it up. You gave yourself to me?"

She rubbed her face in his neck, feeling the silken slide of his hair. There wasn't the slightest feminine thing about the way it felt. More like a warrior of old holding her captive. A willing captive, but she knew she couldn't escape whether she wanted to or not and that was thrilling to her.

"I did give myself to you," she admitted, knowing he was waiting for her answer. Holding himself still. Her heart beat fast. Thudded.

"*All* of you?" he confirmed.

"That was what you asked for, honey, and that's what I've given to you."

"You know there is no taking it back once you give that gift." That was a warning, pure and simple.

She pressed a kiss over his pulse. Rock steady. Hers. "I'm well aware of that."

"Give me your mouth, right now."

She smiled against his neck. "You're going to be unbearably bossy, aren't you?"

"Absolutely. Now give me your mouth. I have to go hunting and I want the taste of you with me while I'm gone."

She did what he asked, kissing him with everything she

had. Hot. Wild. With absolute confidence. She opened her mind completely to him, giving him what he wanted. Letting him see how much she loved his body, his kisses, and his cock, and what they could do to her. Letting him see much, much more than that. How he made her feel truly safe, in a world she didn't fully understand, for the first time she could ever remember. How much she needed him and believed he would always stand up for her. How his steady pulse soothed her and gave her the confidence to live her life—any kind of life—with him.

"You just gave me the world," he said softly.

"You are my world," she told him. Meaning it.

Reluctantly, Aleksei's body slipped from hers. "I have to go, Gabrielle. Stick with Trixie and Teagan unless the sun really begins to rise. Go to my room and use that ground. The mists and the gates will protect you. Fane has woven strong safeguards, so do not try to leave this place for any reason. Andre and I will be adding to the safeguards, so you will be fine while we are gone."

She shook her head as he lowered her feet gently to the ground and swept his hand over her, clothing her. He did the same for himself.

"We have gone over how to open and close the earth. You can do it if need be, *kislány*. I expect you to do as I say. I will not be pleased if you disobey me. This is for your own safety."

"But you'll come back. Before we have to go to ground. You'll come back." She clutched at his shirt, suddenly afraid. She didn't like even thinking about him not coming back. She found she was suddenly very anxious, those knots of dread beginning to form in her stomach. Not just beginning, she realized. She'd been tense since they'd first faced the ancients.

"I do not foresee a problem, Gabrielle," he said quietly. "But you have to always be prepared for an emergency. I need to know you can take care of yourself if I do run into trouble and I am delayed. Eventually we will have children. I will need to know that you can protect them."

Gabrielle bit her lip hard. "I am not good with violence,

Aleksei, but I would never allow anything or anyone to harm our children." She rubbed at her bracelet, wanting to cling to him, to keep him with her. She knew he was making sense but the very idea made her uneasy.

"Or you," he persisted. "If they harm you, *kislány*, they harm me. If anything happens to you, it happens to me. When you are protecting you, that is you protecting me."

She nodded slowly. She would never allow harm to come to Aleksei, either, if she could help it. "I'll go to ground if I have to." She wondered if Teagan and Trixie had already mastered that particular stumbling block. If they had, both were a lot stronger than she was. If not, it would be up to her to help them.

Aleksei rewarded her with a smile. "That's my girl."

She couldn't help but feel a warm glow as they made their way back to the other two women. Trixie and Teagan were both wearing their own glows. She wasn't the only one who had been pushed up against the wall. The three women exchanged smiles. Trixie held out her hand to Gabrielle.

"You boys go ahead and find yourselves something to drink. We'll be just fine. I've got my vampire-hunting kit and we're good," Trixie announced, as Gabrielle took her hand.

"Woman. Do not try to use that kit on anyone, especially one of us when we return," Fane warned. His warning would have been far more effective had he not been laughing. Clearly he found his lifemate both entertaining and amusing.

"I want to see this kit," Gabrielle said. "Maybe we can improve on it."

"It needs improving," Trixie said. "Waste of money, most of it."

Teagan burst out laughing. "Grandma Trixie, you're incorrigible."

Fane joined in with Teagan's laughter and then took to the air, following Aleksei and Andre down toward the village where they could find strong men to give them the sustenance they needed.

20

Gabrielle waved her hands so each of the three women had comfortable chairs in which to lean back and take in the last of the stars. The night was cool and she added a fire pit so the warm glow could heat them while the crackling flames brought a kind of comfort. She took a long, slow look around, still feeling uneasy in spite of the fact that she knew the three ancients had triple safeguarded the gates and woven more safeguards into the thick mist surrounding them.

"There are a few things about being Carpathian I could like," Trixie announced contentedly. She stretched her hands toward the fire and pinned her granddaughter with her steely eyes. "You know I came looking for you. And I brought that passel of trouble with me. No fool like an old fool."

"Grandma Trixie." Teagan breathed her name softly. Lovingly. "I think fate brought you here to Fane. I have to admit I never, ever considered that you would be with a man, but the way he looks at you and the way you look at him, it's beautiful."

Trixie scowled at her granddaughter. "That man thinks he can handle me, he's got himself another think coming. He thinks my attitude is cute. *Cute.* Worse, when I get snarky, he laughs. It doesn't faze him a bit. And then he . . ." She broke off abruptly, scowling even more.

"Kisses you senseless," Teagan filled in, and burst out laughing.

"Enough of that nonsense. What are we going to tell your sisters?"

Teagan sobered immediately. She took a breath. "That we both are in love, Grandma, but we can never tell them what we are. We'll have to be careful to always appear fully human. If we choose to live in that world and our lifemates agree to do so for us, we have to follow the rules of the Carpathian people. We're under the rule of the prince, and humans don't know about us—not even family."

Gabrielle held her hand out to the fire. She felt a chill creep down her spine in spite of the dancing flames. She sat up slowly, listening to the two women teasing each other. She took a look around, not understanding the chill, but not ignoring it, either. The safeguards were so strong, she didn't think even a master vampire could penetrate the guards. Her bracelet drew her attention, the low humming it had been emitting becoming stronger. Louder. More insistent. The flames in the links were glowing red now, and it had gone from warm to hot. Not burning her, but definitely hot.

"What is it, Gabrielle?" Trixie asked.

"I don't know. Do you feel strange? Do you hear any notes that just don't sound right?" The feeling persisted, even though she wanted to tell herself it was nothing and she had always been afraid. Too afraid. Aleksei was gone, and it stood to reason why she didn't like him being away from her. Why she suddenly didn't feel safe. She didn't know what her mysterious bracelet could or couldn't do. Maybe it didn't like the ancients and the lingering power there in the monastery.

Before Trixie could answer, she jumped up and hurried across to the gates. "I think I'd feel better if we put up more safeguards," she said. "I've seen it done, but I've never actually done it before." She was being paranoid and showing the other two women she was, but without Aleksei, she couldn't help it. That chill down her spine had developed into a full-fledged shiver that gave her goose bumps all over her body. She had to grit her teeth to resist calling Aleksei back to her.

"Fane, Aleksei and Andre tripled the safeguards," Teagan said.

"I know. I know," Gabrielle repeated. Her stomach churned

so badly she began to search around the compound itself, looking up on the rooftops, all along the wall itself. She had no idea what she was looking for, something out of place maybe.

"I've unraveled them," Teagan said, watching her closely. "I could probably figure out how to reverse that and set them." She followed Gabrielle to the gate.

Trixie remained seated, closing her eyes for a moment and reaching out to listen to the mountain and the play of the wind. "I hear the music of the mountain," she reported, "and your music, Gabrielle. You're frightened, but I can't find anything for you to be afraid of."

Gabrielle shook her head and halted. She was *such* a baby without Aleksei. She'd promised him she would learn to protect their children. That she'd have his back, but she was such a coward, always afraid.

"I'm just being silly," she admitted. "A bit ridiculous." She tried a small, self-deprecating laugh, her fingers once more dropping to her bracelet, now lit with a steady, angry fire. The links glowed with flames. "I've always been one of those people who are afraid of certain circumstances. I was never a camper like you, Teagan. I wouldn't ever go off by myself and travel. Joie, my sister, and Jubal, my brother, would drop everything and go in a heartbeat. I'm more of a planner and I like four solid walls around me. I'm sorry if I made you all nervous."

Trixie sat up straighter and held her hand up for silence. Gabrielle closed her mouth and then bit her lip—hard. Another chill went down her spine, and this time the air felt heavier. Ominous. The wind stilled. At once she held her breath. The air changed swiftly without the breeze, from clean and fresh to a heavy, oily, very dense atmosphere.

"We need to get inside one of the buildings right now, and, Teagan, you begin weaving safeguards for the house itself," Gabrielle ordered, and sprinted back toward Trixie to yank her out of the chair. "Hurry. We only have a few minutes." *Aleksei! Tell me what to do.* Because now she was certain.

There was a vampire close. Her mind told her that. Her bracelet had been trying to tell her that. *He's inside with us. I feel him, Aleksei. How could he get through the safeguards? How could we not spot him?*

Stay calm, Gabrielle. Look around. I feel the danger through my link with you, but I have to see it to give you aid. If he was floating, molecules in the air, above the monastery all the time you were working with the ancients, it could be done. He would have been inside already. But he would have to be very old and very skilled. Aron would have been his servant.

Oh. God. That means he has to be extremely powerful, right?

I am on my way to you.

His voice steadied her. Calm. Like a rock. Her anchor in a storm. She took in a breath of tainted, foul air as she pulled Trixie from the chair and pushed her toward the relative safety of the four walls. If they could get inside and weave safeguards, they could hold out until the hunters returned. As Trixie ran toward the nearest building—which was Fane's—she looked scared.

"I can't hear his song."

Trixie can't hear his song.

She will not be able to because he is in a form that would not have one. He is part of the air. You feel the thickness. The foulness. He is there.

"Just get inside. Teagan, hurry," Gabrielle hissed, as she shoved Trixie inside.

She took one step toward Teagan and felt a hand in her hair. The vampire dropped from the sky, forming as he did so, his hand reaching down to grip Gabrielle's long hair in a terrible fist of iron. He yanked her so hard she went flying back against him, coming off her feet, unable to turn her head to look at him, to give Aleksei what he needed.

Teagan skidded to a halt and backed up, both hands up in a placating position. "Let's all calm down," she said softly.

I can't see him, Gabrielle told Aleksei. *He's got me and I can't get away.*

Do not fight him. Stall. We are on our way back. He will want to brag. To talk. Let him.

Gabrielle closed her eyes for a moment and then made herself obey. She sagged against her captor as if in surrender. Without warning he bent his head and drove his teeth into her neck. She screamed. It hurt beyond anything she could imagine. The burn was fierce, like an acid dripping all the way to her bones while teeth tore at her flesh.

Teagan screamed as well and ran toward them. Trixie burst out of the building, armed with her gun, firing the wooden stakes. The first hit the vampire in his neck as he bent over Gabrielle. The second hit his throat as he turned, his glowing red eyes finding a new target.

"Get away from her," Trixie yelled.

The bracelet on Gabrielle's wrist released, spinning, the flames dancing in the air in a whirling circle straight at the vampire's thick wrist. It sliced through flesh and bone cleanly, leaving flames behind, flames that swept up the vampire's arm so that he shrieked and let go of Gabrielle.

Teagan caught Gabrielle's arm and yanked her away from the tall vampire, who had his attention centered solely on Trixie. Blood poured from Gabrielle's neck where the vampire had torn great ragged lacerations in her flesh to get at what he wanted most. Teagan continued to drag her as far from the vampire as possible before she helped her to sit on the ground.

Gabrielle turned her head toward the vampire to allow Aleksei to use her eyes in order to see the undead who had lain in wait, keeping hidden, biding his time to wreak his revenge on the three hunters. The action caused more blood to gush from the wound in her neck.

The vampire made a horrible sound, a rattle in his throat as he put out the flames, the sunken holes he had for eyes centered on Trixie as he stepped toward her. Trixie backed up but gamely let loose another wooden stake. This one hit the undead in the center of his chest. He snarled, batted at it and lunged at Trixie, raising his good arm, fist clenched so that his forearm and fist had become a huge hammer. He was so fast there was no getting away from the killing blow.

Trixie threw the gun at him and turned to try to run, knowing it was too late. She heard, as if in the distance, Teagan and Gabrielle scream. She tripped and fell as a blast of hot air burned her skin. Her flesh seemed to shrink in an effort to avoid an unnatural abomination—to prevent it from touching her, let alone striking her.

She rolled to see him standing over her, his hideous teeth jagged and covered in Gabrielle's blood. Black blood dripped steadily from the stub where his hand had been. His skeleton-like face was smeared with blood. His arm raised and descended, and she knew she was dead. She closed her eyes and prayed Teagan and Gabrielle were running.

The blow never came. She heard a grunt and a horrible growling rattle in the vampire's throat a second time, as if he were choking. Cautiously, she opened one eye and saw another man there. He wasn't as tall as the Carpathians she knew, but his hair flowed around his shoulders. He was leaner, but all defined muscle. She could see the ripple beneath the shirt as he backed the vampire well away from her.

"Gary." Gabrielle breathed his name. How he had gotten there, made it through the safeguards and managed to save Trixie was a miracle.

Gabrielle stared in awe at the man she had known and loved for so long as Gary Jansen. That man was gone. In his place was an ancient warrior. A Daratrazanoff. He flowed when he moved. Glided. His strength was enormous as he shoved the vampire's arm up and away from Trixie and backed him up, forcing him away from the fallen woman.

He moved with absolute confidence, his features impassive, his eyes cool as he held the one arm up out of the way like a bridge while he slammed his fist straight into the vampire's chest, driving for the heart.

Trixie scrambled to her feet and made her way cautiously around the two circling fighters to get to the other women.

Teagan was on her knees beside Gabrielle, her eyes closed, and clearly Andre was directing her how to heal the wound in the Carpathian manner.

Gabrielle, making a soft sound of dismay, didn't take her eyes from the scene of combat. Gary had been an academic. More, he was a brain beyond most people's comprehension. He had served the world and then the world of the Carpathians with his ability to see what others could not. She knew he still possessed that brain, but her Gary was no longer there. The ancients had poured themselves into him, giving him their blood and their memories. Good and bad. Skills and darkness.

She wanted to look away from the violence. It seemed such blasphemy when it was Gary, not Aleksei, battling the undead. A scholar with a gentle soul, a poet, a man with such a brain . . .

Kislány. That single endearment whispered into her mind so intimately. She closed her eyes, feeling his love surrounding her. She wasn't lost anymore, not when she had Aleksei.

He's gone, Aleksei, completely gone. I'm looking at him and almost don't recognize him. It's as if he's aged a thousand years.

He has.

She knew Aleksei spoke the stark truth. He didn't sugarcoat the truth for her. She bit her lip hard, wanting to weep for Gary. Inside she was weeping.

Gabrielle. You did not do this. He was converted and then brought to the cave of warriors for recognition. Had Gregori not claimed him, he could have lived a half life. Carpathian and yet not, with no hope of a lifemate. No one knew exactly how it worked. Andre said few males are converted. Until the prince converted his lifemate it was not known it was even a possibility without madness setting in. There was never a reason to convert a human male.

Not until they fell in combat defending Carpathian women and children. She tried not to be bitter.

He is alive, kislány; that is a gift in itself.

He isn't Gary. I don't know this man. Over time, I saw the difference in his build and his combat skills. He had to become a fighter in order to defend the children, but he's completely different now. He looks like . . .

Gregori. The Daratrazanoff family.

Yes.

Because that is what he is. That is who he had to become to come fully into our world. Just as you are changed, so is he.

Aleksei was wrong. Essentially, she was still Gabrielle. She wasn't blind. She knew her looks were enhanced, but inside, she was Gabrielle. Gary was no longer Gary. He was all of those ancients who had gone before.

He was a hunter of the vampire. Skilled. Merciless. Capable of ripping out a heart and throwing it onto the ground. Capable of withstanding horrendous wounds without flinching to get the job done. Capable of calling down the lightning and incinerating the blackened, wizened heart and bathing his arms and torso in the white-hot energy to get rid of the acid-like blood from the undead before he directed the whip of lightning to the vampire's body.

"Eww," Trixie whispered. "So that's how it's done. I don't suppose they can put lightning in a bottle and sell that in their vampire-hunting kits on the Internet."

"I don't think so, Grandma," Teagan said, her voice even softer than her grandmother's. "I saw Andre do that several times and it never feels real."

Gary turned toward them, and Gabrielle's heart thudded wildly. *Aleksei?*

"I'm here, *kislány*," he said, and he was, striding toward her, right past Gary, to wrap his arm around her, to inspect the side of her neck.

I have to go to him.

I know. Give me a minute to make certain this wound is thoroughly cleaned and as healed as possible until we get to ground.

I know. Two little words, but they said everything to her. Meant everything.

She felt him inside her, so bright. No ego. All Aleksei. At once the throbbing in her neck stopped.

"Teagan," Aleksei said softly. "Thank you. You did a great job."

Teagan sent him a smile. "Andre's been working with me."

Andre and Fane stood in front of Gary. Gabrielle could see them greet him in the way Carpathian warriors did one another. Forearms to forearms. Making themselves vulnerable to attack.

Gary had definitely saved Trixie's life. Without him, the three hunters might not have made it back in time to save any of their lifemates, let alone Trixie. His eyes moved from the two warriors thanking him to Gabrielle. She felt his penetrating gaze all the way down to her toes. It was a little disconcerting to be looking into Gary's eyes and see that he wasn't Gary. She saw that so clearly.

His eyes were even different. He'd always worn glasses. Now, his eyes were a deep blue, moving on to a dark inky black and then, when he blinked, a blue green, like the color of the sea. Her heart pounded as Aleksei wrapped his arm around her waist and urged her toward the man.

I don't think I can do this, Aleksei. Maybe if I had . . .

What? Recognized he wasn't her lifemate? Would that have changed anything at all for him? He had not made the decision to become Carpathian. Gregori had made the decision for him, based on his dire condition. She'd been there. She couldn't have stopped Gregori. No one, not even the prince, could have. Gregori had few people he loved in his life. Gary was one of them.

You need to go to him, Gabrielle. I will be with you. Close. Inside you. In your mind. But you need this and you know it. Aleksei stopped walking and allowed her to take the last few steps on her own. *Kislány, you are not to touch him. Not for any reason. I will not be able to tolerate that, so for all of our sakes, keep your hands to yourself. He will not touch you. He is an ancient now, far gone from any of us—even Gregori.*

She hated that. She hated that Gary had given so much of

himself to the Carpathians and now he had lost all of himself. She lifted her chin and stepped close to him. She scented something wild—feral. A trapped animal not familiar with civilization. Gary. Her Gary. So far gone. So out of reach.

Andre and Fane had gone to their women, allowing her a little privacy with Gary. His eyes moved over her face. Impassive. Cool. Remote. She reached out for Aleksei in her mind, needing his strength to get through this.

"You were amazing. Thank you for coming to our aid."

"I had to know you were all right, Gabrielle."

She shivered at the coldness in his eyes. Her Gary was gone for all time. In his eyes burned the hell of centuries of darkness—of battles. He had become a vessel for the ancients, and there was no turning that around and bringing the man she knew back.

She stepped close to him, trying to find the man she loved. Would always love. He was in there somewhere. The gentle soul whose brain had no match. "Gary." She said his name softly, trying to call him back to her. Away from the terrible, unrelenting darkness she'd seen in the ancients there in the monastery.

"Are you happy? Is he a good lifemate to you?"

She shivered and wrapped her arms around herself. Even his voice was different. She had to work to fight back the tears. She nodded. "He's very good to me, Gary. She's out there. For you. Your lifemate."

His eyes changed color again, bleak and cold and gone from her. The ancients, with their despair of finding a lifemate, were already working at him. She knew dawn was close and all of them would have to go to ground. Light was streaking through the gray, heralding the sun. Still . . .

"Teagan helped the ancients, Gary. It is possible she could aid you to hold on. Let us try for you. Trixie can match your song . . ."

"It is not mine alone."

Gabrielle glanced back at Trixie. The two women were already pressing close.

"It is all yours," Trixie replied softly. "I see the notes, and they were originally others', but they've blended with your original song and made another completely different one, unique only to you. Let us try. You saved my life. You saved my granddaughter. Please. Allow us to do this for you."

Gabrielle could see Gary didn't hold out any hope. She had to fight to keep her hands to herself when she wanted to take his arm and tug until he went with them to the map of the world still drawn on the ground.

"It might be worse to know she isn't there," Gary ventured.

"Nothing can be worse than where you are," Aleksei said. "I know. No hope. Only unrelenting darkness. Not even the whisper of temptation. So far gone you know you cannot be around anyone without risking your honor. Give this to them. If not for you, then for them. For Gabrielle."

Gabrielle loved him for that alone, and she had to tell him. Say it. Make it understood that even though Gary stood right before her and she ached for him, wept for him, it was Aleksei. *It's you I love.*

I know, kislány, I feel it. I am in your mind, holding you tight to me. He is close to agreeing. We do not have much time before the dawn is upon us. As old as we are, it is nearly impossible to stand even the early-morning sun. Persuade him. There was a pause. *Without touching him.*

She hadn't even realized she was reaching out toward Gary as if she could hold back the darkness in him. She jerked her hand back and pressed her palm tight against her thigh. "Please," she said softly. "Just do this. If it doesn't work, well, at least you tried. Even if we can't find a direction for a lifemate, Teagan can ease the darkness just a little."

"For you, Gabrielle."

At least the memory of her was still there in his mind. Aiding him in some way. He might not be able to feel the love he had for her, but he remembered it. He had remembered enough to care if she was all right and to do this for her.

Teagan beckoned him toward the map, obviously hoping with him so close to it, they could manage the process faster.

Trixie was already tuned to his song and she pushed the notes toward Gabrielle. Gary's song was dark and foreboding— every bit as dangerous as that of any of the ancients who had been locked away in the monastery. That hurt.

Gabrielle held herself together by leaning on Aleksei's strength. He was there, in her mind, holding her tight. She knew he wanted to be close to her and that it took tremendous discipline for him to hold himself physically away from her. She loved him all the more that he did—that he gave her this time with Gary. That he gave Gary what he needed as well.

Teagan's hands moved through her stones, seeking the one that would fit Gary. Gabrielle held her breath, praying silently that something would be right. She hadn't considered that Teagan might not have what he needed. She'd been in the mountains, collecting various stones that spoke to her, but what if . . .

Teagan frowned and pulled out several stones, cupping them in both hands. "I've never had the pull of more than one," she admitted, "but he needs all of these."

That didn't sound good. Gabrielle bit her lip. Hard. A single ruby drop beaded. Instantly Gary's gaze fastened on her mouth. Aleksei rumbled low in his chest. A warning. He moved, inserting his body between Gary and Gabrielle, his head bending, his tongue removing the single drop of blood as he glided past her.

Do not tempt him again. He is near the end. The ancients who poured themselves into him had no lifemates. They each endured centuries of darkness without any reward at the end. They sought the sun to keep their honor. He is all of them combined. If Teagan does not work her magic, he will have to do the same soon. No warrior, no matter how strong, can take many ancients' demons and stay honorable for long.

She felt his touch all the way to her toes. She felt his revelation all the way to her soul. She shivered and inhaled his scent for strength, because now she knew there was no hope without this. Aleksei didn't tell her lies.

Teagan began her soft chant, and at once, the color green

enveloped her and began to spread from her toward Gary. A
healing, soothing green, right in the center of the color wheel.
Slowly, the other colors began to appear, all of them searching
for a way into the merciless darkness surrounding Gary.
Gabrielle held her breath, terrified the colors wouldn't penetrate at all. At first it seemed as if the dense cloud was impenetrable, but the green found a thread, a single opening, and
wove a thin line, the width of a spiderweb, through the black.

Gabrielle almost bit her lip again, but she felt Aleksei brush
his finger over her lips, stopping her. She realized he was very
aware of her bad habit and was concentrating on her more
than on Teagan and whether she was successful or not.

The colors moved around the thick, solid mass. It seemed
hopeless. Other than the single thread of green, nothing else
could get through. Then Gabrielle felt the subtle boost of
power. First Andre joined with Teagan. Then Fane joined
with Teagan. Last was Aleksei. The three ancients poured
their combined strength into Andre's lifemate.

The burst of power sent a few of the colors pushing hard
at the edges of the darkened aura. One, a deep purple, slid in
beside the green, winding around it, so that the two colors
were woven together. Red slipped in using the same entrance
but branching out, every bit as thin a thread as the green had
been. Indigo found the red and followed the strand, braiding
with it so that it looked as if a spider had begun a web. That
thin. But it was there. Yellow and blue followed, spinning
together, using the same entrance and moving inside, away
from the other two strands.

Teagan swayed and slumped over the stones. She tried
twice to speak, but Andre gathered her into his arms and
turned her away from the others. Gabrielle knew instantly he
fed her. She could scent the blood in the air. Gary's gaze followed them and he inhaled sharply. Instantly she was aware
that his wounds hadn't been healed. He hadn't asked them to
be. Nor had anyone offered him blood to replace what was
lost. She opened her mouth.

Do not!

That was definitely an order. Gabrielle snapped her mouth closed, pressing her lips tightly together.

I will give him blood and heal him once you women are finished. Teagan has helped as much as she can. It is something and will give him relief. How long or how much, I do not know, but you will not allow him to touch you. Not to heal him. Not to feed. Do you understand me?

She knew he expected an answer. Her gaze shifted to him. He looked as if his ferocious temper might erupt at any moment. She even felt it, that fury, right in her mind, beating at her.

I understand. She didn't really. Gary would never harm her.

He is not the Gary you knew.

Trixie had his song, those notes, not silver, not gold. Fierce. Wild. Fearless. Powerful. It was impossible not to feel his song, not to be shaken by it. Trixie surrounded Gabrielle with the notes until she had absorbed them and her palms were filled with him. Her skin tingled. Hurt. Burned. Even her bracelet burned with fire. She gasped and nearly stopped, but she wouldn't let him down. None of the other ancients' songs had given her pain. She knew it was the pain of the ancients that had been poured into Gary.

She breathed through it and moved her hands over the map, trying to let go of herself, of her need to do this, to help him. She couldn't be there, only the strange talent she had. *Please. Please. Please.* She forced herself to quit chanting the prayer in her mind. This had to be right. Real. And if it didn't work, if she didn't find anything, she had to accept that. It would be a terrible blow, but she would have no choice.

She listened for Aleksei's breathing. Strong. Steady. Her rock. He was there with her, his lungs moving, his heart beating. Her left palm jerked toward her left. Subtle, so subtle she was afraid she'd done it. But no, there it was again. Very subtle. She opened her eyes and looked down, carefully drawing a circle with her right hand, the strongest point in the middle of that circle. France. Somewhere in France, Gary had a lifemate. He just had to hang on until he could find her.

She smiled triumphantly. She'd given him something. Hope. A chance. It was done. The best she could do for him.

"I will send the addresses to you of any psychic women Josef finds in the database, Gary," Andre said, "but remember, she may not be in there, so you have to hunt within that circle, and it covers a lot of territory."

Aleksei stepped close to Gary and extended his wrist. Fane glided in between the two men, extending his own wrist. "Let me. For Trixie. For what you did for my lifemate, I offer freely. Take what you need."

Fane glanced in warning at Aleksei, clearly telling him to back off. Fane didn't trust that Gary still wasn't so close to turning that he could keep from draining Aleksei dry, and that made the sorrow pressing down on Gabrielle even worse. She clutched at the back of Aleksei's shirt, connecting them physically. She wasn't certain if she was holding him back, afraid as well, or just that she had to touch him to get through this. To watch Gary leave. Alone.

"Your woman more than repaid me," Gary said.

"Take it," Fane said. "You have a long road ahead of you."

Gary took the offered wrist and drank. When he was finished he stepped back, silently telling them he'd had as much as he could take. He would heal his own wounds. He was a Daratrazanoff.

He leaned toward Gabrielle. "Be well, Gabby," he said softly, and was gone.

One moment he was there, the next he had completely disappeared. The tension went out of the three hunters. Gabrielle hadn't even realized they'd been tense.

"We need to get to ground," Fane said. "I'll weave the safeguards and set the mist. The next rising, we head for the States. Aleksei, you and Gabrielle will join us?"

Gabrielle let out her breath, slumping a little, exhausted. It was business as usual for the Carpathian males. They considered vampires and human hunters, lethal wounds and dangerous ancients an every-evening occurrence.

At least I won't be bored. It was a poor attempt at humor but it was all she had.

I will make certain of that, my little cat.

Aleksei wrapped his arm tightly around Gabrielle, pulling her into the shelter of his body. "We will go to the prince and also talk to Jacques's lifemate, Shea, to ensure she will get whatever samples Gabrielle needs to continue her work. Then we will follow and acquire a house near yours, as well as a laboratory."

Fane nodded and reached out his hand to Trixie. She didn't hesitate but immediately put her hand in his. As they turned away to get to work strengthening the safeguards, Gabrielle heard Trixie.

"Seriously, Fane. We need a real vampire-hunting kit. That silly gun was utterly useless."

"Lady, if I had any sense at all, I would turn you over my knee for even trying such a thing. You put yourself in danger." Fane brought her hand to his mouth. "Still, I was very proud of you."

Aleksei walked Gabrielle into the building that had been his refuge for over a hundred years. Without preamble he waved his hand and the ground opened. Deep. Cool. The soil rich with minerals. Gabrielle could see them sparkling. The cool soil called to her.

"Take your clothes off, little cat," Aleksei ordered. His hands moved up the sides of her breasts, sending an ache through her nipples.

She waved her hand and removed her clothing.

"Float down. Spread your legs for me. I gave you plenty of room."

She opened her mouth to protest, but his eyes glittered, and in any case, her body was already betraying her. She did exactly as he said, feeling her body growing hot and slick. Welcoming him.

He came down over her, completely blanketing her. Pinning her beneath him. The ground was soft and felt amazing against her bare skin. His hard body felt even better on top of her. He took his time, using his mouth and tongue and teeth on her breasts, his finger moving in her, bringing her to the brink over and over. Driving out every sane thought. Taking away the nightmare of the last couple of hours. Giving her something beautiful in return. And then he was inside of her. Hard. Rough. So Aleksei. So perfect.

She screamed out her orgasm, a tremendous tidal wave that swept him up and carried them both into another realm. She lay still, holding him, stroking caresses in his hair, his face buried in her neck.

"I love you, Aleksei." And she did. She was so completely filled with love for him she could barely think straight.

Aleksei kissed her, still buried to the root. Long after he sent her to sleep, he stayed inside of her, the place he loved to be most. He drank in her scent. Kept the taste of her on his tongue. She loved him. A miracle. His. He knew he would spend his life working to make her happy. He also knew she would bend over backward to give him everything he wanted.

He brushed kisses against her throat. "I love you, too, *kessake*," he whispered, and gave the command for the soil to close around and over them. Still buried deep, his body in hers, he laid his head in the sweet hollow between her shoulder and neck and allowed his heart and lungs to cease working until the next rising. He would wake inside of her, right where he wanted to be.

Keep reading for an excerpt from the next
GhostWalker novel by Christine Feehan

Power Game

Now available from Berkley

B ellisia Adams stared at herself in the mirror. Beside her was JinJing, a sweet woman, unaware that the man she worked for was an infamous criminal or that the woman beside her was no more Chinese than the man in the moon. Bellisia's hair was long and straight, a waterfall of silk reaching to her waist. She was short, delicate looking, with small feet and hands. She spoke flawlessly in the dialect Jin-Jing spoke, laughing and gossiping there in the water closet before the chime sounded and they had to get back to work.

She kept her heart rate absolutely steady, the beat never rising in spite of the fact that she knew just by the heightened security and the tenseness of the guards that what she'd been looking for this past week was finally here. It was a good thing, too. Time was running out fast. Like most of the technicians in the laboratory, she didn't wear a watch, but she was very aware of the days and hours ticking by.

JinJing waved to her and hurried out as the chime sounded, the call back to work. Anyone caught walking the halls was instantly let go. Or at least they disappeared. Rumor had it that wherever they were taken was not pleasant. The Cheng Company paid well. Bernard Lee Cheng had many businesses and employed a good number of people, but it was said that he was a very exacting boss.

Bellisia couldn't wait any longer. She couldn't be caught there in the water closet, either. Very carefully she removed the long wig and lifelike skin of her mask and rolled them into her white lab coat. She slipped off the laboratory uniform, revealing the skintight one-piece bodysuit she wore under it—the one that reflected the background around her. Her shoes were crepe soled and easy to move fast in. She removed them and shoved them into one of the pockets. Her pale blonde hair was braided in a tight weave. She was as ready as she'd ever be. She slipped out of the water closet, back into the narrow hallway the moment she knew it was empty. Her acute hearing ensured she knew exactly where most of the technicians were on the floor. She knew the exact location of every camera and just how to avoid them.

Once in the hall, she went up the wall to the ceiling, blending in with the dingy, off-white color that had seen better days. As she transitioned from the hallway of the laboratory to the offices, the color changed to a muted blue, fresh and crisp. She changed color until she perfectly blended in and then slowed her pace. Movement drew the eye and there were far more people in the offices. Most of them were in small open cubicles, but as she continued through to the next large bank of offices, the walls changed to a muted green in the one large office that mattered to her.

She could see the woman seated, facing away from her, looking at the man behind the desk. Bernard Lee Cheng. She was very tempted to kill him, take the opportunity of being so close and just get the job done. It would rid the world of a very evil man, but it wasn't her mission, no matter how much she wished it were. The woman, Senator Violet Smythe-Freeman—now just Smythe—was her mission, specifically to see if the senator was selling out her country and her fellow GhostWalkers, the teams of soldiers few even knew existed.

There was no way into the office, but that didn't matter. She moved slowly across the ceiling, hiding in plain sight. Even if one of the men or women on the floor happened to look up, they would have a difficult time spotting her as long as she was careful to move like a sloth, inching her way to her destination. She positioned herself outside the office over the door. Muting out the sounds around her, she concentrated on the voices coming from inside the office.

Cheng faced her. Even if she couldn't hear his every word because he'd soundproofed his office, she could read lips. He wanted the GhostWalker program. Files. Everything. Including soldiers to take apart. Her stomach clenched. Violet's voice was pitched low. She had the ability to persuade people to do what she wanted with her voice, but Cheng seemed immune.

She wanted money for her campaign. Maurice Stuart had named her his running mate for the presidential election. If elected, she planned to have Stuart assassinated so she would become president. Cheng would have an ally in the White House. It was a simple enough business deal. The origins of dark money never had to be exposed. No one would know.

Violet was beautiful and intelligent. She was poisonous. A sociopath. She was also enhanced, one of the original girls Dr. Whitney had found in an orphanage and experimented on so that he could enhance his soldiers without harming them. She used her looks and her voice to get the things she wanted. More than anything, she wanted power.

Cheng nodded his head and leaned forward, his eyes sharp, his face a mask. He repeated the price. Files. GhostWalkers.

Bellisia remained still as Violet sold out her country and fellow soldiers. She told him where to find a team and how to get to them. She also told him there were copies of the files he wanted in several places, but most were too difficult to get to. The place where he had the best chance was in Louisiana, at the Stennis Center.

Cheng responded adamantly, insisting she get the files for him. She was just as adamant she couldn't do that. He asked her why she was so against the GhostWalker program.

Bellisia tried to get closer, as if that would help her hear better. She wanted to know as well. Violet was one of them. One of the original orphans Peter Whitney had used for his own purposes—a "sister," not by blood but certainly in every other way. She'd undergone the same experimenting with enhancing psychic abilities. With genetics, changing DNA. There was no doubt that Whitney was a genius, but he was also certifiably insane.

Violet's murmured response horrified Bellisia. The woman was a GhostWalker snob. Superior soldiers were fine. DNA of animals was fine. Enhancement met with her approval. But not when it came to the latest experiments coming to light— the use of vipers and spiders. That was going too far and cheapened the rest of them. She wanted anyone with that kind of DNA wiped out.

There was a moment of silence, as if Cheng was turning her sudden burst of venomous hatred over and over in his mind, just as Bellisia was. Bellisia could have warned Violet that she was skating close to danger. Violet was a GhostWalker. Few had that information, but in that one outburst, she'd made a shrewd, extremely intelligent man wonder about her. He had a GhostWalker right there in his laboratory.

Violet, seemingly unaware of the danger—or because of it—swiftly moved on, laying out her demands once again. The two went back to haggling. In the end, Violet began to rise and Cheng lifted a hand to stop her. She sank down gracefully and the deal was made. Bellisia listened to another twenty minutes of conversation while the two hashed out what each would do for the other.

Bellisia calculated the odds of escaping if she killed the senator as the traitor emerged from Cheng's office. They weren't good. Even so, she still entertained the idea. The level of treachery was beyond imagination for Bellisia. She despised Violet.

A stir in the office drew her attention. Guards marched in and directed those in the smaller offices out. She glanced into the hallway and saw that the entire floor was being cleared. Her heart accelerated before she could stop it. She took a slow breath and steadied her pulse just as the siren went off, calling everyone, from the labs to the offices, into the large dorm areas.

Lockdown. She couldn't get to the water closet to retrieve her uniform, lab jacket and wig before the soldiers searched, nor did she have enough time remaining before the virus injected into her began to kill her. She couldn't remain in one of Cheng's endless lockdowns. He was paranoid enough that he had kept workers on the premises for over a week more than once. She'd be dead without the antidote by that time. Cheng would be even worse with his security once the jacket and wig were discovered.

She began the slow process necessary to make her way across the ceiling to the hall. She couldn't go down to the main floor. Soldiers were pouring in and every floor would be flooded by now. She had to go up to the only sanctuary she might be able to get to. There were tanks of water housed on the roof that fed the sprinkler systems. That was her only way to stay safe from the searches Cheng would conduct once her clothes were found. The items would only feed his paranoia. That meant she had to take the elevator.

Cursing in every language she was fluent in—and that was quite a few—she hovered just above the elevator doors. The soldiers would go into the space, but it was confined, a relatively small space, and that meant she would have to be very close to them. The men were already on alert. The slightest mistake would cost her. More, she could blend into her environment, but it took a few seconds for her skin and hair to change. Her clothing would mirror her surroundings, so she would have the look of the elevator over her body, but her head and hands and feet would be exposed for that couple of seconds.

Heart pounding, she edged over to the very top of the elevator. Should she try to start blending into that color now, or wait until she was inside with a dozen guards and guns? She had choices, but the wrong one would end her life. Changing colors to mirror her background was more like the octopus than the chameleon, but it still took a few precious moments. She began, concentrating on her hands and feet first. She was already clinging to the elevator doors now, high up, so as she mirrored the colors around her, she appeared to be part of the doors.

The ping signaled that she only had seconds to get inside and up the wall to the ceiling of the elevator. She waited until soldiers stepped into the elevator, and she slipped inside with them, clinging to the wall above their heads. The door nearly closed on her foot before she could pull it in. The men crowded in, and there was little space. She felt as if she couldn't breathe. The car didn't have high ceilings, so they were mashed together, and the taller ones nearly brushed against her body. Twice, the hair of the man closest to her—and it was just her bad luck that he was tall—actually did brush against her face, tickling her skin.

She rode floor to floor as men got off to sweep each one, making certain that all personnel did as the siren demanded and went immediately to the dormitory, where they would be searched.

The last of the soldiers went to the roof. She knew this would be her biggest danger point. She had to exit the elevator right behind the last soldier. It was imperative that all of them were looking outward and not back toward the closing doors. She was a mimic, a chameleon, and no one would be able to see her, but once again it would take a minute to get there in a new environment.

She crawled down to the floor and eased out behind the last man, her gaze sweeping the roof to find the water tanks. There were six banks of them, each feeding the sprinklers on several floors. She stayed very still, right up against the eleva- tor until her skin and hair adjusted fully to the new back- ground. Only then did she begin her slow crawl across the roof, making for the nearest tank while the soldiers spread out and swept the large space.

Up so high the wind was a menace, blowing hard and con- tinuously at the men. They stumbled as it hit them in gusts. She stayed low to the ground, almost on her belly. She stopped once, when one of the soldiers cursed in a mixture of Mandarin and Shanghainese. He cursed the weather, not Cheng. No one would dare curse Cheng, afraid it would get back to him.

Cheng considered himself a businessman. He'd inherited his empire and his intellect from his Chinese father and his good looks and charm from his American movie-star mother.

Both parents had opened doors for him, in China as well as in the United States. He had expanded those doors to nearly every country in the world. He'd doubled his father's empire, making him one of the wealthiest men on the planet, but he'd done so by providing terrorists, rebels and governments information, weapons and anything else they needed. He sold secrets to the highest bidder, and no one ever touched him.

Bellisia didn't understand what it was that drove people to do the terrible things they did. Greed. Power. She knew she didn't live the way others did, but she didn't see that the outside world was any better than her world. Maybe worse. Hers was one of discipline and service. It wasn't always comfortable and she couldn't trust very many people, but then outside her world, where the majority lived, she didn't see that they had it much better.

The cursing soldier stopped just before he tripped over her. She actually felt the brush of the leather of his boot. Bellisia eased her body away from him. Holding her breath. Keeping her movements infinitely slow. She inched her way across the roof, the movements so controlled her muscles cramped in protest. It hurt to move that slow. All the while her heart pounded and she had to work to keep her breathing steady and calm.

She was right under their noses. All they had to do was look down and see her, if they could penetrate her disguise. She watched them carefully, looking out of the corners of her eyes, listening as well for them, but all the while measuring the distance to the water tower. It seemed to take forever until she reached the base of the nearest tank. For*ever*.

She reached a hand up and slid her fingers forward using the setae on the tips of her fingers to stick. Setae—single microscopic hairs split into hundreds of tiny bristles—were so tiny they were impossible to see, so tiny, Dr. Whitney hadn't realized she actually had them, in spite of his enhancements. Pushing the setae onto the surface and dragging them forward allowed her to stick to the surface easily. Each seta could hold enormous amounts of weight, so having them on

the pads of her fingers and toes allowed her to easily climb
or hang upside down on a ceiling. The larger the creature, the
smaller the setae, and no seta had ever been recorded that was
small enough to hold a human being—until Dr. Whitney had
managed to make one.

Her plan was to climb into the water tank and wait until
things settled down and then climb down the side of the building and get far away from Cheng. She was very aware of time
ticking away, and of the virus beginning to take hold in her
body. Already she knew her temperature was rising. The cold
water in the tank would help. She cursed Whitney and his
schemes for keeping the women in line.

The girls had been taken from orphanages. No one knew
or cared about them. That allowed Whitney to conduct his
experiments on the female children without fearing repercus-
sions. He named them after flowers or seasons, and trained
them as soldiers, assassins and spies. To keep them returning
to him, he would inject a drug he called Zenith, a lethal drug
that needed an antidote or the virus would spread and eventually kill. Sometimes he used their friendships with one another, so they'd learned to be extremely careful not to show
their feelings.

She started up the tank, allowing her body to change once
again to blend in with the dirty background. The wind tore
at her, trying to rip her from the tank. She was cold, although
she could feel her internal temperature rising from the virus,
her body beginning to go numb in the vicious wind. Still, she
forced herself to go slow, all the while watching the guards
moving around the roof, thoroughly inspecting every single
place that someone could hide. That told her they would be
looking in the water tanks as well.

A siren went off abruptly, a loud jarring blare that set one's
nerves on edge. It wasn't the same sound as the first siren,
indicating to the workers to go immediately to the dorms.
This was one of jangling outrage. A scream of fury. They had
found her wig, mask and lab jacket. They would be combing

the building for her. Every duct, every vent. Anywhere a human being could possibly hide.

She had researched Cheng meticulously before she'd ever entered his world. It was a narrow, almost military world, with constant inspections and living under the surveillance of cameras and guards. Cheng didn't trust anyone, not even his closest allies. Not his workers. Not even his guards. He had watchers observing the watchers.

Bellisia was used to such an environment. She'd grown up in one and she was familiar with it. She also knew all the ways to get around surveillance and cameras. She was a perfect mimic, blending into her environment, picking up nuances of her surroundings, the language, the idioms, the culture, and Whitney thought that was her gift. He had no idea of her other abilities, the ones far more important to the missions he sent her off on. All the girls learned to hide abilities from him. It was so much safer.

The guards reacted to the blaring siren with a rush of bodies and the sound of boots hitting the rooftop as they went into a frenzy of searching. She kept climbing, using that same slow, inch-by-inch movement. It took discipline to continue slowly instead of moving quickly, as every self-preservation cell in her body urged her to do.

She relied heavily on her ability to change color and skin texture to blend into her surroundings, but that didn't guarantee that a sharp-eyed soldier wouldn't spot her. The pigment cells in her skin allowed her to change color in seconds. She'd hated that at first, until she realized it gave her an advantage. Whitney needed her to be a spy. He sent her out on missions when so many of the other women had been locked up again.

She gained the top of the tank just as one of the soldiers put his boot on the ladder. Slipping into the water soundlessly, she swam to the very bottom of the tank and anchored herself to the wall, making herself as flat as possible against the side. Once again she changed color so that she blended with tank and water.

She *loved* water. She could live in the cool liquid. The water felt cool against her burning skin. In the open air, she felt as if her skin dried out and she was cracking into a million pieces. She often looked down at her hands and arms to make certain it wasn't true, but in spite of the smoothness of her skin, she still felt that way. The one environment she found extremely hostile to her was the desert. Whitney had sent her there several times to record the effects on her, and she hadn't done well. A flaw, he called it.

The soldier was at the top of the tank now, peering down into the water. She knew each tank had soldiers looking into it. If they sent someone down into the water, she might really be in trouble, but it appeared as if the soldier was just going to sit at the edge to ensure no one had gone in and was under-water. She was fine with that. He could sit there all night, for all she cared. Once it was dark she would be able to slip up to the surface and get air.

Right now she was basking in the fact that the cool water was helping to control the temperature rising in her from the virus. Whitney injected her every time she left the compound where she was held, to ensure she would return. She'd always managed to complete her mission in the time frame given to her, so she had no idea how fast-acting the virus was. The water definitely made her feel better, but she didn't feel good at all. Her muscles ached. Cramped. Never a good thing when trying to be still at the bottom of a water tank with soldiers on the lookout above her.

Night fell rapidly. She knew the guards were still there on the roof and that worried her. She had to be able to climb down the side of the building and she couldn't get out of the tank as long as the guard was above her. She also needed air. She'd risked blowing a few bubbles, but that wasn't going to sustain her much longer. She needed to get to the surface and leave before weakness began to hit. She had been certain the soldier would leave the tank after the first hour, but he seemed determined to hold his position. She was nearly at her max for staying submerged.

Bellisia refused to panic. That way lay disaster. She had to get air and then find a way to slip past the guard so she could climb down the building, get to the van waiting for her and get the antidote. She detached from the wall and began to drift up toward the surface, careful not to disturb the water. Again, she used patience in spite of the urgent demands her lungs were making on her.

After what seemed an eternity, she reached the surface. Tilting her head so only her lips broke the surface, she drew in air. Relief coursed through her. Air had never tasted so good. She hung there, still and part of the water, so that even though the guard was looking right at her, he saw nothing but water shimmering.

A flurry of activity drew the guard's attention, and she attached herself to the side of the tank and began to climb up toward the very top. She was only half out of the water when the shouted orders penetrated. They wanted hooks dragged through the tanks just to make certain no one was hiding in them with air tanks. So many soldiers tromped up onto the roof that she felt the vibrations right through the tank. Spotlights went on, illuminating the entire roof and all six tanks. Worse, soldiers surrounded the tanks, and more climbed up to the top to stand on the platforms, ringing the large holding containers.

Bellisia sank slowly back into the water, clinging to the wall as she did so, her heart pounding unnaturally. She'd never experienced her heart beating so hard. It felt as if it would come right out of her chest, and she wasn't really that fearful—yet. Her temperature was climbing at an alarming rate. She was hot, and even the cool water couldn't alleviate the terrible heat rising inside of her. Her skin hurt. Every muscle in her body ached; not just ached but felt twisted into tight knots. She began to shiver, so much so she couldn't control it. That wasn't conducive to hiding in a spotlight surrounded by the enemy.

She stayed up near the very top of the tank, just beneath the water line, attached to the wall, and made herself as small and as flat as possible. There was always the possibility that she could die on a mission. That was part of the . . . adrenaline rush. It was always about pitting her skills against an enemy. If she wasn't good enough, if she made a mistake, that was on her. But this . . . Peter Whitney had deliberately injected her with a killer virus in order to ensure that she returned to him. He was willing to risk her dying a painful death to prove his point.

He *owned* them. All of them. Each and every girl he took out of an orphanage and experimented on. Some died. That didn't matter to him. *None* of them mattered to him. Only the science. Only the soldiers he developed piggybacking on the research he'd conducted on the girls. Children with no childhood. No loving parents. She hadn't understood what that meant until she'd been out in the world and realized the majority of people didn't live as she did.

All of the girls had discussed trying to break free before Whitney added them to his disgusting program to give him more babies to experiment on. The thought of leaving the only life they'd ever known was terrifying. But this. Leaving her to die in a foreign country because she was late through no fault of her own. She had the information Whitney needed, but because he insisted on injecting her with a killer virus before she went on her mission, she might never get that information to him. He liked playing god. He was willing to lose one of them in order to scare the others into compliance.

Something hit the water hard, startling her. She nearly jerked off the wall, blinking in protest against the bright lights shining into the tank. Her sanctuary was no longer that. The environment had gone from cool, dark water—a place of safety—to one of overwhelmingly intense brilliant light, illuminating the water nearly to the bottom of the tank. The hook dragged viciously along the floor, and she shuddered in reaction.

A second hook entered the water with an ominous splash as the first was pulled back up. The next few minutes were a nightmare as the tank was thoroughly searched with hooks along the bottom. Had a diver with scuba gear been hiding there, he would have been torn to pieces.

She relaxed a bit as they pulled the hooks back up to the top. They would leave soon, and she could make the climb out of the tank and across the roof. Already she could tell she was weaker, but she knew she could still climb down the side of the building and get to the van where Whitney's supersoldiers waited to administer the antidote to the poisonous virus, reducing it to a mere illness instead of something lethal.

The hook plunged back into the water, startling her. She nearly detached from the wall as the iron dragged up the side of the tank while the second hook entered the water. This was . . . *bad.* She had nowhere to go. If she moved fast to avoid the hook, she would be spotted. If she didn't, the hook could tear her apart. Either way, she was dead.

The sound, magnified underwater, was horrendous to her ears. She wanted to cover them against the terrible scraping and grinding as the point of the hook dug into the side of the tank. She watched it come closer and closer as it crawled up from the bottom. The other hook came up almost beside it, covering more territory as they ripped long gouges in the wall.

She tried to time letting go of the wall so neither hook would brush against her body and signal to the men on the other end that there was something present other than wall. She pushed off gently and slid between the two chains, trying to swim slowly so that movement wouldn't catch their eyes. She stroked her arms with powerful pulls to take her down, still hugging the wall as best she could below the hooks. If she could just attach herself on the path already taken, she'd have a good chance of riding this latest threat out.

The advantage of going deeper was that the light didn't penetrate all the way to the bottom. She just had to avoid the hooks as they plunged into the water and sank. Once she was deep enough, the soldiers above her wouldn't be able to see even if she did make a jerky movement to prevent a hook from impaling her.

She'd made it about halfway down when the hooks began their upward scraping along the wall. Once again she stayed very still, the sound grating on her nerves, her heart pounding as the huge hooks got closer and closer. This time she did a slow somersault to avoid getting scraped by either hook. The dive took her lower into the tank. She didn't see how they could possibly think anyone could stay underwater that long, and by now they certainly would have discovered a scuba tank.

The soldiers were thorough, plunging the hooks deep and dragging them up the walls without missing so much as a few inches of space. Bellisia realized they had to have perfected this method of searching the tanks by doing it often. That made sense. The tanks were large and Cheng was paranoid. No doubt the many floors and laboratories were being searched just as thoroughly.

There, in the water, listening to the sound of the chains scraping up the walls, she contemplated the difference between Cheng and Whitney. Both had far too much money. Whitney seemed to need to take his research further and further out of the realm of humanity and deeper into the realm of insanity. No government would ever sanction what he was doing, yet he was getting away with it. At least his motive, although twisted, was to produce better soldiers for his country.

Cheng wasn't affiliated with his government as far as she could tell. He worked closely with them, but he wasn't a patriot. He was out for himself. He seemed to want more money and power than he already had. She'd researched him carefully, and few on the planet had more than he did. Still, it wasn't enough for him. Yet he had no family. No one to share his life with. He didn't work for the sake of knowledge. He existed only to make money.

Bellisia was aware of her heart laboring harder and the pressure on her lungs becoming more severe. That was unusual. She'd taken a large gulp of air and she should have quite a bit of time left before she had to rise, but it felt as if she'd been underwater a little too long, even for her. Of course Whitney would find something that would negatively impact her ability in the water. He didn't want her to use that means as an escape route.

She had no choice but to begin her ascent. She tried to stay to the side of the tank that they'd already dredged. It was terrifying to be in the water as the large, heavy hooks slammed close to her again and again. It was inevitable that she would be hit, given the many strikes the soldiers made at the water, and it happened as she was just pushing off the wall to allow her body to rise slowly, naturally. The hook hit the bottom of the tank and was jerked upward and to the left, right across her back. She folded herself in half to minimize the damage, but it hit hard enough to jar her, even with the way the water slowed the big hook down.

Bellisia felt the burn as the point ripped her skin open. It was a shallow wound, but it stung like hell and instantly there was blood in the water. She had to concentrate to close those cells to keep from leaking enough blood that the soldiers would notice. Under her skin she had a network of finely controlled muscles that aided her in changing the look and feel of her body's surface skin. Now, she used them to squeeze the cells closed and prevent dumping blood into the water, at least until the spotlights were turned off.

It seemed to take forever as she continued to rise, her lungs burning and her muscles cramping. All the while the horrible splash and scraping of the hooks continued. Twice she had extremely close calls, and once more the tip barely skimmed along her body, hitting her thigh, ripping her open. It was much harder to control the bleeding this time, as she was weaker and needed to break the surface before her muscles went into full cramps.

She was relieved when the hooks were dragged from the water and the soldiers began to climb down the ladders back to the roof. Instantly she kicked the remaining four feet to the surface and took in great gulps of air. She clung to the side for several long minutes, resting her head against the wall while she tried to breathe away the inferno inside her. She couldn't keep doing this for Whitney. She wouldn't survive. He made them all feel as if they were nothing. She knew she wasn't alone in wanting to escape because they all talked about it, late at night when one or two could disrupt the cameras and recording equipment and they were alone in the dorms.

She had tried planning an escape with her best friend, Zara, but before they could attempt to carry out their plans, Zara was sent on an undercover mission and Bellisia was sent to ascertain whether or not Violet was betraying Whitney. Whitney had set Violet up as senator, taking over when her husband had been killed. Whitney didn't trust Violet, so he'd gone so far as to "pair" her with him. That meant she would always be physically attracted to Whitney. That attraction evidently didn't stop Violet from conspiring against the man who had experimented on her.

Bellisia began her slow climb out of the water tank. She would have to dry off before she could make the trek across the roof to the side of the building. If she didn't, one of the soldiers might discover the wet trail leading to the edge. From the heat of the high-powered lights, the platform around the tank was really warm and she lay down, allowing her body to change to the color of the dingy planks.

She didn't dare sleep, not when soldiers still guarded the roof, but they seemed content with pacing the length of it in patterns, checking every place that could possibly hide a body over and over. She realized the soldiers were as afraid of Cheng as she and the other women in her unit were afraid of Whitney. Life was cheap to both men, at least other people's lives.

She began her slow crawl down the side of the tank once she felt she wouldn't leave behind a trail. Her body was hot now, so hot she felt as if her skin would crack open. Her muscles cramped and she couldn't stop shaking. That didn't bode well for crossing the roof, but at least it was very dark now that the spotlights had been turned off. If she shook when a guard was close, hopefully the darkness would conceal her.

It took her just under forty minutes in the dark, with her body on fire and her muscles cramping painfully, to climb down the side of the building. The virus he'd given her was vicious, her fever high, her insides searing her. For someone like her, someone needing more water than most people, it was sheer agony, as if he'd developed the strain specifically for her—and he probably had. That only strengthened her resolve to escape.

She rested for a moment to get her bearings and plan out her next step. She needed the antidote immediately, and that meant putting herself back in Whitney's hands. She had no other choice. Bellisia made her way across the lawn to the street where the van was waiting for her. It was parked one block down to be inconspicuous, one block away, which put it right next to the river.

She was staggering by the time she reached the vehicle, and Gerald, one of the supersoldiers sent to watch over her, leapt out to catch her up and get her back into the van. He placed her on a gurney and immediately spoke into his cell to tell Whitney she was back. She closed her eyes and turned her face away, as if losing consciousness.

"I need the information she has," Peter Whitney said. "Get it from her before you administer the antidote. Take her to the plane immediately. Your destination will be Italy."

Her heart nearly jumped out of her chest. She knew several of the women had been taken there to ensure they became pregnant. The GhostWalkers had destroyed his breeding program in the United States. No way was she going to Italy.

"Whitney needs a report," Gerald said.

She kept her breathing shallow. Labored. Eyes closed, body limp.

"Bellisia, honey, come on, give me the report. You need the antidote. He won't let me give it to you until you give him what he wants."

She stayed very still. Gerald and his partner, Adam, were her handlers on nearly every mission. The three had developed a friendship of sorts, if one could be friends with their guards. She knew how to control her breathing and heart rate, and she did both to make him think she was crashing.

"We're losing her, Doc," Gerald said while Adam caught at her arm, shoving up the material of her bodysuit.

"Be certain. She could be faking," Whitney warned.

"No, she's out of it. She got back way past the time she was supposed to. We might be too late to save her. They locked the building down and she was still inside." Gerald's voice held urgency.

"Did you see Violet or any of her people going in or coming out?" Whitney demanded.

"I never saw Senator Smythe. I have no idea if she was there or not," Gerald said. Bellisia wasn't altogether certain he spoke the truth. He may very well have seen the senator, but Gerald and Adam didn't always like the way Whitney treated the women.

"Be sure Bellisia is really out."

Gerald prodded her. Hard. She made no response.

"She's burning up. And she's bleeding on her back and thigh."

"Inject her. She'll need water."

"Adam, give her the antidote fast. We'll need water for her."

She felt the needle and then the sting of the antidote as it went in. She stayed silent, uncertain how fast it was supposed to work. She hated needles, in fact the sensation of them entering her skin often made her nauseous. The double row of muscles caused the needle to spread a terrible fire through every cell.

"Doc says get her water."

Adam held up a bottle. "She's not responsive enough to drink." That showed her how upset Adam was on her behalf; he knew she would need to be submerged in water. He wasn't thinking clearly.

"Not drink. Pour it over her."

The cool water went over her arm and then her chest. She nearly lost her ability to keep her heart and lungs under control, the relief was so tremendous.

"That's not enough. Get it out of the river."

Adam threw open the double doors to the van and hopped out. Her acute hearing picked up Whitney hissing in disapproval.

He didn't like that they'd parked by a river. That was her signal to move.

She leapt from the gurney and onto the ground right beside a startled Adam.

"Grab her," Gerald yelled.

She raced across the street with Adam rushing after her. The tips of his fingers brushed her back just as she dove right off the edge into the river. Water closed over her head, the cool wetness welcoming her.

A MUCH-ABRIDGED CARPATHIAN
DICTIONARY

This very-much-abridged Carpathian dictionary contains most of the Carpathian words used in these Dark books. Of course, a full Carpathian dictionary would be as large as the usual dictionary for an entire language (typically more than a hundred thousand words).

Note: The Carpathian nouns and verbs below are word stems. They generally do not appear in their isolated "stem" form, as below. Instead, they usually appear with suffixes (e.g., "*andam*"—"*I give*," rather than just the root, "*and*").

a—verb negation (*prefix*); not (*adverb*).
agba—to be seemly or proper.
ai—oh.
aina—body.
ainaak—forever.
O ainaak jelä peje emnimet ŋamaŋ—sun scorch that woman forever (*Carpathian swear words*).
ainaakfél—old friend.

ak—suffix added after a noun ending in a consonant to make it plural.

aka—to give heed; to hearken; to listen.

akarat—mind; will.

ál—to bless; to attach to.

alatt—through.

aldyn—under; underneath.

alə—to lift; to raise.

alte—to bless; to curse.

and—to give.

and sielet, arwa-arvomet, és jelämet, kuulua huvémet ku feaj és ködet ainaak—to trade soul, honor and salvation for momentary pleasure and endless damnation.

andasz éntölem irgalomet!—have mercy!

arvo—value; price (*noun*).

arwa—praise (*noun*).

arwa-arvo—honor (*noun*).

arwa-arvo olen gæidnod, ekäm—honor guide you, my brother (*greeting*).

arwa-arvo olen isäntä, ekäm—honor keep you, my brother (*greeting*).

arwa-arvo pile sívadet—may honor light your heart (*greeting*).

arwa-arvod mäne me ködak—may your honor hold back the dark (*greeting*).

ašša—no (*before a noun*); not (*with a verb that is not in the imperative*); not (*with an adjective*).

aššatotello—disobedient.

asti—until.

avaa—to open.

avio—wedded.

avio päläfertiil—lifemate.

avoi—uncover; show; reveal.

belső—within; inside.

bur—good; well.

bur tule ekämet kuntamak—well met, brother-kin (*greeting*).

ćaδa—to flee; to run; to escape.

ćoro—to flow; to run like rain.

csecsemõ—baby (*noun*).

csitri—little one (*female*).

diutal—triumph; victory.

eći—to fall.

ek—suffix added after a noun ending in a consonant to make it plural.

ekä—brother.

ekäm—my brother.

elä—to live.

eläsz arwa-arvoval—may you live with honor (*greeting*).

eläsz jeläbam ainaak—long may you live in the light (*greeting*).

elävä—alive.

elävä ainak majaknak—land of the living.

elid—life.

emä—mother (*noun*).

Emä Maγe—Mother Nature.

emäen—grandmother.

embɛ—if; when.

embɛ karmasz—please.

emni—wife, woman.

emni hän ku köd alte—cursed woman.

emni kuŋenak ku aššatotello—disobedient lunatic.

emnim—my wife; my woman.

én—I.

en—great; many; big.

én jutta félet és ekämet—I greet a friend and brother (*greeting*).

én maγenak—I am of the earth.

én oma maγeka—I am as old as time (*literally: as old as the earth*).

En Puwe—the Great Tree. Related to the legends of Ygddrasil, the axis mundi, Mount Meru, heaven and hell, etc.

engem—of me.

és—and.

ete—before; in front.

että—that.

fáz—to feel cold or chilly.

fél—fellow, friend.

fél ku kuuluaak sívam belső—beloved.

fél ku vigyázak—dear one.

feldolgaz—prepare.

fertiil—fertile one.

fesztelen—airy.

fü—herbs; grass.

gæidno—road; way.

gond—care; worry; love (*noun*).

hän—he; she; it.

hän agba—it is so.

hän ku—prefix: one who; that which.

hän ku agba—truth.

hän ku kaśwa o numamet—sky-owner.

hän ku kuulua sívamet—keeper of my heart.

hän ku lejkka wäke-sarnat—traitor.

hän ku meke pirämet—defender.

hän ku pesä—protector.

hän ku piwtä—predator; hunter; tracker.

hän ku saa kuć3aket—star-reacher.

hän ku tappa—killer; violent person (*noun*); deadly; violent (*adj.*).

hän ku tuulmahl elidet—vampire (*literally: life-stealer*).

hän ku vie elidet—vampire (*literally: thief of life*).

hän ku vigyáz sielamet—keeper of my soul.

hän ku vigyáz sívamet és sielamet—keeper of my heart and soul.

Hän sívamak—Beloved.

hany—clod; lump of earth.

hisz—to believe; to trust.

ho—how.

ida—east.

igazág—justice.

irgalom—compassion; pity; mercy.

isä—father (*noun*).
isäntä—master of the house.
it—now.
jälleen—again.
jama—to be sick, infected, wounded, or dying; to be near death.
jelä—sunlight; day; sun; light.
jelä keje terád—light sear you (*Carpathian swear words*).
o jelä peje kalk hänkanak—sun scorch them all (*Carpathian swear words*).
o jelä peje emnimet—sun scorch the woman (*Carpathian swear words*).
o jelä peje terád—sun scorch you (*Carpathian swear words*).
o jelä peje terád, emni—sun scorch you, woman (*Carpathian swear words*).
o jelä sielamak—light of my soul.
joma—to be under way; to go.
joŋe—to come; to return.
joŋesz arwa-arvoval—return with honor (*greeting*).
jŏrem—to forget; to lose one's way; to make a mistake.
juo—to drink.
juosz és eläsz—drink and live (*greeting*).
juosz és olen ainaak sielamet jutta—drink and become one with me (*greeting*).
juta—to go; to wander.
jüti—night; evening.
jutta—connected; fixed (*adj.*); to connect; to fix; to bind (*verb*).
k—suffix added after a noun ending in a vowel to make it plural.
kaca—male lover.
kadi—judge.
kaik—all.
kalma—corpse; death; grave.
kaŋa—to call; to invite; to request; to beg.
kaŋk—windpipe; Adam's apple; throat.
kać3—gift.

kaδa—to abandon; to leave; to remain.

kaδa wäkeva óv o köd—stand fast against the dark (*greeting*).

karma—want.

Karpatii—Carpathian.

Karpatii ku köd—liar.

käsi—hand (*noun*).

kaśwa—to own.

keje—to cook; to burn; to sear.

kepä—lesser; small; easy; few.

kessa—cat.

kessa ku toro—wildcat.

kessake—little cat.

kidü—to wake up; to arise (*intransitive verb*).

kim—to cover an entire object with some sort of covering.

kinn—out; outdoors; outside; without.

kinta—fog, mist, smoke.

kislány—little girl.

kislány kuŋenak—little lunatic.

kislány kuŋenak minan—my little lunatic.

köd—fog; mist; darkness; evil (*noun*); foggy, dark; evil (*adj.*).

köd alte hän—darkness curse it (*Carpathian swear words*).

o köd belső—darkness take it (*Carpathian swear words*).

köd elävä és köd nime kutni nimet—evil lives and has a name.

köd jutasz belső—shadow take you (*Carpathian swear words*).

koje—man; husband; drone.

kola—to die.

kolasz arwa-arvoval—may you die with honor (*greeting*).

koma—empty hand; bare hand; palm of the hand; hollow of the hand.

kond—all of a family's or clan's children.

kont—warrior.

kont o sívanak—strong heart (*literally: heart of the warrior*).

ku—who; which; that.

kuć3—star.

kuć3ak!—stars! (*exclamation*).

kuja—day; sun.

kuŋe—moon; month.

kule—to hear.

kulke—to go or to travel (on land or water).

kulkesz arwa-arvoval, ekäm—walk with honor, my brother (*greeting*).

kulkesz arwaval—Joŋesz arwa arvoval—go with glory—return with honor (*greeting*).

kuly—intestinal worm; tapeworm; demon who possesses and devours souls.

kumpa—wave (*noun*).

kuńa—to lie as if asleep; to close or cover the eyes in a game of hide-and-seek; to die.

kunta—band; clan; tribe; family.

kuras—sword; large knife.

kure—bind; tie.

kutenken—however.

kutni—to be able to bear, carry, endure, stand, or take.

kutnisz ainaak—long may you endure (*greeting*).

kuulua—to belong; to hold.

lääs—west.

lamti (or lamt3)—lowland; meadow; deep; depth.

lamti ból jüti, kinta, ja szelem—the netherworld (*literally: the meadow of night, mists, and ghosts*).

lańa—daughter.

lejkka—crack; fissure; split (*noun*); to cut; to hit; to strike forcefully (*verb*).

lewl—spirit (*noun*).

lewl ma—the other world (*literally: spirit land*). *Lewl ma* includes *lamti ból jüti, kinta, ja szelem*, the netherworld, but also includes the worlds higher up *En Puwe*, the Great Tree.

liha—flesh.

lõuna—south.

löyly—breath; steam (*related to lewl: spirit*).

ma—land; forest.

magköszun—thank.

mana—to abuse; to curse; to ruin.

mäne—to rescue; to save.

maɣe—land; earth; territory; place; nature.

me—we.

meke—deed; work (*noun*); to do; to make; to work (*verb*).

mića—beautiful.

mića emni kuŋenak minan—my beautiful lunatic.

minan—mine; my own (*endearment*).

minden—every, all (*adj.*).

möért?—what for? (*exclamation*).

molanâ—to crumble; to fall apart.

molo—to crush; to break into bits.

mozdul—to begin to move; to enter into movement.

muonì—appoint; order; prescribe; command.

muonìak te avoisz te—I command you to reveal yourself.

musta—memory.

myös—also.

nä—for.

nâbbŏ—so, then.

ŋamaŋ—this; this one here; that; that one there.

nautish—to enjoy.

nélkül—without.

nenä—anger.

ńiŋ3—worm; maggot.

nó—like; in the same way as; as.

numa—god; sky; top; upper part; highest (*related to the English word* numinous).

numatorkuld—thunder (*literally: sky struggle*).

nyál—saliva; spit (*related to nyelv: tongue*).

nyelv—tongue.

odam—to dream; to sleep.

odam-sarna kondak—lullaby (*literally: sleep-song of children*).

olen—to be.

oma—old; ancient; last; previous.

omas—stand.
omboće—other; second (*adj.*).
o—the (*used before a noun beginning with a consonant*).
ot—the (*used before a noun beginning with a vowel*).
otti—to look; to see; to find.
óv—to protect against.
owe—door.
päämoro—aim; target.
pajna—to press.
pälä—half; side.
päläfertiil—mate or wife.
palj3—more.
peje—to burn.
peje terád—get burned (*Carpathian swear words*).
pél—to be afraid; to be scared of.
pesä—nest (*literal; noun*); protection (*figurative; noun*).
pesä—nest (*literal*); protect (*figurative*).
pesäd te engemal—you are safe with me.
pesäsz jeläbam ainaak—long may you stay in the light (*greeting*).
pide—above.
plle—to ignite; to light up.
pirä—circle; ring (*noun*); to surround; to enclose (*verb*).
piros—red.
pitä—to keep; to hold; to have; to possess.
pitäam mustaakad sielpesäambam—I hold your memories safe in my soul.
pitäsz baszú, piwtäsz igazáget—no vengeance, only justice.
piwtä—to follow; to follow the track of game; to hunt; to prey upon.
poår—bit; piece.
põhi—north.
pukta—to drive away; to persecute; to put to flight.
pus—healthy; healing.
pusm—to be restored to health.
puwe—tree; wood.
rambsolg—slave.

rauho—peace.
reka—ecstasy; trance.
rituaali—ritual.
sa—sinew; tendon; cord.
sa4—to call; to name.
saa—arrive; come; become; get; receive.
saasz hän ku andam szabadon—take what I freely offer.
salama—lightning; lightning bolt.
sarna—words; speech; magic incantation (*noun*); to chant;
    to sing; to celebrate (*verb*).
sarna kontakawk—warriors' chant.
śaro—frozen snow.
sas—shoosh (*to a child or baby*).
saɣe—to arrive; to come; to reach.
siel—soul.
sieljelä isäntä—purity of soul triumphs.
sisar—sister.
sív—heart.
sív pide köd—love transcends evil.
sívad olen wäkeva, hän ku piwtä—may your heart stay
    strong, hunter (*greeting*).
sívam és sielam—my heart and soul.
sívamet—my heart.
sívdobbanás—heartbeat (*literal*); rhythm (*figurative*).
sokta—to mix; to stir around.
soŋe—to enter; to penetrate; to compensate; to replace.
susu—home; birthplace (*noun*); at home (*adv.*).
szabadon—freely.
szelem—ghost.
taka—behind; beyond.
tappa—to dance; to stamp with the feet; to kill.
te—you.
Te kalma, te jama ńiŋ3kval, te apitäsz arwa-arvo—you
    are nothing but a walking maggot-infected corpse, with-
    out honor.
Te magköszunam nä ŋamaŋ kać3 taka arvo—thank you
    for this gift beyond price.

ted—yours.

terád keje—get scorched (*Carpathian swear words*).

tõd—to know.

Tõdak pitäsz wäke bekimet mekesz kaiket—I know you have the courage to face anything.

tõdhän—knowledge.

tõdhän lõ kuraset agbapäämoroam—knowledge flies the sword true to its aim.

toja—to bend; to bow; to break.

toro—to fight; to quarrel.

torosz wäkeval—fight fiercely (*greeting*).

totello—obey.

tsak—only.

tuhanos—thousand.

tuhanos löylyak türelamak saγe diutalet—a thousand patient breaths bring victory.

tule—to meet; to come.

tumte—to feel; to touch; to touch upon.

türe—full; satiated; accomplished.

türelam—patience.

türelam agba kontsalamaval—patience is the warrior's true weapon.

tyvi—stem; base; trunk.

uskol—faithful.

uskolfertiil—allegiance; loyalty.

varolind—dangerous.

veri—blood.

veri ekäakank—blood of our brothers.

veri-elidet—blood-life.

veri isäakank—blood of our fathers.

veri olen piros, ekäm—literally: blood be red, my brother; figuratively: find your lifemate (*greeting*).

veriak ot en Karpatiiak—by the blood of the Prince (*literally: by the blood of the great Carpathian; Carpathian swear words*).

veridet peje—may your blood burn (*Carpathian swear words*).

vigyáz—to love; to care for; to take care of.
vii—last; at last; finally.
wäke—power; strength.
wäke beki—strength; courage.
wäke kaδa—steadfastness.
wäke kutni—endurance.
wäke-sarna—vow; curse; blessing (*literally: power words*).
wäkeva—powerful.
wara—bird; crow.
weńća—complete; whole.
wete—water (*noun*).